The Dark Flood

The Dark Flood

Deon Meyer

*Translated from Afrikaans
by K. L. Seegers*

HODDER &
STOUGHTON

First published in Great Britain in 2021 by Hodder & Stoughton
An Hachette UK company

Originally published in Afrikaans in 2020 as *Donkerdrif* by Human & Rousseau

1

A CIP catalogue record for this title is available from the British Library

Hardback ISBN 978 1 529 37551 0
Trade Paperback ISBN 978 1 529 37552 7
eBook ISBN 978 1 529 37554 1

Typeset in Plantin Light by Hewer Text UK Ltd, Edinburgh
Printed and bound in Great Britain by Clays Ltd, Elcograf S.p.A.

Hodder & Stoughton policy is to use papers that are natural, renewable
and recyclable products and made from wood grown in sustainable
forests. The logging and manufacturing processes are expected to
conform to the environmental regulations of the country of origin.

Hodder & Stoughton Ltd
Carmelite House
50 Victoria Embankment
London EC4Y 0DZ

www.hodder.co.uk

For Marianne.
With love.

We are in danger of destroying ourselves by our greed and stupidity.
Stephen Hawking

As a secular psychological concept, greed is an inordinate desire to acquire or possess more than one needs.
Wikipedia

JULY

I

Captain Benny Griessel heard the racing footsteps, the urgent shout; his Hawks colleague Vusi Ndabeni calling them, come, come quickly, there's a cash-in-transit heist, happening right now.

A Tuesday morning in July. Mid-winter.

He abandoned the dossier on his desk, grabbed his Z88 from the drawer and ran. Vusi was small of stature, the quiet one, always calm. But not now: the urgency in his voice meant Griessel did not hesitate. He fastened his holster around his hips as he ran down the passage. Vaughn Cupido was approaching, long coat flapping behind him – his 'Bat suit', his winter gear.

'Praise the Lord,' said Cupido. Vaughn hated the tedium of police paperwork. They had been buried in dossiers for days. This was a reprieve.

Captains Frankie Fillander and Mooiwillem Liebenberg emerged from their shared office, shoes drumming on the bare tiled floor of the Directorate for Priority Crimes Investigation – the DPCI – in Bellville, a herd stampeding to the armoury on the first floor.

Ndabeni was already inside, passing out R5 assault rifles and spare magazines, Warrant Officer Bossie Bossert scribbling hurried notes in his inventory.

'I want a Stompie,' said Cupido.

Vusi gave him the short Beretta RS200 shotgun with the pistol grip, and a cartridge belt.

'You always gotta be otherwise, hey,' said Fillander. 'It's a cash-in-transit heist, not a bank robbery.'

'Method in my madness, uncle,' said Cupido. 'Just wait and see.'

'Just bring them back,' Bossert shouted after them.

At morning parade over the previous five months, they had been kept informed of Vusi's investigation. He had been working on the flurry of in-transit heists in the Western Cape. The same gang, the same modus operandi; ten men in four stolen cars would ambush the transit van. One vehicle, always old and heavy, would be deliberately rammed into the security van, forcing it to a standstill. The other cars would encircle it and open fire with (according to post-action ballistic tests) AK47s and an exotic collection of small arms. Until the guards surrendered. Or explosives would be used on the rear doors if they would not. An estimated fourteen million rand had already been stolen.

The robbers were phantoms, they left no solid forensic evidence behind. Ndabeni was at his wits' end, and under extreme pressure from his commanding officer, Colonel Mbali Kaleni.

So now the five detectives raced off, at a hundred and fifty kilometres per hour, in two unmarked cars, the BMW X3 leading and the Ford Everest behind. To the N1 first, then heading east.

Griessel's phone rang. It was Vusi, from the leading BMW, driven by Fillander.

'Vusi?'

Ndabeni had to shout over the wailing of the sirens: 'I believe the robbers have a police radio, so we'll restrict comms to the phone. It's a very hot tip from my new informant, very credible. They're going to hit a Pride Security van on the R45, between Malmesbury and Paarl.'

Griessel repeated the lowdown to Cupido behind the wheel, and Liebenberg, both of them in the Ford with him.

'I've notified Paarl, they're dispatching their task force,' said Ndabeni.

Griessel shared the update with his colleagues.

'Shitshow,' said Cupido. He had little faith in the rural police force's abilities.

'I called Pride Security, they'll reroute the van,' said Vusi. 'So, we're hoping to get the gang while they're waiting.'

'Do we know where they'll be?' asked Griessel.

'At the junction of the R45 and the Agter-Paarl road,' said Vusi. Adding: 'The chopper is coming too.'

They drove with majestic blue mountains looming ahead, the Boland beautiful in the clear light of the brisk, bright winter's day.

★   ★   ★

It was, as Cupido described it afterwards, 'a clusterfuck of majestic proportions'. Right from the very start.

Because the thieves had a radio, tuned to the frequency of Pride Security. The van's new route was broadcast straight to them.

Because Vusi chose the R44, reckoning it would be quicker than driving through Paarl, sirens or no sirens.

And because Mrs Barbara van Aswegen, farmer's wife in the homestead just sixty metres from the scene of the crime, would hear the shots and immediately phone the Paarl SAPS, who in turn would notify the task force where the action was. And then she would unlock the safe and take out her husband's .308 Winchester hunting rifle.

But first the robbers overtook the van. They struck just past the Windmeul Kelder wine cellar, where the dual carriageway flowed like the confluence of two rivers into a single road. An old, solid, 1995-model Mercedes S500 rammed with a dull boom into the side of the armoured security vehicle. The Pride driver, pumped up on adrenaline, fear and desperate determination, was driving too fast. He over-compensated in his response to the collision, spinning the steering wheel to the right, but at that moment the Mercedes wasn't in contact, and the van swerved too sharply. It rolled. Two, three, four times, and scraped across the tar, sparks flying, metal screeching, a high-pitched keening. Finally, it came to rest on its left side, in the middle of the road.

The four heist vehicles encircled the van – the Mercedes in front to fend off any approaching traffic, two on the sides and one behind. The robbers leaped out and began firing at the security van. Their usual tactic. They knew the van's windows and panels were bullet-proof, but the hammering hail of lead was so terrifying that guards would usually surrender. They emptied their magazines and in the silence of reloading gave the men in the van a chance to emerge with their hands in the air. So that the rear doors could be unlocked without further exchange of fire.

But not this time. The guards were hanging in their seatbelts, injured, shocked, afraid.

The robbers went for Plan B. The two from the rear vehicle ran to the van with the explosives. They pressed the package expertly against the joint between the doors, ran back to shelter behind their car, and hit the detonator. The blast boomed across the winter-bare vineyards, so that the children of Slot van die Paarl Primary School looked up at their teacher in alarm. A ballooning cloud of flame and black smoke rose up from the van. Ears ringing, the hijackers didn't hear the sirens of the approaching Hawks.

Vusi Ndabeni was the first to spot the smoke from the explosion. '*Ndiyoyika*,' he said, pointing it out to Fillander.

'Bastard!' said Frankie, the old veteran. He looked back at the passenger seat, where his rifle lay.

Their hearts began to race. Fillander braked instinctively.

Vusi phoned Griessel. 'Do you see the smoke?'

'Yes,' said Benny and pointed it out to the other two in the Everest.

'*Fokkit*,' said Cupido. 'Party time.'

Griessel felt an intense craving for the calming effect of a Jack Daniel's. He was a rehabilitating alcoholic, more than two hundred days now since his last drink.

He and Liebenberg smacked back the folding butts of their R5's, and cocked them. Thumbs on the large safety mechanisms. Cupido braked to keep his distance from the BMW.

The two gangsters standing guard at the Mercedes, looking out for approaching traffic, saw and heard the Hawks simultaneously. They yelled to the other eight, who were carrying the cash boxes out of the back of the Pride van, but it was too late. When they fired the first shots at the SAPS cars, the BMW and Everest had already screeched to a halt – sideways across the road. The detectives piled out on the safe side of the vehicles. They sheltered behind the cars and returned fire. Cupido, whose 'Stompie' wasn't built for this range, had his Glock 17 in both hands.

The crackle of gunfire, lead smacking against all three of the vehicles and the road surface. Bullets whizzed past the men, some only a whisker away, the chemical tang of propellant charges heavy in the air.

A moment of hesitation for the eight cashbox carriers, as they weighed up their options: should they help shoot, or get the loot into the getaway vehicles as fast as possible? The road to Paarl was still open behind them. The leader – sinewy, clever and fearless in his orange beanie – had many hits' experience behind him. He didn't rate the ability of policemen, was sure his mates could keep them busy long enough. He shouted at the others to get the boxes into the cars.

He had no idea of Frankie Fillander's talents.

Fillander was one of the top marksmen in the DPCI – better known as the Hawks – in the Cape. And his previous experience with the SAPS in Mitchells Plain had taught him to be calm under heavy fire. He set his R5 on semi-automatic, and lay on the ground at the back of the BMW. His colleagues provided covering fire. He waited for his chance, lined up the first Mercedes man through the larger foremost ring sight of the rifle. He shot him high in the right shoulder. The man jerked and dropped his AK.

Fillander swung the barrel to the left. He could see only one arm of the other man by the Mercedes, where the elbow bent as he cradled the AK. He aimed, taking the constant movement of the arm into consideration, and fired. The 5.56 ×45 round shattered the elbow: the man screamed out his pain and shock.

No one was shooting back at them now.

That was the moment that Benny Griessel thought, we've got this under control, today the good guys win.

Then the cavalry thundered in.

2

The Boland Task Force arrived from the direction of Paarl. East.

The Hawks had come from the direction of Butterfly World. West. A perfect pincer movement. If they had planned it in advance, it would have been a deadly flanking strategy that would have caught the gangsters neatly in the crossfire.

But they hadn't planned it in advance. The radio silence, the smoke of the explosion and gunfire, the thugs running back and forth to load boxes, blasting off wild shots in between, meant that at first the task force commander, Lieutenant Colonel Phila Zamisa, wasn't even aware of the Hawks on the far side of the commotion.

He and his troops, in their black, bullet-proof, urban combat jackets, Heckler & Koch MP5N machine pistols, R5 rifles and a McMillan TAC-50 sniper rifle, stopped and jumped out and began shooting. The eight remaining robbers dived under and behind vehicles, and most of the task force's shots smacked into the Hawks vehicles. One hit Mooiwillem Liebenberg – whose good looks meant he was known as the Hawks' 'weapon of mass seduction' – on the cheek. Mercifully it was a mere scratch, a bloody streak below his left ear. And the task force kept on shooting.

The Hawks ceased fire; they could see the task force.

'What did I say? Shitshow!' yelled Vaughn Cupido.

'Fuck,' said Griessel.

'I'll call them,' shouted Vusi, he had Colonel Zamisa's number. He lay just under the nose of the BMW, wiggled his phone out of his jacket and called.

It took a while before the officer answered, Ndabeni screamed as hard as he could over the clatter and booms, and eventually Zamisa understood.

Silence descended on the scene. And in the homestead right next to the road, farmer's wife Barbara van Aswegen had been listening intently to the running battle. She was alone at home, but she was ready, the hunting rifle firmly in her hands. Now was the time, she decided, to act, to protect hearth and home. She lifted the gun and let rip. At the white unmarked Hawks cars directly in her line of sight. To her it was obvious that these men were part of the gang of hijackers.

Benny Griessel heard the shot somewhere from the left as the round smacked into the Everest directly above him. He cursed and dropped to his haunches.

Another shot. Again, into the Ford.

'*Jissis*,' said Cupido.

Frankie Fillander could see Van Aswegen. 'It's an aunty,' he yelled. And then, to her: 'Aunty, we're the police this side.' But she kept on shooting.

Griessel heard Vusi's phone ring, most likely Colonel Zamisa calling from the other side to hear what was going on. And then he saw the raiders exploiting the confusion, making a run for it. South, away from the farmer's wife, over the fence, into the vineyard. 'Come on, Vaughn, Willem!' he shouted as he reloaded his R5, jumped up and ran after them.

The gangsters were younger, more agile. Griessel was cycling fit, but he'd never been a sprinter or a fence hurdler. Cupido was much more of an athlete, but that was before he'd piled on sixteen kilograms over the last few years. And Mooiwillem Liebenberg wanted to help, but at that moment Mrs van Aswegen shot out the passenger window near his head, glass showered over him and he dropped down flat.

Benny was first over the fence and racing through the long row of poplar trees hemming the road. He could see the eight robbers running past the whitewashed outbuildings of the farm on the crest of the slope. And, out of the corner of his eye, the task team people also coming up on his left flank. He looked back. Cupido's stylish long coat had snagged in the fence as he leaped over, carrying the pistol grip shotgun in his hand.

'I'm coming, Benna!'

Griessel ran. The ground was sodden from the recent rain, and slippery. He reached the top at last. He would have to stop at the outbuildings, take a careful look around the corner. He skidded to a halt, feet slipping out from underneath him, and he came down hard. Leaped up, trousers, elbows muddied.

The raiders were in full flight. He wanted to raise his R5 and shoot, but there was a row of labourer's cottages up ahead. Four task force officers were approaching rapidly along the farm road, but still too far off to intercept the robbers.

He ran on, breath rasping, lungs on fire.

At the cottages he had to stop again to look. The fugitives were running down into the hollow beyond the dam, at full speed. He lifted his rifle, fired three shots. It made no difference.

Something wasn't right. He counted the running figures – there were only seven robbers between the long rows of winter-bare vines. And they had split up. One group swung right, the other three kept straight on.

The task force men reached him. He recognised Colonel Zamisa.

'Ah, Benny,' said Zamisa. 'Come with me, we'll take those three.' He motioned to his team mates to follow the group of four.

Griessel looked back. Cupido was thirty metres behind. 'Vaughn, one of them has gone into a worker's house here,' he shouted.

'Leave the fucker to me,' said Cupido. Gasping for breath.

Zamisa took off. He was in his forties, but he was fast. Griessel had to push hard to keep up.

'There's a primary school there,' said Zamisa while running, and pointed east.

'Shit,' said Griessel, as that could mean hostages and a whole load of trouble.

But the three fugitives swung north suddenly, towards a stand of pine trees.

'They want to double back to their vehicles,' said Zamisa.

Griessel didn't have the breath to answer.

Cupido stood close to the labourer's cottage at the top, leaning his hand against the wall while he caught his breath. He would have to lose weight, it was a long time since he'd been this fat and unfit, what was he going to do? His Banting diet just wasn't getting off the ground. He blamed his girlfriend. Desiree Coetzee loved cooking and dining out. There were always sweet treats in the house, and he couldn't resist.

He saw them sprinting away over the rolling landscape, his colleague, and the task force guys.

From across the road he could still hear single shots. The farmer's wife shooting at Vusi and the rest of them.

He shook his head.

Clusterfuck.

He peered around the corner, looked down the road that ran between the row of four small buildings and an avenue of trees.

All quiet.

A movement in the trees. He lifted the shotgun, although he knew it was too far for that particular weapon.

It was a child – a small coloured boy, maybe five years old – peeping out, a frightened little face.

Cupido crept around the corner, keeping close to the wall, towards the boy.

Shots rang out in the distance, to the south.

The child jumped, startled.

Cupido tried the door of the first house. It was locked. The robber could have locked it from inside.

The boy was motioning to him. Vaughn looked. A tiny finger pointed, at the third house.

He jogged closer, as lightly as he could, up to the boy.

'Is he in there?'

Little head nodding.

'Is there someone else in there?'

'The baby.'

'The baby? Where's his mama?'

The child pointed again, this time towards the farmyard. He whispered: 'She went to fetch wood, uncle. It's cold.'

Cupido nodded. 'Stay there behind the tree. Lie flat.'

The child nodded solemnly and lay down, hands over his ears.

Vaughn walked across the little stoep, to the closed door of the cottage. He put the shotgun down on the cement, pulled off his coat. Put that down beside the firearm on the stoep. He didn't want it to get in his way. He picked up the RS200 again. Stood to the side of the door, back against the wall.

'Come out, and I won't shoot you,' he shouted.

Shots boomed from inside, the wooden door splintered, an AK47 on automatic. The baby inside began to wail.

Cupido waited until the magazine was empty. Then he kicked the door open and dived inside. He rolled once, aiming the shotgun at the robber from his prone position, flat on his belly on the floor. The living room was small, the man standing behind a couch. The baby lay on the couch, its high-pitched shrieks slicing through marrow and bone. The gangster had a pistol in his hand, the barrel pressed to the baby's cheek.

'I'll kill the baby,' he said to Cupido, his eyes wild.

Vaughn realised Fillander had been right. The Stompie was the wrong choice. If he fired now, the shot would hit the baby too.

3

'Take it easy, brother,' said Cupido.

He held his left hand up high, spreading the fingers of his gun hand open in a gesture of surrender, and rose slowly to his feet.

'Drop the gun,' the man said. The pistol pressed against the baby was shaking. The child shrieked louder.

'Okay,' said Cupido. 'Easy.' He slowly shifted the Stompie to his left hand as he crouched, never taking his eyes off the man. He lowered the shotgun to the floor, slowly, inch by inch. He knew the moment he let go of it the man would lift his pistol and shoot him.

'See, I'm going to put it down softly,' he said, wanting to keep the robber's attention on the shotgun, so he could reach his right hand into the back of his belt.

He had to get the timing right.

'You want me to kick it over to you?' he asked, just before he put the Stompie down.

The baby screamed. Ear splitting.

He asked again, louder: 'You want me to kick it over to you?'

The man didn't answer, he was wound tight as a spring, but his eyes followed the RS200.

Outside Cupido heard a woman's voice, full of fear. 'My child, my child.'

Vaughn dropped the gun, the last few centimetres to the floor; his right hand grasped the butt of the Glock 17 behind his back. He pulled it out. The man raised his pistol. Cupido dived and shot.

Two shots rang out in unison.

Colonel Zamisa was seven strides ahead of Benny at the long stone wall. The pine trees were still a short distance ahead.

Griessel's lungs were burning; he had to lean up against the cold stones for a bit. His hair, as usual one haircut behind, now messier than ever. His almond-shaped eyes, which had been described as 'Slavic', were squinting in the bright sunlight. He thought, I'm too old for these shenanigans, forty-six, but *Jissis*, the mileage on him was much more than that.

'The shooting has stopped,' said Zamisa.

The farmer's wife had come to her senses. Griessel nodded.

'It's a cemetery,' said Zamisa. He had to stand on tiptoe to see over the wall and peer through a few cypress trees.

Griessel did the same.

The Slot van die Paarl churchyard was about a hundred metres long and fifty wide. The wall ran right around it, with a gate on the opposite side from where they were standing. A few hundred graves. Then a flash of movement. The barrel of a Russian assault rifle only just protruding from behind a large marble headstone. One of the gang, hiding.

'They're in there,' he said.

Zamisa hesitated for a moment. 'Benny, you go around to the gate. I'll wait for you to cover me. When you start shooting, I'll come over the wall. Catch them by surprise.'

'Right,' said Griessel. He took off, crouching slightly to stay below the wall. He crept around to the right, the shorter route to the gate, trying to keep his footsteps as quiet as possible. It was relatively easy on the moist, soft soil and grass.

Around the first corner, he ran along the short side of the church-yard. No sound, just pigeons cooing in the cypress trees. A lizard scut-tled across the ochre stones as he approached.

Around the final corner.

One of them on guard at the gate, crouching, AK in his hands. But he was looking north, away from Benny. Then he heard the detective approach, and turned. Griessel dived flat to offer the smallest possible target, aimed and fired, two rapid shots.

The man toppled over backwards.

Shots from inside, smacking harmlessly against the other side of the wall.

Benny realised Zamisa would think that was his covering fire. The colonel would be jumping over the wall now. Griessel leaped up, headed for the gate.

On the other side of the wall he heard shots, the task force commander's R5 firing.

Outside the labourer's cottage the mother of the baby screamed, a shrill lament over the wailing of the child.

Cupido heard her footsteps, running over the cement. 'Stay outside,' he shouted; he didn't want her to see the hijacker with a gaping wound where his right eye should be. He jumped up, pushed the Glock back into his belt, picked up the baby, very very carefully, and turned round.

She was standing in the doorway, a small, delicate woman, barely in her twenties. A keening, high and continuous, from her mouth as she held out her arms for her child.

He passed the baby to her, still wailing inconsolably. 'Come,' he said. 'Everything is okay.' He walked back, picked up the Stompie, steered the woman outside. He looked at the hole in the wall left by the gangster's bullet. It had missed him by millimetres.

Fokkit.

He went out, to go and say thank you to the boy.

Griessel charged in through the churchyard gate.

A shot hit the wall right beside him, stone shards and dust flew into his right eye. He crashed down behind a grave. More bullets whacking, all around. Tears blinded him and he dropped the R5, trying to wipe the dust from his eyes.

A moment of silence; the shooting ceased.

He heard the footsteps just in time. The hijacker thought he was hit, Griessel reckoned, he was coming to finish him off. He grabbed the rifle, rolled onto his back, lifted the R5, waited. His sight was blurred, his eyes still not clear.

The man appeared in the pathway with a murderous look of intent. He fired hastily, too soon, the rifle still swinging down, so that the clattering rounds hit the gate and the wall.

Griessel's heart was galloping, the impulse to pull the trigger overwhelming, but he waited, took the man's movement into account, shot – once, twice. The man crashed down on top of him, finger still on the trigger, the Russian weapon carrying on firing until it was empty.

Benny shoved him off violently, barrel to the robber's chest. Fired once more. The body went limp.

All quiet.

Benny got to his knees, shaking from adrenaline. He raised his head above the gravestone and saw Zamisa, sixty metres away. Helpless, the R5 in his hands, the magazine apparently empty. In front of him, the scrawny man in his orange beanie – his back turned to Griessel – walking towards the task force leader, pistol in hand.

He had one chance, Griessel knew. Seconds.

His right eye was full of tears, there was no time to wipe them away. He propped his elbow on the grave, aimed through the blur, and shot.

The skinny gang leader lay groaning. The wound high up on his shoulder was bleeding, his hands cuffed behind his back. He didn't say a word.

Griessel and Zamisa watched the task force vehicles approaching.

'Fancy gun,' said the colonel and poked the AK47 propped against the wall with the point of his boot. 'I'm assuming – and hoping – you'll be doing the Buddy Fick?'

To 'Buddy Fick' a weapon meant the detective had to prepare the firearms documentation for the SAPS's Confiscated Firearms Store in Silverton, outside Tshwane, headed by Colonel Buddy 'The Flash' Fick. Fick was a meticulous, somewhat dictatorial ruler of his little kingdom, not very popular with the men on the force because he often sent their forms straight back, embellished with corrections and cutting comments. He came by his nickname because his uniform buttons – and his car – were always polished to a high shine.

'I suppose I'll have to, now,' said Griessel, as he looked at the assault rifle. The pistol grip behind the trigger had been replaced with carved ivory. A single word was inscribed on it: *Ukufa*.

'It's Xhosa,' said Zamisa. 'It means "death".'

SEPTEMBER

4

19 September. The coming of Spring.

The season when the West Coast displayed its floral beauty in shades of white and orange and purple, from Bloubergstrand to beyond Springbok. A time for Cape radio DJs to play easy, breezy, *loslit* music and burble away with bubbling enthusiasm, encouraging their listeners to joyfully make the most of the season's first proper heat. To go out and celebrate the de facto end of winter, with a spring in the step and a song on the lips. Because they can see clearly now, the rain has gone, it's gonna be a bright, bright, sunshiny day.

And early on this bright morning in Paradyskloof, Stellenbosch, it did indeed seem to any onlooker as though Sandra Steenberg was a woman with a light-hearted spring in her step.

Her heels clicked over the paving in front of the preschool, the dark grey handbag swinging from her shoulder. At first glance she was simply another rushed, purposeful mother dropping off her children, running a little late for work, perhaps. In her grey checked skirt and navy-blue sweater over a white buttoned-up blouse, she was the very image of a successful professional. She was dressed for cooler weather, as though experience had taught her not to trust the weathermen's optimism. Unmistakeably a sensual woman, with slender ankles and full calves, a pretty mouth, her thick, dark hair swinging loose and long. Somewhere just north of a very vital and dynamic thirty, full of confidence and energy.

But appearances can be deceptive.

For at that moment, Sandra was a fugitive. She lengthened her strides, anxious, walking as fast as her dignity would allow, to the safety of the trenches – her car. Hounded by the fear of the head of the nursery spotting her, and confronting her about the overdue fees. Three months' worth.

Seven metres from her car, six, five, four, perhaps she would escape again this time, one more morning.

'Mrs Steenberg. Please,' came the call, in that cool, refined Stellenbosch tone of courteous firmness.

Sandra halted, mustering a smile before she turned, her excuses and empty promises ready. She would deliver them with a controlled, defensive aggression.

Her cell phone rang.

She snatched it from her handbag as if grabbing a lifebuoy. She threw an apologetic look at the frowning principal who had almost reached her, and though she didn't recognise the number, answered the call.

'This is Sandra.'

'The estate agent.' Not a question, a statement. A man's voice. Businesslike.

'That's right.'

'Jasper Boonstra,' he said. A pause after the statement, as though allowing time for the momentous impact of his identity to sink in.

It took her a second, because the principal was now standing right in front of her – her indignation evident, ready to pounce. Then Sandra realised it was *that* Jasper Boonstra. The crook. With the principal looming, and her fierce desire for escape it didn't even occur to her that it might be a joke. She felt a shot of adrenaline in her blood.

'Hello,' she said. 'How can I help you?'

'I want you to come and see me. As in now.'

She knew she was going to say yes. She *had* to say yes.

'Of course,' she said. That was the moment that Sandra Steenberg's life changed, irrevocably.

There was little brightness in the bedroom of the beautiful old Victorian house at 47 Brownlow Street, on the slope of Signal Hill. Benny Griessel's mood was sombre and heavy. He had hardly slept a wink. His temper was frayed. His nerves were gnawing away at him, eating him up.

He dressed in his only suit, the black one, grey tie and white shirt.

His fiancée, Alexa Barnard, clucked over him. She kept tugging at his collar, smoothing his hair until it looked a little tidier.

'You look lovely, Benny.'

He knew how he looked, but he held his tongue. He didn't want to be fussed over. Not today. And looking 'lovely' was no help to him at all.

'Come on, I'll make you a delicious omelette. And a nice cup of coffee.'

Coffee wasn't the beverage he wanted. Coffee wouldn't slake *this* thirst. He didn't want an omelette either; he had no appetite at all. Besides, cooking wasn't one of Alexa's great talents. And he didn't want to be stuck in the kitchen with her now. He knew Alexa, she would want to rehash last night's difficult conversation. Try to soothe him. Encourage him, coax him on. There was nothing that could soothe or encourage him now.

He trailed her down the stairs to the kitchen. Gritting his teeth, because he would have to pick his battles with her on this particular matter.

He went over to fetch the coffee pot from the filter machine, but she stopped him. 'Sit down and let me spoil you a little.'

Alexa, in her mothering mode. He could forget about trying to stop her now.

He sat down at the table. She poured out the coffee. 'Thanks,' he said and checked his watch. Another seventy minutes before the hearing.

'You'll see, they'll never fire a master detective like you,' she said cheerily as she fetched the eggs from the fridge.

He wasn't going to have a rerun of last night's argument. He loved this woman. More than words could say. But, Lord knows, she was bloody persistent. She didn't understand the police, and her overwhelming optimism blinded her to the nonsense that was going on in the country. Two weeks ago, at a very expensive restaurant outside Stellenbosch, he had asked her to marry him. She had said 'yes', to his immeasurable relief. Last night he had sat down with her on the sofa in the sitting room for a serious talk. He told her, if he was fired today, they would have to postpone their wedding plans. Until he found another job. No matter how long that took. He wasn't going into a marriage unemployed.

She replied that he was much too negative, and there was no reason to worry. She point blank refused to move the December wedding date. 'No, Benny, I've already booked the little church, and I'm not cancelling it.' She was revelling in the wedding plans, like an excited child. He granted her that, but she had to understand . . .

He watched her beat the eggs.

'Benny, last night I spent a long time thinking . . .'

As he'd suspected.

'And I might have a plan. If the worst comes to the worst, and I know it won't, you've always got your music. And good bass guitarists . . . Well, we have a constant shortage.'

He sighed. Alexa was the owner of the AfriSound record company she had inherited from her late husband. They met when Benny was investigating the murder of her ex. She'd survived and risen from the wreckage of that tragedy, got her alcoholism under control, and made a tremendous success of the business. She was a wealthy woman. Now she was offering him session work in the studio. But let's face it, his bass guitar playing wasn't good enough. Never had been, never would be. Good enough to play golden oldies with *Rust* on Friday or Saturday nights at wedding and parties. But nothing more than that. Session work would be a nonsense. Alms. Charity. Crumbs from her table. And he wasn't up for that. He still had *some* pride.

'I'll get investigative work,' he said. Without conviction. Because the economy was going down the drain, and what private eye firm or security company would appoint an ageing former drunk, when they could pick and choose these days?

'I know you will. And that's why I don't want to mess with the wedding date. Some lovely bacon on your omelette?'

'I'll have cheese instead, please,' he said. It was a safer bet.

The headquarters of the South African Police Service in the Western Cape are housed at 25 Alfred Street, Greenpoint, an ugly old building reminiscent of a Communist-inspired block of flats. Seven storeys of white-painted walls, rows and rows of small steel windows, rusty air conditioning units and a motley array of sun-bleached blinds.

The conference room where the disciplinary hearing would be held was right at the top, just down the passage from the Provincial Commissioner's office. Griessel waited to be called into the small office next door. It wasn't a cheery room, to say the least.

His hands were sweating, he rubbed them down his trousers and felt in his inner jacket pocket. His police ID card was there, in his wallet. So that he could hand it in when they sacked him. And his statement, which he would read out. Without much hope. He had handed in his Z88 yesterday to Warrant Officer Bossie Bossert at the Hawks armoury.

His cell phone kept buzzing – WhatsApp messages from his Hawks' colleagues wishing him well: Vusi Ndabeni, Mooiwillem Liebenberg, Frankie Fillander, even Major Benedict 'Bones' Boshigo from the Statutory Crime Group and the press officer John Cloete.

He got a lump in the throat. Hell, he was going to miss them, this brotherhood, the camaraderie, built up over years of going through deep water together.

Vaughn Cupido hadn't arrived yet. His hearing wasn't until 10:00. Then they would sit and wait for the outcome.

Griessel's charge letter said that the disciplinary committee consisted of five people. He knew that Brigadier Musad Manie, commander of the DPCI in the Western Cape, would be on it. And the provincial commissioner. And the brigadier in charge of Human Resources. And an officer from the legal department. And one other policeman. An interpreter was on standby.

He could expect sympathy from Manie. Some mercy. Manie knew him, Manie was a good man. But he'd have no luck with the commissioner. He was a political appointment, a supporter of the president. The corrupt, state-capturing president of the country. The commissioner would demand Griessel's head on a platter; that was a fact. Maybe the HR brigadier would too. At least he would get a fair hearing from the legal officer.

His lot would depend on who the fifth committee member was.

He took his statement out of his pocket. It had taken him two weeks to write it. Painstakingly. Over and over. Vaughn wanted to see it. He had refused. With good reason.

He read it through one last time.

5

I am Captain Benjamin Griessel. I am a member of the Directorate for the Priority Crime Investigation's Unit for Serious and Violent Crimes, based in Market Street, Bellville.

I am subject to a disciplinary hearing according to Article 24(1) of the 1995 South Africa Police Service Act's addendum of 1 November 2016, and specifically Article 5(3), which determines that any member of the SAPS who:

(b) performs any act or fails to perform any act with the intention –

(i) to cause harm to or prejudice the interests of the Service, be it financial or otherwise;

(ii) to undermine the policy of the Service; or

(iii) not to comply with his or her duties or responsibilities;

Also under Article 5(3):

(j) fails to carry out a lawful order or routine instruction without just or reasonable cause.

I understand the charges against me. I choose not to have union or legal representation. I plead guilty as charged. I wish to testify as to extenuating circumstances.

On 29 August of this year, along with various colleagues from my unit, I investigated the death of Mr Menzi Dikela in his house in Nuttall Street, Observatory*. At first it seemed to be a suicide. In my career as detective over approximately the past twenty-six years I have investigated more than seventy cases of suicide. On the basis of this experience I made certain deductions at the Nuttall Street scene that led me to suspect foul play was involved. This included the absence of shells from the pistol with which Mr Dikela was shot, and soil samples from footprints that were found in the sitting room and kitchen of the house.

---

* These events are fully described in the crime novel *The Last Hunt*.

There was also the testimony of relatives and neighbours and evidence from the traffic cameras of the Cape Town Traffic Authority that lent weight to my suspicion. Without encouragement from any of my colleagues, I decided to investigate it as a murder case.

I admit that my direct superior Lieutenant Colonel Mbali Kaleni ordered me to shut down the investigation two days later, as the State Pathologist could find no evidence to support my theory of foul play. I admit hereby that I am guilty of failure to carry out an order by continuing the investigation. The reason for doing so was that new evidence, in the form of a hidden room in Mr Dikela's garden shed, stolen computers, and forensic results from the soil samples which I have already mentioned, confirmed once again that this was not a suicide.

On Sunday, 3 September this year I received further information about a BMW X5 that had been seen at Mr Dikela's house on the day of his death, and the origin of the soil sample, indicating that the identified suspects were hiding on the farm Kleingeluk between Philadelphia and Malmesbury. I wish to declare that I decided independently, and without the knowledge of Lieutenant Colonel Kaleni or the influence of my colleague Vaughn Cupido, to confront the suspects.

I wish to declare that I influenced Captain Vaughn Cupido inappropriately to persuade him to accompany me. I further declare that I had no reason to believe that the suspects were members of the State Security Agency, the SSA. I wish to declare that I acquired no information in my investigation that could have led me to believe that the members of the SSA were involved in an official operation.

I wish to declare that I had no intention of interfering with an SSA operation through this arrest. This was simply an unforeseen coincidence of circumstances.

Captain Vaughn Cupido and I confronted three members of the SSA in the farmhouse. They confessed that they were involved in the death of Mr Dikela, which had a great influence on my subsequent actions. I realised that justice would not be served via the usual channels, and out of frustration, I decided to handcuff the members of the SSA to their vehicle. They were also aggressive, and I wanted to be sure they would not use firearms against us. It was solely my decision. My colleague Captain Vaughn Cupido had nothing to do with this.

I wish to declare that even today I believe that the SSA agents must be held accountable for the death of Mr Menzi Dikela. I have devoted my entire career to the fight against crime. In all the hundreds of cases that I have investigated over the years, my sole objective was to bring criminals to justice. I confess that I did not always do my work according to the standards that my commanding officers set for me, or within the prescribed regulations of the South African Police Service. But with every difficult decision I genuinely tried to ask myself in what manner justice could best be served.

With regards to the Dikela dossier I did the same, because that was my duty.

I ask you to take my record as a detective, my arrest figures and my years of service into account when you decide on my punishment. Finally, I wish to ask you to acquit my colleague, Captain Vaughn Cupido of all charges. I was the senior team member in terms of years of service. I improperly influenced him and take full responsibility for that.

I thank you.

He sighed. He knew the hearing was a sham. Vaughn and Mbali Kaleni did too. But it's what you wrote – and how you plead – when you were innocent, and up against the dark forces of state capture and corruption in the highest police echelons. All their efforts in the Dikela investigation, and nothing had changed.

He had wondered whether he should ask for some clemency because he was solely responsible for the very high fees for his son Fritz's studies at the AFDA film school. Or merely say that he still had one dependant to support. But either way it felt like begging, emotional manipulation. And that was something he could not abide.

Footsteps approached. He took a deep breath. Today, right here, his career, nearly thirty years in service of justice, was about to come to its end.

The constable opened the door for him. He entered.

The blinds were drawn and one of the strip lights above didn't work. The room was gloomy. They sat at a long table, in a row side by side. Commissioner Mandla Khaba, a fat toad of a man, in the centre. Musad Manie sat on the far left. He nodded encouragingly to Griessel.

But it was the man on the far right who gave Griessel the most courage, who made him believe he might perhaps have a chance. Lieutenant Colonel Phila Zamisa, commander of the Boland Task Force. The man whose life Benny had saved two months earlier.

But Zamisa did not make eye contact; he stared down at the documents before him. Not a good sign.

'Good morning,' said Griessel and stopped at the isolated island of a table facing them.

There was no response. The Legal Services captain stood up. He asked Griessel if he was certain he wanted no representation.

'I am certain, thank you.'

'You understand the nature of the charges against you?'

'Yes.'

'You may sit down.'

Griessel nodded, sat down.

'Captain, you indicated that you wished to read a statement.'

'Yes.' He removed the document from his pocket.

'Please proceed.'

Griessel cleared his throat, unfolded the paper, and began to read.

Sandra made her excuses and promises, swiftly and apparently smoothly and convincingly enough. The nursery school principal listened attentively and empathetically, then put a gentle hand on Sandra's forearm. 'Just remember, Mrs Steenberg, I also have children. And accounts to pay. And you're not the only parent in arrears.'

As she drove away, Sandra burned with shame and guilt. The chances of her being able to make any payment were increasingly slim. The lie was growing bigger, and how glibly it slipped from her lips every time. And now she was acutely aware that her default was causing hardship to others. That wasn't who she was, it wasn't who she wanted to be. She wasn't her father.

And you're not the only parent in arrears.

She bit her bottom lip, remorseful. She had been so intent on her own needs these past few months. But the entire town was suffering. Which reminded her of Boonstra's call. She took out her phone and rang her boss.

'Yes, my darling?' Charlie always answered as if he was cheerily grateful for her call. An affectation. But that was Charlie.

'I'm on my way to Jasper Boonstra,' she said.

He was quiet for what seemed like an eternity. She enjoyed the rare silence *'Jitte Krismis,'* he said at last, the closest Charlie ever came to swearing. Then, more firmly: 'You're pulling an old man's leg.'

'You're sixty-two, Charlie. A mere spring chicken.'

'You should know, good looks can be deceiving. Tell me you're pulling my leg.'

'No. He called me. Five minutes ago.'

'Directly? On your cell phone?'

'By name.'

'You know what that means, Sandy-san.' He never called her just plain 'Sandra'. Though some of his 'nicknames' bordered on harassment. 'Honey-bun', 'sweety-pie', 'baby doll', and the one she hated most: 'sexy thing'. At first she reprimanded him crossly, but he would just shrug and say, 'It's harmless, babe. Anyway, I'm too old to change.' Though she suspected his breezy flirtation was a form of camouflage. Charlie's sexuality was somewhat ambiguous, even though he was married. So she held back. Besides, she couldn't afford to lose this job. Especially not right now.

'Yes,' she said. 'I know.' The website of Benson International Realtors displayed the photos and contact details of Charlie and his five estate agents. All five were women. Four were clearly older than fifty, only Sandra was thirty-two. By Charlie asking her if she knew what that meant, he meant that Jasper Boonstra might have chosen her from the group deliberately.

'You be careful. He has a reputation. With younger women.'

'Among other things.'

Another silence. Then again: *'Jitte Krismis.'* Still amazed.

'Surprising, hey?'

'I'm bowled over, Longoria. Bowled over.' As in Eva Longoria. Charlie thought there was a resemblance. But only when he wanted something, or was especially pleased with her. 'Wouldn't that be ironic. Where are you meeting him?' he asked. 'Baronsberg?'

'Yes.'

'*Jitte Krismis*. Maybe he wants to sell. That place is worth eighty million, Sandy-san. Minimum.'

'This time I want seventy-five per cent, Charlie.' Benson regularly got four per cent commission. Three point two million. Her usual share was fifty per cent of that, the rest went to Charlie. But Boonstra had phoned *her*. Personally.

'We'll talk about that, my darling. See what he has to say first.'

No, she thought. Not this time, you manipulative old scoundrel.

6

The entrance to Baronsberg was just past the Stark-Condé estate, out on the Jonkershoek road. Sandra stopped at the impressive gate, the name picked out in elegant sans serif letters against the stone pillar. The word 'Baron' accentuated a bit more than the rest.

She wondered if there would still be any press lurking about. There were none that she could see.

She pressed the intercom button just below the eye of the CCTV camera. Nothing happened.

Even the name of the wine estate was a bit of a con, she thought, like the rest of Jasper Boonstra's life, so thoroughly documented after his fall from grace. He had come to study here in Stellenbosch, first a BComm in Economics and Law, then an MBA. The clever son of an agricultural co-op man from Dordrecht. His first job was as assistant manager of a small motor parts chain in Gauteng. He was always blessed with burning ambition and a silver tongue, and quickly developed an eye for a gap in the market and a sharp nose for a good deal or a canny merger. His astonishing talent for manipulation and shady dealing came to full fruition later. His rise was swift and impressive. First with the development of a business conglomerate in South Africa, over two meteoric decades, and then the great international breakthrough – the merger with the Dutch business giant Schneider-König.

He'd brought the merged company's headquarters to Stellenbosch. Where all the Afrikaner corporate top dogs were gathered. He so badly wanted to run with that pack.

Over the last eight years, as his fortune grew, he'd bought three adjoining tracts of land on the slopes of Botmaskop Peak, one after the other. In shameless imitation of the other top dogs. He'd consolidated the properties and christened them afresh as one grand new wine estate. Launched it with a great deal of fanfare, pomp and ceremony.

The incomer, the gossips said, who so badly wanted to be part of the Stellenbosch elite, that he even manipulated history: Baronsberg's brochure and website claimed the estate was named after the administrator of the Dutch East India Company, Baron Hendrik Adriaan van Rheede, who in 1683 issued the order to establish a town where Stellenbosch was today. The link to this land in particular because the Baron rode his horse up this very slope where the farm was situated, gazed out on the valley below, and made his plans there. A professor of history at the university wrote to the *Eikestadnuus* to denounce that claim as pure fabrication.

That was five years ago. When Jasper Boonstra still walked on water. When Schneider-König's share price was reaching new heights each week. Everyone chose to ignore the professor back then, while they counted their profits.

The gate slid silently open, without a word from the intercom. She drove through, and up the winding paved road to the big house, vineyards on either side. Beyond stood the Jonkershoek mountains: the green flanks rising up towards the grey rock formations of Botmaskop on the left and Square Tower and the Twin Peaks to the right, magnificent, brooding. Past a small guard house, where two security guards waved at her. She waved back. She felt the unsettling, puzzling buzz of adrenaline again. After all he was just another client.

But he wasn't.

He was Jasper Boonstra. Rand billionaire. Worth three hundred and fifty million dollars. Still. After everything.

Jasper Boonstra, former chief executive of Schneider-König. The biggest corporate swindler in the history of the country. Or so they alleged. Because he hadn't been found guilty yet, hadn't even been charged. His fraud was so complex, so entangled in countless transactions and cleverly woven spider webs of front companies and shell companies and hidden bank accounts that they reckoned there wasn't a team of state advocates or policemen in South Africa with the knowledge and experience to unravel it all.

Jasper Boonstra, the most hated businessman in the country. Hundreds of thousands of people had lost billions of rands when Schneider-König's share price crashed from fifty-four rand to two rand in a single day. The day that the bubble and the bombshell burst, the auditors revealing 'irregularities'. Investment funds, pension funds, private investors, employees, it was financial carnage, everyone suffered.

The most hated man in this town. Because Schneider-König's head office was in Stellenbosch. Several hundred of the company's top and senior management had big homes here, where they lived with their families. They spent big money, in clothes boutiques, restaurants, art and car dealers. At home decor shops, at businesses that installed fabulous kitchens and luxurious bathrooms. They had enormous mortgages on very expensive homes, with Schneider-König shares as the only security. On Fridays strings of Porsches and Ferraris crawled along Church Street looking for parking, ahead of the regular wine-and-dine and flash-your-cash show at the street cafés, so that often it looked more like a luxury motor show parade.

And then everything imploded. Overnight. Literally.

And the property market imploded with it. The banks wanted new security that the home owners could not provide.

Boonstra was the reason that the preschool fees for Sandra and Josef Steenberg's twins, the cute five-year-olds, Anke and Bianca, were four months in arrears. The tip of the debt iceberg. Nobody could sell a house in Stellenbosch any more. The market forces were turned upside down, the tide turned, too many expensive houses on the market, too little demand. Three estate agencies had already closed their doors. At Benson International Realtors, Charlie had encouraged two of his agents to retire. And the rest lived in fear that they would be next. Sandra too.

And now she was going to meet him face to face. This scoundrel, this swindler, this enigma. This man who since his great fall had been hiding from the media in his fabulous house at Baronsberg. Or in his billionaire beach house in Clifton. Or sometimes, the gossips said, at the luxury pad of his much younger, super-sexy mistress in Franschhoek. Apparently his wife knew about it, and did nothing.

Wouldn't it be ironic? Charlie had said. And Sandra had instantly understood what he meant. If they stood to gain, to make a packet, from the man who had wreaked so much havoc.

Yes, she thought. It would be the most delicious irony.

★　　★　　★

Griessel found Cupido in the room where he'd been told to wait. His colleague was in his charcoal pinstripe, with a bold, upbeat, blood-red tie. But he was strung taut as a wire. Benny knew, to Vaughn, the Hawks were everything.

'How did it go, Benna?'

Griessel lied, because it was the right thing to do. 'Okay,' he said. 'Zamisa is the fifth member.'

Fleeting relief as Cupido recalled the cash-in-transit fiasco. 'Then we've got a chance.'

'You can come through,' said the constable to Vaughn. 'They are ready for you.'

'Keep cool,' said Griessel.

'Ain't I always?' and Cupido was gone.

Griessel sat down. He could only hope the commissioner wasn't so hard on Vaughn. The man had been ruthless. 'You don't belong in my Police Service,' he'd said before he dismissed Benny from the room.

Sandra pressed the button next to the front door and heard the melodious chimes sounding from somewhere deep in the house.

She was expecting a servant to answer the door. In the period costume of a colonial lackey? She smiled at her absurd imagining, but you never knew with the super-rich. Perhaps a footman would invite her in and show her to an ornate drawing room, keeping a watchful eye so that she didn't slip a Ming vase or Pierneef painting in her handbag. Perhaps he would bring her exotic tea in a golden cup while she waited forty minutes for the lord of the manor to appear with a royal flourish of his cloak.

She tried to remember the images she had seen in photos of this overwhelmingly impressive house, an architectural masterpiece that had graced the pages of so many glossy magazines.

She didn't hear footsteps, lifted her hand to ring the bell again but the door swung open. Jasper Boonstra himself stood there, startling her. She knew, to her chagrin, that he could see she'd been taken unawares.

He was in jeans, with a blue shirt hanging loose over his slight belly. Barefoot, a dark three- or four-day beard. He was slimmer than he'd seemed at the last press briefing. Slightly shorter than she'd expected.

Apart from that it was the same Jasper Boonstra in all his notorious glory.

He didn't greet her, just looked her up and down. Shameless, direct, chauvinistically appraising her like a stud cow, his eyes lingering over her bosom. Then he opened the door wider, with a slight, smug grin and said: 'Come in.' A tone of measured warmth, as if she were an old girlfriend. As he closed the heavy door behind her, he rested the palm of his hand briefly on her back. She stiffened: he was too close to her, she could smell him, a blend of soap and deodorant and shampoo and hair oil. Not unpleasant as such, her revulsion was for the man as an entirety.

She felt a flash of rage flare up in her belly over his blatancy, and she knew her temper would make her cheeks flush. She smothered her anger with an effort of will, a frozen grimace on her face. She would have to remain very calm. He had answered the door himself, so perhaps he was here alone, and more challenges lay in store for her.

Then the house opened up in front of her, vast and gorgeous, the beautiful expanse lifting the atmosphere. The hall was spacious, a single Maggie Laubser painting on display, a big, beautiful country scene peopled with farm workers, playful and colourful. The reception lounge that followed on was huge, but decorated with taste, understated. Impressive, broad stairs beckoned to an upper floor. This house, this estate, was worth many, many millions. She could be the one to sell it, solving all her financial problems with one single deal. The thought that it would make her a legend in the Stellenbosch real estate business did not escape her.

'Come through,' he said with a half smile, as if he found her hesitation and tension quaint.

He walked ahead of her, silently. She noticed his thick, black hair, damp and neat as if he had combed it only minutes before. Why hadn't he shaved? Did he think the four-day beard was . . . attractive?

At that moment she remembered how she had quoted from the film *My Fair Lady* on seeing a photo of Boonstra in a newspaper when the scandal broke. 'He's like the "Hungarian",' she'd said to her husband Jozef. '*Oozing charm from every pore. He oiled his way around the floor.*'

And they'd laughed.

★   ★   ★

The only thing Cupido said when he rejoined Griessel in the waiting room was '*Jissis*.' Then he sat down heavily and stared ahead like a man suffering shell shock.

'Coffee?' the constable asked from the door, formal and disdainful, as if they'd already been found guilty.

'Yes, please,' said Benny.

Cupido just nodded.

The uniform disappeared down the passage.

Vaughn slowly lowered his elbow onto his knees. He bent forward. 'You told them it was all your fault, Benna.'

'Yes.'

'That is a bit of a *fokkop*, partner.'

'Why?'

Cupido stared at the bare floor. 'Well, fact number one is, I sweet-talked you into that mess. Fact number two is, I came and told them so too. But that fat *drol* of a commissioner tunes we conspired, and it's a strategy that's gonna sink us both.'

Griessel was afraid that would happen. But he'd staked his reputation as a boozer that they'd put the blame on him, and go easy on Vaughn.

'He's not the only one on the panel,' he said.

'I told you, let me read your statement. Then I could have stopped you.'

'No, you couldn't.'

'You have to get married. That's the big thing, partner.'

'I'll get a job somewhere, Vaughn. Maybe not straight away . . .'

Cupido sat up straight and looked at Griessel. 'Listen to me, Benna. Where you go, I go. Even . . .' And he shuddered at the thought: '. . . even if we have to open our own private eye business.'

7

Jasper Boonstra waved a hand at the breakfast bar in the kitchen, at six tall stools. Sandra hesitated. Then she perched on one, placing her handbag on the stool beside her.

'Coffee?' Boonstra asked.

'Thanks.'

'Cappuccino? Flat white? Espresso?'

'Cappuccino, please.'

Was he really going to make the coffee himself?

The kitchen was magnificent, white cupboards and dark grey wood and stainless steel and glass. Perfectly equipped. There was a view through a glass door to a charming herb garden at the back. Birds chirped outside. A kitchen like this was the first big selling point in any house, she thought. It would be a pleasure to market this wine estate. A privilege, almost. If it wasn't for the owner's reputation.

He slid aside a cupboard panel, exposing an expensive coffee machine with a small full-colour touchscreen and shiny pipes and buttons. He removed two glass coffee mugs, and tapped on the touch screen.

'This isn't the place that I want to sell,' he said with his back to her, as if he could read her mind. The machine began to grind, gurgle and steam.

'Oh,' she said, neutrally, to hide her disappointment.

He turned and looked at her. 'Where do you come from?'

The question was so unexpected and random, and she stumbled over her words. 'From . . . from the nursery school in Paradyskloof . . . I was dropping off my children.' She added the last deliberately, to make the point that she was a married woman. A mother.

He leaned against the counter where the coffee machine was, crossing his arms. 'I mean, where did you grow up.' Clearly amused.

'Oh. Bethlehem. In the Free State.'

'It's a long way from Bethlehem to Stellenbosch.'

'For sure.'

'How did that happen?' He took the cappuccino from under the spout and passed it to her. Followed by a white sugar bowl with an ornate silver spoon.

Did he really want to know her story? This man? Now? Or was it just part of his method? To charm her, in the hope . . .? In the reports of the scandal this man had been described by his victims as a sociopath.

He turned away again, busy with the coffee machine.

'I had . . . I couldn't complete my studies. It was . . . The money ran out. I got a job in the Cape. Then I met my husband . . .' Reluctant, he didn't need to know any more than that.

'What were you studying?' He looked at her again, coffee mug in hand.

'BComm.'

'Where?'

'In Bloemfontein.'

'Why become an estate agent?'

It was all a game, she thought. First, he says he doesn't want to sell this place, then he interrogates her, increasing the suspense. He liked the power of it.

'I . . . my first job was as broker's assistant. In Bellville. I didn't enjoy that . . .'

'Insurance?'

'Yes.'

He nodded. 'A rip-off. And then?'

'Then . . . Everyone was talking about the Cape real estate market that was so . . . on fire in those days. I thought, I can do that. I wanted to work for myself . . . I studied part-time. EQF level four in Properties, then level five and then my FFC.'

'How long ago was that?'

'Seven . . . almost eight years ago.'

'Charlie Benson must have been only too happy to employ a sexy young thing like you.'

'Which property do you want to sell, Mr Boonstra?' For the first time she was unable to hide the distaste in her voice.

He sipped his coffee slowly. 'Call me Jasper. You're married . . .?' An invitation to say more.

'I'd much prefer it if we could talk about the property.'

He gave her another assessing gaze. That little half-smile back on his face. He straightened up, walked past behind her. Was he going to ask her to leave?

He kept on moving, out of the kitchen into the house, with his coffee mug in hand. She watched him go. The arrogance in his body language and in this silent gesture. She felt like picking up her hand-bag and walking straight out. He and this whole set-up made her feel uneasy. It awakened all the old aggression in her that she'd worked so hard to control.

But she remained seated.

Benny Griessel and Vaughn Cupido stood before the disciplinary committee, their hands folded in front of them, as if to form some sort of shield against the verdict.

'You have pleaded guilty,' said the fat commissioner. 'And you are. Both of you. And then you try to win our sympathy by trying to cover for each other. False loyalty. We're not stupid. It did not work.'

When they entered, Musad Manie had given Griessel a near-imperceptible nod. He had taken heart from that. But that hope was quickly dwindling now.

'Not only are you guilty of insubordination, but you have disgraced yourselves, and you have disgraced the Hawks and you have brought the South African Police Service into disrepute. You have embarrassed our minister, and if he knew, our honourable president would have been deeply disappointed.'

Cupido made a sound, soft and disdainful, so that only Griessel could hear.

'And,' said the commissioner, 'you have pissed away your careers.'

Jasper Boonstra came strolling back with the coffee mug in one hand and a document in the other.

'Have you got a pen?' He sat down beside her, too close again, plac-ing the coffee and the A4 sheets, neatly stapled, in front of her.

She read the covering page: *Confidentiality Agreement*.

'Basically, it says that if you ever say anything about our conversations or the transaction or the nature of the ownership to anyone, I will cancel everything and sue you for more money than you will earn in your lifetime.' He said that in an offhand conversational tone, without a hint of hostility. Then he drank his coffee, as if it really didn't matter to him how she reacted.

She read both pages.

The document gagged the agent and the estate agency. In every possible way. Then she saw the final paragraph. It offered the estate agency six per cent commission, but specified that only she – and no other agent at Benson International Realtors – could market the property.

Sandra opened her handbag, found a pen, filled in her name and the details of Charlie's company. He leaned over, checked it all. She signed at the bottom.

'Initial page one,' he said. With a smirk in his tone, as if to suggest he'd known she wouldn't be able to resist the deal.

She initialled the first page, put the pen down.

'Charlie Benson has to sign too. Then give me a ring, and bring the forms right back to me.'

She nodded. 'What property do you want to sell?'

'Donkerdrif,' he said.

'Donkerdrif?' Her heart skipped a beat.

'Behind Kylemore, in the Banhoek valley. Two hundred and thirty-eight hectares, with ninety hectares of vineyards.'

She got her breath back. 'I know it. Doesn't it belong to a German?'

'It belongs to a Swiss company. Huber AG. And you don't need to worry about my . . . reputation.' A slight, fleeting smile. 'It is impossible to connect me to the company.'

She waited for him to explain. Schneider-König had so many subsidiaries, she couldn't remember the details of the spider web.

'Be discreet, and just find a buyer,' he said. 'I will take care of the legal signatures. The paperwork is the easy bit.'

Sandra nodded. 'What is the selling price?'

'A hundred million.'

She had to press her palms down on the counter to hide the trembling. A hundred million. Their commission would be six million rand. Even if Charlie only gave her the usual half share . . .

He misinterpreted her silence. 'It's a good price,' he said. 'Prize-winning wines. Cabernet Sauvignon, Merlot, Malbec, Petit Verdot, Cabernet Franc. Four boreholes, two dams, two permanent springs. The farmhouse is two hundred years old, it's big, it was restored two years ago. The cellar has capacity for four hundred and fifty tons of grapes, about three hundred thousand litres of wine.'

'I can get more,' she said. A small victory.

'No.'

Because he wanted to sell quickly and with as little fuss as possible, she reckoned. She picked the pen up again. 'Why did you choose us?' she asked, as she signed the second page.

The commissioner stared at Cupido and Griessel, at each in turn, his disdain unmistakeable.

'To my great disappointment,' he said, 'this committee does not share my opinion that you should be permanently and dishonourably discharged from the Service.'

Griessel felt relief wash over him. But he dared not show it.

'However, we do agree that you are no longer fit to be part of the Directorate for Priority Crime Investigations, and you are not worthy of the rank of captain. Therefore, you are demoted to the rank of warrant officer with immediate effect, and your posting to the Hawks is hereby terminated. You will be suspended for the rest of September without pay. You will be informed of your new duties in due course. Your personnel files will be amended with final written warnings, and should you be found guilty of similar transgressions in the next twenty-four months, I will personally see to it that you are permanently dismissed. Now, get out of my sight.'

8

Mute and defeated, they walked up Alfred Street towards the Cape Quarter where they had both parked.

Griessel heard someone calling his name. He turned. Cupido did the same. It was Musad Manie hurrying to catch up with them. He was a strongly built man with granite features. He looked around as if to be sure they were not observed.

'Keep walking, I'll walk with you,' said Manie.

'Thanks, Brigadier. You saved our mutual butts,' said Cupido as they walked.

Manie kept his deep voice down. 'It wasn't only me. Phila Zamisa fought just as hard for you. Now, can you hold out for six months?'

'Yes, Brigadier,' they said.

'I hear via the grapevine that we might have a new president in December. There's a chance. A reasonable chance. That means a few changes in the Service too. Do you understand?'

'Yes, Brigadier,' Griessel said.

Cupido posed the question that was weighing on them both: 'Where are we going to lie low, Brigadier? Where are we being posted?'

Manie was silent at first, and that was not a good sign. Then he halted, just around the corner of Somerset Street. 'Laingsburg,' he said.

'*Jirre*,' said Cupido.

Griessel bowed his head.

'That's what the commissioner wants,' said Manie apologetically.

'Laingsburg,' said Cupido in despair.

'It hasn't been finalised yet. I will see what I can do.' But his tone of voice didn't lend them much hope.

They stood in sombre silence.

Then Manie put out his hand to the detectives, solemnly shook hands with each of them. 'Good luck, boys. This too shall pass.'

Benson International Realtors' offices were in the historic Dorp Street. Number 157 had once been a residential home, now an office, it was still attractive, restored, gabled and white-washed. Charlie Benson's office was up in the old attic, where his window looked out on the giant oak that had been flourishing on the sidewalk since the Battle of Waterloo.

'*Jitte Krismis*,' he said, crouching over the Boonstra confidentiality document.

He was a skinny man. He reminded Sandra of a secretary bird, the same careful stiff walk, the somewhat affected air of dignity. Charlie was wearing a peacock-blue cravat to hide his loose neck wattles. It matched, as always, the handkerchief in the upper pocket of his jacket. His hair was perfectly cut and combed, the blond almost all overcome by grey.

'Why us, doll?' he asked Sandra.

'He claims you have the most extensive database of prospective buyers in this price class,' she said.

'He has done his homework,' said Charlie smugly.

He read. She waited patiently.

He looked up. 'You . . . You can't even tell Josef about this.'

'I know,' said Sandra. 'But it's not my mouth I'm concerned about.'

Charlie was indignant. 'San-San! How could you? Discretion is my middle name.'

It was not. Charlie was far too eager to show off. Especially with big sales, in the days when they had those, before the disaster.

He reached the final paragraph. His knee began to twitch nervously, a sign that he was tense or upset or indignant. 'Only *you* can sell it.'

'That is correct. And I want seventy-five per cent of the commission.'

'Hah!' No jokes now.

'Charlie, I'm serious.'

'But it's my database, built up over decades.'

She had anticipated this response. Charlie had financial problems of his own – he had to keep the agency's doors open in this difficult climate. The clause prohibited him from selling the property himself and weakened his position to negotiate her commission.

'I'll tell Jasper that's how you feel,' she said and held out her hand for the contract.

'Wait,' he said.

His knee twitched.

'Fifty-five per cent,' he said, his pen hovering over the place where he had to sign.

'No,' she said.' I want seventy-five.'

'It's my database. Sixty.' Charlie in fighting mode, stiff-back, upright in the chair. 'And that's my last offer.'

She shook her head.

'Sandy-san the bank doesn't want to raise our overdraft facility any more, it's a desperate situation.'

'Seventy,' she said.

'Sixty per cent gives you three-point-six million. That's enough.'

'Sixty-five,' she said. 'My final offer.' She took the contract and headed for her office to show him she was serious.

'Wait . . . You're mistreating the elderly. How am I going to retire? I'm ruined.' Charlie the victim. She knew all his tricks.

She halted in the doorway, crossed her arms. She knew she would never have the upper hand like this again. And Charlie was a well-to-do man. Very well-to-do.

He looked at her spitefully. 'You know that Jasper Boonstra never gives away anything for free.'

'What do you mean?'

'Think a little. He could have used an attorney or some or other obscure go-between to handle the sale on his behalf. Then no one would have known of his involvement in the deal, because you say he can't be connected to the company. He's taking a risk, with all those claims against him.'

'So?'

'So he decided to take the risk. Why?'

'Our client list, Charlie.'

'My client list. But he didn't call me, he hand-picked you. You are going to make big money, he's giving you a lot of power with this contract. Which you are now using against me. The question, sweety-pie, is what he wants in exchange for all of that,' he said and held out his hand for the contract.

She put it down in front of him. 'A quick, quiet sale, Charlie.' But she knew he had a point.

'Well, we'll see what your sixty-five per cent costs you, buttercup.' He almost spat the words at her. And then he signed on the dotted line.

She knew Charlie. And she didn't trust him, not one bit. Twenty minutes later she brought over a new version of their internal agreement on commission sharing and put it down in front of him to sign.

His leg jumped again in frustration. 'This is geriatric abuse, after all that I've done for you.' He pouted and fretted, but she just waited, hands folded on her chest.

Until he signed.

'Warrant officer, Benna? Warrant fucking officer? That's heavy humiliating,' Vaughn Cupido said. 'But Laingsburg. That is purgatory, *pappie*. That's the abyss, that's Heartbreak Hotel, middle of fucking nowhere, end of the road. Do you know the Karoo? If the sun doesn't fry you to death in summer, you freeze to death in winter. That'll be the end of me and Desiree, I'm telling you now. I wanted to pop the question, on New Year's Eve, inspired by your marital valour. But now it's bye-bye, love; bye-bye, happiness. Hello, fucking Laingsburg loneliness. 'Cause why, she's a much desired woman in the Stellenbosch district, I'll be sitting in misery city, attempting a long-distance weekend relationship while another man snaps her up. Life as we know it is over, *pappie*. Warrant officer in Laingsburg.'

They were sitting at a sidewalk table at the Café Charles in De Waterkant's Dixon Street. Griessel drank his coffee; Cupido hadn't touched his yet, he was too upset. Benny knew his colleague's outburst was not necessarily against Laingsburg or the Karoo. It was because he would be out of the Hawks. Vaughn was on record with statements such as 'the Hawks, they are my pride and joy, I would die for them'.

'And you, partner,' Vaughn said. 'You wanna get married. We're in the same boat. It's like one of those sad chick flicks; we have to make the tragic choice – the SAPS or love.'

Griessel looked up the street, above the pretty old Cape cottages, towards Vlaeberg. He sighed, then asked: 'Do you know who Mauritz Lotz is?'

'That dude who played centre for the Sharks before he also went off to France? Part of the Great Brawn Drain?'

'No, the guitar player.'

'Sorry, Benna, don't know him. You know I am more of an Early B kind of guy.'

'When Alexa has a new artist who needs to make an album, she tries to get the best people for the orchestra. She uses Mauritz a lot. He's a genius, Vaughn. World class. A while back, she said I should come and listen, Mauritz was recording a track, they were going to be working late. So I went. I sat there at the mixer desk with Alexa and the sound engineer, and Mauritz sat in the studio, behind the glass. And he played. *Fok*, Vaughn, he played. It's like he wasn't there; he went someplace where it was just him and the music, where the notes and his hands and fingers and his head and everything came together, and you could see that was his place. His home. Where he was what he had to be.'

Vaughn nodded. He understood. He drank his coffee.

'I've been playing bass guitar for over twenty years,' said Griessel, 'and I never ever came close to that place. You dream, you hope, you try, but you know it's not your home, your talent just doesn't crack it. And that's fine. Because my home is to be a detective. That's where I come together.'

'That's where you are what you have to be.'

'That's right.'

'That's deep, Benna. I dig it.'

Griessel kept on staring at the mountain.

'But what are you actually trying to say?' Cupido asked. 'Laingsburg is okay because you're still in the SAPS and you can detect there too? That's crazy, Benna. Laingsburg is domestic violence and Friday night boozers stabbing each other. Livestock theft. Shoplifting at the garage café? That is not detective work, *pappie*, that is for the *blougatte*, the bloody greenhorns, fresh out of police college, wet behind the ears.'

'That's what I mean, Vaughn. I won't be able to do it. I think Alexa and I will be okay if we have to wait a year or six months for the wedding. She's not going to be happy, but I know her. In the end she will understand. The trouble is, I won't be able to hold out . . .'

'You'll start drinking again.'

'That's right. I'll start drinking.'

9

Just after two, Sandra drew up outside Baronsberg's palace again. She parked her white Ford EcoSport in the space where the transparent glass garage doors stood open below the house. Beside that was another pair of matching doors, now closed. But visitors could see the vehicles inside. A white Mercedes Maybach G650 Landaulet and a low yellow Ferrari. She wondered if the place where she had parked now was the spot where Boonstra's absent wife would normally park. Rumours were doing the rounds that the wife was living in the giant beach house at Rooi-Els.

She grinned at the contrast between her humble Ford and the two supercars, and pressed the front doorbell, contract in hand, now in a posh Benson International Realtors binder. She had phoned half an hour ago. Boonstra said she could come, but he had sounded different. More . . . convivial?

He took a long time to respond. She pressed the bell again.

At last the heavy door swung open.

He was still dressed exactly as he had been that morning. Still unshaven. His eyes were a bit bloodshot, hair no longer impeccable. A strand hung down his forehead.

He grinned at her, gestured with his head for her to enter. Again he looked her up and down, shamelessly.

'Mr Boonstra,' her greeting was formal.

Passing him she smelled the booze – and potential trouble.

He shut the door behind her. She walked to the kitchen and he followed. '*Jis*, you're a sexy little thing,' he said.

She stopped, rage washing over her. 'No,' she said. 'You will not speak to me like that. I don't care who you are and how big this deal is. You don't speak to me like that.' She knew her face had turned red.

He laughed, short and guilty. ' "Little thing" is the wrong word. Forgive me. I won't do it again. Come, give me the document.'

He held out his hand. She reined in her temper. It was hard, but she wanted to get out of here. She handed him the folder. Her hand trembled.

He took it, walked ahead, to the kitchen counter. There was an open bottle of red wine, half empty, and a full glass.

'Wine?' he offered.

'No, thank you.'

'You do have something to celebrate.'

She didn't respond. He shrugged as if he didn't care. He flipped the folder open, examined the agreement, the signatures.

'Charlie Benson couldn't have been very happy that I cut him out.' Conspiratorial, conciliatory, seeking to get back in her good books. She wasn't going to fall for that.

'I need to know how I can have access to Donkerdrif.'

He drank deeply from his wine glass. 'The manager knows you're coming. His name is Moolman, he's always there. I'll send you his number.'

'Thank you very much.' She wanted to get moving. 'I'll let you know if there is an offer.'

'No. You will report weekly to me. Here.'

She shook her head. 'I will send you a WhatsApp if there is news.'

'You are stubborn. I like it. But you have signed a contract to report weekly.'

'The contract does not specify that I have to do it in person.'

'I specify it.'

'Goodbye, Mr Boonstra.' She turned around and walked to the door.

'I know exactly how badly you need this, Sandra,' he said.

She carried on walking.

'How is Josef's book going?'

That stopped her in her tracks, from rage as well as surprise.

'You must think I'm stupid,' he said.

She just glared at him.

'I only give this kind of deal to someone I'm sure of. We did an in-depth investigation of you.'

'We?'

'Absolutely,' he said, and poured himself another glass. 'I don't take chances. Not in my . . . situation. I have a whole team of private eyes on retainer. They went over things with a fine-tooth comb. I know things about you both that you don't even know. Your husband is Dr Josef Steenberg, lecturer in English literature, on sabbatical to write a novel. He did his doctorate on Ivan Vladimir, or something. He's a youngest child, two older sisters, his father is a medical doctor, big practice in Mossel Bay. Quite posh people. Your roots are . . . shall we say, less sophisticated? You are Sandra, maiden name Boshoff. The only daughter of Jannie Boshoff, who once played rugby for Eastern Free State. A hooker. Funny, it's always the hookers that are so . . . colourful. All his life he sold second-hand cars, never stayed long in one place. He was charged with fraud, about ten, eleven years ago? Just when he should have been paying your student fees. In any case, a common bunch of thieves, a syndicate that smuggled stolen vehicles to Lesotho. Some talk of illicit diamond dealing too. He got off. Docket disappeared, witnesses never turned up, the usual bribery. A real character, our Jannie. Party guy, joker, everybody's drinking pal, but his daughter is not one of those buddies. Apparently you no longer have contact.'

He was clearly enjoying her dismay. He raised his glass to her before he took another swig.

'They tell me Josef is the complete opposite of your father. Cultivated. Soft chap. Bit of a nerd. Not at all a rugger bugger. That says something, hey, about you . . . In any case, you are the mother of Anke and Bianca, the twins. You all live in a townhouse in Colombar Street in Kleingeluk. You and Josef . . . No, technically that's not correct . . . *you* are four months – maybe five months now – behind with the mortgage. You had trouble with the preschool too. Your Ford EcoSport's instalments were last paid five months ago. Apparently Josef is blissfully unaware of your mutual problems. Because I hear from my people that you are the one who handles the finances, it seems he doesn't have a head for numbers. I suspect it's unlikely that he would be peacefully writing if he knew the depth of the mess you're in. We all have our little secrets, hey? In any case, they tell me you're a strong character. The one who wears the pants in the household, for sure. How do your pants feel now, Sandra? You're this deep in debt,' and he waved his hand against his throat to emphasise his point. 'How long before Ford repossesses the car? Before the bank summons you to discuss the bond? Or have they already? How long before they chuck your kids out of the preschool? How long before Josef finds out? I'm just wondering, will he think the Sandra apple didn't fall far from the Pa-Jannie tree after all? So, you should think carefully about just how difficult you want to be. Just remember one thing: I still have to get the signatures on an offer to purchase. We should rather be friends, don't you think?'

She felt it burn through her, a white-hot flame of humiliation.

He drained his glass, swept back the strand of hair, looked at her with disdain.

She said the one thing that popped into her head. 'Ivan Vladislavić.' She knew it was a pathetic attempt to retrieve a fraction of her dignity.

'What?'

'Ivan Vladislavić. Josef did his doctorate on him.'

He poured himself another glass of wine. 'Go and sell my farm. You know how to find your way out.'

Griessel sat in front of the little old restored house in Boston, Bellville for a long time. In front of Doc Barkhuizen's rooms.

Doc had been his sponsor at Alcoholics Anonymous for years. Doc was seventy-one years old, with a long grey ponytail, and thick glasses. Sometimes he wore an earring. He still practised as a doctor, because 'the drink devil makes plans for idle hands'.

Griessel hesitated, wondering what he was going to say to Doc. The old man was a hard taskmaster, he would want to know: 'What are you going to do, Benny?' And he would have to have a proper answer.

He'd decided to serve his sentence of nine to twelve months in Laingsburg. Musad Manie's question of 'can you hold out for six months' was hopelessly optimistic. The bureaucratic SAPS personnel department never worked fast. At best it would be a year. But he would go to the Karoo. The only alternative was to leave the Service. Find work in the private sector. Security or investigations. But who would employ him? Everyone in the wider industry knew he was a boozer who could fall off the wagon at any moment. He couldn't see himself going round pleading and making promises.

No, it had to be Laingsburg. He would fight against the bottle every day and on his weekends off back in Cape Town he would attend the

AA meetings with Alexa, at the Dutch Reformed Church in Upper Union Street, Tamboerskloof, where the Green Door group fought the good fight on Saturdays at seven and Sundays at five.

Once he had finished talking to Doc, he would go and tell Alexa they were postponing the wedding for a year. She would weep, she would try to persuade him, try to cheer him up with her rose-tinted optimism, but he wasn't going to budge.

Doc would also want to know: 'Benny, how are you going to keep your hands occupied in the month and a half of suspension ahead?'

He would tell him that he was going to paint Alexa's Victorian house in Brownlow Street. And mend the gutters. And cut back the old palm tree in front of their bedroom window. And ride his mountain bike in the mornings.

Doc would tell him: 'You're not a painter's arse, Benny.'

And he would reply: 'Doc, that's the truth. But what else am I going to do?'

Jissis, it wasn't going to be easy.

In spite of Brigadier Musad Manie's promise that he 'would see what he could do', he was not the one to fire the first salvo in an attempt to rescue the mutual butts of Benny Griessel and Vaughn Cupido from six months' purgatory in Laingsburg.

It was Lieutenant Colonel Mbali Kaleni.

She was Commanding Officer of the Serious and Violent Crimes Unit of the Hawks. Griessel and Cupido's former boss. She reported to Manie. She was a Zulu woman and her name meant 'flower'. She was short of stature and since the distressing events that led to her two detectives' disciplinary hearing, she had been gaining weight again. It was the stress. She believed she was really to blame, even though she had told them at the time to drop the case.

When Musad Manie walked into her office and told her the outcome of the hearing, she said: '*Hayi*' in her mother tongue. She never used stronger language than that, even when she was very upset. As she was now. Colonel Kaleni was conservative and proper and painfully law-abiding.

Manie also told her, serious and determined, that he would see what he could do. Then he walked out again.

Mbali leaned back in her chair. She was thoroughly indignant about the injustice to her people. And she felt it was her responsibility to help them in some way. She thought long and hard. Eventually she tapped both palms gently on the desk top, stood up, and unlocked a cupboard against the wall. She took out a dossier from deep in the back, relocked the cupboard, and walked purposefully to her car with the thick folder in her hands.

She drove away from the Hawks offices in Bellville. She never exceeded the speed limit. It was twenty-five kilometres to the Western Cape headquarters of the SAPS in Green Point.

On arrival, she parked, got out, walked into the building and took the lift to the seventh floor, where the commissioner, that large bull-frog, Lieutenant General Mandla Khaba, had his office. She asked his secretary if he was in.

'Yes, but he is busy.'

Kaleni clicked her tongue crossly, walked over to the commissioner's office door and opened it.

'You can't go in there!' the secretary barked.

Kaleni cast her a withering look, walked in and shut the door behind her.

The secretary could not hear what was said. She only heard the commissioner bellowing a few times, and the plump little colonel raising her voice back at him. But then the sound subsided considerably.

Thirteen minutes later Kaleni came out again.

The secretary waited ten minutes to be certain there wasn't more to add to the story, and then she rang her colleague who worked for the Western Cape chief of detectives to share this juicy bit of gossip with her.

10

Sandra wanted to find a place to pull over, so that she could get out and get rid of some of the tension in her body. She wanted to scream out her rage, find relief. She wasn't going to cry, she would not cry. But there was no privacy on the Jonkershoek road for a moment like that, too many joggers and cyclists and tourists. She did it while driving past the Lanzerac, with whitened knuckles on the steering wheel and her face flushed. She made a keening sound, long and drawn out, like an animal in pain. To let the anger out.

She would not cry.

Jasper Boonstra knew how to wound her, where her deepest hurts lay, her weaknesses.

She was going to walk away from this thing, from him. Charlie could handle the sale. Charlie could go and see Boonstra and tell him she had withdrawn, the two of them could do what they liked.

But she knew that was a fantasy, an attempt to process the humiliation of it all.

She simply could not walk away from this.

She parked behind the office, sat in her car, breathed. She didn't want her colleagues to see how she felt.

At last she got out, walked to the office, sat down at her desk. She wanted to phone Moolman, manager at the wine farm, Donkerdrif, to make an appointment for the following day. But then Charlie came over. His antennae were as sharp as ever, he must have picked up some hint of her state, because he put a great deal of compassion and concern into his voice: 'Are you okay, San-San?'

She needed the empathy so badly that it undermined her self-control. She said: 'Jasper Boonstra . . . I'm telling you, Charlie, I could kill that man. With a smile.'

★　　★　　★

Benny Griessel's prediction that Alexa Barnard would cry was incorrect.

She hugged him tightly, in her office at AfriSound in the city centre, consoling him.

He didn't want to be consoled. It didn't help. But he patiently submitted to her embrace, until he felt it was enough.

'It's only four months, every weekend when you come home will be like a honeymoon,' she said. Typical Alexa, she simply couldn't help lining every dark cloud with silver.

'Four months?'

'Yes. You'll only start in Laingsburg in November. We get married in December. So, it's really only January, February, March and April of our married life that you won't be home in the week. Four months, Benny, it will go past in the blink of an eye. And in any case, absence makes the heart grow fonder . . .'

Griessel sighed. He couldn't summon the courage to tell her it would be far longer than four months. He didn't have the strength to stick to his guns and insist on postponing the wedding.

'What colour do you want the house painted?' he asked.

Vaughn Cupido didn't have the courage to tell the woman in his life about the exile to Laingsburg.

He believed Brigadier Musad Manie could still save the day. He had promised, and he was a man of his word. So he only told Desiree about the month-and-a-bit of suspension without pay and the uncertainty of what would happen next. In the Punjab Restaurant in Stellenbosch Square, during her lunch hour.

Desiree was a project manager at a tech company that developed mobile phone applications. She was clever. And very beautiful. Tall and slim, pitch-black hair draped down her back, dark eyes that still enchanted Vaughn with their shades and flecks of copper and gold. Lioness eyes.

'I'm still very proud of you, lovey,' said Desiree. 'For what you've done. For standing by your principles. Now try the prawn curry, it's awesome.'

He looked at her and thought he couldn't lose her, no way he would get a chance like this again. As he kept telling Griessel: 'Desiree is class, she's aristocracy. I mean, I'm from Mitchell's Plain. Humble beginnings. In ordinary circumstances, she'd be way out of my league. But luckily I'm the best detective in the Hawks now, and that makes all the difference. No offence, Benna, you're a very close second best.'

No, he couldn't let her slip between his fingers. If they posted him to Laingsburg, he would resign. That's the way he felt now. He would choose love.

And the prawn curry.

Sandra, tired and hungry, could already smell the food from outside the front door at half past five in the afternoon.

Anke and Bianca heard her key in the lock and came running, dark plaits bouncing on their heads. She had to put her handbag down to get her arms around them both.

'Papa's making pasta,' said Anke.

'Pasta fagoli-fagoli,' said Bianca.

'Isn't,' said Anke. 'Fagoli-fony.'

'Isn't,' said Bianca.

'Pasta fagioli al forno,' said Josef. He came around the corner of the living room, in the denim apron, pasta spoon in hand, his smile broad and welcoming.

'And we're helping,' said Anke. 'I pushed the sausages out of their skin. Bianca couldn't do it.'

'Isn't!' said Bianca. 'I didn't want to do it. It's yucky. It's gross!'

Sandra kissed Josef, from between the two little wriggling bodies. The kiss was more lingering and intense than usual. He looked at her questioningly, but the twins kept up a constant babble, describing their day, fetching the works of art they had made at nursery school. She sat down in the open-plan kitchen with them on either side of her, savouring the aroma of Josef's pasta, laughing and chatting with the children. Every now and then she would glance at her husband who was slicing bread, setting the table. At his beautiful hands, his tall, lean body, at the thick beard that he kept neatly trimmed, his dark hair nearly as long as her own. And his dear, gentle eyes that looked back at her and their children with such contentment.

Soft chap. Bit of a nerd. Not at all a rugger bugger. That says something, hey. Jasper Boonstra was emphasising that Josef was the antithesis of her father, that she'd deliberately chosen him for that.

She hadn't chosen him, she had fallen in love. In a coffee shop in Ryneveld Street. She was new in town, new at her job. Her break from the office, at ten in the morning, coincided with his time off, when he was free from lecturing. It was pure chance. Mostly she was busy on her laptop, doing property research and drawing records on WinDeed and Lightstone. He would always sit and read, every few days a new book. She noticed the way the female students would peer at him, then put their heads together and giggle and speculate. He was so utterly oblivious to it. But not to her. Now and then he had looked up from his book and made brief eye contact with her. Shyly returned to his reading. Over two weeks of that, before he sent a slice of cheesecake to her table. There was an accompanying note: *Roses are red, violets are blue. A good pick-up line? I don't have a clue.*

She looked up at him. He blushed. She sent the note back with her own attempt at rhyme: *It's not bad, it's not sad, makes me (a very tiny bit) glad.*

He sighed theatrically in relief. They shared a cautious smile. He continued reading his book.

The next day, another slice of cheesecake, another verse: *Roses are red, violets are blue. My name is Josef, what about you?*

In that manner, without speaking a word directly to each other, they communicated for more than a week. She liked that he wasn't in a hurry, that he was a reader, playful and good-looking, with good taste in clothes. And that he wasn't bothered by the adoration of the students, although they were so young and fresh and attractive, some- times even blatantly seductive. And then he invited her to dinner at Jardine. She met him at the restaurant, and his voice and hands were beautiful, and he talked with her, listened to her, was interested in her. His eyes were gentle, and his heart too.

Yes, he was different from her father. At their wedding reception, Josef had pacified the drunk and rowdy Jannie Boshoff with wisdom and compassion and led him quietly away, so that her father's dignity was more or less preserved. He didn't let him ruin her big day. Yes, he was soft, but in the right kind of way.

Also, he was no nerd. Early each morning he went running on Stellenbosch mountain. And some weekends he would make minor adjustments to his 1990 Mazda MX-5, the little crimson second-hand convertible that his parents gave him at his first graduation.

Josef dished up the food, and sat down with them.

'Oh,' he said, 'before I forget, the principal says thank you.'

Her brow furrowed. 'What for?'

'For the payment.'

Thoughts raced through her mind. There was no irony in his tone, not a trace of reproof, no indication that the principal of the nursery school was being sarcastic. What payment?

She kept her reaction neutral, in the hopes that he would elaborate.

He began to eat.

'Did you make any headway with the book today?' she asked.

He shook his head. 'Not much. The muse wasn't very generous. But who knows, maybe later,' he said with a meaningful look at her, 'I might be able to lure my other muse into my bed chamber for inspiration . . .'

'Why is your voice so funny, Pappa?' Anke piped up.

'That's just silly,' said Bianca. 'You don't even have a bed changer.'

Sandra and Josef smiled across their heads, though Sandra didn't feel much like laughing at the girls' inquisitive cuteness tonight.

Sandra tossed and turned, long after Josef had fallen asleep. The gnawing sense of guilt, her suspicions about who had made the payment. Boonstra was right, her beloved husband was blissfully unaware of the financial mess they were in. She had tried not to think of it herself. Now Boonstra had put it starkly into words, made it reality. Her reasons for not telling Josef were complex. But the most important one was noble – she didn't want him to be troubled by this. He didn't need the stress, he had only this year of sabbatical to complete the book. He *had* to complete the book. The novel that meant so much to him, that he had been planning for so long, that he had been working so hard at. The book that would establish him as author-lecturer, that would give a massive boost to his career, so they wouldn't have to be so desperately dependent on her variable earnings. She hadn't burdened Josef with their financial dilemma, because she kept hoping and believing that the next property deal was just around the corner, it was only a question of time, of holding on and keeping the wolf from the door until her ship came in. But the only properties selling in this town in the past months, were the cheap townhouses in the developments in Stellenbosch's outer suburbs. And Benson International Realtors were not in that market, Charlie had been too snobbish and choosy for far too long.

How long would it be before Josef began to suspect something? She felt like a deceiver, a traitor; they had never had secrets from each other. And now there were two. Their finances and Jasper Boonstra. Josef had asked her tonight: 'How was your day?' She badly wanted to tell him everything, about her fury, her humiliation, her hope that this deal would turn out to be worth the monster-man's manipulations. And that it would fix everything that was wrong. So she could break free from the secrets.

All she had said was, 'Long.' And changed the subject.

But now, lying in bed beside her spouse, there was a single refrain that sawed and grated her innards: *I'm just wondering, will he think the Sandra apple didn't fall far from the Pa-Jannie tree?*

That was the biggest shame of all. She was starting to become like her father; a dodger of creditors, glib liar, the rationaliser of her sins.

I I

She made a point of seeing the principal when she dropped the twins off the next morning.

'I felt so awful,' the woman said, her hand on Sandra's arm, in a gesture of empathy and apology.

'Oh?'

'I didn't mean you to . . . I realise I was a tad sharp with you yesterday morning, but you needn't have paid a month in advance as well. I know we're all having a difficult time. But thank you very much for that. Thank you very much.'

She could tell the woman meant it. Sincerely grateful.

She knew where the money had come from. She phoned right away, once she was back in her car.

Jasper Boonstra did not pick up.

On the way to the office she wondered: What else had he paid? The arrears on the home mortgage? The outstanding instalments on her car? She would have to check.

She fired up her computer the minute she got home.

He hadn't.

She hated herself in that moment for the spark of hope she had harboured.

Why would Boonstra have paid the nursery school? What was his purpose, his expectation? Just a display of power? Manipulation? A taste of things to come? It filled her with a vague sense of unease.

Charlie Benson knocked on her door frame. Aping concern again. 'What did that man do to you to upset you so much, Sandy-san?'

'He was rude, Charlie.'

'Is that all?'

'Yes. That is all.' Charlie had an agenda and she was going to resist it.

He sidled up to her, his voice a conspiratorial whisper: 'Do you know what I heard the other day? He and his wife went out to dinner, a few months ago, here in town. Shameless, he doesn't care who sees him, after all that's happened. Apparently he walks around with a total eff-you attitude . . . And then there was this young student singing and playing guitar in the restaurant. So he goes over to the poor guy and asks him how much they are paying him to sing. The lad tells him. And he says: 'I'll pay you double if you stop.' Can you believe that, San-San?'

'I can.'

'He's a psychopath.'

'That's possible.'

'Tell me if you need help, Longoria.'

'I'll be fine, thank you, Charlie.'

He hid his disappointment well.

She stood up.

'I'm going out to Donkerdrif with a photographer,' she said and picked up her handbag. 'We have to get a move on with the prospectus . . .'

21 September

Benny Griessel's big painting project didn't start well. The Cape is a fickle creature in September. Unpredictable. Thursday's crystal clear sunshine was gone and Friday dawned dreary, grey with the threat of rain.

He was busy with the walls of the house, the second storey, high up against the roof. Since seven o'clock he'd been clambering about on rented scaffolding, in his new-but-already-stained overalls, a messy painter, hopelessly inexperienced. And probably in too much of a hurry, eager to get it over and done with. This wasn't much fun.

He pushed the roller up and down, dipped it in Plascon's Quicksand shade, Alexa's choice. He avoided looking down, as he struggled a bit with heights. The north-wester tugged at him.

He gradually found a rhythm that suited him, that wasn't too hard on his arm and shoulder. His mind kept returning to Laingsburg. He'd been searching on the internet for a flat to rent, but there was nothing available. Not even a little room somewhere. What was he going to do? He couldn't afford a hotel or a guest house. He was still paying his son Fritz's expensive film school fees, he was paying off Alexa's engagement ring, and for two months he would receive no pay. And in October he would be a warrant officer again, which meant even less pay.

Fuck.

Charlie waited for Sandra to arrive, then beckoned her to his office. Today the cravat was a paisley pattern in burgundy and navy blue – his colour scheme when he wished to make an impression on clients.

He shut the door behind her. Before he'd sat down he was already talking in a hushed but excited you're-never-going-to-believe-this tone: 'He forced himself on a woman, Sandy. Jasper Boonstra. A woman who worked with him. In a hotel room in Berlin.'

'Where do you hear these things, Charlie?'

'What does that matter?'

'Suddenly you've got all these stories about Boonstra. Are you talking to anyone about the contract?'

'Of course not.' Highly indignant. 'I have your best interests at heart. I just . . . did a little research. Discreetly. As ever.'

'I suppose the rumours are running like wildfire.'

Charlie wouldn't be deterred. 'This one is true, my darling . . .' He sat down across from her, elbows on the desk, leaning his thin torso forward: 'It comes from someone who worked in Schneider-König personnel department. Quite high up . . .'

'And this person told you this directly?'

'Sandy-san, my source is above reproach.'

Which really meant that Charlie did not hear it first-hand. She wouldn't be at all surprised if he had sucked it out of his thumb overnight.

'Let's hear it then, Charlie.'

'He says, they employed a very sexy woman in their publicity department. Young, not yet thirty. Curvaceous, lips, the whole shebang. She had hardly started work when Jasper said no, she had to go along, to Germany, for a board meeting or something. And, on the second night in the hotel, he phoned her in her room, very late at night, and told her to come, he wanted to discuss things. When she walked in, he was already into the wine and wearing just his bathrobe. He poured her a glass of wine and told her what he could do for her career, if she was prepared to . . .' Charlie made quotation marks with his index fingers, '. . . "cooperate". And then he let his robe fall open, San-San . . .' He gestured with his hands, and raised his eyebrows to show how shocked he was.

'And then . . .'

'Well he had a huge . . . you know . . .'

Prudish Charlie. She suppressed the urge to say, no, she didn't know. 'And then?'

'She got up and left the room, and when they were back in Stellenbosch she reported him to HR. And she got a big payout. A settlement. Off the record. To buy her silence. We're talking more than a million, sweetheart. Apparently she works in Johannesburg now. For a banking group.'

'He's a pig, Charlie.'

'He's a rapist, Sandy-san. It was that close. I mean, if she hadn't got up and run from the room . . .'

Sandra didn't react.

'Apparently it wasn't the first or the last incident of that kind. Until he got the girlfriend, the mistress. Then he calmed down.'

'I see.'

'I thought I should tell you.' He looked a bit deflated by her calm response. 'Just so you know. Be very careful.'

'I will be, Charlie. At least he's still got his mistress.'

Charlie didn't hear her. He leaned back, his knee twitched. Here comes the card he meant to play, she thought.

'You know, we aren't without leverage in this agreement. The fact that he wants to keep the deal so quiet, means that there are backhand dealings, he wants to channel money somehow, probably means to skip the country ahead of the court cases. And it's *my* address list . . . We have leverage. We can tell him if he wants to make use of us, I will handle it. Then you won't be exposed to any risk.'

She laughed, because she saw through his scheming. 'The second he opens the front door in his robe, we will do that, Charlie.'

'You think it's a joke?' he said indignantly. 'That man is a manipulator, a psychopath, a molester, and you think it's a joke?'

She walked to the photographer's studio in Plein Street. Angry with Charlie and his suggestions, his transparent machinations. The discussion carried on in her head, and in her mind her tone was controlled and firm.

'No, Charlie, I don't think the story is a joke, I think you are a joke. Your tricks, your stinginess, your plan to cheat me, to deprive me of my good fortune. In these tough times. While you are going to score millions anyway. It's funny how you think you're smart enough to cheat me. You with your own form of harassment, honed to a fine art. Your little pet names, your assumption of superiority, your way of constantly reminding your female staff that they are beneath you. It's so subtle, Charlie, just this side of the line so that you can always claim innocence.

'Do you think that Jasper Boonstra is the first man I've had to deal with? The first man who will try to use a situation for sexual benefit? Every woman has been there, Charlie. I've been there. I've known what men are like since I was fifteen, sixteen years old. It's always there. The pressure, trying to take advantage. Mostly in the background, just below the surface, especially when you first start work and there are male colleagues and male clients. Most of them are cowardly, cautious, testing the water. But unavoidable, constant, eventually it just becomes like the background hum of a city. White noise. You learn, slowly but surely, to handle it, you become accustomed to it, you know it's there, you just choose not to hear it all the time. Sometimes it's more direct, then it penetrates your defences, and you have to block it, deal with it. Be polite but firm, or laugh to defuse it, depending on the circumstances. Try to protect your dignity and professionalism and career. I learned the hard way, Charlie. I made mistakes. Lost my temper; I've stored up a lot of rage. I ruined my first job with that rage because I lost my temper with a client who just would not stop. That's when I realised it's not a level playing field. Not a fair fight. Not if you're female and young and poor and desperate and you have no qualifications. Not if you don't have the emotional and financial safety net of supportive, balanced parents. Getting angry doesn't help. Reporting it to your employers didn't help either, although they made all the right noises; it still branded you, branded you as a certain "type". Not a "team player". I learned the hard way, Charlie, if I wanted to win, I had to be smarter. More cunning. A month ago I was showing one of your clients that property in Mostertsdrift. Remember the construction magnate from Johannesburg who talked about demolishing a twelve-million-rand place so he could build "something prettier"? That was probably an attempt to impress me with his wealth. A man close to sixty, he'd been so courteous and respectful at first. He talked about his wife as "the missus", as in "the missus will have to come and take a look as well". But there's something about being alone with a woman in the privacy of an empty house, Charlie, that even a sixty-something baldy with a beer belly and double chin can't resist. "Is there anything you can do to convince me to buy?" he wanted to know. I said we could negotiate with the owners, we could look at the commission. "That's not exactly what I had in mind," he said and looked at me in that way. Then I said with a sweet smile: "Well, perhaps I could talk to the missus" . . . Maybe that's why he preferred to buy in Constantia. Perhaps that agent "convinced" him?

'You know nothing of all those goings on, Charlie Benson, and I know that telling you about them would not help a single bit. So you leave me and my commission alone. I will handle Jasper Boonstra. Without your help.'

12

Ten a.m. High on the scaffolding, Griessel took a breather. He put the paint roller down, took out his cigarettes, struggled to get one to light. He had to turn his back to the wind, bend over and cup his hand around it, drawing quick and deep.

The cigarette tasted of paint. He exhaled the smoke angrily, turned back again so that he could look over the city. That's when his eye caught it, down in Milner Street, a white Honda Ballade with broad tyres and smoked glass windows pulled away abruptly, up, towards Vlaeberg. As if his turning round had taken them by surprise.

The car disappeared behind the house.

Just coincidence.

He finished his smoke. Picked up the paint roller again.

Sandra received the final photographs on Friday. It was an excellent job, displaying the estate in spectacular fashion.

On her computer she put together the Donkerdrif prospectus, and sent Boonstra a WhatsApp to ask for his email address.

He rang her at once. It surprised her; till now he hadn't answered any of her calls.

'You paid my kindergarten bill,' she said.

'I'm sure you'll repay the debt.'

That suggestive ambiguity again, so she said: 'Yes, I will pay back the money. Every cent.'

'We'll see. Why do you need my email?'

He provided an obscure Gmail address when she explained that he had to approve the prospectus.

23 September

On Saturday afternoon Griessel walked Vince Fortuin back to his car outside the Woodstock Municipal Hall.

'Benny, your mind wasn't on the music today,' Rust's lead guitarist said. 'Are you okay?'

The band had been practising in the hall. Griessel knew he wasn't at his best. And what Vince was really asking was whether he was drinking. They had been playing together for many years.

He told Fortuin there was a very strong possibility that he would be transferred and wouldn't be available to play in the band for six months. It wasn't yet official, and that's why he hadn't mentioned it earlier. But it might be wise to start looking for another bass player. Hopefully just a temporary one.

'No,' said Fortuin. 'We'll just wait for you. Six months is not a lifetime.'

'Thanks, Vince. But think about it.'

They said goodbye. Griessel walked to his car, a white Toyota Corolla, ten years old and nearly two hundred thousand on the clock. He had meant to replace it next year, when Fritz completed his studies, but that too would have to wait.

On the door handle was a folded piece of paper stuck down with masking tape. At first he thought it was a new form of advertising, like the annoying pamphlets under the windscreen wipers. He pulled it off, meaning to crumple it up. He waved at Vince Fortuin who was driving away, and looked around for the nearest litter bin. Then he noticed the writing in thick blue ink on the paper: *Captain Griessel*.

He propped his guitar case against the Corolla so that he had both hands free, pulled the masking tape off and unfolded the A4 sheet of paper.

It was a black-and-white photo of a firearm being held by someone. It seemed to be photocopied. The photo occupied two-thirds of the page. Below, in the same blue ink, was written: *I can only trust you and Captain Cupido. There is an adder in our bosom. Be careful of phone calls.*

Griessel scanned the parking lot, and the park beyond, then up and down Aberdeen Street. There were no obviously suspect people or vehicles. Just the usual, constant traffic over in Victoria Street.

He examined the photo more closely. Two large hands held a revolver, fingertips under the barrel, while the grip lay in the palm of the other hand. It looked like the inelegant shape and stainless steel of Smith & Wesson's brutal S&W 500 model, reputed to be the most powerful revolver in the world.

The underside of the synthetic grip was damaged; a small section was broken or shot off. The rest of the weapon was in good nick. The way it was held, led one to believe that it was being displayed for the photograph.

The only other detail in the photo was just above the revolver. A button on a dark jacket. With the eight-pointed star of the South African Police Service on it. Someone in uniform holding the weapon in front of his body, perhaps.

He looked around again, searching for whoever delivered the letter. There was nobody to see.

Griessel unlocked the Corolla, picked up the guitar and put it on the back seat. He took his cell phone out of his trouser pocket and phoned Cupido. It took a while before his colleague answered with: 'Howzit, partner, paint job done yet?'

'Not even a quarter. What are you up to?' He heard the buzz of a soccer match transmission in the background.

'Benna, I'm being domesticated, and the sad thing is, I like it. With Desiree doing overtime and all, I'm helping her out a bit. With the boy and the housekeeping and so on. I've just taken a batch of chocolate muffins out of the oven, and Donovan thinks they're better than his ma's . . .'

In the background Desiree Coetzee's son pronounced emphatically: 'Nay, uncle, I said they are just as *lekker* as my ma's.'

'He's just loyal to his ma, Benna. What's up?'

Be careful of phone calls. Was it really a risk? 'No news?' he asked Vaughn. Just in case.

'Nada, zilch. Word has it, we are still going to be catching the Transkaroo.'

'Call me if there's anything.'

'I feel you, Benna, I feel you.'

Cupido would have told him if he had received a similar letter.

*   *   *

A couple from Pretoria raised Sandra's hopes of a fast, uncomplicated sale. And restored her faith in humanity somewhat.

She showed them a house in Brandwacht Street in the suburb of the same name, Benson International had a sole mandate over the property. The house was forty years old, but spacious and in good condition. It helped that the house was still furnished with tasteful furniture, because André and Joan Schoeman – the owners – were already in America, applying for permanent residence. André Schoeman had started working there as a science lecturer.

The prospective buyers were in their forties, polite and sophisticated. On the front veranda the woman held her breath when she saw the view of the mountain in the late afternoon light. She grasped her husband's hand. 'I can live here, Papa,' she said. He put his arm around her shoulders and they stood for a moment, looking like a pair of young newly-weds.

She wanted to be like that with Josef, at their age, Sandra thought. Still loving and in love.

They liked the kitchen, and that there was a room for each of their three children. The quiet neighbourhood, and the fact that the neighbour on the left held a high position at Distell. Sandra said nothing about the house on the right. It was an Airbnb rental, people coming and going; some buyers were scared off by that.

The couple chatted with Sandra, explaining their desire to get away from the poor service delivery and the never-ending crime in Gauteng, they hoped to build a new life here. And they didn't need to wait for their current house to sell, they had cash. Did she think the owner would accept six million?

It was nine hundred thousand less than the listed price, but she knew for a quick sale Charlie would agree to a smaller commission, and the owners' price was negotiable.

'We'll try,' she said. 'Let me get the offer forms.'

Griessel parked inside the garage. Before he got out he read the message once more.

I can only trust you and Captain Cupido. There is an adder in our bosom. Be careful of phone calls.

There were four things that made him suspect it was a policeman who had stuck the note to his car. The first was the statement that the writer could only trust him and Vaughn – most likely someone who knew they were a team, and both in hot water over the SSA matter, both suspended, trustworthy when it came to state-capture affairs? Because information about their hearing had never been in the media, but was widely known in the SAPS.

The second was the reference to 'Captain' Cupido. On the whole, members of the Service were more inclined to refer to rank than members of the public.

The third was the 'our bosom'. Surely that was a reference to the police?

And the fourth was the uniform button. There was something about the photo that led him to believe it wasn't taken for public consumption in the mainstream media, or on social media. The way the revolver was held, he couldn't put his finger on it. An internal photo, internally shared?

The reference to the 'adder' – did that mean there was a member of the SAPS who was corrupt? A senior member, because you wouldn't go to all this trouble to nail a mere constable.

He folded the letter and put it in the glove compartment. There was nothing he could do now. He would have to wait for further communication.

24 September

While Alexa was reading the Sunday papers, Griessel used her laptop to google the S&W 500 revolver.

That was the type of revolver in the photo for sure.

He tried various combinations of search words to see if the specific photo existed on the internet. Or at least a reference to a crime that had been committed with it.

He found nothing. He went back to his painting, ignoring the protests of his fiancée that he ought to rest at least one day of the week.

Sandra sat in the shade at the picnic table at Blaauwklippen family market and watched Josef and the twins laughing and playing on the bouncy castle. Love for them made a warm glow inside her.

He was a wonderful father. From the beginning he'd said he would love to have daughters. He was involved from the birth. He had often got up with her at night when she had to breastfeed, and was more deft with the nappies than she was. More patient with the children.

He deserved to know the whole truth, she thought. Lord knows, he deserved the full truth.

Her cell phone rang.

It was the couple from Pretoria. They had found another house, closer to the schools. Through one of the big, national estate agencies. They were sorry. Thank you for the excellent service, they said.

13

Sandra noticed the date on her laptop and her heart rate skipped a beat. Another month end. Another month behind.

The sale of Donkerdrif was going to come too late to save her. Two months before everything was completed? Three? The only silver lining was that deals of this nature and size – in contrast to regular mortals who had to wait for their bond to be approved and registered – were paid in cash, and usually completed promptly. If she was very lucky, a month and a half? Would that be too late still?

She opened her email.

Her heart leaped. Charlie's address list had yielded its first fruit. There was a response from two potential buyers to her discreet presentation of the nature of the Donkerdrif property without identifying it. Two influential people with existing wine estate interests. Their response was enthusiastic.

She forwarded the confidentiality agreement to each, with the promise of a prospectus as soon as it was returned.

That made her feel better about the Brandwacht disappointment. A month and a half seemed more doable now.

At 11:24 Griessel was standing on the corrugated iron roof of 47 Brownlow Street, with the north-wester doing its damnedest to pluck him off, and grey paint on his face, hands and blue overalls. His arm was knackered, his left leg uncomfortably braced against the gutter to prevent him hurtling off the edge. It was a long way down, two storeys.

His cell phone rang. He had to put the roller carefully down in the paint tray, wipe his hand off as well as he could before touching it.

It was Cupido.

'Vaughn?'

'Where are you, Benna?'

'At home . . .'

'Can't you hear the *fokken* doorbell, partner? I've been ringing it till I'm blue in the face.'

'I'm on the roof.'

'What roof?'

'The house roof, Vaughn. At the back. Hang on, I'm coming down. It will take a while. It's a *moer* of a long ladder . . .'

He clambered down the ladder, and then had to go through the garage and the house before reaching the front door. He opened up. Cupido was standing there in jeans, T-shirt and trainers. The T-shirt was tight. Vaughn burst out laughing when he saw Griessel, took out his phone immediately.

'*Jissis*, partner, I gotta get a *photie* of this. Even if it's just to blackmail you if you want to drink.' He snapped Griessel in the paint-smeared overalls, while Griessel stood there meekly. He knew he was a sight.

He beckoned Cupido inside. While he carefully climbed out of the overalls in the sitting room, Cupido removed a folded sheet of paper from his pocket.

'Benna, I got a weird letter . . .'

Griessel knew instantly what it was. 'Welcome to the club,' he said.

'You too.' A confirming nod, without surprise. Cupido unfolded his and handed it over. Same photo. Different message: *I can only trust a brother. And Captain Griessel. There is an adder in our bosom, gahzie. Be careful of phone calls.*

'About the same,' said Griessel. 'What's a *gahzie*?'

'That's Cape Flats slang for a *tjommie*. A friend. Which is a bit weird, look how formal the "Captain Cupido" is on the outside. Not "Captain Vaughn", not "Cappy": very respectful. And then he throws a "*gahzie*" inside.'

'How did he get the letter to you?'

'Special delivery. Very crafty.'

'Oh?'

'He's *kwaai* cunning, this dude. That worries me. You know I'm the live-in lover at Desiree's now, there in Welgevonden. You've been there, you know, it's an estate with a boom barrier and good security and all, so you can only get in if you've got an appointment and a code. And there's cameras, Benna. This morning, the gate guard called me and said there's a brother who dropped off a letter. So I walked over to fetch it, and this is it. In an envelope. Just your common garden variety envelope. I read it and I asked the dude what the delivery man looked like. And he said, *nay*, it's a brown brother, youngish, with a green beanie. So I said, can we look at the camera footage? He knows I'm a Hawk, so he said, no problem, come see. Now the camera is high def, but the screen they have there, it's not great. But good enough so we could see a dude stop with a white Honda Ballade, like late nineties model, I would say, fat *takkies*, looks a bit pimped up, like a Cape Flats wannabe drag racer. But he stopped far away, Benna, other side the circle, about a hundred metres. And you could see him calling another man who was walking this way, the one with the green beanie, and they talked a short while, and the guy in the Honda pointed, and gave him the letter and maybe twenty rand, and Beanie brought the letter to the gate. So we don't know anything about the Honda driver, and the guard said he thinks maybe the beanie is a gardener up at Squirrel Close, he's seen him around there.'

Griessel thought about the white Ballade that he had seen down in the street. He told Cupido about it, invited him to the kitchen for coffee, but first he collected his own letter from his car's glove compartment.

While Benny was firing up the coffee machine, Cupido examined the letter and said: 'What worries me, Benna, is this dude knows our ins and outs. He knows where we go, he knows where we live. He's made it his business. And he was clever enough to sidestep the cameras. Sharp. All that indicates a certain dedication. Or a certain level of fear.'

Griessel shared the four conclusions he had drawn, that he was a policeman.

'Check. And number five, the *ou* who wrote the letter is coloured.'

Griessel nodded, that's what he thought too. 'I googled to see if I could find anything about the weapon in the media, a crime or an arrest or something, but there's nothing.'

'I scheme it's state-capture-related, Benna. Everyone in the Service knows about our thing with the SSA, that's why he contacted us. And he knows the SSA eavesdrop on the phones. And that uniform in the background. It's only the brass who walk around in full dress uniform all day. It's some high-up, I'm telling you.'

'Could be. But we'll have to wait. This was just his way of getting our attention.'

'It could be our ticket out of Laingsburg, Benna. If this pans out . . .'

'I thought about that too. It could also be an ambush . . . I don't trust this thing, Vaughn.'

'I don't trust anyone any more. But we have to have a code word. If he contacts one of us, we can use it over the phone.'

26 September

Charlie came past her desk with a copy of *Die Burger* in his hand. The cravat and handkerchief were olive green, usually a sign that he was going to discuss the month's books with the auditors.

'Look here, Longoria.' He spread the newspaper open on her desk with a theatrical flourish.

It was a front-page article with three paparazzi photos of Jasper Boonstra's mistress, Jenna Abbott, moving out of her luxury Franschhoek pad. She was standing on the sidewalk in a svelte track-suit, beside the removal van. Men were busy loading furniture in the van. Her long blonde hair was tied back and she looked angry, hands on her hips. But still sexy, athletic.

BOONSTRA'S LOVENEST ON THE MARKET, the headline trumpeted. According to the report the house belonged to a company, and Abbott was one of the company directors. Consequently neither Schneider-König nor the authorities could stop the sale. *Abbott has declined to talk to Die Burger. The five-bedroom house was listed on the Pam Golding Properties website for R18 950 000. (More photos on page 3.)*

'Five bedrooms,' Sandra said. 'For a love nest. That's so . . . South African . . .'

She turned to page three. The photos showed a tasteful, beautiful house.

'He's cleaning up,' said Charlie. 'First Donkerdrif, now this house. I think he wants to skip the country.' And then, with feeling, while tapping his finger on the photos of the house: 'Pity we couldn't have sold that little nest as well.'

'If he wants to skip the country, why isn't Baronsberg on the market yet?' asked Sandra.

'Because it's in his name, doll. And Schneider-König will get an interdict at lighting speed to stop the sale. There are enormous claims against him.'

'That's true,' she had to admit.

'Maybe he isn't running away,' said Charlie and gave her a significant look. 'Maybe he's making room for a new mistress.' He strutted out looking smug.

Sandra felt the aggravation rise, but she refrained from saying anything. If the Donkerdrif sale went through and she had her commission, it might be time to start her own agency. This situation was bringing Charlie Benson's true colours to the fore. She wouldn't be able to stand it much longer.

Griessel scraped the old paint and varnish off the window frames at the rear of the house. It was tedious and demanding work, the monotonous repetition making his arms ache. But in a way he liked it – slowly exposing the oak until the wood was clean and dark brown again. The work was straightforward, the results directly proportionate to the effort and dedication. Detective work was not like that, where you might work for weeks, months even, and make zero progress.

He thought about the life of a police detective in Laingsburg. Far removed from a specialist unit's teamwork, as in the old Murder and Robbery, or the Hawks. In his younger years he'd cut his teeth at Parow police station, and Caledon Square in the City. The single greatest difference was that the levels of knowledge, integrity and work ethic varied considerably between police station colleagues. Plus there was the nature of the work – which scared Cupido just as much – the countless cases of domestic violence to investigate, only to have so many charges withdrawn. Thefts out of vehicles that led nowhere, house burglaries that led you back to drug-addicted children, booze-fuelled Friday night violence – it was soul-destroying work, it wore you down, made you feel you couldn't make a difference, you could never turn the tide.

He would be able to do it again. But how long would he hold up?

He heard Alexa calling. He swept the paint scrapings off the face of his watch to check the time. Just after one. She'd said she would bring Woollies food, and they would eat together, because later in the afternoon she had to fly to Johannesburg for a few days.

He carefully descended the ladder, began taking off the overalls. Alexa came out the back door. 'Benny, there's mail for you . . .'

He saw the envelope she was holding. *Your common garden variety envelope*, just as Cupido had described it. With something written in blue ink.

'Hello, Benny, look at you!' Alexa began wiping the dust off his face before kissing him on the mouth. 'My handyman, you work so hard, come and eat, I bought your favourite.'

That meant chicken and broccoli with cheese sauce.

She waited until he had wriggled out of his overalls before handing him the envelope.

It was addressed to *Captain Griessel*. Just like the previous letter. 'Someone must have delivered it by hand,' Alexa said as she walked ahead into the kitchen.

He shoved it into his trouser pocket. He didn't want to involve her in this. Not before he'd seen what was in it. 'I'm just going to wash my hands,' he said.

In the bathroom he ripped open the envelope.

The same photograph, but this time a larger picture – the police officer holding the Smith & Wesson. It was the fat Western Cape commissioner, Lieutenant General Mandla Khaba.

'Fuck,' said Griessel.

At the bottom, hand-written: *Saturday. 12:30. Green Dolphin, V&A.* Nothing more.

Only once Alexa had left did he google *Green Dolphin, V&A*. He found it was a restaurant and jazz bar at the Waterfront. He rang Cupido.

'Have you got muffins in the oven?' That had been Vaughn's suggestion, their prearranged code; meaning: Did you get a letter too?

'No, Benna, but I can put some in. Then you can come taste. I'm here with Desiree.'

'Around four o'clock for coffee? Before the traffic gets too bad.'

'Stellenbosch traffic is always too bad, partner. Chocolate, chocolate mint, blueberry or bran?' That wasn't part of their code.

'*Jissis*, Vaughn, your repertoire is more extensive than Rust's now.'

'And I don't use the ready-mix packets any more, *pappie*. I've progressed to the real thing.'

14

After lunch Sandra took the two clients who had responded to the prospectus, to Donkerdrif separately. Both were foreigners living in the Cape, a German and a Frenchman. Their interest didn't surprise her. Nearly twenty per cent of South African wine farms were already in foreign hands, more than thirty per cent of Charlie's database were prospective international buyers.

They waxed lyrical over the estate, from the pretty old Cape Dutch farmhouse, postcard picturesque between the oaks, to the cellar's up-to-date equipment and the state of the vineyards. They expressed much interest, but first had to 'consult' before making an offer. She understood that as a euphemism for securing capital. She confirmed once more with each that the price was not negotiable. They said they understood.

She drove back to the office, heartened – this transaction could go through before October after all. But she mustn't get her hopes up, she had experienced too many disappointments over the past year. It just got worse as her debts mounted. But there truly was a good chance.

She sent Boonstra her first weekly report via email. No response.

Griessel drove to Bellville first, to the Hawks' headquarters in Market Street.

He parked at the Municipal Library and walked across, told DPCI reception that he just wanted to pick up a last few items from his office.

But he went to the first floor instead, to the armoury.

Bossie Bossert, the gunsmith to the Hawks, still addressed him as 'Captain'. He was surprised to see Benny. 'This suspension is rubbish, Captain. Total rubbish. It will blow over. Everyone says so. Come in, come in . . .'

Griessel said he didn't want to bother him, he was just in the neighbourhood, and had a small question. He took the first letter out of his pocket, the one with the photo of the firearm, and showed it to Bossert. He had used a pair of scissors to trim off the part with the writing.

'*Ja*, the five-hundred Magnum,' the gunsmith said in awe. 'It's a cannon.'

'Have you seen this photo somewhere?'

'No, Captain.'

'Do you know of a five-hundred that's been damaged like this one?'

'No. It's quite rare. It has a sturdy butt, well built. It looks to me as if it's been hit by another large calibre. That's about the only thing that could cause that sort of damage.'

'Do you know of any crimes committed in the past year where a five-hundred was involved?'

Bossert thought about it. He was a gun fanatic with encyclopaedic knowledge. If there was something in the SAPS bush telegraph about an S&W 500 he would know about it. He shook his head. 'They are rare, Captain. It's a beautiful piece, but it's an awkward thing. Too big to tote around, too clumsy for self-defence. On the heavy side too. And kicks like a horse, even though Smith & Wesson claim the muzzle compensator reduces that. In America there are people who hunt with it. Big game. It has helluva stopping power. And it's expensive for a handgun. Here in South Africa they go for over thirty thousand. Your typical owner is a collector, an enthusiast. With money. Who locks up his collection properly so they don't get stolen. And if a criminal gets his hands on one . . . He will battle to get the ammunition on the black market . . .'

'Thanks, Bossie. That's all I wanted to know.'

Griessel could see he had made the warrant officer curious about the nature of his query, but all Bossert said was: 'Captain, if I can help. To get you guys back here with us. Anything . . .'

Cupido opened the door of the townhouse and the pleasant aroma of fresh baking wafted out to greet Griessel.

Vaughn's black T-shirt was dusted with flour.

'Afternoon, ma'am, is the man of the house at home?'

'Benna, that's sexist. Just so you know, all the best bakers in the world are men,' he said and stood back to let Griessel enter.

The fruit of Cupido's labour was displayed on the kitchen counter, blueberry and chocolate mint muffins.

'You're really serious about this baking,' Griessel said.

Donovan, Desiree's son, came in from the passage.

'Hi, Uncle Benna, it's the start of an industry. We're in business now, me and Uncle Vaughn.' He was eleven, tall and skinny, deep blue eyes with the cafe-au-lait skin and dark hair like his mother. He shook Griessel's hand. 'I sell the muffins at school. Ten rand a pop, our profit margin is twenty-three per cent . . .'

'If you don't sample the goods, *ja*,' said Cupido.

'Quality control, Uncle.' Donovan took a muffin before exiting again.

'That is the only upside of this suspension, partner. Me and the boy are bonding *lekker*.'

'I see that,' said Griessel and took the new letter out of his pocket, unfolded it and passed it to Cupido.

'Hit me with a *snot snoek*,' said Cupido when he saw the photo of the commissioner. '*Fokken maaifoedie*, that bloody scoundrel . . . And the Green Dolphin? The tapas place at the Waterfront?'

27 September

Sandra woke with a sense of unease, and the anxiety kept her in its grip. As if she knew this day would bring some calamity.

Since yesterday, the sickening, growing realisation, how weak the response was to her emails to all the people and companies on Charlie's list.

Interest in a wine estate of this size just wasn't what it had been four, five years ago. Only the Frenchman and the German had made contact: nineteen others had not even taken the trouble to acknowledge receipt.

Perhaps the secrecy around it was a factor? But that wasn't that unusual. The poor economy definitely played a role. And the chaos the government had caused with state capture, the endemic corruption in the country, meant that fewer foreigners wanted to invest here, more and more wealthy South Africans were moving their money offshore. Add all that to the Boonstra hurricane and you had the perfect storm.

Had some of the potential buyers smelt a rat about Boonstra's involvement in the deal? People with big money weren't stupid. They knew all the Cape wine farms of this size and extent; despite the vagueness of her emails they would draw their own conclusions as to which one it might be. Did they know something about the mysterious company ownership of Donkerdrif?

Just after eleven her phone rang. She saw that it was Ford's finance department. Her heart skipped a beat. It wouldn't be good news, not this time of the month.

She didn't answer, put the phone on silent, gnawed at her thumbnail.

The vultures were beginning to circle.

How long before her financial house of cards collapsed?

At twenty to twelve the Frenchman called. He was charming and apologetic. He thanked Sandra for showing him the farm. It was a magnificent property, but he didn't believe the climate was currently right to buy.

At twenty past twelve, just as she wanted to grab her bag and walk to Basic Bistro for her weekly Wednesday lunch date with Josef, the email from the German dropped into her inbox. The same angle, but Teutonically frank and direct: Donkerdrif was an outstanding wine farm. But they had lost confidence in the South African government. The corruption, looting of state enterprises, the gradual collapse of rail, water and power networks and the National Prosecuting Authority placed the investment at too great a risk. Given the circumstances, they would refrain from making an offer.

She suppressed her feelings, the disappointment, and then the despair when she realised: South Africans would not have the capital, foreigners would not have the courage. Donkerdrif would not be a quick sale. Donkerdrif would not sell at all.

That made her make up her mind, on the way to the restaurant: she was going to make a clean breast of it. Tell Josef everything. Now. She had to unload the burden. And she was ready for it, she had been composing her speech, a confession, in her mind for days already.

'Why didn't you tell me?' That was what he would say.

And that was the most difficult question to answer, because there was no excuse, no extenuating circumstances. She could say, 'I didn't want to trouble you, you're working so hard on the book, you don't need the stress and distraction'. It was part of the truth and it would hurt him. It would upset him that she didn't trust him enough, that she wasn't open, that she had carried the heavy burden alone. But that argument was only a small part of a much larger, more complex truth. She had been a diligent, conscientious manager of their finances. It had been a question of pride for her, her part in their success and peace of mind as a family. Her *gift*, she was good with numbers. Josef wasn't. He was grateful that she'd taken over the money matters, he had often mentioned how good it was that she was doing it. And excelled at it. And then she failed. She was ashamed. Her silence was also because of pride.

There was the spectre of her past, always in the background, the shame of a family home where creditors were constantly lied to and evaded, bailiffs arriving to reclaim the furniture, another move to yet another house because of unpaid rent. Whispers in the school corridors, Jannie Boshoff is a crook, a slippery customer. Humiliation in front of her friends, her teachers. Her father bragging about how he'd conned yet another person, he was always the hero of his own slick stories. Her mother never spoke up. Not one word. Never found the courage to stand up to her man or leave him. Never told Sandra that 'just like you, I die inside at every story'. It was this haunting spectre that drove Sandra to build up a nest egg, to carefully calculate every time they had to borrow, on the house, her car. Josef's salary wasn't large, and her commission earnings always variable and unpredictable. She'd amassed nearly two hundred thousand in the savings account. Sometimes it dwindled to barely a hundred thousand when the real estate market lagged, but it always improved again. Always, four years now.

And then the fiasco of the Schneider-König collapse.

No one could have predicted how enormous the impact on the local Stellenbosch economy would be. Nor how long it would endure. Not even she. She drew on the nest egg. As usual. In a responsible way, based on past history. It ran out, and she still believed that the big sale would come, there were more expensive properties on their books, it had to come, it *had* to.

Until it was too late. Until she started avoiding creditors, with all the déjà-vu of her youth.

Why hadn't she sat down with her husband then and there, explained what had happened?

Because he would have said 'we'll ask my father to help'. And that was the heart of the matter. The thing she couldn't talk to her husband about.

Josef's parents were prominent people. And *grand*, as Jasper Boonstra had said. The Steenbergs of Mossel Bay. Her father-in-law was a beloved, well-to-do GP, her mother-in-law a member of the town council for many years. They were supporters of the arts, big donors to the Cape Town Philharmonic Orchestra, they never missed an arts festival in Oudtshoorn or Stellenbosch. At first glance they were humble people without affectations. But constant admiration, years of being looked up to and respected, is not without consequence. Those on the receiving end of adoration always come to believe in the impression of their own status. When Josef brought Sandra to meet his parents the first time, they received her warmly. There was some gentle probing about her parents, their occupation, their circumstances. They showed apparent sympathy for her 'unusual' childhood – she had euphemistically explained how her father 'had a little trouble' after his rugby days were over, that he was a colourful character. But Sandra had also overheard her future mother-in-law behind the closed kitchen door asking Josef: 'Are you sure she's the one for you? You don't think the differences are too great? After all,' she heard the barely lowered voice, 'she's not from our side of the tracks.'

The differences. Josef and she spoke the same language, shared the same faith, culture. There was only one difference.

Money.

She had watched how Dr and Councillor Steenberg had to grit their teeth when they met her parents for the first time in Stellenbosch. Jannie Boshoff was at his wine-slugging braggadocio best, her mother pathetically inappropriate in her attempts to talk about books and music. It marked a turning point. From then on, Sandra could see that Josef's parents merely tolerated her. They did it gracefully, she conceded, but she could tell that they were merely resigned to their son's choice.

They enjoyed their grandchildren immensely. But the relationship with her was never genuinely warm.

Asking them for financial support, would confirm all their misgivings. That *the differences* were too great, that *the Sandra apple hadn't fallen far from the Pa-Jannie tree.* That was the major reason that she hadn't talked to Josef about their predicament while the wolf was approaching, nor even when it was actually at the door.

But now, as she walked to Basic Bistro, she knew her father-in-law was their only solution. She would have to swallow her pride. It was the price she had to pay for her sins. And to be free. Of everything. Her dependence on Jasper Boonstra as well.

She was determined not to cry when she confessed to Josef. She would not. She would not feel sorry for herself or make excuses. She would just admit that she'd made a huge mistake, and she took responsibility. It was the one thing that would make her different from her father.

She walked up Ryneveld Street, turned left in Church Street, feeling the weight of it all bear down on her. They needed a few hundred thousand. It was going to cause havoc to Josef's writing schedule, he would have to put the book on hold, and that would break his heart.

In front of the pretty Hofmeyr Hall her phone rang. She took it out of her handbag, didn't recognise the number. 'This is Sandra,' she answered.

'Mrs Steenberg?' A woman's voice.

'Yes.'

'My name is Mareli Vorster. I'm calling from Stirling and Heyns in Cape Town.'

She knew the name, it was a large law firm. Her insides contracted, it was either Ford or the bank suing her over the house bond.

'Yes?' she said.

'We represent the local interests of Demeter Capital in San Francisco. Mr Hurwitz asked us to just phone you to let you know that we are interested in the wine estate . . . They wanted us to take a look at the confidentiality clauses first, and it was . . . We were somewhat delayed, to be frank, and they are concerned we may have missed the opportunity. I am forwarding the signed documents immediately; could you please send me the prospectus as a matter of urgency.'

Sandra's heart leaped. 'Of course,' she said. Then she looked up, and saw her beloved husband standing on the veranda of the bistro, looking at her with such appreciation and love. And she thought, I won't ruin this lunch today. There was still a tiny sliver of hope.

15

Griessel was down in the garage mixing more paint when Cupido phoned.

'Vaughn?'

'Volvoville, *pappie*,' he said jubilantly.

'What?'

'We're going to Volvoville. Not Laingsburg. Volvoville. Praise the Lord and pass the champagne, Benna, purgatory can go to hell.'

'Volvoville' was Cupido's name for Stellenbosch, because of the multitude of residents driving around in that car brand, a fact that made Vaughn's head spin. 'Benna, I mean,' he said often, 'if the world is your oyster, and you can buy any luxury car, why buy the most boring one known to man? Rich whiteys. I just don't get them.'

'How do you know we're going to Stellenbosch?'

'Contact at HR, middle-aged coloured aunty who really likes me. She phoned now, just now. But wait, there's more. We are starting on Monday. On full pay, so we've only been docked a half month's.'

'Are you sure?'

'Damn straight I'm sure. *Jissis*, Benna, what a relief, partner.'

'I won't have finished the paint job.'

'Wait, let me get this straight, no more purgatory, a month's pay reinstated, and *you're* worried about a fucking house painting job that won't be finished?'

'Yes, right. I'll have to get my ass in gear the next few days . . .'

'Now you can look forward to marital bliss, and I can pop the question to Desiree. I have decided, on Christmas Day, I'm getting down on bended knee.'

'How did it happen, Vaughn?'

'Love found a way, *pappie*. Like always . . .'

'No, I mean about Stellenbosch.'

'Oh. I scheme The Camel pulled a few strings. Had to be. He said he would see what he could do. That man is a *king*.'

Griessel was not convinced. 'Vaughn, are you absolutely sure?'

'The aunty was sitting with the forms in front of her, Benna. Relax, it's a sure thing.'

'None of it makes sense.'

'Why?'

'Stellenbosch is . . . It's hardly punishment. A good station. Only an hour's commute in the morning for me, and you can stay with Desiree. And only losing a fortnight's pay? Something doesn't feel right, Vaughn.'

He vividly remembered the commissioner's rage and derision.

Cupido was silent a while. 'I feel you, Benna,' he said with a less exuberant tone.

'It's . . . Let's wait until The Camel calls. Until it's official.'

'Okay. And, if it's gospel, remember to sound surprised when he tells you. See you Saturday?'

'See you Saturday.'

Griessel rang off, lost in thought with the phone in his hand. Cupido's source must be mistaken. He still believed they were going to Laingsburg. Or else there was a snake in the grass.

He wouldn't breathe a word to Alexa until it was official.

Just before ten that night Sandra's cell phone rang. A man with an American accent. He introduced himself as Gregory Hurwitz from Demeter Capital in San Francisco. He had examined the prospectus, and they were very interested. He just wanted to be certain, were there other offers on Donkerdrif? Was there still time?

Sandra had done her homework on Demeter since the attorney's call. She now knew they already owned two wine-producing properties in the Boland, they certainly had the capacity to buy the estate. 'We're awaiting two offers at the moment,' she lied, 'but I haven't received any paperwork yet.'

'Excellent. I'm flying out this afternoon. I'll be in Cape Town on Friday morning. Could we make an appointment for a full appraisal?'

'Of course,' she said. 'I'll keep the whole day free for you.'

'And please don't accept any offers yet.'

28 September

Brigadier Musad Manie, aka 'The Camel', only phoned Griessel after nine, just as he was screwing the new gutter to the wall.

'Benny,' he said, 'I've got excellent news for you. You and Vaughn are starting Monday morning at Stellenbosch.'

'Stellenbosch, Brigadier?' Even now he could scarcely believe it. 'Monday?'

'That's right, Benny. October second. I think the only bad news is that you'll be there a year at the least, it seems. Before we can think about bringing you back.'

'Brigadier, thank you, thank you, I . . . It couldn't have been easy, I don't think.'

'Benny, I'll be honest, all I did was write to the commissioner and politely ask for clemency. On the grounds of your good service, knowledge and experience. I never expected such a swift response, nor one so positive. I'm . . . Really, I'm quite surprised. But I'm truly delighted as you are. Anyway, Benny, you're starting Monday morning half past six. Report to Colonel Witkop Jansen, he's chief of detectives there. You know their office?'

'Yes, Brigadier.'

Manie said goodbye, Griessel thanked him again, and they rang off.

It took him some time to chew over it before he eventually just said '*fok*', with a mixture of massive relief and vague unease. It didn't make sense, something was off. Then he called Alexa, and after that, Cupido.

Sandra was evaluating a house in Paradyskloof. She was vying for a sole mandate. When she had finished, she phoned Josef and told him she would pick up the twins, it was on her way home.

'There's a registered letter for you . . .' he said with a query in his voice. 'It's from Ford.'

Her heart stopped. Had he opened it?

'Must be the terms for the residual finance,' she said in the hopes that he hadn't. 'It's coming up to that time.'

'Okay. Love you, see you soon . . .'

She drove to the nursery school, tense now. Would he look at the letter before she got home? How easy she found it to lie. To everyone, even to her husband now. The web she was weaving was getting denser, tighter, the consequences could be more serious, she was starting to put her marriage at risk.

If Josef were to know the truth, he would never be able to trust her again.

It was a warning, perhaps a final notice that they intended to repossess the Eco Sport. Then the whole matter would be revealed in any case. If he opened the letter, she would tell him everything tonight. Also the hope that the sale of Donkerdrif offered, a slender hope, dangling from the single silken thread of Demeter Capital.

Anke and Bianca were tired and hungry, whining in the back seat. She had to grit her teeth and take deep breaths to stop herself from venting all her anxiety on them.

She pulled in beside Josef's little Mazda in the garage, unclipped the children from their safety seats, waiting for her husband to appear in the doorway between the garage and the kitchen, the open letter in his hand.

Or would he be sitting and waiting for her at the dining room table, head in his hands in disappointment and despair?

The twins charged ahead, opened the door shouting: 'Papa, Papa!' She went inside.

Josef hugged the children, picked them up and squeezed them tight, looking up at her entering with gentle eyes and a loving smile.

He hadn't opened the letter.

She felt soiled, worthless and a traitor.

When she had given Josef a kiss and a hug, she quietly hid the Ford envelope in her handbag.

29 September

The gutter was skew, Griessel could see that now. For fuck's sake, he was no handyman.

And to be honest, the paintwork was sloppy as well. The window frame's colour had bled over into the wall here and there, on the roof a dark patch of undercoat was visible where he hadn't applied enough layers. And there was no way he would be able to fix that or do it over before Monday. Alexa kept on praising his handiwork, but he wasn't blind. They would have to hire someone to fix his bungling.

But he couldn't be negative this morning. Not after yesterday's good news. The truth was they had saved close to twenty thousand rand because he had tackled the lion's share of the maintenance himself. And he was going to Stellenbosch. Stellenbosch was good. Stellenbosch was fantastic. Stellenbosch was not Laingsburg. He would be able to sleep at home at night. Be a real detective, surely he would get the chance to investigate serious crimes occasionally, the Eikestad – the Town of Oaks – had its share of those too. He would be working with a good team, Stellenbosch station's detectives had an excellent reputation. All of that meant a much easier battle with the bottle.

Last night in bed he'd been thinking; Stellenbosch meant that he would have to forgo his early morning bike ride on the slopes of Table Mountain. The traffic in the student town was a nightmare, especially at rush hour, so he would have to leave home at half past five to be in time for work. Perhaps he could take his bike along, go for a ride in lunch hour? He heard there were super routes along the mountain and in Jonkershoek. But if that wasn't possible, that sacrifice was the only price he would have to pay, along with the demotion and salary decrease, of course.

Temporary. A year, Brigadier Musad Manie had said. He could do it. Absolutely.

With a burst of renewed energy he began unscrewing the gutter.

Sandra opened the Ford envelope at work. Josef hadn't even mentioned it last night. They'd eaten, bathed the twins together, laughing at the children's antics. She told him about the Paradyskloof house, a pretty place at a good price. He discussed his progress on the book with her, he'd had 'a very good day'.

There was a lot of red print. A final warning. Unless the arrears were paid in full before 15 October, they would repossess the EcoSport, as agreed in the hire purchase contract.

Three weeks. She had three weeks.

16

Donkerdrif was a picture postcard.

The vines were just budding, the subtle, fresh shades of the new leaves in perfect harmony with the mountain's dark green after the winter rains. In the background loomed spectacular, snow-white cumulus clouds. The scenery served as nature's frame for the classic, stately farmhouse, as if the universe wanted Gregory Hurwitz and Demeter Capital to snap up the place and rescue Sandra Steenberg from her terrible dilemma.

The American was a dignified man in his fifties. He was courteous to Sandra, engaging, he made her feel important. He was accompanied by two of his countrymen and Mareli Vorster, the legal representative of the Cape Town firm Stirling and Heyns.

In the shade of the large wine cellar she stood and listened to Hurwitz questioning Moolman the farm manager, and the young lady winemaker about their relationship with the Swiss company that owned the estate. Moolman said they were relatively autonomous, directors came to check up five or six times a year, make use of the facilities, evaluate the vintage and go through the books.

'We had a quick look at the financials. They're not . . . spectacular,' Hurwitz said.

Sandra's heart sank.

'We make a profit every year,' Moolman shrugged. 'Look, it's a tough industry. Our numbers are as good as most vineyards around here. The owners, they're . . .' Moolman hesitated and looked guiltily at Sandra, as if she represented them.

'Yes?' Hurwitz asked.

'We believe they use Donkerdrif as a sort of . . . I don't know, a kind of tax write-off. They haven't been very . . . involved. Especially in the marketing. What we need, is owners who can help us to introduce the wine internationally. The wine is superb, we really believe it's world class. Our King Red Madiba, that's our Bordeaux blend named after a famous protea that grows up there,' he pointed at the mountains, 'won a Sommeliers Choice in the USA last year, and a Decanter World Wine Award two years ago. We would love it if you tried it, with lunch.'

'So, I take it you will both remain with the vineyard, should a new owner be supportive, and assist in the international marketing?'

Moolman and the winemaker both said a hearty yes.

Hurwitz was thoughtful: 'We will certainly take a closer look at the financials.'

They spent longer and took a more in-depth look at the farm than the previous interested parties had. A promising sign.

After four they asked Sandra to excuse them, they wished to consult, and study the past few years' accounts with close attention. She waited in an armchair on the broad veranda looking out on Botmaskop, while they met behind closed doors in the homestead dining room.

She recalled a Bible verse from her childhood days. *I will lift up mine eyes unto the hills . . .*

'Please,' she whispered to the ether. And then she waited, her mind dwelling on her problems and her family.

At six she sent a WhatsApp to Josef to let him know she was still with the clients.

It was gone seven when they opened the doors again. Hurwitz came out with a broad smile, his hand stretched out to her. 'We'd love to make an offer for the place,' he said. 'Let's get the paperwork done.'

She found Josef and the girls in front of the TV. He was watching *Frozen* with them, for the umpteenth time.

She apologised for being so late; they were overseas clients who first had to consult. He stood up, came and hugged her.

'Is it a biggie?' he asked. She had simply told him she was showing a property in Banhoek. 'Come on, I'll warm up your dinner.'

They walked to the kitchen.

'I can't talk about it.'

'Oh?' He put the covered plate in the microwave oven, pressed the buttons.

'It's . . .' The urge to tell him was so strong; to offload a tiny fraction of the burden. And to explain why she was being so secretive. 'It's an . . . odd situation. The seller made us sign a confidentiality contract.'

He took a bottle of white wine out of the fridge. 'Only in Stellenbosch,' he said with an understanding smile. She had often told him about the odd and wacky clients she worked with in this town, their outlandish sale and purchase requests, their preposterous behaviour. People from the academic and business world, even two members of the so called 'Stellenbosch Mafia', as the informal club of billionaires who lived in the area were called.

'Wine?' he offered.

'Please. It's . . . such a strange story. When this is all over . . . someone could write a book about it.'

He poured the wine and brought her a glass, kissed her on the cheek. 'Are you allowed to say if it was a good day?'

'I am. It was. And now it's getting even better.'

She felt a little lighter.

30 September

Cupido came to pick Griessel up just before noon.

He chatted to Alexa first. They liked each other, those two. She enjoyed Vaughn's self-confidence and his sense of humour, and she was eternally grateful to him for the many times that he had protected and stood by Benny when he succumbed to the bottle. Vaughn was crazy about her because she laughed so easily, was so down-to-earth, in spite of her erstwhile superstar status.

Griessel had to hurry him up, so they could head to the Waterfront. On the veranda, on the way to Cupido's car, Vaughn cast a quick glance at Benny's handiwork. 'Don't give up your day job, partner.'

Griessel chuckled. 'I know. If only I had a talent for muffins . . .'

'Damn straight, *pappie*. I'm an artist.'

They drove down Buitengracht, the Saturday traffic mercifully quieter than the usual weekday chaos. They talked about Stellenbosch, and the fact that neither of them knew anyone on the detective team there. It was a younger generation of policemen, mostly coloured, and they speculated about how they would be received in that circle. Their conclusion: not positively.

About a hundred metres before the Dock Street intersection an ambulance raced past, lights flashing and sirens wailing. Followed by a SAPS patrol vehicle. Both vehicles turned left, to the Waterfront.

'*Aitsa*,' said Cupido. 'Looks like there's some action at the V&A.'

Sandra walked into the bedroom in her yellow, sleeveless sun dress. There was a bubbliness in her, hope and optimism. And she knew she looked good. She had made an effort, because today she had to compete with fourteen always impeccable Stellenbosch mothers.

'Come on, you lot, we have to go,' she called the twins.

They came running in their party frocks, red ribbons tied to bouncing braids, shrieking. She was taking them to a friend's birthday party so Josef could concentrate on writing.

Josef came out of the spare room, where he worked every day. His table was an old door that he had propped on two trestles, his computer and books surrounded him.

He gave her an appreciative look. 'Hello, sexy, what's your name?' he teased while moving his eyebrows suggestively.

'Papa! Her name is Sandra,' said Bianca.

'I'm a married woman, sir,' said Sandra and walked towards him. 'Control yourself.'

He held her around the waist. 'Then you shouldn't have worn that dress, miss.' He kissed her.

'Yuck! She's not a miss, she's a housewife,' said Anke.

'They're so lovey-lovey, silly,' said Bianca.

'Yuck,' said Anke.

'Mamma, come on, we'll be late,' Anke did her best imitation of her mother's stern voice.

Sandra's cell phone rang. She motioned to the children to be silent. 'Mister Hurwitz, good morning.'

'Good morning, Sandra. How are you?'

The Americans always asked how you were, first, while your heart was in your throat in anticipation of good or bad news. Hurwitz had only said they wanted to make an offer, but hadn't indicated whether they had taken the non-negotiability of the price into account.

'I'm good, thank you. How are you?'

'Well, I'm great, thanks, but I'll be even better if you tell me you haven't accepted any offers since yesterday.'

'Not yet,' she said.

'Good. Sandra, we have our offer, all signed and sealed, and ready to go. We're keen to get it to you as soon as possible. Could you help me with an appropriate address for hand delivery?'

Cupido and Griessel drove in the same direction as the emergency vehicles. At the South Arm intersection the traffic was suddenly dense and very slow. It took them ten minutes to reach the large Dock Road circle. A SAPS van obstructed the road to the Waterfront. A constable in uniform indicated they could not go through, they had to go around the circle and back, to the Silo district.

Cupido stopped beside the constable and wound down his window. 'Brother,' he said, 'I'm Warrant Officer Vaughn Cupido, this is Warrant Officer Benny Griessel, we're with the Stellenbosch detective branch. What's going on?'

He looked them over first, then nodded his satisfaction and said: 'Gang shooting, Warrant. Half an hour ago. One of our own.'

'A policeman?' Cupido asked.

'Just so. Warrant officer from Mitchells Plain. Drive-by, two cars, he didn't stand a chance.'

'*Jirre*,' said Cupido.

'You have to move on, Warrant, sorry.'

Cupido put the car in gear.

'What car was he driving?' Griessel asked. He didn't believe in coincidences.

'White Honda Ballade.'

They looked at each other. Vaughn drove on.

Behind them two people jumped out of a car and wove through the traffic on foot, on the way to the crime scene. The man with a large TV camera on his shoulder, the woman with a microphone in her hand.

17

'What the fuck, Benna?' said Cupido and turned left, towards the Silo district.

'White Honda Ballade . . .' Griessel repeated.

'*Jissis*,' said Cupido. 'We'll have to take a look.'

'There are cameras, Vaughn, the media have just gone past.' Their faces in the background of a TV report was the last thing they needed in the circumstances.

'Check.' And then, almost in a whisper: 'Benna, you know what this means.'

'I know.'

They drove on in shocked silence. Griessel tried not to jump to conclusions. But it was a struggle. The provincial commissioner had been in the photograph. A confidante of the president. And now a policeman had been gunned down, apparently because he wanted to pass on information about that officer.

Premature conclusions could be dangerous, especially in their current situation.

'We will have to be very careful,' he said.

Cupido didn't answer. He parked in the Silo Parkade.

They watched from a safe distance.

The Honda Ballade was just past the entrance to Merchant House, on the wide turn that Dock Road made to the Waterfront. Half on the sidewalk, its bonnet crumpled against a tree. Otherwise free of traffic, the SAPS vehicles and ambulance had stopped in the road. Policemen in uniform diverted the growing crowd of curious rubberneckers behind yellow crime tape. A few detectives were at the car and the television team were standing on the wall in front of Merchant House to gain a better view.

From where they were standing, it looked like the same white car with the wide wheels that had been on the corner below Griessel's house, the one that Cupido had seen on the video monitor.

'It's no coincidence, Benna,' said Cupido.

'We need more,' said Griessel. 'Let's go and wait at the restaurant.'

'Okay.'

When they turned to walk to the Waterfront, they saw the minibus, the elite Provincial Crime Scene Investigative unit that usually worked with the Hawks, arrive. That was always the case when the victim was a member of the Service.

Josef phoned her just after one. She had to walk away across the lawn far enough to hear him over the din of screeching children.

'Your parcel is here,' he said. 'A big white envelope.'

She wished she could ask him to open it and tell her whether the offer was for the full amount. She wished she could bundle the children into the car and go and see for herself.

'Thanks,' she said. 'I'll have a look once we're home.'

'How's it going there?'

'The *girls* are enjoying it immensely.'

'Say no more.'

Cupido and Griessel waited half an hour. They ordered tapas. Nobody turned up.

They talked about the various possibilities. It could have been a straight gang hit. The deceased was a detective from Mitchells Plain. There was always that risk. At least two lawyers with Cape Flats connections had been mown down in the past year by organised crime. It might have nothing to do with the letters delivered, or the fat commissioner.

But if it did, then a line had been crossed, an unwritten rule of blood was broken. And that was what disturbed them at a deep level.

Just after two, Griessel phoned Jimmy, the tall, thin forensic scientist of PCSI, also known as 'Thin'. Because his partner Arnold was short and round, they were commonly known as Thick and Thin, and always joked that 'the PCSI will stand by you through Thick and Thin'.

'Benny! Well I never,' said Jimmy. 'The Outcast. Great name for a movie, right? Wait a minute, they already did that. Now that I think of it, you sort of look like Nicolas Cage . . .'

Thick and Thin thought they were hilarious. The detectives who had to work with them, usually tolerated their humour, because the two PCSI members were extremely good at their job. Griessel hadn't seen the film nor did he see the resemblance. He merely said: 'Good one, Jimmy. Are you at the V&A scene?'

'No, I'm off this weekend. Why?'

'Policeman shot here an hour ago. *Ou* from Mitchells Plain. Could it be . . . Jimmy, I need your discretion here. There's a case that Vaughn and I are looking at, but you know our situation . . .'

'I know. How can I help?'

'We can't go near the crime scene. Any information would be helpful.'

'I'll see what I can do . . .'

Seventeen minutes later Jimmy sent Griessel two colour photos via WhatsApp.

They were taken with a cell phone. The first showed the Honda Ballade against the tree. The second showed the Smith & Wesson Model 500 on the floor of the vehicle, on a piece of clothing, between shards of glass and a few drops of blood.

The butt of the weapon wasn't chipped any more. It looked like someone had filled the hole with epoxy resin and tried to disguise it with black paint. Poor workmanship, plain to see. He and Cupido were still studying it when Jimmy rang.

'Here's what I have,' he told Griessel. 'The deceased is WO Milo April. His nickname is "Venus". He is . . . he was with Mitchells Plain detective branch. Eye witnesses say he was driving towards the Waterfront, when a car passed him, and a *bakkie* drove up alongside him. They forced him to slow down, and then shot at him, from both vehicles. The witnesses can't agree on what make the vehicles were; the *bakkie* was white, the car light blue. At least two men in the *bakkie*, maybe three in the car. Automatic weapons, maybe one assault rifle of some or other kind. The car collided with a tree, but he was already dead, bullet wound to the head. Sounds to me like a gang hit, Benny.'

'And the Smith & Wesson?'

'They found it in the footwell of his car, on the passenger side. On top of his jacket, they thought it must have been under the jacket, and when he drove into the tree, it fell there.'

'Did he have his service pistol with him?'

'He did. On his belt. Didn't have time to draw it.'

'Anything else?'

'His cell phone was with him.'

'After they shot him . . . Did they just drive away?'

'Yip. Both vehicles made a U-turn, down by the aquarium, and headed back to the N1. They are busy checking the traffic cameras, but I wouldn't hold my breath . . .'

'Jimmy, have you seen that revolver before?'

'I'll have to hear from Ballistics.'

'Thanks, Jimmy . . .'

'Benny, we give you and that arrogant partner of yours a lot of grief . . . But I'll have you know, we are just as fed up as you are. Our reputations are all gone to hell. If there's anything, anything, we will help . . .'

'Thanks, Jimmy. It's going to be hard for us to get information about this case. You heard we're starting Monday in Stellenbosch?'

'We heard.'

'We . . . Let's just say we'll have to stay far away from this one, but any information will be welcome.'

'You can bet on it.'

Sandra came home at half past three, the twins worn out and fast asleep in their child seats in the back of the EcoSport. She unlocked the front door, called Josef, and they carried the girls inside, put them down in their room. She saw the envelope on the breakfast counter.

'How did it go?' he asked as they came back down the passage together.

'I think Bianca is in love with little Ivan, Hope Beneke's son.'

'Oh?'

'She gave him fourteen marshmallows.'

'Bianca did?'

'Our very own, stingy Bianca.'

'It's true love. I'm going to have to buy a shotgun.'

She laughed, her eyes on the envelope. She walked up to it, opened it, had to force herself not to be too hasty.

Josef stood watching her while she took out the OTP document.

'And?' he asked.

She scanned the forms quickly. It was for the full amount, an uncomplicated offer. Relief flooded like crystal-clear water through her.

'And now you can kiss me,' she said. Because she had just saved this family from the abyss.

18

At five she sent Jasper Boonstra a WhatsApp: *Signed offer, for full amount.*

He answered simply: *Bring.*

Now?

Please.

Yes, she thought. You can say 'please' when I've got an offer in my hand, you greedy pig.

She stood there holding the telephone and weighing up her options. She wasn't keen on driving out to him. She was worn out after the children's party. Watching the frenetic twins drained her but that wasn't all. Navigating the waters of Stellenbosch's social channels was challenging. Especially in the competitive thirty-something sphere where everyone was essentially a newcomer. They competed for status, a pass into the Eikestad upper echelons, nirvana, inclusion with the elite. At these events Sandra was usually the only one without an academic qualification. No matter how friendly they were, no matter if they began with an interest in the state of the property market and the value of their homes, it wasn't long before the conversation would move on to weightier subjects that did not really include her. With an air of condescension, possibly unintentional, but she felt it all the same, especially when Josef was not with her.

When it became known that her husband was writing a book, there was a subtle shift; that could be the Steenberg's passport to the Stellenbosch inner circle. She began to present better value, potential coattails to ride on. But it also meant more pressure: you were watched more closely, one faux pas committed by you, or your children could quickly became the talk of the week.

And then there were was the faux political correctness that irritated her so much. Nearly everyone in this circle of friends was white, and no one had the courage to say outright that the government was a nest of corrupt kleptomaniacs looting the country into bankruptcy. This town in general and especially the university – the largest employer – were oh, so liberal and terrified of offending the authorities and pressure groups. While more and more they were squeezing Afrikaans into oblivion. Sandra's philosophy was that it had nothing to do with race or colour, it was a question of right and wrong, and in a country that professed a commitment to freedom of speech, you had the right to say so. Directly. Call it by name. But not these people. They would hint, make nuanced jokes, sigh, shrug and roll their eyes, but nobody would open their mouth and say anything direct. She was fed up.

She decided she would have to shake off her fatigue. The sooner she got the envelope to Boonstra, the sooner she could seal the deal. And get her commission.

She told Josef she had to deliver the offer to her client. She quickly smoothed her hair and touched up her lipstick in the bathroom, and then went to her car.

There were two minibuses parked in front of the Baronsberg house, preventing Sandra from parking under cover.

New Broom Cleaning Services was written on the side panels of both vehicles.

She rang the bell, papers in hand. It felt like a much longer wait before Boonstra opened the door at last with a solemn: 'Hello, Sandra'. He waved a hand to invite her in. He was sober, clean-shaven and wearing bright Nike trainers with jeans and a white golf shirt. Vacuum cleaners hummed in the background, and when she walked through to the lounge, she saw people everywhere hard at work; women with buckets and cloths, vacuum cleaners, brooms, feather dusters. She was relieved and thankful not to be on her own with him.

She still wondered where Boonstra's wife was.

For the first time he led her up the ostentatious staircase that swept up from the reception lounge. 'Sorry about the racket. Come to my study, they've finished there.'

He climbed the stairs. She followed him in without speaking, her heels loud on the marble.

The first-floor passage was wide and high. Doors led off into rooms. Paintings decorated the walls.

She saw the life-size knight in armour on the left, brightly polished, at the corner of the stairs, but it was a painting on the wall that captured her attention. It was large and colourful, African women dancing, in mixed media, with a strange, beguiling depth to it. Without thinking, she stopped to stare at it.

He noticed. 'It's a Ben Enwonwu,' he said.

'I haven't heard of him,' she said, and in her enchantment she momentarily forgot the circumstances. 'It's beautiful.'

'He was a Nigerian. Brilliant. And it's a good investment. Bonhams are going to auction one of his Tutu paintings next year. It was discovered in a middle-class flat in London, it's going to attract a lot of attention.'

'Bishop Tutu?'

He smiled. 'No, it refers to a Nigerian princess. And they think she's still alive. They're looking for her. Nice story . . .' Something happened to Jasper Boonstra as he spoke. As if he became human, a person with interests and knowledge. More relaxed. More comfortable. Civilised.

'That's interesting,' she said, still on her guard.

'Do you like art?' he asked.

'Yes.'

'Then I will have to show you my whole collection one day.'

No. Thank. You, she thought.

It was a study, but enormous. A window looked out on the valley. The view was a panorama of vineyards and mountains in the soft late afternoon light. A bookshelf covered the opposite wall. Photos of Jasper with politicians and business leaders and Springbok rugby players were displayed behind the big, dark, gorgeous blackwood desk. In one corner was a lovely old liquor cabinet, and in the other an antique chess board on a coffee table, surrounded by leather chairs.

He held out his hand. She realised he wanted the offer. She handed it over.

'Please sit down,' he waved at the leather chairs, walked over to the desk, sat down behind it and opened the envelope, taking out the document. He quickly looked at each page. She noticed a halved ostrich shell on a mount just in front of the desk blotter. In swirling script: *Half an egg* . . . Inside the bowl formed by the shell was a handful of colourful jellybeans. It was an odd thing for Jasper Boonstra to display there. She hadn't pegged him as a 'half an egg' sort of man.

Sandra sat down and looked at the photos. Not a single one of him with his family. Just Jasper Boonstra, the Very Important Person, with other VIPs.

He looked up. 'This is good work, Sandra. It's a good offer. From a good source. Well done.'

'Thank you.'

He stood up again. He was restless, as always, she thought.

'We will accept the offer. Your financial affairs are going to improve dramatically . . .'

She merely smiled at him in relief.

'Sherry?' he asked.

'Oh, no, thank you.'

He put the papers down on the desk, and walked to the liquor cabinet, pulled the stopper from a crystal decanter, poured dark sherry into two glasses. He said: 'When your commission arrives, I can advise you on art investments. Io Makandal from Johannesburg, Wangechi Mutu, the Kenyan; hell, her work is good. There are a few here around Stellenbosch who also have potential . . .'

He brought her the glass. She took it resignedly.

'This is a Portuguese oloroso, you must swirl it and breathe it.' He sat down opposite her. 'Do you know why I chose you, Sandra?'

'No.' She began feeling uneasy again. She would prefer to talk about the offer. Or just get out of here, but at least there were other people in the house, that made it relatively safe. And this version of Boonstra was different. He talked to her without the arrogance he'd shown before.

He inhaled the aroma of his sherry, and sipped. 'Because you have ambition. The right sort.'

'Oh?'

'It's a rare thing. The kind where you believe you can be *something*. You believe you have . . . a kind of destiny. It's here in the back of your mind, not exactly defined, you are still busy finding out what it is. You're not arrogant about it, and you are prepared to work for it, to search until you find it. Am I right?'

He wasn't entirely wrong, but she was definitely not going to admit it. She took a tiny sip of the sherry as her response. It was dry and delicious.

'We both come from . . . shall we say "humble origins"? I thought the same when I was young. That I could become something. Something more than people thought I could. Maybe it was because they underestimated me, that made me want to show them. And then . . .'

He stood up again, walked to the window, sipped his sherry and stared outside. Drank a bit more.

'Let me give you some advice,' he said and looked at her again. His expression was sympathetic, with a compassion that surprised her. 'If you get there, if you've become what you can be, don't try looking for more.'

Like you? she wanted to ask.

'Like me,' he said.

The moment was surreal. Jasper Boonstra's confession. Sort of. And the way it sometimes felt that he was reading her mind.

The silence between them lengthened. She couldn't offer him any sympathy.

He drained his glass suddenly. 'I will get the directors' signatures. It shouldn't take long. I'm sure you are just as eager as I am to get this done.'

'Thank you very much.' She stood up.

'Come, I'll walk you to the door.' He politely waited for her to exit first. She couldn't help wondering what had happened since she had been here last. Something must have caused this about-turn.

He opened the front door for her when they reached it. 'Thank you, Sandra,' he said.

'Goodbye,' she said and went to her car.

She was some distance away when he called out: 'I think that yellow dress suits you very well. You look lovely.'

And then he shut the door.

OCTOBER

19

1 October

Vaughn Cupido sat on the edge of the sofa, eyes fixed on the front page of the Sunday paper spread open on the coffee table.

Donovan stood opposite him, with an irritated scowl.

'I'm waiting, Donovan,' his mother said.

'Mommy,' he said. That single word carried in it a whole universe of injustice.

'You can play PlayStation when you've recited the poem. Finish and *klaar*.'

'Poetry is for girls,' Donovan said.

'No poetry, no PlayStation,' she shrugged.

Donovan sighed theatrically. Then he began, with a sulky mumble:

'O hushed October morning mild,
Thy leaves have ripened to the fall;
Tomorrow's wind, if it be wild,
Should waste them all.
The crows above the forest call;
Tomorrow they may form and go.
O hushed October morning mild,
Begin the hours of this day slow.'

'That's lovely, Donovan,' said Desiree. 'But you should try to sound melancholy when you do your oral tomorrow. It's a very melancholy poem.'

'It's not melancholy, it's weird,' said the boy. 'Fact is, all poetry is weird. I just don't get it. Tomorrow the teacher will ask us, what does that mean, that the leaves are ripe? I mean, leaves are not fruit.

So it must mean something deep. In poetry it always means something, and it's always something mysterious and deep, and it's always something I don't get. The girls get it, but not me. Poetry just isn't a guy thing.'

'Are you done moaning?' Desiree asked.

'I'm not moaning, I just said it's weird.'

'It's about the leaves turning to autumn colours. It's a metaphor.'

'A metaphor?'

'Yes, when you say one thing is another thing. He's saying leaves are like fruit, but they ripen in autumn.'

'So why doesn't he just say the leaves are changing colour?'

'Don't act dumb, Donnie. That's what makes it poetry.'

'Whatever. A dude who writes about leaves. What sort of dude is that?'

'A sensitive soul,' said Desiree. 'In touch with his feminine side.'

Cupido looked up from his paper, and rolled his eyes.

Desiree punched him on the shoulder. 'Don't encourage the child in his nonsense, Vaughn. It's okay to be a sensitive soul.'

'Mommy, we aren't saying it's wrong to be sensitive,' said Donovan. 'We're just saying we aren't like that. Me and Uncle Vaughn, we identify as red-blooded male.'

'Red-blooded male, you say,' said Desiree, amused. 'You two muffin bakers.'

'Damn straight,' said Cupido. 'Best bakers in the world are red-blooded male.'

'Sensitivity has nothing to do with masculinity, Vaughn, tell the boy. You can be a real man and still be in touch with your feminine side.'

'Fair enough,' said Cupido. 'You can, but you don't have to be. Don't force it if you don't feel it. Just be yourself.' He pointed at the newspaper. 'We have much bigger problems in this country than understanding poetry and sensitive souls.'

The main article was about the head of the National Prosecuting Authority finding yet another excuse not to charge the president with corruption.

'That dude is captured,' Donovan said.

'True, that,' said Cupido.

'And not an oil painting either,' said Desiree when she glanced at the photo. 'That's the silver lining of leaving the Hawks. You don't have to worry about the state-capture stuff any more.'

'We all have to worry about the state-capture stuff,' said Cupido. He flicked through the newspaper. The story about the fatal shooting of Warrant Officer Milo 'Venus' April at the Waterfront was on page five. There was a photo of the Honda Ballade against the tree. The paper labelled it 'gang violence'. There was a picture of April's weeping fiancée, Chriselda Plaatjies. They were going to get married in December.

Cupido wanted to swear, but Desiree didn't allow cursing in front of her son. He swallowed the words.

Just before twelve, Griessel finished his last section of painting. He wanted a quick shower, before he and Alexa went out for lunch at the Black Sheep restaurant a little way up Kloof Street. He put his phone down on the bedside cabinet, climbed out of his overalls for the last time, and walked naked to the bathroom to toss them in the laundry basket.

His phone rang. He turned around, squinted at the screen. It was skinny Jimmy from Forensics. He answered: 'Jimmy?'

'Hello, Benny, some quick news about the Smith & Wesson five-hundred; there's no record of a five-hundred being tested by ballistics. There was one, about two years back, that was tested for fingerprints in a burglary case, but the record says it was returned to the original owner, in Saldanha. I can get his particulars for you . . .'

'No, it's okay, Jimmy . . .'

Alexa walked into the bedroom and found Griessel in his birthday suit. She approached him with a contented smile. 'Hello, my love,' she whispered. It never ceased to amaze him that she could find him attractive, with all those miles on the clock, that unflattering paunch.

'The only other thing . . .' Jimmy said.

'Yes?' said Griessel, as Alexa took the overalls out of his right hand and dropped them on the floor.

'Milo April worked on a whole series of carjackings in Mitchells Plain. There was quite a spike last year, ninety-five, highest ever. Then they made him part of a small task team, that's where most of his time went, the last ten months. I'm not sure you can call it "gang activities".'

Alexa came up close, put one hand on his bum, and with the other began caressing what she called his 'rascal'.

'Thanks, Jimmy, thanks a lot, I appreciate it, really, I have to run, talk to you soon,' he said and rang off. He knew his fiancée.

It was going to be a very late lunch.

Sandra Steenberg took the golden-brown roast chicken out of the oven.

At the breakfast counter Josef looked up from the Sunday paper and said: 'My goodness, that smells good.'

'It's the lemon and marjoram,' she said. It was a Jamie Oliver recipe, whole chicken stuffed with herbs, one of the few dishes that the children also loved. 'You can carve for us.'

Josef stood up to fetch the electric carving knife. Sandra saw the photo on page three of the paper. She pulled off the oven gloves and took a closer look.

It was a paparazzi shot of Jasper Boonstra and his wife, Lettie, in a restaurant at Clifton, Friday night.

She quickly scanned the article.

It speculated whether Boonstra and his wife were reconciled now that the billionaire swindler – still apparently worth three hundred and fifty million dollars – had sent his mistress packing.

Sandra examined the photograph. Boonstra and his wife on the terrace of The Bungalow. Boonstra leaning forward, seeming fully attentive to his wife.

She looked serious.

She could be anybody's aunt, Sandra thought. Plump, a little old-fashioned. She looked older than her husband did. As if she had worked harder.

Was this, she wondered, why Boonstra was different yesterday? More easy-going, pleasant? Because his wife had taken him back? Then he wasn't an insensitive monster after all.

And why would the wife take him back? After all she'd had to endure, including the public ridicule. Why?

'What's on your mind?' Josef asked, watching her expression.

'I think it's easy to forget that a fraudster like Jasper Boonstra is also just human. With feelings.'

Her husband raised his eyebrows, but didn't comment.

20

Appearances can be deceptive.

Stellenbosch doesn't seem like a large town. Even when the students – over thirty thousand of them – are in residence.

Perhaps it's the effect of the encircling mountains' breathtaking beauty and the close proximity to the pomp and splendour of so many grand wine estates. Or the fact that so much of the municipal area is made up of farms, golf courses and sports fields. The myriad oak trees, the babbling Eerste River and the whitewashed historic build-ings might have something to do with the enchanting intimate country atmosphere. An aura of old-world courtesies and innocence.

So the size of the large police station was a surprise to most people on their first visit. The nerve centre of law enforcement filled an entire block, just a stone's throw from the town centre – should you have the nerve to throw a stone here. To some, this huge SAPS presence evoked a feeling of disappointment, even unease. As though it somehow diluted the enchantment of South Africa's second-oldest European settlement, contaminated it. With all this charm there really ought not to be any crime.

Mrs Annemarie de Bruin did not share this sentiment now.

At twenty-five minutes to eight on Monday, 2 October, when she parked in Du Toit street and jogged to the single door entrance of the police complex, she was fleetingly aware of the expansive building behind the high white wall. She thought that here at least there ought to be enough people to help with the search.

She hurried to the charge office, where seven people waited at the counter to offer assistance.

A constable spotted her and noted the distress in her body language, her anxious expression. She did not look like the hordes of people reporting a stolen cell phone or laptop for insurance purposes. Her need was obviously real.

'Can I help you?' he asked.

'My son,' she said. 'My son is missing.' Then she burst into tears, breaking her resolve to be strong.

Three kilometres west of the police station in the Eikestad's town centre, its forty-two detectives were seated in the old Stellenbosch Commando Headquarters in the Lower Papegaaiberg suburb. Set to one side, as if they were the black sheep of the greater SAPS family.

It was a two-storey complex, about sixty years old, reminiscent of a school hostel. A long, dignified structure set in spacious grounds, surrounded by lawns and trees. The investigators weren't based there because of their importance. There were simply too many of them: they had outgrown the police station in town, so they had been relocated here.

On the first floor, in the eastern corner, was the office of Lieutenant Colonel Waldemar 'Witkop' Jansen, branch commander of the detectives. He was just as old as the building, a real little terrier, compact, bad tempered. As a young man his hair and Charlie Chaplin moustache had been light blonde, hence his nickname that meant 'white head', but now they had greyed to the colour of snow. At twenty to eight he looked up irritably from his desk and said, wagging a warning finger: 'I won't put up with any nonsense. Not from either of you. You receive me?'

Griessel and Cupido sat across from him, each dressed in his best working clothes. Cupido was wearing the charcoal-grey suit with fine grey stripes, white shirt and rose-coloured tie. Griessel was in the navy-blue J.Crew jacket – his newest, two years old already – with khaki chinos and a light blue shirt and no tie. It was the outfit that Alexa liked the most.

'Yes, Colonel,' Benny said. Cupido merely nodded solemnly.

'You come with a history,' said Jansen. 'And a helluva reputation. Listen closely, gentlemen, there will be no high-profile cases, no Hawks-style glitz and glamour and no TV cameras.' He consulted the case register on the desk in front of him. 'Last night we had three robbery commons, three break-ins, four thefts from vehicles, one ATM fraud complaint, one assault GBH, one assault common, three thefts common, of which one was a mountain bike that disappeared three years ago, I ask you . . .' He shook his head. 'Not the sort of thing that will get your name on the front pages. Ordinary work, foot work, hard police work. And if you don't like it, then you had better leave now. Read my lips: there's no space here for prima donnas or provocateurs, or for idlers, drunkards and contrarians.'

He glared at them. They sat poker-faced.

'You receive me?'

'Yes, Colonel.'

'There's no room for any kind of *attitude* here. You receive me?'

'Yes, Colonel,' they both said meekly.

'Loud and clear?'

'Yes, Colonel.'

Jansen sighed. 'Only forty-eight per cent of our dockets make it to court, and now they send me two troublemakers.' He closed the case register and looked intently at them. 'Show me your appointment certificates.'

The warrant officers took out their SAPS identification cards and showed them to the colonel.

He nodded in satisfaction. 'Show me your notebooks.'

They took out the standard-issue black notebooks that detectives used to record notes throughout the day, to be transferred to dockets later in the administration process.

Witkop Jansen nodded, growled his approval. 'Good start. But if I catch you without your appointment certificate and your notebook, there will be trouble. You receive me?'

'Yes, Colonel.'

'Basics. Here we do the basics right. By the book.'

They were silent. He continued: 'We work shifts, six to six, four days on call, four days off. You are on call the next four days. From six in the morning. Six. Not quarter past or half past. Six. At the Crime Office. At the station. In town. Go and report to Captain Geneke now. You are dismissed.'

They stood. 'Thank you, Colonel,' said Griessel.

'I'm watching you,' said Jansen, making a two-pronged fork with his fingers, first pointing them at his eyes before swinging them round in their direction. 'With my beady eye.'

Only once they were outside in the corridor, and the door shut behind them, did Vaughn Cupido let out a long, slow and loud breath. '*Jissis*, Benna,' he said.

Cupido struggled with authority sometimes. Especially this kind, that made him feel like a schoolboy.

'Count your blessings, Vaughn,' Griessel said. 'Just count your blessings.'

A team of four Eikestad detectives were available every day at the Stellenbosch police station in town. In what was generally known as the 'Crime Office'. In reality just a demarcated area right beside the charge office, with a collection of battered government-issue wooden tables and chairs for work space. It was where the team 'on call' could give immediate attention to the cases that the senior detective at work would allocate to them.

On this Monday morning the senior detective was Captain Rowen Geneke. He was a coloured man who had moved up the ranks over twenty years, and he had heard *all* the legends about Benny Griessel and Vaughn Cupido, often over a tall beer with colleagues who had heard the stories from other members of the Service. Thus it felt a bit awkward to give them a 'fifty-five'. Investigators of their stature and experience were not going to be crazy about the idea of a fifty-five. Especially one where the missing person was a male student. Captain Rowen Geneke was expecting that, WO Cupido at least – widely known as a bit of a cocky son-of-a-bitch – would throw a tantrum. He was braced for it. He was just going to shrug his shoulders and say: 'Brother, I'm doing my job, you do yours.'

But to his relief the two former Hawks took the fresh docket without complaint and sat down at a table opposite Mrs Annemarie de Bruin. He heard the first words of the conversation, and could tell they were treating her well.

Captain Geneke wondered fleetingly if he shouldn't have hung in and given them the stolen mountain bike too. The one where the bike had been stolen three years ago and was only being reported now. Just so that he could tell the story later. One day over a tall beer.

'I'm so grateful they gave me such senior officers,' Annemarie de Bruin said sincerely, looking from Griessel to Cupido and back to Griessel.

She was in her forties, painfully thin. Her attire was simple and she wore no jewellery. They could see how distraught she was. Fine worry lines around her eyes and mouth, a weary resignation clinging to her like an old garment, as if she had been accustomed to bad news all her life.

'Ma'am,' said Vaughn Cupido, pleased that she had noticed their senior status, 'that is protocol now.'

'What do you mean?'

'With a fifty-five,' Cupido said.

'A fifty-five is what we call a case when a missing person is reported,' said Benny Griessel.

'Because of this,' said Cupido and pressed his finger on the completed form that lay between them. 'SAPS Form fifty-five A.'

'In the old days it was handled like any other complaint,' said Griessel, 'but last year the police took a new approach where minors are involved.'

'Your missing person is a priority at once,' said Cupido, 'you skip the schlepp of working with uniforms, you get detectives straight away. And we are under orders, we have to involve the Department of Community Safety, and the station commissioner, that's the big boss of this police station. And even higher up, the cluster commander has to be informed, all the way to the provincial commissioner. The SAPS doesn't take a fifty-five lightly any more.'

'That's wonderful,' she said. 'But Callie is not a minor any more. He's already twenty.'

'We understand that,' said Griessel. 'But the fact that he is still a dependant and a student, means that it is still seen as a priority. Only we won't involve FCS. That's the Family Violence, Child Protection and Sexual Offences unit.'

'Ma'am, but because it escalates up high, because you are getting the full force and might of the SAPS, we have to make absolutely sure that it is a genuine missing person case,' said Cupido.

'Of course . . .'

'Young people . . .' said Griessel. 'Your son . . .' He consulted the form in front of him. 'Calvyn . . .'

'Callie'

'He's a student . . .'

'Yes.'

'The thing about students . . .' said Cupido warily, 'well, with boys in general, especially those between sixteen and twenty-four . . .' He left the sentence hanging.

'No, no,' said Annemarie de Bruin. 'You don't understand . . .'

'Ma'am, we understand, it's just . . .' said Griessel, searching for euphemisms, 'there is a certain degree of experience with them . . .'

'No. Not Callie,' she said, panic in her voice. 'He never . . . He would never, he wouldn't just . . .' She put a hand to her face, fingertips touching her cheeks. A gesture of despair, alarm, self-comfort. She looked from one detective to the other. She began to weep quietly, overcome. 'He has a bursary,' she said, 'Callie has a Dimension Data bursary and . . . It's his only chance, he knows that . . .'

'Ma'am, I'm sorry, I never meant that he . . .' said Griessel and thought how very out of practice he and Cupido were in dealing with front-line complainants. And how important it was that they did not stuff up their very first case at Stellenbosch station. 'We are going to investigate the case thoroughly,' was the best he could do for now.

She scrabbled in her handbag for a tissue. 'Excuse me, I'm just . . . very upset. Very worried. He never . . . I'm just scared it's something serious . . .' She mopped her tears then blew her nose gently. Then in a very quiet voice, as if it was a secret between the three of them: 'We have nothing, sir. *Nothing*. He doesn't have a father, we are poor, he knows this is his only chance . . .'

'Ma'am,' said Cupido, 'it's all right. I'm sorry . . .'

'There is no question, we believe you,' said Griessel.

'I just wanted to say, that is our duty, to ask a lot of questions, to make sure it's a genuine fifty-five,' said Cupido. 'Because the statistics say that *outjies* of this age, you know . . . ?'

She nodded, dried her tears.

'Please don't take offence.'

'Excuse me. I'm sorry.'

'It's fine, ma'am,' said Griessel. '*We're* sorry.'

A moment of awkward silence.

'Can we get you a cup of tea?' asked Cupido.

'No, thank you, I'm . . . Yes. Some tea, that would be good, thank you.'

'With a little bit of extra sugar?' asked Cupido.

21

The cup trembled in her hand. She sipped and told them she was a single parent, had been ever since Callie was born. She put the cup down on the table and put her hands in her lap, in tiny clenched fists. The C that her body formed in the chair reminded Griessel of a drawn bow.

For the past sixteen years she had lived in Robertson, she told them. She worked as a freelance bookkeeper, doing work for a small supermarket, a panel beater, a garden services operation, a take-away fast food shop, and she did the tax returns for a few private individuals.

Her son, Callie, christened Calvyn Wilhelm de Bruin, after his late great-grandfather, was the light of her life. She took out her cheap Chinese cell phone from the worn brown handbag and showed them the photos of her and her child. With a certain degree of pride. And something more. Griessel recognised it: faith, a passionate conviction that these photos were proof of life, that Calvin was merely temporarily missing, mislaid, they had simply to go and find him. He saw that often with parents when something bad might have happened to their children.

'He's twenty,' Cupido read from the completed form.

She nodded, kept paging through the photos on the phone and showing them.

The similarity between Callie de Bruin and his mother was obvious. The same lean body, the same prominent hawkish curve of the nose. But he was a head taller than she and blond, in contrast to her nearly colourless brown hair. His eyes were also unnaturally large. In some of the photos they made him look innocent, in others somewhat surprised, but mostly he looked younger than twenty years. In every photo his arm was protectively around his mother, their heads inclined to each other. She looked proud, he looked cheerful, happy and full of life and slightly awkward, as a son of his age would be when having to pose for his mother's selfie against his will.

Cupido wanted to move the process along and said: 'Ma'am, you last spoke to him on Friday?'

She reluctantly put her phone down beside the mug. Wait, she said, please, she wanted to tell Callie's story, she had to tell his story, so they could understand why she was so deeply concerned.

They just nodded in agreement. Sometimes you had to let a *haas*, a rabbit – as members of the police called the public – give their information in their own way.

Callie was clever, she told them. She didn't know where he got that from, it was grace from above, but even in primary school Callie outdid everyone. In all subjects, actually. But especially in mathematics, good grief, that child was just brilliant in maths. So brilliant were his results back then in Robertson Primary School that Paul Roos, the elite high school in Stellenbosch, had offered him a residential scholarship. Callie accepted. He would have easily been the academic number one in the boys' school, from Grade Eight to Grade Twelve, if he hadn't developed an obsessive interest in computers. He was still top in maths, still in the academic top ten. Before his Matric year he was a fluent programmer in Python and Java, and others too, she couldn't recall all the unfamiliar terms. He earned eight distinctions in his final exams. Ninety-eight per cent for maths. Companies were literally queuing up to offer him a bursary. She wanted him to become an actuary, Nedbank offered him a bursary for actuarial studies. But Callie's heart and soul were in computers. He accepted a bursary from Dimension Data and he studied BSc in mathematical sciences, in the computer science stream, as they say.

Always in the clear understanding that he needed to continue to excel in order to qualify for the bursary each year.

Again and again Callie de Bruin told his mother that he had this one chance in life, and he wasn't going to mess it up, she must not worry. He didn't drink, he didn't party, he didn't even have a girlfriend. He was here to study, to graduate.

'He likes girls, there's nothing "wrong" with him in that way,' Mrs de Bruin said and made quotation marks with two fingers before the hands rested in her lap again. With no apparent awareness or irony.

She said Callie didn't have a steady girlfriend, he always told her there was still plenty of time for that. In the future. He wanted to get the BSc done this year, and then do honours, and then master's, his eyes were fixed on A-eye . . .'

'A-eye?' Vaughn Cupido queried.

'Sorry, I didn't know either. It's Artificial Intelligence,' Annemarie de Bruin said. 'AI, Callie says it's the next big thing, they are teaching computers to think like people. Callie says it's going to change everything. He says he will eventually make more money than as an actuary, and then I can retire, and he will buy me a big house at the sea, and everything I want, because AI is the next revolution.'

'Check,' said Cupido, though his patience was wearing thin, while he waited for her to reveal why it was so important that they should hear the whole story.

'It's just, Callie wouldn't take any chances with his future. He never misses a class. Never. He stays in at weekends, to study. Or, if he does come home, he's at his books or the computer all the time. He's not one for partying and such like. He always calls me back. Straight away. And a packet of biltong? He would never turn that down, good heavens no. Something has happened. We have to find him. Please. You have to help me.'

They said they believed her. They believed everything. But she must describe to them everything that had happened over the past seventy-two hours. So they could know where to start searching.

She told them that she had talked to Callie on his cell phone on Friday afternoon. He was in his room at the hostel. Eendrag, the men's residence. On campus.

'What time did you call him?' Griessel asked.

'About . . . five. A little after five, I had just finished work.'

'And then?'

'He said he didn't want to come home for the weekend, the final exams were just around the corner. We didn't talk long. He sounded like he always sounds. Full of jokes, he's always telling jokes. He was always so good to me, so loving and patient. I'm quite serious, too serious, always worrying about him, too much. I know it irritates him, but that's just the way I am. It comes from wanting to mother him too much, I know that. That's what happens when you raise a child completely on your own, twenty years of single parenthood. I told him, on Friday afternoon, if he wasn't going to come home, I would try to send him a parcel. He . . . The one thing that always worries me is that the boy doesn't eat. He's so engrossed in the computer and his studies, he forgets to eat. So I always send him a little something, when I can.'

She phoned again on Saturday, just to tell him she was sending him biltong and rusks and six Bar Ones that afternoon via a lift, but he didn't answer. Which wasn't unusual, but he always would call her back. Within the hour, mostly. Sometimes two. Never later than that. Especially on weekends.

The biltong and rusks and chocolate bars arrived with a female student whose parents lived in Robertson. It was important they understood that there was no reception at Eendrag residence to drop off anything. Nowhere you could ask them to call someone for you. The residents used an electronic card to go in and out. So the only way to get the parcel to Callie was for him to meet the girl at the door. Or to collect it at her residence.

Later, Annemarie de Bruin sent her son WhatsApp messages to tell him the girl will be at the hostel at five, just wait for her outside. Why aren't you calling me back?

He did not reply.

She and the girl arranged that Callie would fetch the parcel from her hostel.

And still no call from Callie.

By late Saturday night, she was already very worried. She realised she didn't have the phone numbers of Callie's hostel mates, and she didn't want to bother the warden, the 'hostel father'. She waited until Sunday. And when she had heard nothing from Callie by lunchtime, she phoned him. The warden reassured her and said he would get back to her, and by four o'clock he said, no, Callie was not in his room. They'd checked, his bed was made up, a bit rumpled, but no Callie. None of his friends knew where he was. But not to worry, they were like that, these young men. They just took off sometimes, did the craziest things. Drove off to the Cedarberg for a few days, or to Cape Town, especially over the weekend. Sometimes they only came back on Tuesday or Wednesday. She must stay calm, they were looking into it now.

Annemarie de Bruin already knew they were wrong. She knew her son. It was only her wish not to embarrass him that kept her silent.

At ten last night, the hostel father phoned her and said no, no one knew where Callie was.

What was a mother to do?

She decided to wait one more night. The next morning at four she would drive through to Stellenbosch if she had no further word.

And now here she was.

'Ma'am, does he have a car?' Benny Griessel asked.

'No, there was no money for a car, I wished I could afford one. Callie rode a bicycle. In the holidays he worked at Tom's Computers in Robertson by day and sometimes at the Four Cousins new wine-tasting venue, where they have the restaurants too. He bought himself a second-hand bicycle, with his earnings. And he would use Uber, on my credit card if needed, if it was too far to cycle.'

'Where would he Uber to?' Griessel asked.

'Butterfly World,' she said.

'Butterfly World?' Cupido asked.

'The butterfly zoo near the N1,' she said.

'Why was he going there?'

'Sometimes there are people driving from Cape Town to Robertson. But the traffic in Stellenbosch is a nightmare, and they don't want to come in from the highway to pick up Callie or drop off a package. He would take an Uber to Butterfly World, and they would pick him up there. That's what you do when you're poor. You make a plan. We always make a plan, Callie and me. Doesn't matter what, we make a plan. That's why I'm so worried now. If he could have phoned me, he would have made a plan.'

'Ma'am, these are our cell phone numbers,' said Benny Griessel and pushed the sheet of paper he had torn out of his notebook across the table to her. 'Please send us that photo of Callie by WhatsApp.'

She solemnly complied.

'Callie has his own cell phone?' Griessel asked.

'Yes.'

'May we have the number, please?'

She shared it with them. Griessel wrote it down.

'Is the contract in his name?' Cupido asked.

'Yes, but I pay the account.'

'Ma'am, we will have to pull his phone records from the service provider, and ask them to track the location of the phone for us. Would you be able to sign a form for us to authorise that. As his parent and guardian?'

'They can tell us where Callie is now?'

'If his phone is on.'

'Merciful heavens, that's good news,' she said. 'Callie's phone is on most of the time.'

'And we will be able to see who he has spoken to over the weekend. If he has perhaps gone somewhere with his friends . . .'

'You will see he's only talked to me. He would have told me if he was going away. Callie tells me everything.'

The bank rang Sandra at 09:01.

The relationship manager's tone of voice was formal. She said they were aware that the Stellenbosch property market was under pressure. They knew the lion's share of the Steenberg's income consisted of Sandra's commissions. But the Steenberg's bond repayments were now, with the passing of another end of month, more than a hundred and twenty thousand rand in arrears.

Could Sandra and Josef come in to see them so they could look at possible solutions?

'Of course,' said Sandra, her heart in her throat. 'We feel so awful. When do you want to meet?'

As soon as possible. Today would be good.

'What time suits you?' Sandra asked.

They agreed to an appointment at two o'clock.

22

Sandra decided not to tell Josef about the bank appointment. She would go on her own, and tell them he was unable to make it. She would play for time. A week or two. Hopefully that was all she would need. When all the paperwork for Donkerdrif was completed. She would take them – and Ford's finance department – documentary evidence of the immense windfall coming her way soon.

Twelve minutes later her phone rang. She recognised the number. It was Stirling and Heyns, the law firm representing Demeter. She answered.

'Sandra, this is Mareli Vorster.' The attorney who had called her to tell her that Demeter were interested. And who had been with Hurwitz on the farm nearly a week ago.

'Hello, Mareli.'

'Do you have a moment? We have a little problem.'

Captain Rowen Geneke waited until Annemarie de Bruin went out before he went over to speak to Griessel and Cupido. 'Don't escalate this docket yet,' he told them.

'Escalation is the protocol, Captain,' Cupido said. 'And you know about our . . . position. The colonel says we are on a very short leash.'

Griessel could tell that it was tough for his colleague to take orders from a detective who had the same rank as him until barely a month ago.

'I will phone the colonel and tell him it's my call,' Geneke said patiently. 'With students disappearing . . . We usually find them quickly.'

'Usually? How often do they go missing?' Cupido asked.

'There's one or two every month,' said Geneke. 'Especially just before or just after the weekend. Often the boyfriend coming to say that his girlfriend is missing. And turns out she had gone on a dirty weekend with some other guy. Or they went for a piss-up in Hermanus.'

Then it's embarrassment all round, so just handle this with discretion. About ninety-five per cent creep out of the woodwork after a day or two. Your best bet is to clock in with Campus Security first. Sixty-two Merriman.'

'How will Campus Security help?' Griessel asked. Ever sceptical of private services.

'They are quite jacked up. There are a couple of former policemen who work there. Know the story. But the point is their systems. The municipal CCTV is fairly useless, but the varsity's is top-notch. Over a thousand cameras, in the buildings and on campus. And all the students have cards that they have to swipe to get in and out.'

'At the hostels too?' Griessel asked.

'Most of the buildings. Their systems can tell you what time the people entered or left, about all of them.'

'What sort of problem?' Sandra asked Mareli Vorster, the tension building up in her again.

'Are you private enough right now? Can we speak in confidence?'

'Yes, absolutely.'

'Listen, I'm going to talk directly to you. Is Jasper Boonstra involved in the Donkerdrif deal?'

A hammer blow, it rocked her. But she knew her response now was critical. She attempted to remain calm, breathe. She tried to recall what Boonstra had said to her, the first day. That the farm belonged to a Swiss company. *Huber AG. And you needn't worry about my . . . reputation. It's impossible to connect me with the firm.* She would have to believe that he was sly and devious enough to pull it off.

'Jasper Boonstra?' She did her best to sound surprised. Could the woman hear the hoarseness in her voice?

'That's right. Demeter is one of our most valued clients, and we must . . . We have a duty, a responsibility, to examine every aspect carefully, due to the size of the purchase price. We have done our research thoroughly . . .'

'Yes . . .'

'One of our researchers picked up something. Just a small red flag, but there it is. Huber . . . One of their British directors had connections with Boonstra, in another company, a London-based one. Quite obscure, seems like one more that Boonstra used as a smokescreen to make his profits look better. About two years back.'

'Mareli, I have no knowledge of the Huber directors' connections to Jasper Boonstra.' Technically true.

'I understand that. We are just concerned that . . . Demeter cannot afford to be seen to have anything to do with Boonstra. Not now, you know how much emotion there is surrounding that man.'

'I know. Listen, I can try and find out . . .'

'No, not necessary, we have already decided we will have to withdraw the offer . . .'

'Oh.' She knew her disappointment could be heard in that single syllable. Her entire world was slowly imploding. It felt as though the universe was punishing her, forcing her to take responsibility for her lies and deceit. 'I see . . .'

'I'm truly sorry, Sandra. The problem is, a transaction of this size . . . it will attract the interest of the media. Even if only the wine industry media to begin with, it won't remain there. Donkerdrif is one of the crown jewels of the Boland. And once the cat is out of the bag . . . Demeter already owns two other South African wine farms. There is too much at risk.'

'I . . . I don't know what to say to you.'

'There is good news too, however. All is not lost. The fact of the matter is, Demeter is still keen to acquire the farm. We just want to approach this from another angle. To better protect our client. Consequently, could you enquire of your clients if Huber AG is for sale? It seems that Donkerdrif is their sole asset. If we can do it that way . . . It is only the company ownership that will be replaced per Swiss regulations, if you get my drift . . .'

Sandra grasped it. By selling the shares of Huber AG in Switzerland to Demeter – or an affiliate of Demeter – there need be no registration of title deed in South Africa. The farm ownership remained the same. If Demeter also retained the wine maker and farm manager, nobody local would be any the wiser. It could work, if Boonstra agreed.

But then she realised there would be huge repercussions for her and Charlie. Especially for her. It would not be a property sale, Benson International Realtors would be completely side-lined. 'I can't do that,' she said swiftly.

'Because you don't want to lose the commission,' said Vorster. 'We foresaw that. It is negotiable . . .'

Sandra knew that her knowledge of this type of offer and the potential implications was limited. She played for time. 'We would first have to be satisfied with your offer before I can present the possibility to my client.'

'You are a clever woman,' Mareli Vorster said, respect and amusement mingled in her voice. 'Here is what we thought to do: Demeter agrees to pay Benson International Realtors a finder's fee of two million rand, and offer Huber AG ninety million to purchase the company in Switzerland. Demeter will be paying a better price, but think of the saving in tax and transfer and legal fees. And trouble. And you won't have to wait until title registration before you receive your money. You can have it in your hand this week.'

The big fat golden carrot. They would get the money sooner. What a temptation. If she received the money promptly, all her shabby financial secrets were secure. But it meant four million less than the commission that Benson International Realtors would have received. Sandra would lose two million on the deal. A great deal of money. Her heart was in her throat. Should she take this offer to Charlie, as it was, and save the deal? Or try to insist on the original amount? What about the very real risk that Demeter would simply walk away? There were no other buyers on the horizon.

The big question was, how seriously worried were the lawyers at Stirling and Heyns about the Boonstra connection? And how badly did they want Donkerdrif?

'We will have to think about this,' she said.

'I understand. But we would like clarity by the end of the day.'

Sandra terminated the call. She stood up, walked out of the office with her cell phone in her hand, down the stairs, out onto the pavement, in search of fresh air and shelter from the storm.

They drove up Dorp Street.

'Hell, this is a pretty place,' Griessel said to Cupido as he gazed out at the historic whitewashed houses that had been converted into offices, street cafés and clothes boutiques. A beautiful woman in white blouse and black skirt walked out of an estate agency and came to a standstill on the pavement. 'You're probably used to it already.' While Vaughn owned a house in Bellville South, even before the suspension he had begun spending a lot of time with Desiree in Stellenbosch.

'Benna, the traffic drives you crazy, the students are irritating, and there's never any fucking parking, but it's a true thing you say there. The place oozes charm.' Then he added philosophically: 'There's no other town in this country like it, partner. Weird place. The very rich and the very poor, shoulder to shoulder, a *moer* of an income inequality. For all practical purposes it should have been a powder keg, but somehow they get along.'

They turned left into Drostdy Street, then right into Van Riebeeck. Students streamed by, carefree and relaxed, in skimpy summer outfits. 'Look,' said Cupido. 'Black, white, coloured, the entire lot together. The New South Africa in all its youthful glory. And they're all universally inappropriately dressed.'

Standing on the pavement, Sandra saw and heard nothing.

She went over everything again. Should she go and talk to Charlie? Ask his advice? Call Jasper Boonstra and check? She recalled his words again. *It's not possible to connect me to the firm.* He was a swindler, but for many years he had led a great deal of extremely intelligent people up the garden path. He was still not in jail. If he said there was no evidence, there was no evidence.

Why the lawyers' great concern then?

The truth dawned on her: Mareli Vorster was playing a game. She was sure of it. She thought back over the conversation. First the lawyer told her that they were going to withdraw the offer, to throw Sandra off balance, to evoke anxiety. Then waited for it to sink in. Only then did she bring in the alternative, the lifebuoy so generously thrown her way, so that she could grab on to it. The evidence of a Huber AG connection to Boonstra would be extremely slim at best. Stirling and Heyns were just looking for ways to save Demeter a million or two, most likely upping their own legal fees at the same time. There were probably bonuses at stake.

Cunning.

But two could play this game. Her need for the money was too desperate.

She accessed her call register on her phone, rang Mareli Vorster's number. She had to hold until a secretary put her through. Her heart pounded in her throat. She rolled the dice: 'Mareli, we have consulted. And our decision is that that will not be acceptable. We have two other buyers interested. And the Boonstra story sounds like mere speculation to me. It's surely not true.'

A long silence followed on the line.

'Would you consider the alternative transaction at all?' asked the lawyer.

'We would, if the figures were adjusted.'

'That's what I wanted to hear. I'll get back to you.'

Sandra balled her fist and made a small gesture of triumph.

'I'll await your call.'

23

Cupido and Griessel flashed their identity cards, introduced themselves to Veronica Adams at the University of Stellenbosch Campus Security.

'You're new,' she said, beckoning them into her office.

'We started today,' said Cupido. 'Formerly from the Hawks,' he softened the truth, so she would know they were not just anybody.

'Really, hey?' she said, looking impressed. 'Please sit down.'

The detectives sat across from her at the desk. 'You were in the Service?' Cupido asked.

'I was. Criminal Intelligence at Provincial. But you know how it's going there, when the state-capture thing began . . .'

'I feel you, sister,' said Cupido. It was widely known in the police that Criminal Intelligence was one of the SAPS branches that was most abused by the country's corrupt politicians. 'We had our own innings with capture shenanigans.'

'How may I help you?' she asked.

'We have a fifty-five on one of your students.'

She nodded as if this was fairly routine and shifted into place in front of her computer screen and keyboard. 'What is her name?'

'It's not a "her", it's a "him".'

Adams looked up and raised her eyebrows. 'A male student?'

'Calvyn Wilhelm de Bruin. His mother calls him "Callie". Is that unusual, for a young man to go missing?'

'It happens. Once in a blue moon. It's usually the girls. In which residence is he?'

'Eendrag.'

'Student number?'

'We don't have that, sister.'

'Okay, no problem . . .' She typed on her keyboard. 'Yes, he's on the system . . . When did he go missing?'

'His mother spoke to him the last time about five o'clock Friday afternoon,' Griessel said.

'And then?'

'That was the last time. She hasn't heard from him again. He's not answering his phone.'

Adams tapped on the keyboard, waiting for results. Then she frowned. 'That's funny,' she said.

'How so?' Cupido asked.

'The system log says he used his card yesterday at Eendrag's front door, around 18:42.'

'Yesterday? Sunday?'

'That's right.'

'Could it be an error?'

'Not on my system.'

She turned the screen around so they could see. Griessel and Cupido leaned forward. 'Look. There are his last two records. Yesterday at 18:03 he clocked in to the hostel. There's an electronic lock at the front door, they have to swipe a card to open the door. And then he left again, at 18:42.'

'So he didn't sleep in the hostel?' Griessel asked.

'That's the way it looks. Must have been with the girlfriend. Happens all the time.'

'His mother says he doesn't have a girlfriend,' said Cupido.

'Let me tell you the biggest lesson I learned in this job. The moms and dads don't know ten per cent of what's going on in their children's varsity lives.'

Griessel checked his watch. Twenty past nine. 'Have lectures started already this morning? Would he have clocked in for class?'

'First class was at eight already. He's final year BSc, they have fewer classes. And they skip a lot of them too.'

'Will your system show if he went to class?'

'Not always. Only certain lecture rooms have electronic locks. And the library.'

'We will have to talk to the hostel father, sister,' Cupido said.

'We haven't called them that for ages, it's perpetuation of the patriarchy.'

'I see, said the blind man . . . What do you call them now?'

'Residence coordinators. Eendrag's is Dr Paul du Toit. He's at Sports Science.' She consulted her computer again, then gave them the number.

'Can we have all Callie de Bruin's movements, from Friday?' asked Griessel.

'Okay.' She worked the keyboard. 'I'll print it out for you.'

They walked to the car with the information that, according to the university system, Callie de Bruin was not missing after all.

The previous Friday he exited the front door of Eendrag at 17:56. As did approximately a third of his fellow residents, departing late afternoon. Callie went somewhere for the weekend. As did a third of his fellow residents. He only returned on Sunday evening around three minutes past six. More or less in step with his comrades. The only anomaly was that he left again thirty-nine minutes later, and still had not returned.

'He doesn't drink, doesn't party, doesn't even have a girlfriend,' said Cupido sarcastically as he and Griessel climbed back in the car. 'Those are the mother's winged words. I ask you, where was the little angel the whole weekend?'

'I'm starting to wonder if his cell phone hasn't been stolen, Vaughn. That would explain everything. He doesn't know about his mother's WhatsApps, that's why he hasn't called her back.'

Cupido switched the engine on, then off again. He looked at Griessel in frustration. 'Benna, explain one thing to me: where's the logic? We live in a country with one helluva crime rate, the SAPS has had the biggest brain drain and loss of experience in history in the last ten years, there's a massive problem with corruption in the Service and they have the two best former Hawks detectives in the land looking for a student who is still jaunting about somewhere after a weekend piss-up during which his phone has been stolen. Where's the fucking logic?'

'That's something I've been pondering the whole weekend. There's a snake in the grass here, Vaughn.'

'What do you mean?'

'The entire story makes no sense. You heard the commissioner, at the hearing. And saw him. If he could, he would have locked us up. He wanted to exile us to Siberia. Laingsburg was the closest they could get to that. And then Milo April contacted us about the Smith & Wesson, and all of a sudden they turned around and sent us here. It makes no difference whichever way you look at it, Stellenbosch is heaven on earth compared to Laingsburg. Stellenbosch feels like a *reward*. Why not Khayelitsha or Mitchells Plain, if they wanted to keep us in the Cape, but still punish us? And then someone shot Milo April at the Waterfront? You know I don't believe in coincidences. But what I want to know, is how it all connects. Is someone trying to solve a problem? What problem? Is there a message in it somewhere? "Keep your mouths shut and enjoy Stellenbosch or you can end up like Warrant Officer April?"'

'Fuck, partner, I hadn't thought of it like that.'

'If I have to look for drunken students for the next twelve months until a new president tries to fix this mess, that's okay by me. But one of our brothers has been shot, and I think one of our other brothers has had him shot, and we can't just leave it there. Even if that means Siberia for us.'

'Amen, brother.'

'So, what do we do?'

Cupido sighed. 'Good question. I will have to think about it.'

'I've been thinking for three days already. And I still haven't got a solution.' He took out his notebook. 'But while we're thinking, let's try and find Callie de Bruin's hungover little ass.' Griessel looked up Calvyn Wilhelm de Bruin's cell phone number, called it and put the call on speaker phone.

'The subscriber you have dialled is not available at present. Please try again later.'

'So, his phone is switched off,' said Griessel. He consulted his notes again, then called Annemarie de Bruin. She answered almost instantaneously.

'Ma'am, this is Warrant Officer Griessel from the police. Do you have a moment?'

'Have you found him?'

'No, ma'am, we are still busy with the investigation. I just want to ask you: when you phoned Callie on Saturday . . .'

'Yes.'

'Did his phone ring? Or did you get the voice saying he is not available?'

'I can't remember. I think . . . Sometimes, when he's studying, he switches his phone off. But then I send him a WhatsApp to ask him to call me. Then he phones back. Always. Within an hour or so. I think . . . If I remember correctly, that's what happened. That his phone was off. That's why I sent him the WhatsApps.'

'So, his phone was off the whole weekend?'

'I think so. Yes, I think that's right. Why? What does that mean?'

'Ma'am, it doesn't mean anything yet, we just want to know, for when we try to track the phone.'

'Haven't you done that yet?'

Griessel suppressed a sigh. 'It takes a while to get all the documentation to the service provider, ma'am.'

Mareli Vorster phoned Sandra back before lunch.

That was a very good sign.

'I just want to say that we understand your point of view very well. It's a large amount of commission to lose. And we want the best deal for all parties.'

Yes, yes, Sandra thought. Of course you do.

'So, here is where we stand now: we pay Benson International Realtors a finder's fee of four-point-five million, once the contract is signed. And for Huber AG ninety-two million to buy all the shares. How does that sound?'

It sounded better to her. She would lose about a million, but she could get the money this week. Jasper Boonstra would receive about two million less, but at least the sale would go through. It could work. If everyone agreed.

'I will speak to my boss immediately.'

24

'Look at those wheels,' Cupido said, pointing at the parking lot in front of Eendrag residence. There was a fleet of relatively new cars, even a few large *bakkies*, a Mini Cooper and a Range Rover Evoque. 'You and I can't afford any of those luxury rides, but Daddy coughs up so his golden boy won't suffer at varsity. *Jissis*, Benna, the world we live in . . .'

'*Ja*,' was all he said. Griessel was thinking about his son, Fritz, studying film-making at AFDA in the Cape. Fritz didn't have a car, because his policeman father couldn't afford it. He could barely afford the expensive class fees, especially now that he was only earning a WO salary. He had been thinking of Fritz since they got the Form 55 that morning. His relationship with his child was not good. He did his best, but Fritz was still angry about his alcoholism. It made no difference how long he was on the wagon, no difference how he tried to explain the shrink's diagnosis of post-traumatic stress and survivor's guilt that made him resort to drink. He didn't blame his son, because Griessel had done a great deal of damage over the years. To his ex, Anna, his daughter, Carla, and especially to Fritz, the youngest, the son who had been looking for a role model. Who was probably still searching for one.

The irony was, if Fritz took a week to phone him back, he still wouldn't imagine the boy had gone missing. Maybe it was his feeling of guilt about that which spurred him to tackle this docket with more energy than Cupido now.

They got out and went across to wait at the residence's front door.

It was a building from the same era and in the same style as the old Stellenbosch Commando headquarters that housed the Eikestad detective branch: white walls, pink-red roof. And the old, ugly steel window frames. Students were going in and out. They noted that when two or three students were in a group, only one swiped his card through the reader.

'It's not a perfect system,' Griessel said.

'Look at the cameras,' said Cupido and pointed out the two electronic eyes, one outside and one visible through the glass beside the locked wooden double doors. 'Big Varsity Brother is watching.' And then: 'Residence coordinator, Benna. Super woke, and that's cool, but the PC thing is a mystery to me sometimes. Perpetuation of the patriarchy. I ask you. Does that make "hostel mother" a perpetuation of the matriarchy? I mean . . .'

'No, I don't get it either. But we will have to make peace – we are the dinosaurs here.'

'Speak for yourself, grandpa. I'm in my prime, and a metro man through and through. Exhibit number one: muffin baker.'

'Aren't you turning forty? It's all downhill from there . . .'

'For you mere mortals perhaps, *pappie*.'

A man in a jacket hurried up from the parking area. He was tall, broad-shouldered and clearly very fit, more or less Cupido's age. 'Are you the police?'

'We are,' said Griessel. 'Doctor du Toit?'

'That's right. Paul, please.'

They introduced themselves. He swiped his card through the reader and invited them in. 'How can I help?'

'We want to see his room, please,' said Griessel.

'And talk to his friends,' said Cupido.

'Yes,' said Du Toit. 'I talked to a few guys in his corridor yesterday, Callie isn't . . . very sociable. But hang on, I have to get the key to his room, excuse me . . .'

They waited. Later they strolled through into the large inner courtyard. In the bright sunshine tables and benches were arranged on the paving and lawn. Students sat chatting, drinking coffee and tea. From some window, music played. Nobody bothered with the detectives.

Paul du Toit hurried back holding a bunch of keys. 'Sorry to keep you waiting. Come, I'll show you.'

'Doc, how well do you know Callie?' Griessel asked.

Du Toit answered as they climbed the stairs to the second floor. 'To be honest, I don't know him well. There are nearly two hundred and eighty residents . . . I mean, I know exactly who he is, we have talked in passing, but he isn't terribly involved in hostel activities. He's what the students call "a lurker". But academically he is extremely strong, he's never been a troublemaker, so I . . . There was never a particular need for contact.'

'We saw at the front door that they don't all swipe their cards,' Cupid said.

'They are supposed to, but you know how it is . . .'

Charlie Benson's cravat was navy blue, as was the handkerchief peeping from his blazer pocket. His knee twitched. While Sandra waited for his answer, he sat staring blankly at the framed poster on the wall. It was an advertisement that had appeared two years ago in the *Eikestad News*. A photograph of him in front of the Moederkerk, lit dramatically in the late afternoon sun. He stood dapper and upright, arms crossed, self-confident smile. Below the words: *Forty years of service to Stellenbosch. Let our experience work for you.* And the logo of Charlie Benson International Realtors.

'I'm not going to argue with you again,' he said at last. 'Fifty-fifty. And that's final.'

She'd known he wouldn't be able to resist the temptation to renegotiate. She simply got up and walked out.

'Sandra,' he said in his sternest voice, but she ignored him. She went to her office.

Callie de Bruin's room was something of a train wreck.

It smelled of stale food and sweat and dirty laundry. The crumpled, but more or less made bed was the only bit approaching order. In the corner beside the bed was a heap of clothes. The built-in cupboard door was ajar, and more clothing was protruding from it. Under the bed a pair of trainers and dirty socks were visible. There were textbooks on a shelf, randomly inserted, more books and files and papers underneath on the floor.

'*Fok*,' said Benny Griessel. ''Scuse me, Doc,' he said when he realised he had spoken out loud.

'Does it always look like this?' Cupido asked. He looked at the desk with the large monitor, colourful keyboard and mouse. Cables led to the desktop case which was under the desk against the wall, beside a small wastepaper basket, overflowing with empty fast food containers, predominantly McDonald's and Steers, and Coke cans.

'I don't know,' said Paul du Toit from the doorway. 'I was only in here yesterday afternoon, after his mother phoned. To see if he was all right. It looked like this.'

'But he wasn't here,' said Griessel.

'No, he wasn't.'

'What time did you come to check?'

'About three o'clock.'

'The system shows he popped in about six o'clock last night,' said Cupido. 'He for sure didn't come back to tidy up.'

Griessel pulled the open built-in wardrobe door wider. Clothes, toiletries, an electric shaver and cord, a few towels, everything seemed to have been shoved in hastily and carelessly. A couple of jackets and trousers hung up, an attempt at order. A toiletry bag with toothbrush, toothpaste, shaving cream, razor and a plastic soap container gaped open at the zip.

'Yesterday I talked with some of the guys who live in the rooms next to him. They say he was almost always on the computer. They never knew when he was here.'

'Can we talk to them?'

'I will have to see if they are here. Excuse me,' Paul du Toit said and walked down the passage to start knocking on doors.

'Looks like a smart computer system,' said Cupido from the desk. 'Razer Blackwidow Elite,' he read. He bent down to look at the computer case. 'No-name brand, looks like.'

He took out his cell phone, began snapping photos of the computer equipment, and the room in general.

Griessel felt through the clothes in the wardrobe, looking for drugs, or signs of them. That was one subject they had not touched on with Annemarie de Bruin – Callie's possible use of illegal substances. When young men went missing, that was all too often part of the problem. But his mother had rattled on so much about the virtues of her son that neither he nor Cupido had had the courage to raise it.

In the sweater drawer, right at the back, he felt something hard, pulled it out. A cordless PlayStation hand control.

Paul du Toit reappeared in the doorway. With him was a short, sturdy student with a wild bush of curly russet hair on his head and the optimistic fluff of a fledgling beard on his chin.

'This is Lucius. He's our first rugby team hooker, he lives in the room next door.'

They greeted him.

'Does Callie's room always look like this?' Cupido asked.

'*Ja, Oom.*'

'I'm not old enough to be an uncle. My colleague here, Dinosaur Griessel, on the other hand . . .' Cupido pointed at Griessel.

'Did you see him yesterday afternoon?' Dinosaur Griessel asked.

'No, *Oom*, I . . . His nickname in the hostel is "The Ghost". Because you never actually see him, you just hear about him.'

'And what do you hear about him?'

'Actually just rumours, *Oom.*'

'Like what?'

'He's super clever, *Oom.* So they say. And he's cool. Makes jokes when you see him. And he hardly ever eats.'

'Not according to this,' said Cupido and pointed at the fast food containers in the waste-paper basket.

'Yes, *Oom*, he has them delivered sometimes, with Mr Delivery. That's when you see him, going to the front door to collect.'

'You have no idea where he was this weekend?'

'No, *Oom*, it must be two weeks since I saw him last. He's either at class or here, on the computer.'

'Has he got friends in the hostel?'

'No, *Oom*. I think his friends are outside.'

'Oh?'

'One *ou* sometimes comes here. But I don't know who he is.'

'Lucius, Callie is missing, and his mother is very concerned about him,' said Griessel. 'If there is anything that could help . . .'

The student frowned seriously. 'I understand, *Oom*, but I really don't know.'

They thanked him. Lucius looked at Dr du Toit, who nodded that he could go. He left. But barely a moment later he was back. '*Oom . . .*'

'Yes?' said Griessel and Cupido simultaneously.

'There's a rumour. I don't know if . . .'

'Tell them,' Du Toit urged him. 'Maybe it will help.'

'They say he's the only one who ever hacked into the varsity system. Then they paid him to make it better.'

25

Charlie phoned her on her landline, less than a quarter hour after she had walked out. 'Sandy-san, come talk to me please.' As if nothing had happened.

She walked to her office. He had adopted his martyred look.

'Charlie, you're right about one thing. We're not going to argue any more. We have an agreement. We are going to stick to it.'

'You've changed,' he said. 'You weren't always like this.'

'Circumstances have changed, Charlie. I can barely make a living out of this work.'

'And me, Longoria? And me? My retirement is just around the corner. You are the one who must take over from me when I go, and you do this to me?'

So he was offering her the business now? Was there no end to his machinations?

'Can I talk to Boonstra? Are you happy with the new offer?'

There was something in the look that Charlie darted at her, just a glimpse, like a shooting star. Hate. Brief, unmistakeable, before he pulled himself together. Melodramatic as ever, he sagged his shoulders in exaggerated hurt and resignation. 'Well I suppose I have no choice.'

Outside at the car they discussed what they knew.

'His wallet is missing,' Cupido said. 'And his cell phone and charger.'

'His toothbrush is in the cupboard,' said Griessel. 'But his PlayStation has gone.'

'Do you think he's gone to an electronic games party somewhere? Maybe they're not super concerned about dental hygiene at those get-togethers?'

'Could be . . .'

'It worries me that they can go in and out without swiping, Benna. We must go and see if they have footage from the cameras over the weekend. They might show that he actually was here.'

'I will drop you off, I want to go to court for a two-oh-five.' To access cell phone data from a service provider a detective needed an article 205 subpoena signed by a magistrate or judge.

They climbed into the car, drove back to Campus Security. 'Maybe the video can show us if someone picked Callie up outside the hostel,' Griessel said.

'Check.'

Cupido thought for a moment. 'Do you think his mom would be able to see if he took an Uber? On her credit card?'

'I have no idea.'

'Lithpel will know. Surely there's no reason we couldn't still consult him.' The eccentric Sergeant Reginald 'Lithpel' Davids was part of the Hawks Information Management Centre – or IMC – in Bellville, and the closest to a technological genius that the detectives knew. Davids, thin as a reed with a massive afro hairdo, had a speech impediment for years before it was surgically corrected, and that was the origin of his nickname.

'Ask him about the PlayStation. There was only one . . . joystick, is that what you call it? There was only one in his cupboard.'

'And about the fancy computer,' said Cupido.

Sandra sent Jasper a WhatsApp, just after 11:00. *Demeter wants to alter the offer. May I come and talk?*

It took twenty minutes before he answered, rudely brusque once again. *At 2.*

She had to be at the bank at 14:00. She replied: *Can only be there at 3.*

Not if you want to do business with me.

The old Jasper was back, she thought, and felt her temper rise. She wanted to write back, *Fuck you, see you at 3,* but she restrained herself. *Emergency meeting at the bank at 2, I will come straight after.*

And then she took a copy of the offer to the photocopier. She would take out the names of those involved as well as the name of the farm.

Then she would show the document to the bank manager. She hoped it would be enough to keep the wolf at bay.

While she placed the pages one by one in the machine, she confronted her other growing unease. Charlie's words. *You've changed. You weren't always like this.*

It was true. She had changed. The last few years, before the perfect Boonstra storm hit this town and her life, she had been happy. A happy wife and mother and estate agent, everything going well, the future looked bright. She had shaken off the demons of her youth. The feelings of inferiority, insecurity, but above all, of rage. At her crooked father and spineless mother and the damage they had done to her. At the unfairness of life, preventing her from completing her studies, that others had a much easier time.

She could rise above it all due to Josef's love, his gentleness, the way he made her feel precious.

And the twins.

But now? Now the old feelings were back, and it didn't matter how hard she tried, it felt as though the downward spiral was gaining momentum.

It might all be over, so soon.

She walked back to the office, checked her phone.

Jasper Boonstra had still not answered.

While Cupido waited for them to prepare the video footage of Eendrag's front door from Friday afternoon for him, he sent the photos he had taken in Callie's room to Lithpel Davids, and then phoned him.

'Warrant Officer!' said Davids. 'If you go on like this, one of these days you will be a sarge, like me. Won't that be something? But I'll be honest, the DPCI isn't the same now that you're gone. It's become a very classy place.'

Vaughn had known he would get an earful from the cheeky techie. 'That's just your way of saying how much you miss me, Lithpel. I'll be back, and give you a bloody good kick up the butt.'

'Because I'm such a kick-ass techie, that's why.'

'If you're so kick-ass, tell me about that computer gear in the photos.'

'Serious stuff. Gamer stuff. Who's the lucky guy?'

'Student in Stellenbosch, on a fifty-five. He's dirt poor, says his ma.'

'Bullshit. Those accessories don't come cheap, Warrant. The Dell monitor alone is close to seven thousand. The keyboard and mouse go for three thousand new, and I'm not talking sum total, I mean individual pricing.'

'*Aitsa*,' said Cupido. 'And the computer?'

'Hard to say. The case looks like an InWin seven-oh-seven, that's not big money, depends what's on the inside. But one thing I can tell you, it's a serious gamer's rig. I will bet money he has radical stuff inside that casing.'

'He's a computer science student at the varsity. Rumour has it he hacked into their system, and they paid him to make it better.'

'Aha, my brother from another mother. That makes sense, Warrant Officer, hackers are gamers, a lot of the time. But dirt poor, him? Not so much.'

'Another thing, Lithpel: Benna only found one joystick for a PlayStation . . .'

'You call it a controller, Warrant.'

'Whatever. We only found one, but no PlayStation. We want to know what that means.'

'Doesn't mean much. Most of your PlayStation bundles come with one basic controller, but serious dudes prefer a more fancy one. Scuf or Razer. This brother, it seems, is into Razer, so it could be that he sold the whole lot as a bundle and only kept the old controller.'

'Could he have gone to a PlayStation party, for the whole weekend? Do they still do that stuff?'

'Warrant, you're a dinosaur, you know that, hey?'

'You're confusing me with Benna. Why?'

'PlayStation is all about online play these days. You sit in your bedroom and you challenge the world. But it might be the case that this dude took his PlayStation to a place with bandwidth, 'cause why, maybe his connectivity is a bit iffy where he hangs.'

'Okay.'

'But you could be right about the whole weekend games. The

serious guys do that. There's money in it, if you're good. Big money. Maybe that explains the expensive PC gear.'

'Maybe. And Uber? Do you know Uber?'

'What do you want to know?'

'The kid's mother says he can Uber, but she pays. Will she know if he took an Uber over the weekend?'

'Yes, as far as I know, Uber sends an SMS every time someone takes a ride. To say the money has gone through.'

The video operator beckoned to Cupido that they were ready for him.

'Thanks, Lithpel, we'll talk again.'

'Pleasure, Warrant. And hang in there, hey? We miss you. But only a little.'

Griessel was waiting outside the magistrate's office when Cupido phoned him.

'Benna, there's something weird going on here.'

'How so?'

'I'm looking at the CCTV footage. I thought I'd begin with last night, when little Callie popped back in to the Residence for R and R. At exactly 18:03, the record says. Lo and behold, at 18:03 some guy clocked in at the front door, all on his own, so it's not a gang bang on entry. And that *outjie* used Callie's card, no doubt about it. But the problem is, it doesn't look like our little Callie. It looks like a coloured *ou*, under a hoody.'

'*Bliksem,*' Griessel said.

But wait, there's more. When Hoody came in, his hands were empty. But when he went out, at 18:42, again using Callie's card, he had a sports bag with him. Nice and full of stuff. And suddenly he was wearing gloves.'

'How sure are you that it's not Callie?'

'Naturally that was the big issue, since it's not very hi-def. Coming in it was still nice and light outside, but our friend is too cunning for the outside camera, his head is turned away. When he went out, it was dark, so we don't have what I would categorise as a pin-up shot. But it's enough. 'Cause I checked, the system said Callie left through that door on Friday at 17:56. And when I watched the Friday footage, it shows the real Callie, that skinny one with the Bambi eyes and a nose like his mother. Obvious, Benna. Callie is shorter than the Hoody, and Callie is as pale as any nerd who never sees the sun. No doubts.'

'Fuck,' said Griessel.

'My sentiments exactly,' said Vaughn Cupido.

26

'What do you say, *pappie*?' Cupido asked.

Griessel's mouth was stuffed with burger, so he nodded enthusiastically instead.

'Best burgers in the Cape,' said Cupido with pride, as if he had made the food himself.

They were seated on the benches outside De Vrije Burger in Plein Street. Benny had a Melrose-and-biltong burger, Cupido had chosen the standard model, ''cause I have to watch my weight, partner, I overdid it a bit with the muffin testing the last few weeks'. He had brought Griessel here deliberately, because Benny was a loyal burger man. Everyone who had worked long police-hours with him knew that.

'This is the best since . . .' said Griessel when he had finished chewing. 'Hell, you remember the Steers Dagwood burger, back in the day?'

'Nah, Benna, back then I was a gatsby man, there was this place in Long Street, just around the corner of Wale. Fresh bread, fresh chips, and a peri-peri sauce if you liked. And chili bites, at a place behind the Cape High Court. Just enough bite, always fresh, it was a pleasure to wait at court . . .'

'Your Steers Dagwood burger was pure art. Along with those *lekker* thick chips of theirs. And then they went and changed the menu, took away the Dagwood. Just in that time after the divorce, when it was one of life's few pleasures.'

'No wonder you hit the bottle.'

Griessel laughed. Only Cupido could talk to him like that. 'Exactly. But this . . .' Griessel took another bite and said through a full mouth: 'This is better than the Dagwood . . . I think I'm in love, Vaughn.'

They didn't want to talk about the Form 55, because they knew the big question now was escalation, according to the protocol. Notices to the Department of Community Safety, the station commissioner and his immediate superior, the group commander of the Boland, and eventually the provincial commissioner. Which was not a problem in itself. The domino that they didn't want to topple was the media attention. Missing children and youths were always news. A missing student in Stellenbosch was big news. And a young computer genius, academic achiever and child of a poor single parent was sensational news.

The stranger who'd used Callie's card was the main reason why they felt they had to escalate it now. One of the possibilities now was drugs. And that changed everything.

But before they could escalate the case, they would have to call Annemarie de Bruin and ask her some awkward questions. The way she'd been that morning, led them to believe that she would be pretty upset, at the very least. Her anxiety levels were about to hit the roof.

And Griessel would have to do it. Because, as Cupido often said, his 'bedside manner' was so much better.

Benny was procrastinating on purpose. Because it didn't matter how good his 'bedside manner' was, it remained a difficult thing, every single time. And it played havoc with his mood. He took another bite of hamburger: 'I'm telling you, this Stellenbosch thing is no punishment.'

'*Ja*, partner, speaking of why we're sitting here enjoying the local pleasures . . .' Cupido said. 'I was thinking what we could do. About Milo April and the Smith & Wesson. So here's my question: who do you trust the most? Present company excluded, of course. In the Service, I mean.'

Griessel pondered that. 'Our people in the Hawks. Uncle Frankie, Mooiwillem, Vusi . . .'

'A bit higher up?'

'Mbali,' he said.

'Bingo. That's what I say too. She's a pain in the neck, but she's a straight arrow. Don't take me wrong, I trust The Camel too, but he may be just too close to the fire, so to speak. So here's what I scheme: we go talk to her. But discreetly, I still don't trust the phones.'

'It will have to be tonight, at her house. If she's there.'

'You know The Flower,' said Cupido, using Colonel Mbali Kaleni's nickname. 'She's always home.'

'Okay,' said Benny Griessel, and polished off the burger.

★   ★   ★

Sandra drove as fast as she could to Jasper Boonstra.

The unpleasant atmosphere of the meeting with the bank's relationship manager clung to her. *Relationship manager*, she thought. There is no relationship with a bank to manage. Only the eternal tension of pay, pay, pay. If they could lend you money when times were good, then the 'relationship' was warm and friendly. Hugs all round, look how cute we are, how we care for each other. But when you were struggling, it was a one-sided 'relationship' that said, if you don't cover your overdue payments, we'll take your home away from you.

The woman was chilly from the start. Where was Sandra's husband? Why wasn't he also here?

'His head of department wanted to see him, about his future,' she lied glibly, so glibly. 'It was at short notice, he's very sorry.'

The woman interrogated her, with the reproving tone of a primary school teacher: 'And tell me, why does your home loan look like this?'

All the pent-up rage of the last week bubbled up: 'You know why it looks like that. For the same reason there were four "relationship managers" here before the Schneider-König debacle, and now there's just one. You have lost clients, we have lost clients. The whole town is haemorrhaging, and you ask me *why*?'

The woman's tone was icy: 'The rest of the town has made arrangements, ma'am.'

'How can I make arrangements when I don't know when the next house will sell? Explain that to me.'

And then she took out the documents for Donkerdrif, smacked them down on the table and said: 'Here are my arrangements. It's a sale that has gone through, it will be a month or two before the commission arrives. And if that's not good enough for you, come and take the house. Put it with all the other houses that you have repossessed in Stellenbosch and can't sell. Do you think I'm stupid? Do you think I don't know what's going on here? But let me tell you now, if you want to talk to me again about the arrears, then drop the attitude and talk to me like a valued customer who has been banking with you for ten years, who always paid, a valued customer who is going through a rough patch. Do you understand me?'

The woman's face shrivelled like a prune. Sandra stood up, and walked out. Something she was becoming quite good at lately.

'Ma'am, this is Warrant Officer Griessel of the police,' said Griessel. He was calling from the parked car. Cupido sat beside him listening.

'Is there any news?' Her voice was already pitched higher and anxious.

'No, ma'am, but we are making progress. Are you still in Stellenbosch?'

'No, no, I'm at home. It's too expensive to stay over there. Why do you ask?'

'We . . . We went to look at Callie's room, ma'am, and we wanted to just make sure about a few things . . .'

'Yes?'

He would have to proceed with caution. 'Callie carries a wallet, I assume? Because we didn't find one.'

'Yes. He has a brown leather wallet. He always has it with him. That and his cell phone. Have you found his cell phone?'

'No, ma'am. And he has a black sports bag . . .'

'That's right. It's his weekend bag. Is it still there?'

Griessel was not ready to answer that yet. 'We also want to make sure about his computer, it looks like a very expensive model . . .'

'That's Callie's life, that computer. He used all his extra bursary money and holiday money to build it up. Did it himself, everything, he bought the parts on the internet, second hand, where he could. You must understand; he has to have a good computer.'

That at least explained the expensive accessories that they'd seen. 'I understand, ma'am . . .'

'Is the computer there?'

'Yes, ma'am, it's there. He must have bought his PlayStation with his bursary money too?'

'What PlayStation? Callie doesn't have a PlayStation. Is there one in his . . . There can't be.'

Griessel had to backtrack. 'No, no, we found a . . . a . . .'

'Controller,' Cupido helped him out.

'We found a controller in his cupboard, but it must be someone else's. Do you know if he might have gone to play computer games with his friends sometimes?'

'No. Callie did play, he loves the computer games, but he played them on the internet, when he could. The university charges a lot to use the internet, so when he sees he's over his limit, then he doesn't play.'

'Do you know some of his friends?'

She was silent for a moment. 'I . . . Callie didn't actually . . . He worked so hard, sir, he put all his time into his studies. Every now and then he said there were people studying with him, they had projects to do, and there are the boys in the hostel with him . . .'

'But no one specific whose name he mentioned? No one who came home with him ever, or whose home he went to for a weekend?'

'No, no, he never said anything like that. He would have, if there was. Callie shared everything with me.'

Griessel knew he would have to tell her now. He took a deep breath. 'Ma'am, yesterday someone used Callie's student card to get into the hostel. It looks like a young man, possibly a student, and it seems that he took Callie's sports bag, and that he put something in the bag before he left . . .'

'Oh, merciful heavens . . .'

'We don't think it's anything to be worried about . . .'

'Of course it's something to be worried about, someone carrying Callie's things away!'

'Most likely it was a friend fetching something for him. Maybe he went somewhere where there was faster internet, to play games . . .'

'So his computer is gone?'

'No, ma'am, his computer is here.'

'Then that is not what happened.'

'Ma'am, is it possible for you to come back to Stellenbosch? To see what might have been taken from there in the black bag?'

Just a momentary hesitation. 'I'll come right away.'

27

She found Jasper Boonstra outside the garage's glass doors, next to his canary-yellow Ferrari parked in the driveway.

The car's engine bonnet was open at the rear. Boonstra was wearing shorts and a golf shirt, barefoot. Dark glasses and a Ferrari baseball cap. He was polishing the two black air intake pipes with silicone spray and a cloth.

She parked, picked up the spreadsheet that she had printed out for him, and got out of her car.

He checked his watch. 'It couldn't have been a very long bank meeting,' he said.

'It wasn't,' she said.

He walked away from her, to the garage, reflected in the eye of a CCTV camera looking down on them. A fraction unsteady on his feet. She spotted the cause: a bottle of wine and a glass were inside on a table. He left the spray and cloth there, picked up the glass.

'I take it you don't want to drink with me.'

'No, thank you.'

He gulped the wine, put the glass down again, walked up to her with a wry smile. Although she could not see his eyes, she felt him eyeing her up again.

'Do you know what car this is?'

To merely name the make would be senseless. She shrugged.

'It's a four-eight-eight Spider. Top speed around three hundred and twenty-five kilometres per hour. You and she have two things in common.'

She wasn't going to take the bait.

His smile widened. 'You both cost me six million rand. And you're also built to ride hard.'

'Fuck you,' she said. She listened to her words come out sounding matter-of-fact, not a trace of rage. She realised she had control; a peculiar calm had come over her. Part of it was the way the bank meeting had transpired, as if she had thrown the dice and won, in some way. At least she had survived. Another part was that he was showing weakness now. He was probably drinking because his wife wouldn't take him back. And here he was fondling one of his status symbols like a dummy, a big baby's comfort blanket. He's really a weakling, a swaggering bully, she realised. In that instant he reminded her of her father. Boonstra's fraud was just on a much larger scale than Jannie Boshoff's, but it was the same dynamic in front of her, with all his insecurities and inferiorities and his desire to camouflage them with money and possession and status. She knew it. And Boonstra needed her to sell the farm. The process was too far advanced for him to pull out now. The realisation liberated her. The threat that Jasper Boonstra posed to her, his power over her, was diminished.

He laughed at her, fetched his glass and raised it in salute. 'You're fucking sexy, Sandra. Live with it. So tell me what Demeter's story is.'

She crossed her arms and laid out the details for him. As she spoke, he turned his back on her again and walked back in to the garage, still swigging from his glass. He came back again, closed the engine hood. Then he leaned his butt against the door.

Explanation over, she handed him the spreadsheet. He glanced at it.

'And you're happy with this?'

'There's nothing else on the table.'

'You're naive.'

'Oh?'

'Let me teach you something about business today. They're bluffing. There are lots of people who had a finger in a Jasper Boonstra pie, and they know it. The fact that they found one from the past means nothing. Hell, I owned a yacht with one of the Stirling and Heyns senior partners six years ago. Maybe you should ask them if Demeter knows about that. We bought Donkerdrif via a Swiss company because it offered certain tax benefits. And that's also why they want to do it. In the long term it's a helluva advantage for Demeter. Even in the short term it's cleaner and cheaper for everyone. They're taking you for a ride, they're banking on you being just a little local agent who only sells local properties. That you won't understand anything about Swiss AG transactions. The lower offer is purely manoeuvring. Ten to one they have a contact with a legal firm in Geneva that will give them kickbacks for the business. And if they can push the price down, they show the Americans how sharp they are. So they can get more business from Demeter. And raise their fees.'

She nodded just to acknowledge that she understood.

'You like this deal because you get your money sooner,' he said.

He's a weakling, he's pissed, but he's sly as a fox. Don't forget that, Sandra, she thought.

'Yes.'

'Go and tell the vultures Huber AG will accept the deal if they still get ninety-four million out clear. I will take care of the directors' signatures. You can decide if you want to take less.'

'How long?'

'To get the signatures?'

'Yes.'

Again that odious smile. 'So, the meeting with the bank was hard today, Sandra? Tick-tock, tick-tock, your hour glass is running out.'

'How long?'

'It depends. You know, if you ask me very nicely . . .'

She just shook her head.

'A day or two, three.'

He straightened up from the car, and grinned at her, suggestively. 'But it's not for free, Sandra. You must know that. Nothing comes for free.'

Captain Rowen Geneke sat behind the day's growing stack of dockets as Griessel informed him of the state of their investigation. When he heard about the stranger in the hoody he said: 'Shit. That really worries me.'

'It worries us too,' said Cupido.

'How big a problem are drugs on campus?' Griessel asked.

'No, not too bad,' said Geneke. 'You have your dagga, yes. Some of the *manne* smoke a lot of weed, but you know how it is – it's freely available, friction-free transactions, it doesn't cause trouble. A bit of ecstasy at the clubs, a bit of magic mushrooms, now and then we get a Nigerian peddling cocaine. But I can't say we lose any sleep over drugs on campus. Alcohol is the problem. They booze, these students. *Kwaai.* So it's drunk and disorderly, drunk driving is up thirty-five per cent on last year, now and then you have guys throwing a few punches under the influence, motor vehicle accidents. The problem with drugs in Stellenbosch is in the disadvantaged communities, I'm sorry to say. Like everywhere in the Cape Flats. We are running at around one thousand five hundred drug-related crimes per annum, have been for a few years. Methamphetamine. Tik. The big poison, and all that goes along with it . . .'

'If not drugs, what worries you about Hoody?' Cupido asked.

'Look, I'm not saying that's what happened, but petty theft is quite a thing here. Laptops, cell phones and bicycles. They steal those like nobody's business. In the streets, out of cars, from the hostels, even out of the varsity library. Every day, you can take a look, here in the register. So, if Hoody went in there with the sole purpose to steal it's not unusual. That he found a student card somewhere to swipe in with isn't the weirdest thing that has happened in this town. What worries me is that the chappie whose card he swiped has been missing since Friday. That's not looking good. And this *outjie* came out with gloves. That's quite sophisticated for your average local petty thief. There seems to be some planning behind it.'

'He knew where Callie's room was,' said Griessel. 'He had Callie's card, and he knew exactly how to get to Callie's room. That's what bothers me.'

'Amen, brother,' said Cupido. 'We'll have to find out, do these guys lock their rooms? He might have had Callie's key as well. Maybe he tried other rooms.'

'Have you sent the two-oh-five to Vodacom?' Geneke asked.

'We have,' said Griessel.

Geneke nodded. 'Escalation is a bitch,' he said. 'Before we go there, talk to them again. Tell them it's a priority investigation, they must get their butts in gear. But let's just look at the phone records before we go nuclear on this.'

Greed. That was what drove her father, that was what drove Jasper Boonstra, Sandra thought on her way back to work.

She would not allow it to become her sin. Her passion. Her dark passion, *donker drif*, she thought, and smiled. Maybe it was the lesson that the universe wanted her to learn through this farm deal.

She weighed up everything again. Point one: Boonstra had confirmed what she had suspected – Stirling and Heyns were bluffing. They would accept the deal in any case if they could simply buy Huber AG, as there were enough benefits for them and Demeter.

Point two: Boonstra still wanted his ninety-four million.

Point three: Stirling and Heyns were looking for a way to look good to Demeter.

Point four: Charlie already agreed to a lower commission of four and a half million.

Point five: *You are the one who has to take over from me when I go.* Those were Charlie's words. Maybe he was being manipulative but . . . In a way it made sense. At sixty he'd already said he only wanted to work another five years. Charlie's wife wanted to go to Hermanus, where they owned a house, and had a wide circle of friends. All four of the other agents at Benson International Realtors were women in their fifties, sweet people, but without any great ambition or drive, comfortable in their roles.

She was the only one who really had a chance.

Which brought her to point six: she didn't want to be greedy.

So she would go to Charlie now, and she was going to tell him they should take five million as commission. And she would put a new agreement in front of him to sign, one that said she was lowering her share to sixty per cent. That meant three million for her, two million for him.

An olive branch.

So that in a week or two, three, when she had the money in the bank, she would take Charlie to the Bird Cage for the lemon meringue tart, a firm favourite of them both. And tell him she was prepared to buy a million rands' worth of shares in the agency, with the condition that she had right of first refusal to buy the rest when he retired.

'I'm so sorry it looks like this,' said Annemarie de Bruin, gazing around her son's hostel room in dismay. She was clearly embarrassed and upset. 'He . . . Callie . . . He must have been so drawn into the computer, and forgotten about being clean and tidy . . .

Griessel and Cupido nodded in sympathy.

She saw the fast food containers in the bin. '*Ai*,' she said. 'He . . . It's a waste of money. He knows better . . .'

She picked up the trainers that were poking out from under the bed. Scrutinised them. Refrained from comment.

She opened the wardrobe doors, looked inside. Shook her head, held some items of clothing longer than others, especially where Callie's trousers and jackets were hanging.

'Something's wrong,' she said.

'Are there things missing?' Griessel asked.

'No,' she said with a world of worry in her face. 'There are so many clothes here that I don't know.'

28

'Those trainers don't belong to Callie,' Annemarie de Bruin said.

She selected a dark blue jacket from the wardrobe. 'This one . . . I have never seen it before.'

Cupido turned the jacket's lapel over to inspect the label inside over the pocket. 'Hugo Boss,' he said. 'Snazzy.'

'It's not Callie's,' she said.

'Those things cost a lot of money,' said Cupido, a bit of a dandy himself. 'Five, six thousand rand.'

'It's not Callie's,' she repeated and put the jacket on the bed.

'How big is this bursary he got?' asked Griessel.

She took more items of clothing out of the wardrobe, arranging them on the bedspread. Jeans, another two jackets, a few shirts. Calvin Klein, Tommy Hilfiger, Lacoste, Polo, a few cheaper brands as well. Then she stared at them, her whole body clenched with worry. 'Something is very wrong,' she said and began to weep.

They stood uneasily in the chaos of the room, smelling her light perfume mingling with the odours of stale fast food and sweat.

'Ma'am,' said Griessel, 'we will find out.' Hoping it sounded at least vaguely encouraging.

'I know my son,' she said. 'I know my son.' She took tissues out of her bag.

'We understand,' said Griessel.

'I'm sorry,' she said, trying to mop up the tears with the tissues.

'I take it the bursary was not large enough to cover these clothes?' Griessel asked.

She shook her head.

'Maybe there's an explanation that we are just missing,' said Cupido.

'What are we going to do?' she asked, her voice filled with despair.

★   ★   ★

What they did was to ask her to give them an hour or two, to go and wait in a coffee shop until they could make a few plans.

Then Cupido dropped Griessel off at the detectives' headquarters so that Benny could download the Vodacom report from the email and start to analyse it.

Cupido drove back to Veronica Adams at Campus Security, to bring her up to speed with the investigation, to tell her they were going to escalate the fifty-five, and ask if the university had facilities to accommodate Callie's mother for a night or two.

She said they had, and he should leave it in her hands.

'Okay, sister, we have to get moving now. How do I get that whole residence together, 'cause why, I need to get everyone together who knew Callie or anything about him.'

'It's going to be difficult, they come and go. We might not be able to get everyone together. But with social media, the message that Callie is missing will get out very fast. I will make arrangements with the residence coordinator and the house committee. Maybe eight o'clock tonight.'

'Thank you. And I want a printout of the man in the hoody. Can we get that out on social media as well? Someone might know him?'

She nodded. 'What about the media?'

'I'll have to check with my people first. I don't know how they work with the newspapers here.'

'Let me know. The media are going to pick it up from Facebook and Twitter. The university will have to issue a statement. It's a long process.'

'Okay. Let me call quickly.'

Charlie signed Sandra's new commission agreement, as cocky as a bantam rooster. 'I always knew that you would come to your senses, Longoria,' he said.

Sandra phoned Mareli Vorster at Stirling and Heyns with the news that she, Charlie and the client had a final offer. And then she presented it.

'That's not what we expected,' said Vorster dissatisfied.

'That's what's on the table,' said Sandra. 'We would like to have your confirmation before closing time today. The other two potential buyers are getting impatient.'

'It's seven in the morning in San Francisco. I will need more time.' Mareli Vorster's voice was stiff.

Sandra ignored the antagonism in her tone. She made the time calculations in her head. 'Shall we say just before nine o'clock tonight, South African time?

'I'll see what I can do,' the woman said and rang off.

Let me teach you something about business today. They're bluffing. She hoped with all her heart that both half-sloshed Jasper Boonstra and her own intuition were correct. Throwing the dice of destiny twice in one day was a dangerous game.

The cellular records from Calvyn Wilhelm de Bruin's service provider showed that his phone was turned off on Friday evening, 29 September at 18:07, and never turned on again.

Griessel studied the Vodacom documents in his and Cupido's 'new' shared office in the detective headquarters at Onder-Papegaaiberg, the first time he had actually seen the space. The room was like any other SAPS office: two government-issue desks, a chair each for the detectives, three chairs for visitors, a few cabinets for documents. Old notes and clippings up on the walls, relics from previous incumbents.

He sat at the desk with the information spread out in front of him. One printout gave the times when the phone was active, another provided the location, and the last pile was the call register.

Over the past three months Callie's cell phone was almost never off. Until Friday evening.

That worried Griessel.

The location didn't help much. All through Friday the phone registered on Vodacom's mast with eNB identification 961021, which according to the accompanying printout was in Simonswyk, just adjoining the campus.

On Friday afternoon just after six the signal jumped to eNB 919521, in the Cloetesville industrial area, for less than two minutes, after which it reconnected with the previous mast close to the university.

Following that the phone's location according to triangulation, was given as stationary in the region of Paradyskloof, until 18:07, when it was switched off.

Callie de Bruin left the residence and went to Paradyskloof. Not by Uber. And not by bicycle; the movement was too fast.

Somebody picked him up. And then he and his cell phone evaporated like mist in the sunshine.

At sixteen minutes to five Captain Rowen Geneke informed the station commissioner about the fifty-five-A on Callie de Bruin. The station chief escalated it immediately to all the appropriate branches and ranks.

Just before five the liaison officer of Stellenbosch SAPS and the university agreed on a news briefing. At 17:19 the message went out on Twitter, Facebook and Instagram that Calvyn 'Callie' Wilhelm de Bruin was missing and that the police had allocated a team of detectives to the investigation. It was accompanied by the photograph that Annemarie de Bruin had forwarded to Griessel and Cupido that morning.

Ten minutes later the liaison officer sent a tweet with the screengrab of the young man in the hoody who'd used Callie's card at the residence door. It was the best one they had, a low-resolution semi-profile shot as the man entered in the late afternoon light. Along with the picture was a request for anyone who knew the individual to please make contact with the Stellenbosch police. The university repeated the tweet. At 17:28 various memes began circulating on social media with the hashtag 'whereiscallie?'

When Cupido returned to the detectives' office at 17:32, there were still no meaningful responses.

Griessel examined the records of Callie de Bruin's calls for the past three months.

There were two numbers that stood out: Callie called them regularly. One was his mother's. The other was unidentified. Callie had called it four times in the past week, and at least three times a week before then. On Friday afternoon just after five the call lasted almost eight minutes.

Benny rang the unknown number from the office, on the fixed line.

It rang for a long time. There was no voicemail, only the service provider's recorded voice telling him the subscriber was not available, an SMS would be sent to notify them of his call.

He tried another two times, without success.

Then, on the spur of the moment and because the whole investigation was beginning to play on his parental concerns, he called his son.

'Pa?' Part surprise, part concern.

'Hello, Fritz. I just want to check in, see how things are?'

'Why?'

Griessel sighed inwardly. He'd known it would be difficult. 'Because I was thinking about you.'

'Oh. What's wrong, Pa?'

'Nothing's wrong, Fritz. What are you doing?'

'I'm editing. My project.'

'The short film?'

'Yes, Pa. For the grad fest. It's on 15 November. I already told you, Pa.'

He hadn't: it was the first Griessel had heard of it. Fritz had probably told Griessel's ex-wife, Anna, about it. His relationship with his mother and her new husband was good. Because they were always sober. Benny pinched the phone between his ear and shoulder and took out his diary, so he could make a note of the date. 'I'll be there.'

'Okay.' There was a hint of irony in the word. Which really meant, 'if Pa's not too drunk.'

'I was wondering, if you're not busy on Sunday, we could get something to eat.'

'What's going on, Pa?'

'Nothing's going on. I just thought . . . I would really like to work on our relationship, Fritz.' He suppressed the urge to say 'please'.

A long silence. Then Fritz said: 'I really have to edit on Sunday. I want to get the rough cut done early, so we can see if we need any reshoots. And ADRs.'

'What are ADRs?'

'That's when we have to record the actors again because the sound man made a fuckup. And the sound man always fucks it up.'

He was in no position to say anything about Fritz's language, he didn't have the right. 'I understand,' Griessel said. 'If you want to take a break on Sunday, let me know.'

'Pa, are you sober?'

'Seven months already, Fritz.'

'Okay.' But with scepticism in his voice.

29

After Dr du Toit and the hostel's student leader had said a few words, Cupido addressed the Eendrag residence meeting.

More than one hundred and fifty students had come to listen. Griessel stood to one side against the wall, with a bundle of printed photos of Hoody in his hand, while Cupido spoke to the students. Benny could tell his colleague was in his element.

Vaughn stood in front of the group in his charcoal suit, a tight fit nowadays, with rose-pink tie, his legs planted wide. In a ringing voice full of authority and drama he told them that he and Griessel had been 'transferred' from the Hawks. They were investigating the disappearance of one of the residents' 'comrades'. They needed cooperation and solidarity now, because with 'what we call a fifty-five, that's law enforcement code for a missing person', time is of the essence. 'The first seventy-two hours are crucial, but that's already behind us. We are working against the clock, and time is running out. You . . .' and he pointed a finger at the audience, 'you can make the difference, between life and death.' Then he paused for a moment to let the thought sink in.

You could hear a pin drop.

Cupido nodded at Benny, who stepped forward and began handing out the photos. 'This is the *outjie* who swiped Callie's card last night to get in your front door, and took Callie's stuff away,' said Cupido. He asked if anyone recognised the man in the hoody. Was anyone, especially in Callie's section of the hostel, missing anything from their room? And lastly, if there were students who knew Callie reasonably well, or had information about where he might be, would they please remain behind. Any information could be valuable. 'It doesn't matter how trivial, come and talk to us. *Life and death*,' he said again. 'You can make the difference. Thank you very much, class dismissed.'

They sat a while, a quiet hum of voices as they discussed the events. Then a few stood up, and came up to the front. Eventually there were nine of them who came to talk to Griessel and Cupido.

It was take-away night at the Steenbergs. Josef had fetched McDonald's for the kids. They were addicted to the Chicken McNuggets, and their parents reluctantly ate the bland chicken burgers with at least the consolation that neither of them needed to cook tonight.

Sandra went to bath the twins. She made certain her phone was within earshot.

Josef came to sit with her while the children splashed in the foamy water.

'Pappa, let's play crocodile-crocodile, please, Pappa,' Bianca pleaded. That was a game when Josef's hand disappeared under the bubbles, a crocodile hunting for 'soft juicy meat' and tickling their toes.

'In a bit, Bee,' he said. He looked at Sandra and asked her in his compassionate way: 'Are you okay?'

'Yes. Why?' She heard the curtness of her tone, and was instantly regretful. 'Sorry,' she said.

'That's what I mean. This past week or so you've not been yourself. I can see that you . . . Is there some tension at work?'

'What's tension, Pappa?' Anke asked.

'I'll explain to you later, sweetheart' he said and looked back at Sandra.

She bit her lip before nodding. 'We're really counting on one big deal. It's kind of . . . make or break. But we should hear tonight.'

'What do our finances look like?' he asked.

Her heart began to race. What did he know? 'If this one doesn't go through, we will have to rethink.'

'I don't want you to stress, please. It's not necessary. We'll be okay,' he said.

He meant they could always borrow money from his parents. She didn't want to start that argument now. 'There's still hope,' she said. And then she heard her phone ringing. She stood up from the edge of the bath and went into the bedroom where the phone lay on the bed.

A cell phone number.

'This is Sandra,' she answered.

'Sandra, it's Mareli,' the lawyer said. 'We have a deal.'

From the bathroom she heard Josef tell Anke: 'Tension is when the crocodile disappears under the water . . .' The twins' excited shrieks were earsplitting.

The student was burly and a bit overweight, with a bushy beard. 'My name's Frikkie, but everyone calls me Freaky,' he told the detectives. 'I'm studying with The Ghost.'

They thanked him for coming to talk to them.

'Callie's gaming avatar is a wolf. His gaming profile is El Solo Lobo.' Serious, solemn, as though it was valuable information.

'El Solo Lobo?' asked Cupido.

'It means "lone wolf". In Spanish.'

'Okay,' said Cupido.

'That's what he is. Always solo. I think it's because he's so clever. I mean, he's nice enough, I'm not saying he's not nice. When you talk to him, he's cool. But . . . he's next level. He codes like a demon.'

'What does that mean?' Griessel asked.

'Oh. Sorry. He . . . He's an unbelievably good programmer. Better than any of us.'

'Is it true that he hacked into the varsity system?' Cupido asked.

'That's the rumour, that he got root access with a keystroke logger on one of the administrators' machines. I asked him, and he just laughed. But I can believe it.'

'Were you friends?' Griessel asked.

'No, no, we just attend the same classes, and we worked on a project together in second year.'

'How often do you see each other?'

'Every day, in class.'

'Frikkie, it looks like he was earning extra money from somewhere. Do you know anything about that?'

'No.'

'Do you know anything about his disappearance?'

'No. Nothing. But there is one thing that I thought, maybe . . .'

'Yes.'

'He has one friend.'

'Yes?'

'I don't know him. He's not studying with us. But I saw them together three or four times. On campus. And here.'

'At the hostel?'

'Yes, the *ou* visited him here, I saw them once together at the front door, about a month ago.'

'Is it the hoody man in the photo?'

'I . . . No. I'm not absolutely sure, but I don't think so, no . . .'

'Does the hoody guy look a little like this friend?' Cupido asked.

'Maybe . . . His friend is also coloured, but he looks . . . nicer.'

'Nicer?'

'Yes . . .' Frikkie lifted the screengrab printout and looked at it 'This *oke* . . . He looks . . . *scaly* . . . Callie's friend, looks . . . nice.'

That was the most useful information they got out of the house meeting.

It was already gone ten p.m. when they finished up at the office with the paperwork for the docket. They knew Colonel Witkop Jansen's meaning that morning: *Basics. Here we do the basics right. According to the book.*

All SAPS dockets consisted of three sections: Part A, B and C. They filed Annemarie de Bruin's statement, the information that Freaky Frikkie had provided, and the photos of the room and Hoody in Part A, where they belonged.

The copy of the article 205 subpoena and Vodacom's information went into Part B. And in Part C – the investigation journal on the SAPS5 form – they diligently entered the events of the day, as they had recorded them in their notebooks. Then Griessel phoned Annemarie de Bruin in one of the university guesthouses to tell her that unfortunately they had no news and she should get some sleep.

She thanked him, but he could hear her anxiety. She was on the edge of tears again.

One more time Griessel tried the number that the missing student had phoned so frequently. Still no answer. Tomorrow he would find out who it belonged to.

'It's too late to knock on Mbali's door now,' said Cupido. Their former commanding officer lived in a townhouse in Bellville, half-an-hour's drive away.

'Let's see how things go tomorrow,' Griessel said.

They walked to their cars together. 'For all the excitement, I wish we'd rather found him lying drunk somewhere, Benna. It's not looking good.'

'Not good at all,' said Griessel.

They said goodnight, and left.

Griessel thought about the ritual waiting for him at home. Alexa would still be awake, with supper for him. They would sit in the kitchen, he would eat, and in between mouthfuls he would tell her about his day. According to the psychologist's prescription he had to make his loved ones part of his working life, share his stress with them. And it had helped, before he had been fired from the Hawks. Today was the first time in weeks they would do it again – you couldn't have that sort of conversation about painting the roof. In a way he was looking forward to it.

Halfway to Cape Town, at twenty to eleven, his phone rang. He saw it was his daughter, Carla. She worked on a wine farm near Franschhoek. They had a good relationship. She looked on her father's weakness with a much gentler eye than her brother. Why would she phone now?

'Carla?'

'Are you okay, Pa?'

'Yes, I'm okay? Why do you ask?'

'Fritz called. He said something must have happened, because you want to take him out for dinner.'

Griessel sighed. Then he explained everything to her, all the way home.

Only then, when he was getting out of the car, did he wonder what had happened to Callie's father. And he felt ashamed. He and Vaughn should have known better. But at the Hawks they hadn't been investigating fifty-fives, they were out of practice. When you began searching for a missing person, the best place to start was with immediate family. The stats showed that the cause of the disappearance most often stemmed from there.

30

3 October

In the time before the storm Sandra would often exercise early in the morning at the Virgin Active Gym in the Eikestad Centre, with a personal trainer. She started doing it to shake off the extra kilograms after her pregnancy, later just because she enjoyed it.

That was the first contract she had relinquished when she had to scale back, and she missed it. She still tried to stay slim and trim, lifting light weights in the lounge, early morning, before the twins or Josef woke up. Her routine was three consecutive days training, followed by one rest day, before the cycle repeated. It was also her me-time, reloading her batteries before the day began, her time to think, as her pulse rose. She liked the feeling in her muscles, the slow build-up of resistance and discomfort as she worked her way through the repetitions, breathing deep into her lungs, the fine sheen of perspiration the exertion brought. The way her body came alive.

She did it for herself. And for Josef. To be attractive to him, keep him looking at her with desire when she came out of the bathroom naked. So he would tell her he couldn't resist her. Before the twins that was often the case, wherever they were in the house. After the girls' birth, less often, and now, in these last difficult months, even less so.

She longed for that time, his defenceless surrender to his desire for her: the greatest, most delightful compliment. Even though she didn't really understand it – she'd never thought she was particularly sexy. Her hips and thighs were too generous to her mind, too round and wide. She would have liked to have had more slender arms, delicate hands, prettier knees. More prominent cheekbones.

Standing here now, at eighteen minutes past six in tracksuit pants and a T-shirt, flexing her biceps, she blamed herself that she and

Josef were having sex less often. It was the stress, and the blow that her deception had made to her self-image. She didn't feel sexy. That was something a caveman like Jasper Boonstra would never understand. Even if he had said: *You're fucking sexy, Sandra. Live with it.* That praise meant nothing to her, and not just because it came from him. Why didn't men understand that a woman only felt sexy when a man made her *feel* like that? Did men not realise that their unsolicited, crude and often clumsy advances had precisely the opposite effect? It made her feel cheap, common, easy. Everything she had fought against her whole life, because that was her father. Cheap and common.

And then she thought about Josef, who, in an echo of Charlie, had said yesterday: *You've not been yourself this past week.* He, of all people, didn't deserve the Sandra she was now. Not the one he experienced at first hand, not the one he didn't even know about, the lying, deceiving Sandra.

Lord, would she ever get out of this mess?

Boonstra had not responded at all last night. She had sent him a WhatsApp to say he could have all the documents signed now, Demeter had accepted the offer.

Probably too drunk.

She would phone him as soon as she got to the office.

Morning parade at the Stellenbosch detective headquarters was in the old meeting hall, at 07:30. Colonel Witkop Jansen, Vaughn Cupido would say afterwards, 'was not a morning person'. Jansen opened with a prayer, and then berated them mercilessly, crapping on them from a dizzy height, all sixteen detectives around the table. In English but with an Afrikaans accent. According to him no one had made enough progress with their cases. Because less than fifty per cent of their cases made it to court. Because more detectives had left their SAPS vehicles in a mess, not even bothering to remove the empty pizza boxes, 'you know who you are'.

Everyone had to report on the progress of their cases. Griessel spoke for Cupido and himself on where they were with the Callie de Bruin search.

'And that's all you've got?' asked Colonel Jansen.

'Yes, sir.'

'I drive to work and I see newspaper headlines all over the lamp posts about this missing student. I'm getting calls from the provincial commissioner's office and they tell me the media is all over this like a rash, and what are we doing? I'm getting calls from the provincial crime detection commissioner, who wants to know who is working on the case, because the DA politicians are all over him like a rash too, and we've made no progress. I'm getting calls from the university, saying they are very worried, because we're not making any progress. But what really upsets me, is that Paarl keeps calling me and asking me if they can lend us a bloody hand,' he said.

Griessel knew Stellenbosch SAPS was not terribly pleased with the fact that they fell under the Boland cluster, which was managed and controlled from the smaller town of Paarl.

'Yes, sir,' he said.

'And I tell them all, I have these two ex-Hawks detectives working the fifty-five, don't worry, and now you don't even know who the person is that the boy called regularly on his telephone? This is not a holiday resort for you two. This is a serious matter, and I need serious detectives. You receive me?'

'Yes, sir,' they replied in unison.

They walked back to their office.

Griessel could see that Cupido wasn't happy after that dressing down. It had been years since they had been spoken to like that in front of colleagues.

In the office Griessel checked the unidentified number, getting ready to call again and then send a request for identification to MTN.

Cupido wouldn't sit down. He paced up and down.

'What is it, Vaughn?' Benny asked.

'No, *Jissis*, partner, I don't know how long I can stand this.'

'Witkop is old school, Vaughn, that's his way.'

'Old school? This isn't fucking high school with a principal who definitely isn't a morning person. I mean, what more could we do?'

'You know how it is, he's under pressure from the head honchos and he's passing it on down. That's how it works.'

'I know, I know.' But Cupido kept on pacing, from one wall to the other.

Benny knew his colleague very well. He knew there was something else eating at him. It would come out in time. In the meantime he called the number. The phone was still switched off.

Cupido stopped, hands on hips. 'Benna,' he said, 'I can't go on like this.'

'Like what?'

'Benna, I'm fat. Overweight. Too much, *pappie*. This morning, when I wanted to put on my Rex Trueform suit, that snazzy one with the grey and maroon pinstripe, I couldn't button the trousers. And then I was scared Desiree would see, I mean, the embarrassment. And then it dawned on me: she is this sleek and sensual creature, she can pick and choose. And now she's got this fat slob of a boyfriend who can't even spoon with her because his bloody belly gets in the way. How long do you think that's going to last? But then you think, okay, okay, it's not that bad, the trousers were narrow from the start, I will cut back on the muffins and then you get to morning parade, and you look over your new team and you click that the whole class is fat. Did you see, Benna? You are the thinnest of the lot. And let's be honest, it's not like you are a candidate for anorexia treatment. I'm sitting there looking, and thinking – very condescendingly, I know – what a chubby brigade this is, and my conscience tells me, no, *pappie*, you fit right in, the pot is as fat as the kettle. Fokkit, partner, this is where it ends. I mean, I understand why policemen battle with the scales; there's never any time for a healthy lifestyle, just fast food, most of the time, but I can't afford to get so fat. I might be a Stellenbosch detective right now, but my soul is a Hawk, and hawks are sleek and deadly. And I don't want to lose Desiree. Not through being obese. This is where it ends.'

'You're not obese, Vaughn.'

'That's not what the internet says. I looked it up, I'm borderline, Benna, right on the edge. I didn't want to believe it, so I tried four different health sites, and the results are the same every time. Borderline obese. Fuck.'

It took effort for Griessel to remain serious. 'What are you going to do?'

'I'm going to call Desiree. Honesty's the cornerstone of a relationship, that's her mantra, so I'll be painfully honest. She will have to
advise me. She eats anything, but she stays slim. There's a secret,
Benna, and I want in.' He took out his cell phone and called.

Griessel tried Callie's mysterious contact again. The phone was still
off.

He heard Cupido say to Desiree: 'Lovey, I need your help right
now. And I'm very serious, you're not allowed to laugh at me.' He
listened for a moment and then said: 'Okay, brace yourself, lovey: how
do I get thin?'

Griessel shook his head and called MTN, with Annemarie de Bruin
the next one on his list.

Jasper Boonstra was curt on the phone. 'Huber AG's Swiss lawyers
will have to draw up the documents. I don't know how long that will
take. I'll call them when I have time.' Then he cut the call abruptly, and
Sandra thought, he's an arsehole. A beastly, chauvinistic, deceitful
bastard of an arsehole.

Her stomach contracted. What was she going to do if it took weeks
to prepare the documents?

She realised her anxiety was not just about money. It was because
she had lost control of the deal. Other people were going to control the
direction and speed of this now.

She hated not being in control.

Griessel and Cupido felt the pressure, the urge to make something
happen, speed things up, push the investigation on.

They sat with Annemarie de Bruin on the veranda of the guest
house in Neethling Street, curbing their impatience. This was a necessary hurdle, information they had to test.

The worry lines around her mouth and eyes were deeper this morning, and her eyes were bloodshot. When they came in, she'd asked if
there was news, and accepted their answer with resignation, as if she
had been expecting it. She was sipping her tea now, telling them she'd
hardly slept. Then she waited for them to tell her why they had come.

Griessel had done enough interviews under similar circumstances
to know that behind an absent father there was usually a sad story.

And trauma. You had to ask close relatives the questions, but you did it cautiously, like crossing a minefield. Even if you were impatient and in a hurry. Even more so when the source of the information was under extreme strain.

He cleared his throat politely and then said: 'Ma'am, I am truly sorry that we have to touch on this subject, but with young missing persons there are often domestic circumstances that contribute, one way or another.'

'Oh, no, no,' said Annemarie de Bruin too quickly, with emphasis. 'Not with Callie.'

'You said he grew up without a father.'

She sat up straight, nearly motionless, fists in her lap, and looked back at Griessel with a determined look in her eye, a look that said she meant to cross this bridge with dignity. 'Yes. He died. Before Callie was born.'

They waited, for more information.

Eventually: 'In a motor car accident.'

'Does Callie have contact with his family?'

'No.'

Again they were quiet, giving her space to speak.

This time it took longer before she responded. They could tell she was grappling with some inner struggle. She shifted her gaze to the wall behind them when she added: 'We were not married.'

They nodded sympathetically.

She looked down at her hands. She drew a deep breath, fortifying herself. 'I am not a pretty woman,' she said. Her voice was almost inaudible. 'I never was pretty. You make your peace with it . . . I was in Mossel Bay, back then. Twenty-one years ago. I had just begun working, I was new in town and very lonely and I . . . We are all looking for . . . I never really went out. I was too shy. And then I thought, I can sit in a corner and feel sorry for myself, or I can . . . If I want to meet people . . . There was the old Diaz Hotel; it had a ladies' lounge. I . . . I just went to drink a shandy. And then Mike was there. Michael. Michael Taylor. An older man. We . . .'

She sat with her head bowed. 'The following Thursday, there was a little report in the newspaper, about the accident on the national road, the day after we . . . Then I saw he was a married man. With three children, in Johannesburg.'

Griessel realised that was all that she was going to say. He gave her time to recover, because he had one more question. 'Ma'am, does Callie know that he . . . has those relatives?'

'No,' she said. 'There are only three people who know now. And it must stay that way.'

31

They headed back to the office, swiftly, in silence, but didn't reach it. MTN called back to let them know that the number Callie had called so often belonged to a Mr Roland Parker. He lived in Raziet Street in Cloetesville, on the north side of Stellenbosch.

Cupido made a U-turn. Griessel typed the address into Google Maps, and navigated. Traffic was dense, slow and frustrating. It took them fifteen minutes to drive just four kilometres. 'I told you the traffic is a nightmare in this town,' Cupido said. 'Where the fuck is everyone going?' His mood had clearly not improved.

The Parker house was small and modest, raw brick with asbestos sheet roofing, like most of them in that neighbourhood. The garden was neglected, washing hung from a line beside the house, with a concrete wall on either side. A dog barked at them from the barred gate in the driveway.

They opened the gate and walked through to the front door while the dog leaped up at them, wagging its tail.

'Some guard dog,' said Cupido reproachfully.

They knocked.

A hefty woman in her sixties opened the door. She was wearing an apron. A waft of beguiling culinary aromas drifted out of the house behind her.

'Morning, aunty,' Cupido said. 'We're from the police, we're looking for Roland Parker.'

'Roland doesn't live here any more,' she said bluntly.

'Is he family of yours?'

'He's my son.'

'Where can we find him? He's not answering his phone.'

'What do you want with Roland?'

'A friend of his has gone missing, aunty, we just want to hear if knows anything about it.'

'What friend?'

'Callie de Bruin.'

'Doesn't ring a bell.'

'Where can we find Roland?' Cupido asked again.

She shrugged.

The two detectives between them had more than forty years' experience of people's body language when they were lying. They could tell the woman was not being truthful.

She made motions to close the door: 'I have food on the stove.'

'Do you live here alone, aunty?'

'Yes.'

'Then why's there men's clothing on the line?'

She bit her lip.

'Roland Parker talked to a missing person on the phone, last week, and he can be of assistance to us. We have just come from Callie de Bruin's mother, and she's broken, aunty. If Roland disappeared, what would you want someone else's mother to do?'

'Ay,' she said. 'Ay, ay.' She hesitated. At last she pulled the door wide for them and shouted over her shoulder: 'Rolster!'

Roland Parker was clearly not the Hoody Man in the CCTV recording.

He walked into the sitting room. He was in his late twenties, strongly built, broad-shouldered. And extremely nervous. On his feet were the same kind of trainers as the ones under Callie de Bruin's bed, and he was wearing a pair of Levi jeans, like the ones in Callie's wardrobe.

'The detectives are looking for a Callie de Bruin,' his mother said, and then walked off to the kitchen, stiff and tense.

All three men stood in the room.

'Sit down, Rolster,' said Cupido.

'I don't know any such *ou*,' said Parker.

'Sit.'

Parker sat.

The detectives assumed positions on either side of him.

'Why is your cell phone off?' Griessel asked.

'Is there a law now that says I have to keep my phone on?'

'We know you know Callie. We know you talked to him on the

phone four times last week. The longest call was nearly eight minutes, Friday afternoon. In the previous three weeks you spoke to each other at least three times a week.'

He crossed his arms and stared past them.

'What line of work are you in, Rolster?' Cupido asked.

'I'm self-employed.'

'Doing what?'

'I do what I can. Bit of this, bit of that.'

'Who paid for those nice *takkies*?' Cupido looked at his shoes.

'Why was your phone off from yesterday?' Griessel asked.

He stared mutely in front of him.

'Listen carefully to me, Rolster,' Cupido said. 'We're not in the mood for your *sights*. We're here for Callie de Bruin. We know you had contact. So here are your choices. You can keep on pissing us off, and we will make your life a living hell. For starters, obstructing justice is more than enough to arrest you for right now. Or we can do this the easy way. So what's it going to be?'

Parker shifted in his seat, weighing up his options. 'I helped Callie.'

'How?'

'Computer parts.'

'Go on?'

'I helped him to get computer parts.'

'How?'

'Callie didn't have a car. So he called me, and said there's an advert on Gumtree, he wants me to go look. So I would drive to Cape Town, or Bellville, and have a look, and phone him and say if it's genuine. Callie would make a price, I would do the deal, and bring the parts to him.'

'What did he do with the parts?'

'He must have built PCs from the stuff, and sold them.' With a shrug to suggest it was just a guess.

'Where did he build the PCs?'

'In his room, I suppose'

'There's no evidence of computer parts in his room.'

'Then I don't know. I was just the courier,' Parker said with a shrug.

'What was in it for you?'

'He paid me a flat fee and a cost per kilometre.'

'How?'

'Cash, most of the time.'

'What were you talking about on Friday afternoon?' Griessel asked.

'He said there were a couple of high-end graphics cards that an *ou* in the Flats was advertising, but he was worried it might be stolen goods, would I take a look.'

'And then?'

'I said okay, send me the address. But I heard nothing, Saturday, I called him. Sunday too. But his phone was off.'

'How would you tell if they were stolen goods?'

'You suss the brother out who's selling. It's not so hard.'

'How do you know Callie?' Griessel asked.

'Droppa.'

'Droppa?' said Cupido. 'Who's Droppa?'

'Droppa. The app.'

'What app?'

'It's like Uber for *bakkies*. You register if you drive a truck, and then people can hire you and your *bakkie* to load stuff.'

'You have a *bakkie*?'

'I have. Ford Ranger. It's in the garage.'

'So Callie hired you on Droppa?'

'Last year in April already.'

'What did he load on the *bakkie*?' Griessel asked.

'An old wardrobe.'

'An old wardrobe? To do what with?'

'That you must ask him. I loaded it up from an aunty in Franschhoek, and then I dropped it off at an antique shop in Bellville. Then Callie sent me a message with his number and said he was looking for a regular driver. If we dealt direct then we wouldn't have to pay a percentage to Droppa. So from then on we talked direct.'

'A wardrobe is not computer parts.'

'With Callie it's usually computer parts. He wheels and deals as he can, I suppose. Now and then it's something else.'

'Like what?'

'Furniture. Stuff. In March it was an old car, rust bucket, no engine. Borgward or something, but it was too big for my *bakkie*, I had to get a contact here in Plankenbrug who has a lorry.'

'Did he say he was going away for the weekend somewhere?' asked Griessel.

'No. We didn't talk about that sort of thing. It's a business relationship.'

'Has he had things loaded in Paradyskloof before?'

'Not that I can remember.'

'Rolster,' said Cupido, 'if your partnership was so innocent, why did you tell us you didn't know him?'

'Don't pretend you don't understand. That's what a coloured man does when the cops come knocking. Never admit to anything.'

32

They asked him why his phone had been off the past few days.

'My *bakkie* has a flat battery,' he said. 'I had to hire a charger, it's charging now; go and look if you like.'

'What has that got to do with your phone?'

'I don't need any bad ratings for unavailability on Droppa. If my phone is off, people can't rent me.'

Cupido looked at Benny. The explanations felt weak and fabricated, but they needed ammunition before they could test them. They stood up.

'Turn your phone on,' said Cupido. 'We want to talk to you again.'

Parker remained seated. 'What for?'

''Cause why, you are not what we would call a credible witness, Rolster,' Cupido said. 'We will check everything you said, and if anything doesn't look *lekker*, then we want to have another chat. So keep it on. Unless there's something you'd like to add right now?'

He shook his head.

They walked towards the door. He didn't get up, just stared after them.

Roland Parker's mother followed them with a packet in her hand. 'Samoosas,' she said. 'Freshly fried.'

That explained the aromas that lingered in the air.

They thanked her. She walked with them to the door. When they said goodbye, she said: 'My son is a *frans*. He walks a good path, and that's not always easy.' In Cape Flats Afrikaans a '*frans*' was someone who didn't belong to a gang.

'It's all right, aunty, our interest is not in him. We just want to locate Callie. Time is running out.'

'I really hope you find him.'

★　　★　　★

Back in the car Griessel said: 'It doesn't make sense. Where are all the "computer parts"? And the computers that Callie built?'

'What was he doing in Paradyskloof on Friday evening? How did he get there? The varsity people can help, Benna. They should look through their video footage, and quit phoning Colonel White Hot Jansen.'

'Rolster isn't telling the full truth.'

'I know. But what is he hiding? We'll have to see if he generates a CR.' When detectives wanted to determine whether a suspect had any prior convictions, they used the computerised Krim system that provided a CR number if any criminal record existed.

'And we will have to check with Droppa to see if he really does work for them.'

'Callie's bank account,' said Cupido. 'And the other numbers that he phoned . . .'

They fell silent, each realising they were clutching at straws, that they really had nothing. Most of the obvious clues and possibilities had been followed up already, and all that remained was speculation, wishful thinking and hope. The pressure was mounting. All dockets ran this course, when there wasn't a quick breakthrough. They hated it, because it felt like swimming against the current – hard work, with no progress. And that was a strong indication of a case that would never be solved.

The aroma of food filled the car. Deep in thought, Griessel picked up the packet and took one out. It was still warm. He bit into it. '*Bliksem*,' he said, 'this aunty can make samoosas,' and then he ate the rest of the triangle.

He held out the packet to Cupido, who was driving.

'*Jissis*, Benna,' said Vaughn reprovingly. He did not take one.

'What?' asked Griessel.

'Samoosas are part of my culture. My DNA. That smell, that taste, and now you go and eat one in front of me.'

'I thought she gave it to us both.'

'That's not the issue. The issue is, I'm fat.'

'But you're going to work on it. What did Desiree say?'

'What I didn't want to hear. She said losing weight is a very simple equation. You have to burn more energy than you eat. So I said, how do you measure that? And she said I must download this app on my phone: Lose It! I did download it. You have to put in your age and height and weight. And then put in how thin you want to be. The app tells you how much you can eat every day. And then every fucking thing that crosses your lips you have to log on the app, and it counts the kilojoules automatically. I schemed, that's very nifty, I can do this, give me two weeks and I'll be lean and mean. But then, before we went to Callie's mom, I put in the Coco Pops and milk I had for breakfast. That's half of my daily allowance, in its *moer* in, *pappie*. I shudder to think what a samoosa is going to cost me. And here I sit in the car with that smell and a partner eating what he likes, while I have to first check Lose It!, because I'm obese. No, oh *bliksem*, partner, this is going to be living hell.'

'I don't think you're that fat,' said Griessel, who was feeling guilty now about eating a samoosa.

'It's just because we're homeboys that you say that. The facts are the facts. You have to embrace your fatness.'

'If you think about it, Vaughn, your diet is only fair,' said Griessel.

'What do you mean?' he asked indignantly.

'You can't eat, and I can't drink. We are the perfect partnership.'

'I'm happy you see the humour in it. Because I sure don't.'

When they stopped at a traffic light at the big crossroads beside the train station, Griessel handed the remaining samoosas to the *bergie* who came up to the window begging.

Sandra explained to the van der Merwes of Oranje Street in Uniepark that the market was very weak.

They wanted to move to a retirement resort at the end of the year, but first had to sell their house. They had banked on a good price, it had formed part of their retirement planning. The price that Sandra suggested was 'a disappointment'.

She said she would do her very best. They could test the market at a higher price, but to get it sold before December would be unrealistic. There were already newer houses of the same size on the market at lower prices.

When they said goodbye the man asked if she would mind if they requested valuations from other agencies. She could see he didn't trust her.

'No,' she said, resigned, as this was happening more and more often these days, 'please do go ahead.'

She drove down Merriman Avenue and Ryneveld Street, back to the office.

She saw the blood-red Mazda MX-5 parked in front of the Kruis Church. It was exactly like Josef's car, she thought. Then she saw the registration. It was Josef's.

Odd. That morning he'd said he wanted to keep his head down and write, he'd really got into the swing of things with the book.

She parked directly behind the Benson International Realtors offices, rang Josef's numbers, curious, keen to talk to him.

He didn't answer.

Griessel phoned Annemarie de Bruin to find out if the name Roland 'Rolster' Parker meant anything to her.

'No,' she said, her tone anxious and high-pitched.

'It's just one of Callie's friends,' he tried to pacify her. He wanted to ask about the wardrobe and the old Borgward and building computers, but without adding to her anxiety. He picked his words with care: 'Ma'am, did Callie perhaps buy and sell goods for extra money?'

'All I could think about all night was where the child found the money to buy all those expensive clothes. What I do know is that he sometimes helped people with their computers. Every December and July holiday he worked at Tom's Computers in Robertson, in the workshop. Perhaps he was doing that here too?'

'We would like to examine his bank statements, maybe that would help.'

'Very well. Is there something I should sign?'

'No, ma'am, we just want to know where he banked.'

'Oh. He's at FNB. The account is at the Robertson branch.'

'Thank you, ma'am. And I promise we will let you know if we have any news.'

*   *   *

Cupido drove to Campus Security. Griessel stayed at the office. He rang all the other numbers that Callie had called in the previous two months, even if only once. He recorded the results in a table in his notebook.

Slowly a pattern began to emerge. Most of the calls were on Thursdays or Fridays, and practically always to businesses that bought expensive items direct from the public: antique shops, gold and jewellery dealers, pawn shops. Each time he received more or less the same answer: 'No, I don't know anyone of that name. I can't remember a call like that. A lot of people phone here every day.'

'All the social media did was make #whereiscallie? trend on Twitter,' Veronica Adams of Campus Security told Cupido. 'A lot of inappropriate jokes, and the usual trolls with a lot to say about Callie's looks.'

'No tip-offs at all?' Cupido asked.

'Nothing. Nobody is taking it seriously, everyone believes he will turn up tomorrow or the day after. That's how students are. I already talked to his lecturers; in the classes Callie attends they will make announcements and ask if anyone knows anything. But don't hold your breath.'

'Okay. We want to see if there is any CCTV footage of how Callie went out on Friday evening. Someone giving him a lift, anything like that . . .'

Adams frowned and shook her head. 'We did look. Eendrag's front door faces Merriman Avenue. The cameras at the residence door only cover a section of the parking area. You can see Callie walk out and across the parking area, towards the street, and then he turns left, in our direction. And then he's gone. The next cameras are at the entrances of Helshoogte and Simonsberg – two other men's residences. We did look there. In the next thirty minutes Callie does not walk past there. Somebody picked him up. The video camera team are busy making a list of all the number plates of cars that drove east and west in Merriman in that time period, and not all the numbers are clearly visible. It's going to take a long time, but we will send it on to you.'

'Shit,' said Cupido.

'Yes,' she said and added philosophically: 'He's an enigma, this little man.'

Before Cupido could ask her what enigma meant, his cell phone rang.

33

'Are you still at Campus Security?' Griessel asked.

'*Yebo*, yes,' said Cupido.

'Pick up Callie's computer at the hostel, Vaughn. We should ask Lithpel to take a look at it.'

'Have you found anything?'

Benny explained to his colleague about the pattern in Callie's call register. 'Here's my theory, Vaughn: it wasn't just computers. He was speculating with everything that might possibly have value. He only phoned businesses that he could sell goods to. You don't buy an item for potential resale from a gold dealer or an antique shop, because the price is already loaded.'

'Check,' said Cupido.

'Now the question is, how does he get hold of the stuff in the first place? Not one of his calls was to enquire about goods that private individuals had for sale. I think he did that on the internet. Adverts on Gumtree, Facebook, OLX, that sort of thing. Then he sent the sellers an email. Which we will hopefully find on his computer. Maybe on Friday evening he went to look at something he could make money on . . .'

'Cool, Benna, I'll take the PC to Lithpel. I mean, the Hawks can't say no if we ask for help, this fifty-five has been escalated now.'

'If you see Mbali, see if you can have a quick chat, if you know what I mean . . .'

'Check. But then you will have to go to court for the bank subpoena.'

Sandra arranged for the photographer to take pictures at the Oranje Street house and filed the documents that the Van der Merwes had signed. Then she rang Josef again. Just curious.

His phone was still off.

A vague sense of unease began to grow in her.

On a Tuesday morning in this town it might have been the closest to the bank that he could find parking.

Griessel waited in front of the magistrate's office for the subpoena to access the bank statements. He was thinking about the boy growing up without a father.

Did Callie ever ask questions? Had his mother lied to him? Or said she didn't want to talk about it?

The child must surely have wondered whose genes he carried. Wondered about what sort of man his father had been.

Wouldn't he eventually have gone looking? Especially now, at this age?

If the genius technology student could break into the university computer system, he was surely capable of accessing information on the Home Affairs' National Population Register network? Would Annemarie de Bruin have registered Callie under his real father's name at birth? Would Callie – angry at his mother's lies or evasion – not perhaps have discovered the truth and gone searching for his family? Was that where he was now? On a rebellious young man's journey to the truth? Funded by the money he had made from what-ever he was trading in?

It was a possibility. Keeping Benny from considering the tragic alternative.

The magistrate's clerk came to call him. He handed over the forms, got the subpoena signed and walked the two blocks to FNB. He explained the seriousness of the case. The bank told him they would have to contact head office first and asked him to come back in an hour or so. He sighed, walked back to his car, and stood for a moment, indecisive. He wanted to make progress, *do* something, gain a bit of momentum. Callie de Bruin had been missing for ninety hours now, so something had to be done, and fast.

He decided to drive to Paradyskloof.

On the way he remembered: last year in December* was the last time he went on a drinking binge. Just before the investigation into the

---

* These events are fully described in the crime novel *Icarus*.

murder of Ernst Richter, the internet entrepreneur who ran the controversial website Alibi.co.za. Richter had owned a house in the exclusive Mont Blanc development.

In Paradyskloof, the newer, tree-rich southern suburb of Stellenbosch.

Where Callie de Bruin's phone had last been on.

Because Griessel had not been sober then, his memory of the suburb was hazy. Consequently he drove up and down the streets to get a feel for the area, to feed his visualisation of various possibilities. Because that – and the patience for endless footwork – was his only detection talent, the careful mental reconstruction of a crime. And he thought about the Richter case back then, the initial technological angle of attack of the investigation that yielded nothing, but at least brought Cupido and Desiree together.

Before his death, Richter had become involved in a fake wine fraud. He was murdered up in the Blaauklippen valley and his body found in the dunes on the far side of Table View.

Had Callie become embroiled in something? In his buying and selling, in the peddling of something to someone who had connections to the wrong sort of people? In this country it was not a far-fetched thought. There were plenty of scams on the internet. You advertise a car, a faceless someone with a fake digital identity says they would like to come for a test drive, and then they shoot you in the driveway as soon as they have the car keys in their hand.

That was a strong possibility. His instinct and his prescience told him ninety hours was too long. They were not going to find Callie alive. And he would be the one who would have to break the bad news to Annemarie de Bruin.

He drove through the whole Paradyskloof area. Neat upper-middle-class homes behind walls and with alarm systems. There were a few guest houses and restaurants, a fuel station, a smallish supermarket, a hair salon and Specialized's big bicycle shop – which he dared not enter, because all he would see was beautiful mountain bikes that he could not afford. Not now, and not even when he was still a captain.

And he wouldn't be able to ride them either, there was simply no time.

He looked at the vineyards, north and south of the suburb. The pine plantation at Eden on the eastern side was dense and ominous. If you wanted to get rid of a body . . .

He drove back thinking of his son. He wondered if Fritz would contact him about Sunday. He wondered, on the subject of Callie de Bruin's father, what Fritz would reply if his friends asked him 'what does your father do?' or 'how is your pa?' Perhaps it was better for him that he didn't know.

Back at the bank the FNB official said head office had approved the request, and they were sending Callie's statements to him via email.

He considered mentioning that head office had no choice in the matter. But it would make no difference.

Vaughn Cupido had a strange feeling when he walked into the DPCI head office in Bellville. The poorly lit corridors, the hollow sound of his footsteps on the tiles . . . He remembered times when the building vibrated with activity, before the president and his fellow looters of the state gutted the Hawks to protect themselves. This was his house, his home, but now he was an intruder. It reminded him of how it had been, a lifetime ago, when he went back home to his parents for the first time after he had completed his training at the Police College in Pretoria. His father and mother and their house were still the same, but he wasn't.

Thinking of all this made him even more depressed, so that even his old colleagues' hearty welcome failed to cheer him up.

He first asked permission from Captain Philip van Wyk, head of the Hawks IMC, to let Sergeant Reginald 'Lithpel' Davids examine the computer. It took him nearly fifteen minutes to reach Davids; everyone wanted to ask him about what life was like these days at an ordinary police station detective branch.

Lithpel was in his usual, happy mood. He rapped in a nasal voice: 'Bring it to my lab, and set it on my slab. I'd like it a lot, if it showed me what it's got,' and took the computer case from Cupido.

'Browser history and email, Lithpel, that's what we're looking for,' said Cupido, subdued.

Davids was determined to get a laugh from Cupido: 'You can get high now, 'cause I'm the right guy now, but you must fly now, or I might start to cry now.' He clicked his thumb and middle finger together to keep the beat.

'Nice, Lithpel. I'm going to drop by The Flower now, let me know if you find anything.'

'If you find the bubbly, bickering, and braggadocio former Captain Vaughn Cupido we've come to know and love, tell him we say hi.'

The bubbly, bickering, braggadocio *formerly slim and trim* captain, thought Cupido as he walked away.

Colonel Mbali Kaleni was genuinely glad to see him.

Cupido found that oddly touching. He could see she was still having a hard time. She had put a lot of weight back on – even more than he had – and she looked older. Weary and run down. It must be due to the ongoing state capture, which went against everything she stood for. And she was also so proud of the new South Africa, so blindly loyal. And now the rot was eating away at her, and he felt truly sorry for her. He had had such a strong dislike for her when she had been promoted above him, because she was the direct opposite of him: strongly conservative and cautious, the letter of criminal procedure law was her bible, she didn't swear, drink or smoke and disapproved of such behaviour in her team mates. But he learned over the years, that she was fair, that she supported her people steadfastly. Even when her career was in jeopardy.

She came out from behind the desk and took his hand. 'I'm happy to see you, Vaughn. You're looking good.'

It was on the tip of his tongue to say: 'Colonel, I'm looking a little too good, but I'm on Lose It! now,' but he realised she might not want to talk about weight problems. She had her own history of dieting, which had once been a source of great merriment for her team. But they ate their own words when she managed to lose a great deal of weight.

So he merely said: 'You too, Colonel. I need to talk to you, but not here.' He swung his index finger in a small circle to indicate possible bugging devices.

'Of course,' she said.

They walked silently to the staircase, and Cupido gained a sudden insight: if the old bubbly, bickering, braggadocio Vaughn would have stepped out of his office and spotted these two tubbies, one short and one tall, he would have had a great deal to say about it.

You live and learn, he thought. Fat keeps you humble.

Back at the office Griessel made the first tiny breakthrough with Calvyn Wilhelm de Bruin's Form 55 investigation, but it would be some time before he became aware of its full significance.

He sat down at the computer to see whether Roland 'Rolster' Parker had a criminal record.

34

Down in the DPCI basement was the Hawks 'club room', a legendary, hidden room where only members of the unit were allowed. So many times Cupido used to gather there with his Serious and Violent Crime team members to *braai* on a Friday afternoon, and it was there that he described the sequence of the Milo April saga to Mbali Kaleni. He barely raised his voice above a whisper.

At the appropriate stage of the story he produced the two folded letters from his jacket pocket and showed them to her.

She didn't say a word; her body language was the only indication of her concern. She stared at the photos, deep in thought. He waited for her response. At last he said: 'Benny thinks this is the reason why they didn't send us to Laingsburg, Colonel. A sort of carrot and stick strategy, to keep us quiet about it . . .'

She shook her head.

'You don't think so?' he asked.

'I know why they did not send you to Laingsburg. And that's not the reason.'

'You know?' Stunned.

'I do.'

'What is the reason?'

'When the time comes, I will tell you. But not now.'

'Oh . . .'

'This Milo April matter is very serious, Warrant Officer. I feel exactly like you and Benny. No stone should be left unturned to bring the killer or killers of a police person to justice. It might be the forces of state capture, that is possible, and that will make an investigation very difficult. But it hasn't stopped us in the past, has it?'

'No, Colonel . . .'

'But I don't think the provincial commissioner is involved.'

'How can you be sure?'

She gave him the familiar forbidding look. 'Because I know the man. I also know why the corrupt and crooked politicians have control over him. He has his . . . weakness. But he is a career policeman, and he is not evil. I cannot believe that he would have a fellow member of the Service killed. I just cannot believe that.'

'These are strange days, Colonel . . .'

'I know, Warrant. But that photograph of him and the gun is not proof of anything yet. Let us investigate first.'

'Okay.'

She gave him back the letters.

'Hold on to them. I will make a few discreet enquiries at Mitchells Plain station. What April was working on, who he was working with . . . Then I will let you know.'

'We will have to use some sort of code.'

'Yes,' she said. 'When I call you to say that there is a box of your stuff you need to collect, you must come to my house that night.'

Roland Parker did not have a criminal record.

Griessel carefully typed the identity number he had received from MTN into the Krim system, and retrieved nothing.

Just to be sure, he typed in Roland Parker by name, nickname and surname, and still no result was forthcoming.

Next he phoned Droppa, the truck rental company, at their head-quarters in Centurion, and explained who he was, why he was calling and that it was extremely urgent. They eventually put him through to the managing director, who listened patiently. He said he would look into it and call back.

Griessel went outside to smoke, and when he went back inside, Callie de Bruin's bank statements were in his email inbox.

He opened them. There was a current balance of R5,629.64.

No withdrawals had been made since Friday afternoon. The last one was the previous Wednesday at 13:07 at Roman's Pizza in the Neelsie, the student centre on campus, and for less than ninety rand.

He studied the previous three months' income and expenses. There were only two deposits made: On 7 August an amount of R7,048.00 was paid in by 'Britehouse'. And on the first day of August, September and October 'A. de Bruin' paid R700 into the account. His mother.

Callie spent his money on food and cellular data, insignificant amounts for the most part. And in September one expense at Van Schaik Bookshop in the Neelsie, for R423.99. There were only a few cash withdrawals, small amounts under a hundred rand.

That was all.

No expensive clothing purchases, no extravagant computer equipment. Only food and airtime.

'Fuck,' said Griessel. It wasn't going to be any help in tracing the boy. And in addition it meant that Callie did his trading in cash, or had another bank account, or a combination of the two.

The only clue was Britehouse. It sounded like the name of a pawn shop. He opened a browser on the computer and googled it.

He found that Britehouse was a large technology company. And a division of Dimension Data, the business that was paying for Callie's studies.

The R7,048.00 was bursary income. It didn't help Griessel at all.

'Very funny, Warrant, very funny,' said Lithpel Davids, bristling with annoyance, when Cupido found him again.

'What now?'

'You can cut that all innocent vibe, Warrant, you know very well. Coming in here with your funeral face, I should have known.'

'Lithpel, I don't know what you're talking about.'

'*Ja, ja*, sure. Should I throw the case in the rubbish, or do you still want to play someone else for a fool?'

'How have I played you for a fool?'

Davids paused, doubtful. Cupido really did look puzzled. 'The hard drive,' he said.

'What is on the hard drive?'

'It's not about what's on the hard drive, it's because there isn't a hard drive inside.'

'In the PC? That I brought?'

'That is correct, your honour.'

'But then how's the thing working?'

'It's not working, because there's no bootable system drive, there's nothing. You can see, inside the box case there's nothing but brackets for a two-and-a-half-inch SSD drive, so maybe there was one. And there's an open bay for a three-and-a-half-inch HDD, but both the bays are as empty as Eskom's bank account.'

'Damn,' said Cupido.

'I thought you were messing with me,' said Lithpel.

'We are sitting with a fifty-five that's escalated, I don't have time for messing. So we have nothing?'

'Well, not exactly. We have a state-of-the-art NVidia GTX 1080 Ti graphics card and we have four state-of-the-art Corsair Vengeance LED 3466 RAM sticks of eight gigabytes each. So, if I pop a system drive in there, we have a mean machine that would be worth about forty thousand rand. And that's without monitor and peripherals. I don't call that 'nothing'. But if you want to know this dude's email and browser history, then yes, we have sweet Fanny Adams.'

'Damn,' said Cupido, who understood nothing of the terminology, but grasped the essence of the message very well.

'Looks like the dude was in a hurry to get the drives out though.'

'Why?'

Lithpel brushed a few little screws closer across the desk surface. 'We call these screws "sixes", short for hashtag six stroke thirty-two UNC screws, a.k.a. computer case screws. And if you're a computer nerd you put them away carefully, because you're always short. But these seven sixes were just lying in the bottom of the case. Rush job.'

'Fuck,' said Cupido.

'Two "damn"s, a "why" and a "fuck" ... I really miss Captain Motormouth Cupido.'

The managing director of Droppa rang Griessel back. He said he could confirm that Roland Parker of Raziet Street in Cloetesville, Stellenbosch, was registered with them as a *bakkie* owner and driver. He could also confirm that Parker had been active with them for the past eighteen months, and had built up a four-and-a-half-star grading through his clients.

'Is there a problem with this man that I should know of?' asked the managing director.

'No, sir, we are just covering all the possibilities.'

He rang off and leaned back. Discouraged.

Was it possible that both he and Vaughn were mistaken about Rolster Parker? Both their instincts were telling them he wasn't telling the truth. At least not the whole truth.

He built PCs from the stuff, and then sold them. And later a 'wardrobe' was added, and an old Borgward, it seemed as though Parker just supplied information to make his story work.

Cash, most of the time. But there was no sign of significant cash withdrawals from Callie's account.

Griessel jotted notes in his book, writing down what he knew, trying to build a picture that made sense, a scenario that matched. He found nothing, only more questions without answers. Would Callie have another bank account somewhere? What was he hiding? Nobody worked cash only today, it was just too easy to make electronic payments. Why didn't Annemarie de Bruin know anything about her son's buying and selling of goods and his computer building? Because he hadn't told her. And then the question arose: why not? After all it was something to be proud of, helping his cash-strapped single mother, earning pocket money by canny trading.

Griessel did not like the only logical explanation: Callie de Bruin was involved in something illegal.

And it had had fatal consequences.

His computer would have to provide the answers.

And that was when Vaughn Cupido walked in and said he was coming back empty-handed, because there was no hard drive in Callie's PC.

'And Benna, get this: The Flower knows why we were saved from Laingsburg, but she won't say. And it's not because the commissioner wants to keep us away from Milo April's murder.'

'How does she know?'

'It's an enigma, *pappie. Moer* of an enigma.'

35

Just before four p.m. Sandra Steenberg received a WhatsApp from Jasper Boonstra that made her heart leap.

Come tomorrow morning at 09:00. Documents will be ready. Tell S&H to sign the cheque so long.

Her mind said, don't count your chickens, wait till you have the papers in your hands, and the money in the bank, but the good news bubbled through her, and the relief, Dear God, the relief. It was almost over, this whole mess was nearly over, never again would she let herself get into a mess like this, never again would she lie to Josef. She had learned so much from this experience, and she was going to take every single lesson to heart.

She wrote back to Boonstra: *Thank you!* Genuine and heartfelt. The old fox, she could forgive him for a great many things now.

Her phone beeped again. She checked.

It's not for free. Look sexy.

At twenty to four Griessel and Cupido sat in the parade room with the brigadier in charge of the Boland cluster in Paarl, the full colonel who served as Stellenbosch station commander, and Lieutenant Colonel Witkop Jansen.

The two senior officers were irritable. 'It can't go on like this,' the Paarl brigadier said. 'Province is on my case every ten minutes,' he said. 'The rector's office keeps calling. Now my people tell me the premier is also trying to get hold of me.'

'Absolutely unacceptable,' the station commissioner agreed.

'Not to mention the newspapers and TV people,' said the brigadier. 'What do I say to them? What do you have for us?'

'We have nothing, Brigadier,' said Benny Griessel, because he knew it wouldn't help to beat about the bush.

'You have nothing? Two former Hawks, with one helluva reputation, hot shots, and you have nothing? What do you think this is, a holiday camp?'

'For God's sake,' the station commissioner said. 'Nothing? How come?'

'It's a difficult case, Brigadier,' Jansen said in their defence, to Benny and Cupido's surprise. 'We have to work with what we have, and there isn't much to go on.'

'So do you want me to say that to the premier, Witkop? And the media? Sorry, boys, it's a difficult case, we give up?'

'No, Brigadier . . .'

'What about your SVCI team? The ox is in the pit, why don't you bring them in?' Stellenbosch station had eight top detectives who were part of the Serious and Violent Crimes group, generally known as SVCI, short for Serious and Violent Crimes Investigations.

'I have faith in this team, Brigadier.'

The brigadier looked at Cupido, then at Griessel, clearly not convinced. 'So what do you need?'

'A lucky break, Brigadier,' said Cupido. 'Because this *laaitie* is an enigma.' Shamelessly borrowing the word from Veronica Adams.

'What is that supposed to mean?' asked the brigadier.

'Brigadier,' said Griessel, who also wasn't absolutely sure what 'enigma' meant, 'his phone is off, the hard drive has been taken out of his computer, his bank account offers no clues, his lecturers and classmates and his hostel mates have no idea where he could be . . .'

'We put his photo and disappearance on the varsity social media channels,' Cupido said. 'The newspapers were full of the fifty-five this morning, but we didn't get a single useful lead. Nothing.'

'He has expensive clothing in his room,' said Griessel, 'but his mother has no idea where it all came from. He was trading in second-hand goods, but we don't know how he bought them. He paid a transporter in cash to move the goods for him, but he doesn't seem to have withdrawn more than a hundred rand per week in cash from his account. When Colonel Jansen came to call me now I was busy sending a bulletin to all the banks, to find out if he had another account. It's the only other thing we can do, besides monitoring his phone, and hoping someone responds to the media.'

'An *outjie* wearing a hoody used Callie's student card on Sunday evening to gain access to his room. We don't know if Callie sent him or if it was theft,' said Cupido. 'Hoody's photo has also been circulated. Zero response.'

'As with all fifty-fives there are two possibilities,' Griessel said. 'He's run off of his own free will, or there was foul play. We're not sure which.'

'He could have taken the hard drive out of his PC himself, or Hoody could have taken it, because he had a full bag of stuff with him when he walked out.'

'And then the big question, why remove the hard drive? What was on it?'

'*Bliksem*,' said the brigadier.

'Difficult one,' said the station commissioner.

'Didn't the *laaitie* have a girlfriend?' asked the brigadier.

'Not as far as we can tell,' said Griessel.

'Or a boyfriend. That's also a thing nowadays.'

'No, Brigadier.'

'*Bliksem*,' said the brigadier.

'An enigma,' said the station commissioner.

'Amen,' said Vaughn Cupido.

Lieutenant Colonel Witkop Jansen had a habit of rubbing his moustache with his index finger when he was angry – two short, powerful, horizontal motions just under his nose, a kind of Morse code distress signal, every minute or so.

'Colonel,' said Benny Griessel, 'we're doing our absolute best with this case . . .'

'I don't want to hear it. And this is not about what the brigadier says, or the premier or the rector who's phoning or whatever. We don't work for them. We work for the boy's ma, and we work for him. It's our job. To serve the people of this town. With all that we've got. And if you don't want to serve them, if your minds are still on the Hawks or the state-capture mess that you made, or whatever, then you can bugger off to Laingsburg. You receiving me, loud and clear?'

A swift, to-fro rubbing of his moustache.

'Yes, Colonel.'

'Right then. Go and find the boy.'

Sandra picked up her girls at the kindergarten.

On the way home they sang her a new song they had learned. She sang along smiling; their enthusiasm was contagious, but she was still trying to shake off her concern about spotting Josef's car.

Had he been at the bank? Was it because he suspected something? Or did the relationship manager call him behind her back? She wouldn't be surprised.

She parked the car, took the twins out of their child seats, and walked to the front door.

What was she going to say?

He was in the kitchen busy making supper. He smiled at her – a little stiffly? – but first had to listen while Anke and Bianca sang him their song too. He clapped his hands, hugged and kissed them.

She walked to him. 'How was your day?' she asked, held close in his embrace.

'Good,' he said. 'I made good progress. Yours?' Was his body a bit tense?

She searched for signs of normality, his open-hearted self. She sensed a reserve in him, and felt her own tension rise. 'I saw your car parked in Ryneveld,' she said.

'Oh, *ja*. A master's student who wanted some advice. We went for a coffee at Häzz.'

And then he squeezed her, and said: 'I missed you.'

She relaxed, but not entirely. Because there was something a tiny bit different about him.

At half past five Griessel and Cupido drove to Fishaways to get take-out. They hadn't eaten lunch; Vaughn's hunger was gnawing at him.

'And now I'm a fish eater, because Desiree says hake is low kilojoules, but no chips, only salad. And then the CO threatens to send us to Laingsburg? What more could we do, what stone did we leave unturned? I know I struggle to take a whipping, I have a real problem with authority, but you know me, partner, if I'm guilty I say, okay, I'm guilty. Sorry. But this is ridiculous. I feel the mother's pain, and I know you feel the mother's pain, but now he comes with "we serve the people of this town", as if we're wet-behind-the-ears blue bums who don't know the first thing about policing? Sure, send me off to Laingsburg then, so I can squander my elite crime-fighting skills on petty theft and domestic violence. But don't come and falsely accuse me of not giving a damn.'

'He's just transferring the pressure,' Griessel said. 'The way they're all doing.'

'We also feel the pressure, partner, but we don't go around blaming anybody. "You receiving me?" Ha, like he's a fucking radio station.'

Griessel couldn't help himself, he had to laugh. 'And with that body, he's definitely transmitting in short wave.'

Cupido's anger dissolved and he laughed too. 'Fuck them, Benny. We've seen worse. This too shall pass. If only I can get some food in my belly.'

At Fishaways, they ate quickly – Cupido had five hake fillets, the app had told him the whole lot were only two thousand kilojoules, which he could easily afford, and Griessel tried the Calamari Slider.

He didn't enjoy it, but he knew if he said a word, Cupido would point out that he had no right to complain – after all he'd already wolfed down a delicious samoosa.

They discussed the docket, going through the whole investigation from the beginning again to be sure they hadn't overlooked anything.

'This *outjie* is like The Phantom, Vaughn. It's like nobody saw him.'

'Maybe he didn't want to be seen.'

The remark prodded something in the back of Griessel's mind, a possibility that was there for an instant and then slipped away before he could fully get a grip on it.

Just before six they decided to go back to Eendrag one more time. The residence coordinator let them in. In Callie de Bruin's wing they walked from room to room, asking each student they came across if they had ever seen Callie constructing computers or carrying them around. Or if they remembered anything else, perhaps.

All they could get was one of the residents who said his girlfriend thought she had seen Callie getting into a car, on Friday morning.

'What sort of car?' Griessel asked.

'She said it was a small one, *Oom*.'

After eight Benny phoned Annemarie de Bruin to tell her there still was no progress.

'All I can do is keep praying,' she said. 'You'll see, it will help.'

He wasn't so sure.

Then they brought the docket up to date at the office. And Benny drove all the way back to Cape Town to tell Alexa about his frustrating, fruitless day.

36

4 October

A dreary Wednesday, grey with rain.

Sandra looked out of the living room window before she began her exercises. She was grateful for the weather, because she could dress conservatively, in the black trouser suit with her white blouse buttoned up to her neck. Jasper Boonstra was sure to get the message: Monday was a turning point in the dynamics of their relationship. She had the power to make the transaction go forward. To keep his name out of it. He had no leverage, he couldn't force her into anything. He could be as much of a nuisance and a sex pest as he liked, it wouldn't help him.

She had the power.

And yet she was aware that her confidence about the day that lay ahead was fragile. Because of Josef.

She picked up the weights, began to exercise in the hope that she could shake off her doubts.

Was she imagining things? Was her guilty conscience creating a feeling of distance between her and her husband? Last night at supper, and afterwards. As if something had come between them. A knowing.

And yet, Josef was the sort to speak up when something bothered him.

Or was he still trying to process the extent of her deception?

No, no, it was all in her imagination.

And so as she sweated her way through the workout, her thoughts circled back and forth around Boonstra and Josef, but with no real premonition, no hint of the cataclysm that this day would bring.

★　　★　　★

Vaughn Cupido stood at the window of Desiree Coetzee's house while he waited for the water to boil. He saw how grey it was outside. And grey was exactly how he felt. He wanted with all his might to solve this fifty-five and find Callie de Bruin; he was an athlete at the starting blocks, cocked, ready for battle, but the gun would not fire. Grey, because he had to attend morning parade to be hauled over the coals again. Grey, because he had to eat oats for breakfast. Eight hundred and three kilojoules for fifty grams. With almond milk. Desiree said almond milk had a third of the kilojoules of dairy.

Almond milk. And oats. And a teaspoon of honey.

Him. Like a vege-fucka-tarian. And he would be hungry again by nine a.m.

But if that is what it takes . . .

His gloomy mood stemmed from his growing concern. Why was Desiree so eager to help him with this diet? Because she agreed he was fat? Then clearly she didn't like him being fat. Which meant his fears that he could lose her were well founded.

He poured the boiling water over the oats and thought his grey and gloomy thoughts, totally unaware of the massive upheaval this day would deliver.

Griessel was stuck in traffic.

He was not happy. Because when it rained, Capetonians drove like sheep.

He could be late for morning parade. Which would be a further blow to his already very shaky relationship with Colonel Witkop Jansen.

He thought about Annemarie de Bruin, waking up in the guest house to this grey morning, without any hope. If they could just have a touch of luck on their side today, find some little thread to tease at and pull on until the mystery began to unravel. Then at least he would be able to look her in the eyes and say, yes, there was hope, they had made some progress.

Fritz hadn't said anything about Sunday either. Griessel didn't want to phone or send messages; the boy had to make his own decision. But he was increasingly doubtful that Fritz would turn up. How was he meant to build a relationship from one side only?

He sat in the traffic on the R43 and thought this was not a day he was looking forward to. He had a feeling that this really was not going to be a good one.

Griessel made it just in time, two minutes before the start of morning parade. He hurried in and sat down beside Cupido, who also looked pretty damn sour.

Witkop Jansen opened with a prayer in English. 'Help us through this day, Lord. Guide us.'

Then he began with the most urgent case on the roll: Calvyn Wilhelm de Bruin's fifty-five. It was Cupido's turn to report. Vaughn sketched the main outlines of their lack of progress, and mentioned Roland Parker's name casually, not because it was essential detail, more out of frustration that this was yet another dead-end lead. And also to show that they hadn't just been sitting on their backsides twiddling their thumbs.

'The Rolster?' said Sergeant Erin Riddles, one of the female detectives at the table.

'Yes, Rolster,' said Cupido, surprised that she knew the name.

'No, he calls himself "The Rolster", it's only his mommy who calls him plain "Rolster". Slippery one, that. I put him away, four years ago. Or is it five already . . .'

'Put him away?' Griessel asked.

She nodded. 'Fancies himself as a cat burglar. He robbed a bunch of houses here and in Somerset West, we got him on a single fingerprint, with sixty thousand rands' worth of stolen goods in his ma's garage.'

'He was found guilty?' Benny asked with a sinking feeling that he must have messed up his query on the Krim System.

'For sure,' said Erin Riddles. 'First offence, he was young, his mother is a dependant and the judge was sympathetic. He got two years, suspended for five. So he didn't do time, but I knew he would pop up again.'

Witkop Jansen glared furiously through his eyebrows. Griessel felt the shame burn through him.

'Then we will have to take a closer look at him,' said Griessel.

'Get your asses in gear,' said Jansen. '*Now.*'

*   *   *

Griessel apologised to Cupido when they walked into their office.

'Don't worry, partner. Shit happens.'

Griessel sat down in front of the computer, reached for the MTN documents again, and opened the Krim system interface on the computer. 'I'm telling you, I was careful. With his ID. And his name and surname. I didn't make two mistakes one after the other.'

'It happens, Benna, don't beat yourself up.'

Griessel tapped in Roland Parker's identity number, name and surname again.

Again the Krim system said that 'The Rolster' Parker had no criminal record.

'You see,' Griessel said.

Cupido came and stood beside him, staring at the screen. 'Wait,' he said. 'Read me the data, I'll type it in.'

Griessel stood up and let his colleague take the seat. He read out the number, digit by digit, spelled the name and surname carefully. Cupido typed it in.

The result was still negative.

'This is fucking weird,' said Cupido.

'The ID number is wrong,' Griessel said. 'It's MTN's fault . . .'

'Wait,' said Cupido, and typed just 'Roland Parker' into the database.

The system showed there was no citizen of that name and surname with a criminal record.

'*Jissis*,' said Cupido.

'Let's try NaTIS,' Griessel said. 'Just to check the ID.'

Cupido opened up the database of the National Traffic Information System and typed the ID number in.

'Hallelujah,' he said, as NaTIS showed that Roland Parker of Raziet Street in Cloetesville, Stellenbosch, was the legal owner of a 2013 Ford Ranger 2.2TDCi XL. 'The ID was correct.'

'So what is wrong with the Krim System? Griessel asked.

'They must have entered his stuff incorrectly when he was sentenced.'

'Must be,' said Griessel with great relief. 'I'm just going to clear my name with Witkop first.'

He began walking to the door, but stopped halfway, head down. Things in his mind were trying to make sense.

'Partner,' said Cupido, who was staring at the screen. 'I was just thinking . . .'

'Yes?'

'You remember how nervous The Rolster was?'

'Yes?'

'How he wouldn't talk?'

'Yes.'

'He has a history of stolen goods.'

'Yes.'

'And Callie was selling second-hand stuff . . .'

'Yes . . .' But he was lost in thought.

'Benna, are you listening?'

Griessel stood thinking about what his colleague had said last night. About Callie not wanting to be seen. He wanted to connect that to something, but it eluded him again, and he said: 'You're right, it's a possibility, I think we should talk to Erin Riddles. Let me just pop in to Witkop.'

'I'm coming too . . .'

'Dammit,' said Witkop Jansen, staring at the computer monitor on his desk.

'The fault is in the system,' Griessel said.

'It's the people at the courts who don't do their jobs properly,' Jansen said. 'I'm not surprised. The CFR is even worse, full of errors lately,' referring to the Central Firearms Registry. 'Everyone puts in data any old way. No standards any more. Must be driving a control freak like Buddy Fick nuts up at Silverton.'

Maybe that's why 'The Flash' Fick has become such a complete arsehole, Griessel thought. 'I just wanted to show you, Colonel.'

'Okay. Not your fault. Noted. What are you going to do now?'

'We are going to talk to Sergeant Riddles before we bring Parker in.'

'Right you are then. Get a move on.'

37

'The thing is,' said Erin Riddles. 'The Rolster is one smart chappie.'

She was in her mid-thirties, broad-hipped, with an easy smile. She sat behind her desk which was piled high with files, they stood opposite.

'Check,' said Cupido.

'He should have gone to study. But there was no chance, his father died of tuberculosis when he was still in primary school. The Rolster went to work at Helderberg Security Systems, straight out of Matric. First as an assistant, putting in house alarms. By all accounts a good worker, on time every day, quick learner. After only a year they promoted him, and then he was doing the installations with two *outjies* helping him. Franschhoek, Stellenbosch, Somerset West, the whole area. If you ask me, he got bored. Same thing every day, over and over, in all these rich people's houses ... If you're clever, you will get bored, and you're going to see possibilities. And that's what happened. He saw the possibilities. And he began breaking in ...'

'Alone?' Griessel asked.

'So it seems. And he chose his houses very cleverly. Places where he'd installed the alarms himself, where he knew the vulnerabilities. Only rich people, big places, two- and three-storeys. And that's not easy, you have to be pretty athletic to scale those walls. That's why I say he fancied himself as a cat burglar. You could tell, during the interrogation, there was a bit of pride, a bit of "I'm not your common-or-garden-variety thief" idea. And you have to give him credit, it was pure fluke that he was caught, one of those random things that happen, that you don't see coming, no matter how smart you are. He broke into a house here in Mostertsdrift, grand place. Beautiful. Really posh. The people had a thing about pigeons messing on the windowsills. And they installed those spikes to stop the pigeons roosting. And it was those spikes that nailed The Rolster, if you'll pardon the pun. He used to wear these leather gloves to break in. And when he tried to jimmy the window, a spike hooked on one finger of the glove, and the spike hurt him. So when he jerked his hand away, the glove came off, and he grabbed to regain his balance, and that's when he left one fingerprint. Only one, ever. But it was enough. I got him. And when we opened that garage of his ma's the laptops were lined up and there was a Tupperware container of jewellery, and another one for cell phones. He should have sold the stuff . . . Anyway, I connected him to seven burglaries. Case closed.'

'So why didn't he sell the stuff?' Cupido asked.

'That's what I wondered too,' said Riddles. 'Some of those laptops had been stolen seven months before. He wouldn't say a word, but I thought it had to be one of two things: either he just liked the idea of being a cat burglar, and would sit their admiring his loot every evening, or he couldn't find a fence.'

Sandra drove to Baronsberg.

Her self-confidence, her I-have-the-power mojo was shaky. She knew it didn't matter how much she told herself the contrary, it was only partially true. Jasper Boonstra could instruct his Swiss legal team to contact Stirling & Heyns directly and discreetly, without involving him or her at all. If he wanted to.

He still had leverage.

The uneasy feeling was back.

She tried to think of other things. Good things. Like how she would spend the three million. First of all she would pay off the bond on the townhouse, Lord knows, it would make a huge difference not to have that sword dangling over her head, to drastically reduce their monthly expenditures.

The remaining million and a half? The offer to Charlie for a share in the business. A royal Christmas for a change. She would arrange for a holiday at the sea, a cottage on the beach, Stilbaai or Great Brak, somewhere the children could run around and play in the sand and she could get a tan again, and stay sexy for Josef. Erase the distance between them, make him fall in love with her all over again. She wanted to take him somewhere alone for New Year. Leave the twins with the in-laws for a few days, book in at a grand hotel in Cape Town – the Waterfront maybe! – a candle-lit dinner with champagne, and a huge bed where they could have the kind of sex they had in the BT era. The time Before Twins.

No, she wasn't going to wait until then, she would seduce him tonight. Tonight she would tell him that the big deal was clinched, that their financial position had improved dramatically. She would tell him that there were a few things that were a bit in arrears, she hadn't wanted to burden him with all that, but everything was okay now. And then she would seduce him. A foretaste of their New Year's second honeymoon, a practice run, a celebration of this very good day. A closing of the distance she felt.

And still her heart hammered and her nerves jangled.

The rain had stopped, the security personnel at the guardhouse waved her through with broad smiles, as if she was an old friend already. She waved back and drove the five hundred metres to the house.

Still just the Mercedes-Maybach and the Ferrari in the glass-door garage.

Where was the elusive Mrs Boonstra these days? At Rooi-Els, like the papers said?

She parked in the space next to them, part of the garages, below the house.

One minute to nine.

She picked up her handbag and walked to the front door.

He opened the door before the chimes sounded. 'Hello, Sandra,' he said cheerfully.

He was clean shaven, hair combed, and he smelled of aftershave. Barefoot. He was wearing his dressing gown.

She heard Charlie's voice in her head: *When she walked in, he was already into the wine and wearing just his dressing gown. He poured her a glass of wine and told her what he could do for her career, if she was prepared to 'cooperate'.*

Jasper's eyes looked her up and down, despite her demure trouser suit and white blouse. 'God,' he said, 'you're one fuckable woman.'

She was prepared for something like this, she thought. She was strong. She smiled coldly at him: 'That is a privilege you are never going to have.'

He held the door open. 'Come in.' Wide-eyed, all innocence.

'No, thank you.'

He shrugged, stepped back and shut the door in her face. She stood outside, in the drizzle.

Helplessness washed over her. And rage too, now, because he was an arsehole – a complete, total, utter arsehole.

Her mind told her he still had leverage over her. Her mind told her she also had power, turn around and leave, go and tell your husband what you've been doing. Don't let this monster manipulate you.

Her mind said three million rand. He wouldn't rape her. He would try to blackmail her, try to manipulate her, but he wouldn't rape her. Not in his position.

He was just playing his little game, he needed her.

She stood still. Wavering. Minutes ticked by. Birdsong mocked her, so cheerful and innocent.

She pressed the doorbell. He took his time. When he opened, she said: 'You behave yourself. I will notify Stirling & Heyns that you are linked to this. I will make sure everyone knows that you have an interest in Donkerdrif.'

He laughed at her, motioned her in. 'Okay, okay, you have the upper hand, Sandra.'

She walked into the house. He shut the door.

'Come upstairs. Everything's there.' He gestured that she should go first.

She walked through the reception area, and stopped at the foot of the stairs. 'I'll wait here.'

He put his hand in his dressing gown pocket and brought it out again, opening his hand. On his palm lay a key, a peculiar one with a complex notched and ridged blade. 'Then you have a problem. The papers are up there. Locked away. And I don't carry contracts to junior agents.'

He put the key back in his pocket.

There was something in his eyes, in the angle of his mouth. Anticipation, lust. And power. For the first time she felt afraid.

'Come,' he said.

'You will not touch me.' Even to her own ears she sounded vulnerable.

'I swear I will not touch *you*.'

She took a deep breath, began to climb the stairs with a thudding heart. It was surreal, unreal, like a dream, her limbs rigid, her body heavy, as if she had to wade through deep water.

'Never is a long time, Sandra,' he said right behind her.

She didn't look back, didn't stop climbing the stairs. 'Excuse me?'

'You said I would never have the privilege of fucking you. I say: Never is a long time.'

She kept climbing, upwards.

'There are two questions you have to ask yourself. The first one is, how badly do you need the three million? Really, when the chips are down, as they say.'

As much afraid as she was angry, without looking at him, she said: 'Fuck you.'

He laughed. 'We all have a price, Sandra. What is yours? Three million not enough? For a few days' work and a bit of fun.'

'Fuck you.'

Nearly at the top.

'Have I ever told you you have a lovely arse? I think I'll take you from behind. The first time anyway.'

He was just toying with her, just let him carry on. 'Fuck you,' she repeated.

At the top. She kept on walking.

'The second thing you have to ask yourself is why you don't allow yourself a bit of fun too? I mean, your husband is out there screwing all the students . . .'

Her rage exploded, and she turned to vent her terrible fury on him. All that she meant to do, she would tell herself again and again afterwards, was to say to his face: 'Fuck you, you arsehole.'

But she half-turned, and felt Jasper Boonstra's hand on her bottom, urgent and rough.

Fear and hate and rage overwhelmed her and she pushed him hard, both hands on his chest.

And as she did so, as she saw him falling, backwards, down the stairs, she realised it wasn't his hand. It was the life-size knight in armour to the right. As she swung round its sword hand had pressed against her bum.

Jasper Boonstra's head and neck struck the step far below with a sickening thud.

And then he lay dead still.

38

When they stopped in front of Roland Parker's mother's house, he was reversing the Ford Ranger out the garage. The gate was open, the dog barked from inside the house.

They got out and walked up the driveway.

Parker leaned out of the open window. 'I have a gig; you'll have to come back later.'

'We have a missing person, you'll have to do your gig later, Rolster,' said Cupido.

'Sorry, no can do.' He began reversing and they had to jog out the way. 'Unless you have a warrant.'

'We can do better than that,' said Griessel.

Parker just shook his head, kept reversing into the street.

'We will notify Droppa that you have a record, Rolster,' said Griessel.

Parker stopped.

'We know now they don't allow criminals to drive for them, *pappie*,' said Cupido.

'Your choice,' said Griessel.

'Fuck,' said Roland Parker.

Sandra stood at the top of the stairs with the knight, her fury subsiding, but still the dream-like state persisted, because this could not be real.

The house was totally silent, the only sound was the panting of her breath. She was frozen to the spot, all she could do was to grasp the banister as the dizziness swept over her. Her mind was empty, she did not think of anything, could not, would not. Time had stopped, her eyes fixed on Boonstra. His dressing gown had fallen open: he was naked underneath it, his genitals exposed, with a partial erection. She shuddered, why didn't he move, he should cover himself, he had to recover, stand up. A peculiar feeling came over her, a sort of deep satisfaction that he had been hurt, he *should* have been hurt, it was a hard fall, he deserved it.

The suspicion that it was serious grew slowly, creeping into her consciousness like an intruder, an unwelcome guest.

How long she had been standing there, she had no idea.

She descended the stairs. Step by step. He was lying almost at the very bottom, on his back, his head at a peculiar angle to his body, one eye open and staring. Strangely the other was almost shut.

Instinctively she knew he was dead, though still through a haze of disbelief.

She knelt awkwardly beside him on the stairs. She tugged the dressing gown closed. She smelled him, the Jasper-odour of soap and deodorant and shampoo and hair oil, and it made her retch. She ran into the kitchen, threw down her handbag and vomited into the sink.

With her arms braced on either side of the sink, head bowed, she heaved until nothing more would come up.

And so, slowly, she came to her senses, hunched over the sink, the spasms eventually subsiding. Reality seeping back in, and all the consequences bearing down on her.

She would plead self-defence. He was in his dressing gown, naked underneath, he had been harassing her, had threatened to perform a sex act on her, they would believe he had tried to force her. She could scratch him now, bruise her own arms to show he had been physical with her, it wouldn't be fraud, he *had* threatened her. He had. Charlie could tell his story about what happened in Germany, they could trace that poor victim of his, the sexy one that he had appointed to the publicity department, *young, not yet thirty. Curvaceous, lips, the whole shebang*, they would find her and she would agree, he was a rapist . . .

Her resolve on this was clear, when the future came suddenly into focus. The deal was as dead as Boonstra was. She could kiss the money goodbye. Only scandal lay ahead, shame, the lurid headlines. Her reputation in shreds, an indelible stain. This town a hotbed of gossip. Her children would always be marked by the stigma.

Wasn't it your mother who pushed Jasper Boonstra to his death? Really? Is that what she says happened?

The emotion flooded over her. She braced herself against it.

And then there, at the kitchen sink, she straightened up, realising that perhaps there was another way.

She could still save this situation. She just had to calm down and think.

Keep her head.

She splashed her face with cold water. She let the tap run, rinsing out the sink, slowly, very thoroughly. She inhaled deeply, slowed down her breathing. Forced herself to be calm. Then she made her decision.

First she made certain the front door was locked. She walked back to the stairs, with measured urgency now. She fumbled in Jasper Boonstra's dressing gown pocket. First she found the cell phone. Put it aside, on the step. Felt in the other pocket, found the key. She didn't look at the face.

Then she slowly made her way back up the stairs, to his office, to find the drawer where the documents would be.

If he hadn't been lying to her.

The interrogation room at the detective headquarters was on the ground floor, right beside the morning parade room.

Rolster Parker was neatly dressed in designer jeans and a smart white shirt. With a pair of black Nike Vapormax on his feet.

Griessel and Cupido stood opposite him at the table. 'Rolster, it looks to me like Droppa is quite profitable, hey?' said Cupido.

'I don't know anything about where Callie is,' said Parker. 'You're wasting my time.'

He sat leaning back casually, as if he didn't have a worry in the world. But his gaze constantly flickered to the door, the first indication that he was probably lying.

'The fancy clothes, the fancy sneakers. And the weird thing is, Callie had almost the exact same things in his cupboard. And my partner doesn't believe in coincidence.'

'That's right,' said Griessel. 'Not one little bit.'

'Did you two go shopping together, Rolster. Thick as thieves?'

'You're wasting my time.'

'Okay. So, here's the deal, Rolster. You help us, and we don't tell Droppa about your criminal record slip-up.'

'I can't help you. I swear I don't know where Callie is.' The second sign of dishonesty, the classic, 'I swear'.

'So you keep saying. But we think you have info on what Callie was involved in. And that could help us. So, your future is in your own hands.'

'I don't know everything that Callie was doing. He'd call and tell me when I have to load, deliver, and then I'd do it.'

'What kind of stuff did you load and deliver then?'

'I told you, antiques, an old car once. But mostly it was computer parts. And once I fetched twelve computers at an auction house, from a company that went bankrupt.'

The third sign, the sudden extra information not previously supplied.

'And then, where did you deliver them?'

'To a guy in Salt River.'

'What did he plan to do with them?'

'How would I know?'

'And the other computer parts? Did you take them to Callie at the hostel?' Griessel asked.

'That's right.'

'But nobody in the hostel ever saw him with them. Or had any idea that he built computers with them.'

'How is that my problem?'

Cupido leaned forward. 'Here's how it's your problem, Rolster: you're lying. And if you keep lying another ten minutes, we're calling Droppa.'

'Then you'll have to call them, 'cause that's all I know.'

'Okay. Cool,' said Cupido and stood up. 'We'll do that.'

Parker crossed his arms on his chest.

'You're sure?' Cupido asked.

'You're going to take food out of my ma's mouth, but do what you have to do,' he shrugged.

'That won't work on us, Rolster. What about Callie's ma? She is devastated. And when you were out playing cat burglar, where was your worry for your mammie then?'

'I was young and stupid. I've turned over a new leaf.'

'With the help of Callie de Bruin?'

'He's one of many clients.'

'But he's the only one who could get into our Krim system to delete your record,' said Griessel.

'Excuse me? What do you mean?' said Rolster Parker. The fourth sign. Playing for time, trying to think up an explanation.

'That's right, Rolster-boy,' said Cupido. 'We know he's a brilliant hacker. After all, he's the first *oke* to get into the varsity system.'

'I wouldn't be able to say.'

'You're lying when you say that you met Callie through Droppa,' said Griessel. 'You knew each other before Droppa. And he helped you with your criminal record. Then you got the Droppa job.'

Parker glanced with longing at the door. But he shook his head vigorously. 'Bullshit,' he said. 'I lied on my Droppa application. That's my only crime.'

'The question is, what did it cost you? What did you do for Callie, or give him? Because you were on parole, jobless, you had no money. How did you pay for the favour?' Griessel asked.

Parker's arms remained crossed across his chest. He looked at the floor.

'We have a friend,' said Cupido. 'His name is Sergeant Lithpel Davids. He's a computer whizz, just like Callie. He said hackers advertise their talents on the dark net. Is that where you found Callie? We hear you're no slouch yourself. You know about such things.'

No response.

'Who did you send to get the stuff out of Callie's room, Rolster?' Griessel asked. 'To take the hard drive out of his computer, so we couldn't see what you were busy with.'

Parker shook his head, not looking up. 'Don't know what you're talking about.'

'We're going to get your phone records. We'll see who you called.'

Parker took his phone out of his pocket, put it down on the table. 'No need. Look for yourself.'

Cupido ignored the phone. 'They say you were too stupid to sell your stolen goods, that time. Is that what Callie helped you with? Is that why he phoned all the second-hand shops? You steal and he deals?'

Parker looked up at Cupido. 'Tell you what, call Droppa. I don't care. But I'm going now.' He stood up, picked up his phone. 'Unless you want to arrest me. Then go ahead, by all means. But you can't, because you've got fuck all on me.'

And he walked to the door, opened it and left.

39

Sandra found the papers in the top drawer of Jasper Boonstra's desk. The lock on the drawer was unusually large, but the strange key fitted it. The flood of relief made her feel weak; she had to sit down in the chair.

It was all there, on top of other documents – the agreement, the power of attorney, the contact details of the Swiss legal firm and Huber AG's directors, the order to pay Benson International. All signed, everything correct. No reference to Jasper Boonstra at all. Clean and clear.

Thank you, God.

She could not lose focus now, couldn't risk making a mistake.

What time was it?

She looked at her watch for the first time, saw it was 09:44. How long had she been standing at the kitchen sink?

A rush of adrenaline. Someone could turn up at any moment.

And yet, Boonstra had had plans for her, envisaging sex, he would have made sure they would be alone for at least an hour or two. She had time, she had time, use it. Don't mess up now.

She leaned back in the chair, closed her eyes. Think. Plan.

She stood up again at last with the paperwork in her hand and locked the desk drawer. Where to leave the key? Her gaze rested on the mounted half ostrich eggshell full of colourful jellybeans, but now she was seeing it from the opposite side. She saw the saying: *Half an egg* . . . was completed on this side. It read: . . . *is never as good as the whole egg.*

Yes. That sounded like Jasper Boonstra.

She dropped the key into the eggshell, on top of the jellybeans. She walked out, down the stairs, past Boonstra's body, still staring at the ceiling. Found her handbag in the kitchen, put the papers in it.

Opened the kitchen door, the one to the left of the glass back door. As she suspected, it opened into the triple garage. She walked down the three steps between the kitchen and garage, past the Ferrari and the Mercedes-Maybach to her EcoSport. She stood stock still, looking through the glass doors to the outside.

There was nobody, no movement.

She unlocked her car, put her handbag down on the passenger seat. She took off her jacket and laid it over the handbag. Then she opened the hinged door of the Ford at the back. She walked back to the kitchen, then to the stairs where Boonstra was lying.

She picked up the cell phone, tried to activate the screen. *Swipe up for Face ID or Enter Passcode.*

She held the phone in front of Boonstra's face with its single staring eye. She had to look away.

The phone activated.

She went to WhatsApp, found her conversation with Boonstra, swiped the chat back to the beginning. She deleted messages. Not all of them, only those that referred directly to the Demeter/Donkerdrif transaction. She worked swiftly, feeling the pressure to hurry, but frightened of making a mistake.

Scrolled the screen back again, went through it all again. It looked okay, seemed as if it would match her story.

Sandra put the phone back down on the floor. Now for the hard part.

She grabbed him by the collar of the dressing gown and pulled. The gown started sliding out from under him, exposing him again.

She put him down, pulled the gown back down again. She loosened the belt first and then tied it much more tightly around his waist. Took hold of the collar again.

That staring eye.

She let go of the collar, pressed both eyelids down.

Grabbed the dressing gown by the collar, under his neck, and dragged.

His heels thump-thumped down the steps until he lay flat on the floor. She dragged him through the kitchen, thinking how grateful she was that there was no blood. He must have broken his neck in the fall.

Out of the door. Thump-thump-thump down the three steps into the garage. Then past the luxury cars, to the rear of the EcoSport.

Now for the most difficult of all. The dressing gown had to come off; Jasper Boonstra had to go in.

'Shit,' said Cupido, because he and Griessel had played their trump cards and lost this hand.

'He doesn't really care if we tell Droppa about his record because his pockets are full.'

'I'm going to get a warrant to search his mother's house,' said Griessel. 'There has to be something.'

'We don't have enough for a search warrant, partner.'

'We'll have to try. How did he buy that *bakkie*, Vaughn?' Unemployed, suspended sentence, but he can afford a Ranger? You saw the truck, it's no *skedonk*. A 2013 model, even if he bought it a year ago, it must have cost him close to two hundred thousand. How?'

'I repeat: We don't have enough for a warrant.'

'The court will have to take the urgency of the case into account, the nature of the fifty-five. The protocol . . .'

'Like the uncle told the farmers who wanted to pray for rain: You can try, but the wind is blowing west.'

She couldn't take the dressing gown with her.

As soon as Jasper Boonstra was reported missing, his wife or his personal assistant or a housekeeper or whoever would come to see if anything was missing from the house. If the only thing they couldn't account for was his dressing gown, her entire plan would collapse.

So she had to remove the gown and put it away.

That meant she had to get a naked Boonstra into the baggage compartment of the EcoSport. She didn't want to touch him like that. But she would have to.

She untied the belt of the dressing gown. She rolled him, pulled, pushed and rocked him to get it off.

He lay there, with his partial erection, his flabby, hairy, middle-aged body with its pasty skin and paunch. She gritted her teeth, bent down, wrapped her arms around his chest and picked him up, squeezing the last air from his lungs. She almost screamed at the sigh the air made, crossing his lips. She dropped him, and his head smacked on the garage's spotless tile floor.

She wanted to throw up again, panic suddenly a fever that threatened to consume her. It was too much, the sum total of this nightmare, the terror of being caught, and the fear of the cascade of consequences if she didn't push through with what she was doing now.

She clung on to the Ford's rear door, breathing, breathing. She had to regain her equilibrium.

Slowly she calmed down.

The realisation: God, he was heavy.

Grateful that she exercised in the mornings, sorry that she'd already done weights today – she needed every ounce of stamina she could muster from her muscles.

She grabbed hold of him again. Her face against the back of his head, the scent of the hair oil and aftershave was overwhelming: her insides heaved, but she fought the nausea. Pushing and struggling, the body still limp, when does rigor mortis set in?

She got him more or less upright in front of her, shoved his torso in the boot and let go. He started sliding out, she had to prop her hip against his bare bottom, with all her strength. She choked back her revulsion. Until she had the body balanced, half in, half out. For only a fleeting moment she thought that she had a certain capacity, a primitive survival instinct, that allowed her to do this with a certain distance between herself and reality. As if her brain was protecting her from the truth; her entire body knew she had to: this was a case of life and death.

She gauged it with her eye. He wasn't going to fit in.

She couldn't put the seats down, she had to hide him under the black lid, the 'parcel tray', as the Ford salesman had called it, but the space was going to be too small.

Unless . . . If she could fold him in half, like a pocket knife, if he wasn't too tall . . .

Get the legs in first. She grabbed his feet. His toenails were too long. She lifted his legs up and in, having to use her hip as counterweight to keep his bottom inside. She groaned, forced him in, pulled his head and shoulders to the left, pushed the feet to the left as well.

His body lay at an unnatural angle. His butt was going to obstruct the door. She let go of him, grabbed the EcoSport's rear door and slammed it as hard as she could. The buttocks offered resistance only for a moment, then the lock clicked home and the door was shut and she leaned against the car, realising how out of breath she was, grateful that at least for now she didn't have to touch him.

She looked through the car's rear window.

You couldn't see there was a body in there.

And only then it hit her.

Cameras.

Of course there were security cameras.

Benny Griessel had planned to complete the application for the search warrant, but he didn't get that far. Capitec sent him an email – a reply to his enquiry to all the banks – to notify him that Calvyn Wilhelm de Bruin did indeed have an account with them. At the branch in the Eikestad Centre. With an email address and a telephone number of an official who could help.

He rang the number.

The woman answered almost immediately. He identified himself. She spoke quickly. And fulsomely.

'Yes,' she said, 'I heard about the boy who went missing, my daughter is also at the university, she's studying accounting. They're all talking about it. Head office told me you would contact me. I'm sitting right here with it. This child . . . Good heavens, he's . . . Shall I just say, is a valued client.'

'How so?' asked Griessel.

'He has considerable reserves,' she said.

'How much?' asked Griessel.

'There is seventy-one thousand in his transaction account,' she said.

'*Bliksem*,' said Griessel before he could stop himself.

'*Nogal*, hey?' said the Capitec woman. 'And then he has two long-term investments. One on twenty-four months, the other on sixty months,' she said.

'What are the amounts?'

'On twenty-four months he has one hundred and fifty thousand rand, and on sixty months he has two hundred thousand rand.'

'*Jissis*,' he said.

'I will forgive you taking the Lord's name in vain, Warrant Officer,' she said. 'I was quite surprised myself.'

40

Sandra remembered the camera that had been looking down on Boonstra and the yellow Ferrari the other day. Only a metre or two away from her, on the wall outside above the garage door. She didn't pay it much attention then. Cameras were normal in the houses of the rich, commonplace. This one pointed down and outwards.

Had she, while dragging the body to the back of her car, stepped out from under the roof? Could the camera see her?

No, she didn't think so.

She looked around anxiously inside the garage. There was nothing. Only the motion sensor on the wall.

But the alarm was off.

What about inside the house? She walked hurriedly back through the kitchen, the reception lounge. The stairs.

No cameras.

Up to the study.

Nothing.

Relief.

But she couldn't relax now. She still had work to do. She would have to get her story straight, think it through thoroughly, practise it over and over. And leave evidence. So that everything would fit.

She checked her watch.

She didn't have much time. It was Wednesday. The day she and Josef ate lunch together.

She would have to cancel; she couldn't sit down across from him in this state. Not now, not after Jasper had said that he . . .

No! It was of the utmost importance that she keep to her normal routine as far as possible. Like an innocent person. Like butter wouldn't melt in her mouth.

She would go and have lunch with Josef.

It was going to be very, very hard. And she had better be quick.

They drove to court. Cupido took the wheel while Griessel looked through Callie de Bruin's bank statements for the past six months.

'He bought clothing at the Waterfront,' Griessel said. 'A few times. Thousands of rands' worth. He bought something for thirteen thousand nine hundred and ninety-nine rand at the Tag Heuer Boutique. Must be a watch. He also bought things at Computer Mania with the Capitec card, once at Game and a bunch of stuff at computersonly. co.za . . .'

'What makes me the *moer* in,' said Vaughn Cupido, 'is that he bloody well took money from his mother every month, meantime he's sitting in the moolah. What a little shit.'

'The deposits, Vaughn, that's the key. Here are a whole bunch of them from the same sources, a few thousand at a time. But the big ones . . . These are just codes, I don't understand them . . .'

'How much are the big ones?'

'There are four that I can see, all over fifty thousand, two are over a hundred thousand. The bank will have to help us with that . . .'

'And he actually still *wragtig* took money from his ma every month. Maybe he has fucked off to Mauritius, Benna, lying on the beach with a blonde, sipping piña coladas. Little shit.'

Sandra fetched the dressing gown and belt from the garage.

At the stairs she picked up Boonstra's cell phone. She put it down on the desk, lined up with the other items there, and walked to the bedrooms.

The master bedroom was the size of a small auditorium, with a balcony outside and a view over the stunning valley. The lace curtains were half open. The bed was unmade. This must be his room then, all four of the other rooms were undisturbed.

There were two walk-in wardrobes. Massive, each as large as the Steenbergs' entire bedroom. Gorgeous rosewood, extravagantly expensive finishings; for a second she assessed everything with an estate agent's eye, but then the rising urgency again. Hurry up, hurry up, but don't rush, whatever you do, don't slip up.

The cupboard on the right housed a woman's clothes and make-up. Half empty.

Boonstra's walk-in wardrobe was on the left.

Suits in tidy rows. Shirts. Trousers. Ties on display, shoes in neat rows. Drawers of socks, underwear, cuff-links, pyjamas. A vulgar superfluity, more clothes than any man could need, all neatly ordered.

Behind the cupboard doors she found a corner where two other dressing gowns were hanging, and an empty hanger. She hung up the one he had been wearing, draping the belt over the hanger just like the other two.

She found a small carry-on case in a cupboard to the far left. She took it out. Packed a dark blue suit. Six shirts, six underpants, six pairs of socks. One pair of black shoes. Three ties.

She walked into the bathroom.

From her hip pocket her cell phone shrilled, breaking the silence. She leaped, startled.

Took it out.

Josef. Lord, she would have to speak calmly and quietly to him.

Deep breath. 'Hi.'

'Hey. Can we go and eat at twelve? My words have all evaporated.'

A rush of longing for him to hold her, a desire to be comforted, taken care of – 'don't worry, I will take care of everything', that's what she wanted to hear. She bit her lower lip to stop herself from bursting into tears. She fought against it so long that he asked: 'Are you okay?'

'I'm just finishing up with a client,' she said and looked at her watch. It was half past eleven, how time had flown, she was in a daze, it was the shock. Think, Sandra, think, wake up. 'I may be a little bit late.'

'No problem. At Spek & Bone?'

'Will be lovely, thank you. See you.'

'Love you.'

'You too.'

He rang off.

She felt terribly lonely in the big, silent house.

Then it struck her there wouldn't be any time before lunch to do anything with the body in her car.

Her greatest single priority was to carry on as normally as possible with her routine. As if nothing untoward had happened.

How on earth was she going to manage that?

When a detective didn't have a strong motivation, the application for a search warrant was a gamble. If you could get a sympathetic magistrate or judge – or one in a good mood – chances were better.

Griessel and Cupido rolled the judicial dice with the only available magistrate. She was not in a good mood. She was very pedantic. She said no.

They pleaded with her. It was a missing child, it was the new fifty-five protocol, there was huge pressure from the media, it was a race against the clock. She shook her head and said: 'He's not a child. He's twenty years old.'

'Your Honour, it's a matter of life and death,' said Cupido.

'Do you know what Chapter Two of the Criminal Procedure Act states?'

'Yes, Your Honour.'

'It states that, if it appears to me from information on oath that there are reasonable grounds for believing that the maintenance of law and order is likely to be endangered by, or that an offence has been or is being or is likely to be committed, or that preparations or arrangements for the commission of any offence are being or are likely to be made in or upon any premises within my area of jurisdiction, I can issue you with a search warrant.'

'Yes, Your Honour.'

'So, what is lacking in your application?'

'Reasonable grounds, Your Honour.'

'So why are you wasting this court's time, gentlemen? You should know better.'

When they were outside her office door, Griessel said: 'My fault. Sorry. You were right.'

'Some you win, partner, some you lose.'

Out of frustration and the growing pressure to make progress, to achieve something, Griessel said: 'Let's go to Capitec.'

Sandra put the case behind the front seat of her EcoSport. Then she draped her jacket over it, in case Josef walked to the car with her.

She took two sets of forms out of her handbag, the ones that clients signed when they authorised Benson International Realtors to sell a property. Upstairs again in the study she sat down at Boonstra's desk, using one of the pens she found in an unlocked drawer, and signed her own signature on the appropriate places on both forms. She arranged both the documents neatly, diagonal to the blotter, aligned with the meticulous order of everything on the desktop.

She opened the drawers one by one, searching for Boonstra's passport and ID document. She only found them when she retrieved the key from the eggshell bowl and opened the top drawer with its massive lock.

She made sure his signature was in the passport. She picked up the documents, locked the drawer, returned the key to the jellybeans.

She looked around, surveying the study. Everything seemed in order. She walked out, with the ID and passport in her hand.

Stopped once more at the stairs where Jasper Boonstra had fallen to his death, and thought carefully about what exactly happened since she came in. Precisely what she would say when the police came to talk to her. Precisely what she would offer as proof.

Then she hurried down the stairs, to her car.

She made sure she waved and smiled at the two guards in the guardhouse.

Sandra turned right on Jonkershoek Road, taut as a wire. If only she could pause, lessen the unbearable tension, just for a moment, knowing that she had got this far. But she knew it was out of the question. She would start to cry. And she couldn't afford that now. She had to be strong, not give anything away during her lunch with Josef.

She looked up at the Botmaskop mountain peak brooding over her on the right. Focus on that, to take her attention off everything else. She forced her thoughts to the professor who had refuted Jasper Boonstra's story about the origin of Baronsberg's name in the newspaper. He wrote that few people knew where Botmaskop got its name. No, it wasn't from someone named Botma. It was an abbreviation of Bootmanskop. Boat Man's Peak. In the late 1600s the farmers of Stellenbosch were keen to know when there were ships approaching Table Bay, so that they could take their meat and wine and grain and fruit and vegetables to sell. From up there the boat man could clearly see False Bay and Table Bay. And warn the farmers.

That was what she needed now. A boat man. To warn her. When her ship was coming in.

The EcoSport's instrument panel indicated precisely twelve o'clock.

41

The woman from Capitec that Griessel had spoken to over the phone was called Megan Daniels. Brisk, forty-something, her hands spoke along with her – small, busy movements – when she said she was going to give the case her immediate attention. They could wait, or they could come back in about half an hour, it was such a strange thing, the child disappearing, with all that money in his account.

Griessel asked her to handle the matter with the utmost discretion.

'Of course, good heavens, I understand all too well.'

And then they waited, as this was their only hope.

Griessel sat watching the people walking up and down the corridors of the Eikestad shopping centre and thought about the huge sums of money in Callie de Bruin's account, and of the very small balance of his own. The second half of his son Fritz's very expensive film school fees was due at the end of this month, and he was going to be short. Thanks to the lower salary of a warrant officer. How could he cut the boy's allowance, with their relationship already so shaky . . . He would have to cut costs somewhere, ask for an overdraft. But when? His bank branch was in the city, and to ask for leave now, would look really bad in Witkop Jansen's eyes.

In the bank, Cupido jumped up. 'Fuck it, Benna, can you smell that too?'

'What?'

'The Spur steaks. And chips.'

Griessel sniffed. 'Yes.'

'The gods of fat are taunting me, *pappie*. I'm so hungry I could pass out.'

He was sitting inside Spek & Bone, because it was still drizzling. He looked up when she entered, gave her his warm Josef smile, and she tried not to think of the corpse in the back of her car. She could no longer suppress the memory of Boonstra's last words: *I mean, your husband is out there screwing all the students . . .*

It was a lie. It was a lie.

He stood up and opened his arms to her. The craving to surrender herself to his embrace was overwhelming: just let him enfold her, protect her from the demons relentlessly pursuing her.

Don't give anything away, don't behave oddly. She hugged him, kissed him, then said: 'Your words have dried up?' she sat down.

'I have to start a new chapter,' he said, 'and I don't know what I want to do with it.'

'Sleep on it. That always works.'

'The bedroom is part of my planned solution, but not necessarily for sleeping.' Playful, the old Josef.

She forced a smile, with all her will.

'I thought, after lunch . . .' he said.

'Now? This afternoon?'

'My creative need is great,' he said suggestively.

Her thoughts raced in search of a response.

She didn't want to. Could not. Not now. Not in this state. Something was about to explode, a dam wall threatening to burst, pent-up fear, shock and revulsion and self-hatred and things that she had no words for. She could not have sex with her husband now. Not with Boonstra's words echoing in her mind. Not with Jasper dead in the boot of her car. Not with everything that she still had to do, the list of things to arrange, to put in order, was too long. Her mind was screaming at her: Be normal, be normal!

She found the ability to focus from somewhere, put out her hand and rested it on Josef's. Squeezed it. She had to address the first task on her list, laying the foundation of her alibi. 'Do you remember, I told you about the big transaction, the one we had to sign a confidentiality agreement . . .'

'Yes . . .'

'I know these last few weeks . . . I've been a bit absent. And stressed. I'm so sorry about that. Really, really sorry. It was such a difficult time. The sale . . . I'll tell you everything when the sale has gone through . . . It's all a bit surreal . . . No, it's totally surreal. You could write a book about it.'

Only a faint smile; she knew he hated it when people said that, but she didn't care. She had a job to do here.

'I've just come from the client. It's all signed, I have to get the contract to the buyer urgently. Before they change their terms again. It has to go through. We need it, Josef. We need it a lot. Not just Benson International, but you and me and the girls. Then I can relax and be a much better wife, and we can stay in bed for a week . . .'

He squeezed her hand. 'I'm being selfish,' he said. 'You're the best wife in the world. I know it hasn't been easy these past months. I appreciate what you do, a lot, and I appreciate that through it all you have given me the chance to write. Forgive me . . .'

'Nothing to forgive. Thank you for understanding.'

'Let's enjoy our food and then you go and finish up with your contract.'

'Thank you.' Such relief, but she had to keep her emotions under control.

'Did you hear about the student who disappeared?' he asked.

'No,' she said. 'Tell me about it.'

Griessel and Cupido sat in the Spur, with the documentation and explanatory notes from Capitec.

Griessel ordered a toasted sandwich, the cheapest item on the menu. Vaughn wanted a sirloin, 'exactly two hundred grams, no chips, no onion rings, no sauce. Medium rare. And a garden salad,' after he had totted it all up on his dieting app.

Then they examined the annotated bank statements.

Megan Daniels from Capitec first gave them a summary of the origin of Callie de Bruin's income: the smaller amounts all came from businesses in the Cape – gold dealers, antique shops, pawn shops. The smallest figure was just under a thousand rand, the highest nine thousand. There were twenty-seven deposits of that kind.

But what took them by surprise was the origin of the large amounts.

All four were in dollars, from the USA – two were just over fifty thousand rand, one for one hundred and ten thousand rand and one of a hundred and twenty-one thousand rand. Megan Daniels provided a printout of how Callie had declared them to comply with the Reserve

Bank's specifications for foreign exchange. In all four cases it was: *Specialist services, programming.*

Griessel arranged the bank statements on the table.

'It's two different worlds,' he said.

'The American income ... He's a hacker for hire,' said Cupido. 'Those dudes steal credit card details and sell them, there's a thousand schemes ...'

'Remember that *ou* back at Alibi.co.za who made money like that? With the flaws in programs, when he reported them, the people would pay him ...?'

'*Ja, ja* ... Dicky Grobler?'

'No, *Rick* Grobler. You called him Tricky Ricky. His money came from overseas.'

'Zero-day vulnerabilities, that was what he called them. But Benna, that was legit. Above board, good and legal. Why would Callie hide legit money in a secret back account? Along with that other income, which I scheme is ill-gotten gains. Rolster stole, Callie fenced, so sort of an income on the side. And for the big stuff he hacked, call it phishing in international waters, if you get my drift.'

Griessel considered the idea. It was a valid argument. '*Fok*,' he said, because it meant footwork. They would have to go to the gold dealers, all the second-hand, antique and pawn shops. While they waited for Megan Daniels to work through the international bank channels and try to find out where the large sums came from. He didn't hold out much hope. If it was cyber-crime, the trail would go cold somewhere.

Sandra forced herself to eat, although she still felt nauseous. The phrase kept echoing through her mind: be normal, the way you always are. She could feel her strength ebbing, the dreadful tension starting to take its toll, the effort of suppressing everything, acting light-hearted, of not thinking about Boonstra's final words when she looked at her husband, so relaxed and at ease.

She didn't want him to walk to the car with her, so she got up before he had paid the bill. She said she had to go, thank you, this was exactly what she'd needed. Would he pick up the children, please, it was going to be a long afternoon ...

'Of course,' said Josef. He hugged her, kissed her, and she left him there. When she walked out the door into Dorp Street, she looked across to where she had parked, convinced that the police would already be forming a ring around the EcoSport, waiting for her.

But there was only a beggar playing car guard. 'I watched it *mooi*, ma'am,' he said.

She tipped him ten rand. 'I can see you did,' she said.

42

She drove to the house in Brandwacht Street, the one with the owners already in the USA.

She opened the gate with the remote control, drove up to the garage, waited for the gate to shut behind her. Then she sat for a moment, relieved to have made it to this point.

She got out and tried to establish how visible she was.

The two houses on either side were both double storey, just like this one. The property on the right was an Airbnb rental that only occasionally had occupants. The one on the left concerned her the most. The senior Distell manager lived there with his family, which included two high-school children. There might be someone home.

It was still raining, which would help. The neighbouring house looked quiet enough now, and the wall and position of the home's windows were to her advantage. She wasn't worried they would see her in the driveway – she had good reason to be there after all. It was when she pulled into the garage that it might look strange. She prayed that the teenagers were somewhere glued to a screen.

She walked purposefully to the front door, while scrabbling for the keys in her handbag.

She unlocked the door and went in, walked straight to the garage, turned on the lights.

The freezer was in there, the wide, deep chest freezer, switched off. It was for the meat, when he went hunting in the Karoo, the owner had explained to her.

She measured it with her eye.

It seemed big enough.

And there was a catch. She would need a padlock.

The first thing she did was to switch the freezer on at the wall socket. It shuddered for a second and then began to work with a quiet hum.

She pressed the button on the wall to open the garage door.

* * *

At the office the first thing that Griessel and Cupido looked at was the list of smaller payments, comparing them to the numbers of gold dealers and second-hand shops that Callie had spoken with.

There were quite a few matches, so that Vaughn said: 'Progress, Benna, progress at last.'

Then, just before they began to phone the businesses, Mbali Kaleni rang. 'There's a box of your stuff that you need to collect, Warrant Officer, it is cluttering up my office.'

'Would about seven o'clock be okay, Colonel?'

'Yes, that will be fine,' she said.

Cupido put the phone down. 'Let's get this party started,' he said.

Rigor mortis had set in.

In the back of the EcoSport, Jasper Boonstra's body was stiff as a board. His feet were hooking behind one edge of the rear door, his hips on the other side. The flesh was cold under her hands as she pushed and pulled and groaned, the lunch she'd just eaten rising up her throat, the nausea back again, please, she didn't want to vomit on him now.

Sandra let go, went into the kitchen to catch her breath. That urgent, panicky feeling – finish it, finish it, this is the hardest, most horrible part, but it has to be done, *done now.*

She went back to the garage. Soft rain murmured on the corrugated iron roof of the garage. She grabbed him by the ankles, jerked hard, wrenching him free from the obstruction. His entire body turned, stiff, so that he nearly toppled out. Awkwardly, she wedged her hands under his arms. Lord, that hairy chest was so revolting. Dragged him out.

He was too heavy; he slipped from her arms, onto the cement floor.

She began to weep, quietly, in desperation and exhaustion and fear. Fought it, suppressed it. She saw the reddish-blue livor mortis discolouration of the skin on his right side that had been underneath when he was lying in her car. She shuddered. She dragged him by the feet towards the freezer. Opened the lid.

The freezer was starting to cool down rapidly inside. At least it was working. Now to get him up and over the edge. There was enough room for him inside.

She took a deep breath, got a grip around his flabby belly again. Now or never, the last big hurdle, the last intense burst of effort: come on, you can do it, you have to do it. Adrenaline and fear. She made a sound, guttural and desperate, and lifted him up to the edge. For a second it seemed that he would fall back, but she pushed the body forward with all her strength, so that his body landed head first with a dull thud.

Sandra slammed the lid shut. Then she fled into the house, at last able to weep and weep and weep.

The gold and jewellery dealers, pawn shops and second-hand shops all said they would have to consult their records, it would take time to determine whether Callie de Bruin had sold goods to them. Especially if it was more than three months ago.

Only the woman at the Darling Street Gold Exchange asked Griessel to hold on, she would look it up on the computer quickly.

Less than two minutes later she confirmed: 'Yes, Warrant Officer, I have a record. It was jewellery, three gold rings, two sets of gold earrings with diamond studs, and a one-tenth ounce Kruger Rand. Bought from a C. W. de Bruin, he is a registered supplier. For seven thousand two hundred rand.'

'What does that mean?'

'Well, it means that he came in, registered with us by supplying proof of residence and ID, and that we have bought from him more than once.'

'Okay, do you know how he acquired the jewellery?'

'We assume he bought it from someone. But we *do* check all the SAPS bulletins for stolen goods, if that is what you mean.'

'My problem is, there doesn't seem to be any record in his bank account indicating that he bought it. How much would he have paid, more or less?'

'I honestly can't tell you. Some of the suppliers bid at auctions, others keep an eye on deceased estates. It depends on a lot of things. My best guess would be around five or six thousand . . .'

'So how does it work? He brings it in, and you pay him?'

'Oh, no. Goods are paid for after a week or two, sometimes longer. It gives us time to check the bulletins, and do the full appraisal.'

'So, this payment went through about five weeks ago. When did he bring it in?'

'Let me check . . . It says here that he brought it in on Monday, 29 August.'

Griessel thought this through. How would Callie have got to Darling Street in the city? If he took an Uber, his mother would have known about it. 'Are you sure he brought it in himself?'

'I can't tell you right off the bat, of course, but we can look at the video . . .'

'You have CCTV?'

'We do. We keep the footage for three months. It's going to take an hour or so, Warrant Officer, if you don't mind.'

'Of course.'

'Can I send you the footage on WhatsApp?'

'Do you perhaps have any photographs of the jewellery?'

'Yes, we do.'

'Please send that too.'

Sandra lay with her head on her arms at the dining room table, the house deathly silent, only the gentle hiss of the rain outside audible. Her tears had left her empty, exhausted. She didn't think she had strength to stand.

But she must. She was not finished. She still had two tasks to complete.

She got up at last and walked to her car in the garage to fetch her handbag.

She didn't look at the freezer, only listened to its quiet murmuring. She sat down at the table again and took out her phone. She rang Mareli Vorster's number and waited to be put through.

She scraped the energy together to sound upbeat when she spoke to the woman: 'Hello, Mareli. I have all the documents ready for you. May I courier them?'

'Oh, wonderful, Demeter will be delighted. Yes, please send them marked for my attention.'

'It will only reach you tomorrow. We would appreciate it if you would prepare our payment in the meantime, so we can finalise this as soon as possible.'

'If everything is in order, Sandra, we will do the EFT on Friday.'

Sandra thanked her and rang off.

Two days. Then the money would be in.

She took Jasper Boonstra's passport out of her handbag, opened it at the identification page, where his signature appeared.

She put a pen and a few of the mandate forms next to it.

She sat at the table and practised the signature, over and over, until she was satisfied.

Then she signed one of the forms. In his name.

She would add Baronsberg's information at work, after she had researched it on the Lightstone system.

Just before four the Darling Street Gold Exchange sent Griessel the photos of the jewellery and the video screen grab of their delivery.

It showed clearly that it was not Callie de Bruin.

The person who delivered the jewellery was Roland 'The Rolster' Parker.

43

Sandra refreshed herself in the bathroom of the Brandwacht house. She washed her face, brushed her hair, reapplied make-up. It was hard to look at her reflection in the mirror. She didn't know this woman. Didn't want to know her.

She walked to the front door to make certain it was locked, made a mental note to go and buy a padlock for the freezer, just to make doubly sure.

And then it hit her like a hammer blow – the case with Boonstra's clothes was still behind the driver's seat in the Ford. She had forgotten it completely. Lord, Sandra, you can't afford this. One false step, one little mistake and you'll go to jail. The excuse of self-defence, of harassment and the threat of rape, all that was irrelevant now, you can't, you dare not mess up now.

She fetched the case from the car.

She looked at the freezer. She couldn't bear to open it again.

To the right of the freezer were steel shelves against the wall with garden equipment, shade cloth, a few sun umbrellas and swimming pool piping. She lifted up the case, pushed it under the shade cloth, arranging everything exactly as it had been before.

Only then did she get in the car and drive away.

On the way back to the office she had to concentrate very hard on regaining her equilibrium. Charlie was sharp, perceptive when it came to her mood, he picked up cues very quickly. She would have to be careful.

He was in his office, busy with admin. He looked up when she knocked on the door frame. 'Sandy-my-sweet. I'm so glad you're here. We must talk . . .'

'What about, Charlie?'

'Our financial situation doesn't look good. Not good at all. The end of this month . . . I don't know how we are going to manage.'

'Then I have some very good news for you.' She sat down across from him, took the documents from her handbag, and put them in front of him one by one. 'The Donkerdrif deal is sorted, Charlie. Stirling and Heyns say we will get our money on Friday.'

'Longoria! I could kiss you.' His entire demeanour changed from downcast to delighted and his knee stopped twitching.

'Charlie, today is actually the day I would kiss you back.'

He laughed. 'That's a first.'

'Let me tell you why. I was with Jasper most of the morning. He . . .' For a split second she was going to use the past tense and say 'He was . . .' but she stopped herself in time, with a flash of panic, she had to be careful. 'He is very impressed with our work . . .'

She took out the mandate document, the one with Boonstra's falsified signature, and put it down in front of Charlie. 'He wants us to put Baronsberg on the market. Sole mandate.'

'*Jitte Krismis.*'

'He asked me to leave another two contracts with him, because he is considering selling Franschhoek and Rooi-Els. But all on condition that we must never, ever, say a word about Donkerdrif.'

Charlie's mouth moved, but no sound emerged.

Then he jumped up, ran around the desk and planted a kiss on her mouth with his damp old man's lips.

Roland Parker's mother said he wasn't at home, he was at Le Sports, a sports bar down in Anthony Street.

'Aunty,' Cupido said to her, 'phone him, please, and tell him to come, we don't want to embarrass him in front of his pals.'

'What do you want with my child? He's clean. You know that.'

'Aunty, I'm saying again: we are looking for Callie de Bruin, and Rolster can help us. He knows stuff, he just won't say . . . Call him, please.'

She phoned her son, right there at the front door. She was stern with him. 'Rolster, you come now, and say what you have to say, do you understand your mommy? What does it look like if the Boere are here at my doorstep every day?'

Stiff with anger, she invited them in.

They sat down in the sitting room. The scent of cooking wafted in, cumin and cardamom, coriander and curry.

Cupido moaned softly. 'What is aunty cooking?'

'Chicken breyani,' she admitted reluctantly.

'*Jirre*,' said Cupido.

'You don't come into my house and take the Lord's name in vain, I don't care if you're a policeman,' she said and began walking to the kitchen.

'Sorry, aunty,' he said. Then, as soon as she was gone: 'Benna, why do the slimming gods hate me so much?'

Sandra made copies of the Donkerdrif contracts between Huber AG and Demeter, packaged them up, and phoned the courier to pick it up early the next morning.

She filled in the sole mandate forms, with the details of Baronsberg that she got off the Lightstone system, and put them down on her desk.

Then she walked to Charlie's office to tell him she was just quickly going to run a few errands in town before going home.

'Honey pie, I'm very proud of you,' he said.

If you only knew, Charlie, she thought, if you only knew.

Roland Parker smelt of booze when he came in. With a devil-may-care attitude.

'Rolster,' his mother said, curry spoon in hand, standing in the doorway to the sitting room. 'If you know about the Callie boy and you don't tell them, you'll have me to deal with, do you understand?'

'*Ja*, Mommy. I don't know anything.'

'Now sit down and talk to the people.'

She went back into the kitchen. Parker sat meekly opposite the detectives.

'Rolster, we can keep up this dance. We can come back every day; we can make your life very hard. Let me repeat, our beef is not with you. Just help us to find Callie.'

'We've already had this conversation.'

'Take us through all the things you had to deliver for Callie.'

'Are you stupid or what? I *mos* already told you.'

'Tell us again,' said Griessel.

He sighed deeply. 'Computers and computer parts, an old wardrobe, an old car. That's about it.'

'About?'

A sense of wariness came over Parker when he realised they knew something.

'That's what I can remember.'

'Think carefully, Rolster,' Cupido said.

He pondered theatrically, chin on hand. 'There were lots of deliveries for Callie. What if I forgot something? Then you'll just call me a liar.'

'So I'll say it again: think carefully.'

Another pause for thought. 'Maybe there was a parcel once, I don't know what was in it.'

'That you delivered where?'

'I can't remember.'

'Ball park. Paarl? Bellville? Salt River? Where?'

'Durbanville . . . I'm not sure.'

'And that's that?' Cupido asked.

A shrug. 'As far as I can remember.'

'What about Kruger Rands, Rolster?'

Parker's eyes were guarded now. He looked intently at Vaughn. 'Kruger Rands?' Playing for time.

'You know, those gold coins with the springbok on them.'

'They might have been in the parcel. I don't know.'

'You've never seen one?'

'Never.'

That's when they knew they had him.

Sandra bought a hefty padlock at Builders Express in Dorp Street, then drove back to the Brandwacht house.

She parked outside, grateful the rain had stopped.

She went in the front door, walked through to the garage, took the padlock out of its packaging.

A peculiar moment of doubt: was he still inside? She opened the lid of the freezer and knew immediately it was a big mistake to look.

He was lying there, frozen solid, still bent double the way he had been in the EcoSport.

She slammed the lid shut, pushed the padlock through the two eyes of the catch and pressed the lock closed.

She would have to hide the keys somewhere.

They showed Rolster the video on Griessel's cell phone.

The camera was up on the ceiling of the Darling Street Gold Exchange, focused down on the counter and the door. The silent clip showed The Rolster enter, hands empty. He greeted the woman like an old friend, then put his hand in his pocket, took out the jewellery and put it down on the counter. The woman spread the items out. She took out a jeweller's magnifying glass, bent down and examined them carefully. The Rolster seemed to look directly at the camera then, without being aware it was there.

'What do you say now, Rolster?'

'I told you, I can't remember everything.' There was something new in his eyes, in the tone of his voice. Fear.

'But you will, Rolster. You *will*.'

She wanted to hide the key in the wardrobe of the master bedroom, right at the top, right at the back, out of sight. Not that anybody would look there, but she knew it would be a safe place.

She stood on tiptoe, had to stretch to reach, put the keys down. She checked exactly where she had put them, shut the wardrobe door.

At least brief relief. All done. For now. Ready for the storm that lay ahead.

Someone would come and talk to her. The police, for sure, when they began to look for Boonstra. Because she was the last person who had been with him.

Let them come. She had her story ready.

She went to stand in front of the window, staring outside, just to take a moment's breather in this horrible, frenetic day. It wasn't much help, because her thoughts kept returning to the greater, more terrible challenge ahead: she would eventually have to dispose of the body.

How?

She hadn't a clue. In her mind she pictured the freezer sinking into the depths of the ocean, the padlock still on the catch, but she knew that was impossible. Where would she find a boatman who would do that?

Maybe if she had enough money to pay someone?

No, no. No witnesses.

She had time to think. The body was safe here for now.

She slowly became aware of something over there, at the neighbouring house. The Airbnb. A movement caught her eye, something a bit odd.

She focused, looked hard at the house.

It all happened so fast. Just a few seconds, a young man's face in the window, barely thirty metres away, on the first floor. A look of desperation? He looked at her, shouted something, she could see his mouth move, but not hear anything. Two men grabbed him from behind, pulled him down.

Sandra was scared, stepped back behind the curtain. Looked again, cautiously.

Nothing now.

At the window, someone pulled the blinds down.

For a second she thought the young man looked like the missing student, the one whose photo Josef had shown her over lunch, on Twitter.

No, surely not. She was suffering from shock. Seeing things. Or could it be real?

44

'Why are you looking so pale now, Rolster?' Cupido asked.

'I forgot about that one, now you think I'm lying. I'm on parole.'

'Where does that jewellery come from?'

'Callie gave it to me.'

'Where did he get it?'

'I couldn't say.'

'Now we're back doing the same old couldn't-say waltz again. Okay, tell you what. We have a theory, Rolster. Here's a pile of jigsaw pieces, and it's all starting to make a picture, and the picture doesn't look very pretty for you. We think Callie found you on the Krim system. The Krim system is a database that registers all the criminals in the country. If you have a record, you're there. Now, we think Callie hacked into the Krim system, because he was looking specially for an *ou* like you who can break into houses. You're *lekker* close by, here in Stellenbosch, you're a famous cat burglar, a match made in heaven. So he offers you a deal. He takes you out of the system, you do the stealing, he's the fence, the mastermind who gets rid of the stolen goods. How are we doing so far, Rolster?'

'That's your little fantasy, I know nothing about anything like that.'

'So, you took the deal, because then you can get legit work too, we know, it's not easy when you have a record. As an added bonus, with no criminal record, and a legit job, it gives you *lekker* cover if you want to dabble in a spot of cat burglary. And then you began with your little lucrative, multi-skilled partnership. Why are we saying that, Rolster? 'Cause why, there's no payments in Callie's bank account for jewellery or wardrobes or computer parts or old cars. Nada. Zilch. Zero. He never paid for a thing. Except for the fancy clothes that you bought together at the Waterfront. He never withdrew enough cash, never did EFTs or paid with his card. Bottom line, he never paid for this jewellery. Because you went and stole them.'

'Bullshit.'

'Maybe, maybe not. But let me tell you something. Your average police station detective knows, if a guy comes to report they broke into my house, they stole my girlfriend's jewellery, the detective knows the dude really just wants the case number for the insurance. And he and the complainant quickly rattle off the details of the jewellery, and by the time the bulletin goes out to the gold dealers, it's very late and very vague. And we know those gold dealers, they only pay lip service to the bulletins anyway, because a deal's a deal. We know the game. So, here's what we're going to do, Rolster. We're going to trace everything that you handed in at the dealers. Every payment that Callie received. We're going to get more videos, and more photos of the jewellery. 'Cause why, you know there's more. This was just the tip of the iceberg. And we're going to send the photos to every cop shop in the Western Cape, and ask, boys, do these correspond with anything stolen in the past two years? Have a good look, because this is a fifty-five, a missing person case, and with a fifty-five the police look very hard, Rolster. We go to a lot of trouble. No stone unturned. And then we are going to arrest you, for dealing in stolen goods, and you are going to sit for a long time, with your previous conviction and all.'

Roland Parker was extremely pale now. 'I'm not scared of you,' he said, but without conviction.

'If you help us now,' said Benny Griessel, 'if you tell us what Callie has got himself into, if you help us to track him down, then we will drop our investigation of you.'

'Think how happy Mommy will be,' said Cupido and motioned towards the kitchen.

Parker bit his lip. He glanced towards the door, and back, dragged the fingers of his right hand through his hair. As if he was on the point of revealing everything, as though this would be a solution, a relief.

Then he shook his head.

'I don't know anything.'

Sandra drove slowly back to the house.

She was exhausted.

Tomorrow would be a better day.

She had to get back to her children. She longed for her girls, for the warmth of their little bodies, their unconditional love. She had to behave normally, especially in front of Josef, especially when the police came knocking, so that he wouldn't wonder why she was so 'off' today, so absent.

I mean, your husband is out there screwing all the students . . .

Where was Josef when his car was parked down in Ryneveld Street?

Oh, yes. An M student who wanted some advice. We went for a coffee at Häzz.

A female master's student? What sort of advice did she need exactly?

Did Jasper Boonstra lie about it, to help get her into bed? Did he really, really think that would work?

Or had his people, during their research into her and her family and their financial affairs, found evidence that Josef was unfaithful?

She didn't want to think about that now. She didn't want to think about anything. Not about what she had seen at the Airbnb house either. She just wanted to sleep. For a very long time.

But she couldn't do that either. She had to give the appearance of normality. Be a mother. And a happy spouse who had just pulled off a massive business deal.

At first they spoke nicely.

'You're scared of something, Rolster, we can tell,' said Benny Griessel. 'We can help you. We can protect you.'

He just stared at the floor.

'Who have you pissed off?' Cupido asked. 'Some place you broke into? Did you steal something that someone didn't want other people to know about? Gangstas, Rolster?'

No response.

'Only gangstas make people this scared. We have witness protection, for your mommy too . . .'

Rolster's eyes remained fixed on the ground.

'You don't even have to testify, Rolster,' Griessel said. 'Just help us. Nobody needs to know we were here.'

'It's a little late for that.'

'So you *are* scared?'

He just stared out of the window.

Then they began to threaten him with subpoenas, to delve into his bank statements, his cell phone records, with a search warrant because the video material gave them sufficient grounds.

'You can do whatever you like. I don't know where Callie is, and I don't know what he was up to.'

It was hunger and frustration and the pressure from their commanding officer and the race against time and the lack of progress that made Vaughn Cupido lose his temper. 'Fuck you,' he said and got up, pointing a threatening finger at Parker. 'You know, I'm telling you now, if that child turns up dead and I find out you knew something, *anything*, Rolster, I'm going to come after you. With the full weight of the law. Accessory to murder, obstruction of justice, the whole *fokken* toot. I'm going to put you away for so long, you'll need one of those walkers when you come out. I'm going to get you, motherfucker. I'm going to get you.'

They drove to Mbali Kaleni's townhouse in Oak Glen, Bellville.

'Drugs, partner?' Cupido asked. 'Those international payments in Callie's account. Drug-related?'

'I don't know . . . They would have had to have exported drugs, for that money to come back in. All we can export from here is dagga.'

'Why not? Durban poison, treasured and cherished by potheads all over the world. The gangs supply, Callie exports, but he doesn't pay his suppliers. It might fit.'

Griessel nodded. 'But the phone and bank records . . . There's nothing.'

'*Fok*,' said Cupido and slammed the steering wheel with the flat of his hand, out of sheer frustration. Then he repeated the word over and over, for good measure. Griessel knew exactly how he felt.

At last: 'It's gangstas, Benna. Only explanation, that is the only thing that can make a coloured *outjie* that frightened. He's shit scared of the gangstas. He's scared they'll get him and he's scared they'll get his ma. All we have to figure out is how he and Callie got mixed up with the gangstas, and how they pissed them off.'

'The video of Hoody who went into his room. We must send that to the Gangs unit. Maybe they will recognise him.'

'Check.'

*   *   *

Lieutenant Colonel Mbali Kaleni was making pancakes. They smelled them at the door when she opened it, and Cupido's heart sank, because he knew he was too hungry to turn them down, and despair washed over him about his attempt to lose weight. Maybe he was just born to be fat.

She greeted them warmly, clearly happy to see them. And yet, there was something serious in her expression, as if she had some bad news.

She invited them inside. Her townhouse was painfully neat, but by no means minimalist. Photos on the walls, memorabilia of her travels in a display cabinet and on bookshelves. Potted plants, crocheted covers on the small coffee tables. She invited them to sit down at the breakfast bar. 'You must be very hungry, it's such a cold, rainy day. I have made pancakes with cinnamon and lemon. Coffee? Tea? Hot chocolate?'

They said thank you, coffee would be good.

This home, Griessel thought, reminded him of his granny's house in Parow when he was a child. There was that warmth, and a comfortable, cosy feeling, the atmosphere, the scent in the air, the constant promise of something to eat and drink. Mbali's movements in this space were fluid and easy; her house, her home, her domain. As if she could truly be herself here.

'How are you, Benny?' she asked.

'Relieved to be in Stellenbosch, Colonel,' he said, in the hopes that she would add something about why they hadn't been sent to Laingsburg.

Mbali merely nodded and served up four rolled pancakes on a plate for each of them, passing them cutlery.

'We have a great deal to discuss,' she said, switching the kettle on and spooning instant coffee into the mugs. 'Please eat, we don't want the pancakes to get cold.'

They ate. With relish.

'I reached out to the Mitchells Plain station commissioner yesterday,' said Kaleni. 'Carefully. Just to offer the Hawks' help with the Milo April murder. He told me they have nothing. They had a look at all Sergeant April's dockets, and all they could find that was gang-related was a raid on a meth lab in Philippi that Milo April had led. On the eighteenth of September. Which was just a few days before he reached out to you, isn't that right, Benny?'

Griessel took out his notebook, paged through it. 'Yes, Colonel. I got his first letter on the twenty-third.'

'Okay. So, the lab they raided . . . He tells me it was run by a gang called the Restless Ravens . . .'

'The Ravens? Really?' Cupido asked.

'You know about them?'

'Everybody knew about them, back in the day, Colonel. They were quite a force. Had this psycho called Tweetybird de la Cruz as a leader. Bad apple, used to leave budgies in his victims' mouths after he killed them. And then he got killed himself, three, four years ago, and they quickly fell apart. Last I heard, they had a few splinter groups competing for turf, angling for control and leadership. Small-time stuff.'

'Yes, the station commissioner had the same view. That they just do not have the muscle and the numbers to call a hit on a policeman. He says they have an informant in the Ravens, and the word is, it wasn't them.'

'So then, who *was* it?' asked Griessel.

'The colonel told me they've got absolutely nothing, they just can't understand it. And then he said he can't even bear to take calls from Milo April's girlfriend any more. So, I thought, maybe April told her things. I asked for her number, I told him I just wanted to sympathise. And that's when it got interesting . . .'

'What did she say?'

Colonel Kaleni looked at her watch. 'She should be here any minute now. She can tell you herself.'

45

Chriselda Plaatjies was fine-boned and petite. She was reserved, and clearly depressed now, but her voice was musical and something about her suggested that in happier circumstances she would be a lively creature.

She sat holding a cup of tea in one hand and a tissue in the other. She told Cupido and Griessel: 'Milo April was my fiancé. We were going to get married in December.' Her eyes welled up and she dabbed them with the tissue.

'It's okay, my dear, you cry all you want,' said Kaleni and passed Cupido another couple of pancakes.

Plaatjies sipped her tea, then said: 'I don't know much at all. I don't know who shot Milo. But he did tell me he was going to contact you. He believed you were the only policemen he could trust, because you were suspended over that state-capture affair. He said your hearts are in the right place.'

'Do you know why he went to the Waterfront that day?' asked Griessel.

'Yes. He wanted to show you the gun. And tell you the story about the gun. It was that story that made him so paranoid. And so scared. That's the story that got him killed.'

'Tell us, sister. Please,' said Cupido.

The story had been bottled up in Chriselda Plaatjies for a long time, and when she let it out, it was a jumble of feelings and impressions, information and emotion, so that they often had to interrupt her to get a proper chronological sense of her story.

She told them she was a sales assistant at Queenspark factory shop in Salt River. She and Milo April had lived together for nearly two years in Weltevredenvallei in Mitchells Plain. They were saving up for their December wedding. They had a close relationship, an honest and open understanding, because both of them came from broken homes where divorce and dishonesty had resulted in tension and conflict. They wanted to avoid that at all costs. She was telling them this, she explained, so they could understand why Milo would always be sure to tell her these things. But not straight away. He was too careful.

It started in May, nearly five months ago. Milo came home, still pumped from the action; there had been a robbery at Buco, the building suppliers opposite the Mitchells Plain railway station. He was one of the policemen who had raced to the scene, and been involved in a shoot-out with the cornered robbers. He described the chaos, the fear and excitement, and his eventual distress at standing beside the bodies of the criminals.

And then he told her about the 'helse gun', as he called it.

The Smith & Wesson Model 500, Cupido confirmed with her.

Yes, she said. Milo had said you don't see a firearm like that in your everyday robbery, the thing boomed like a cannon, the shots were deafening and hugely destructive as they hit cars and walls.

And two nights later he told her the commissioner had come to visit, to congratulate them. Their actions had even been reported on TV: the robbery that had been foiled, and the robbers shot.

'Are we talking about the provincial commissioner?' Griessel asked.

'Yes. General Khaba,' she answered. 'The one in the photo.' She carried on: Milo showed the big revolver to the general. The general was fascinated by it. He examined it, held it, he said: 'Man, I'd also love a piece like this.' And that's when they took the photo, of the general and the gun. Milo had shown her the photo, on his cell phone.

It had been months since they'd talked about the 'helse gun'. Till the night of the eighteenth of September. Now, just a few weeks ago.

Milo had come home later than usual, tense and quiet. She asked him, Milo, what's going on? At first he wouldn't say. She was concerned. They argued, he kept saying it was better she didn't know. Until she began to cry, and reminded him about their agreement to talk to each other about everything. He went outside for a bit, and a little later he came back in and took her to the bedroom. There he took the big revolver out of the cupboard, and said: 'This is the same one, Chrissie.' The same one he had processed in May, after the Buco robbery. The one with the piece shot out of the butt and here it was again, the butt clumsily repaired, but still the same weapon.

The one that the general so badly wanted.

He told her that the previous day they'd heard about a methampheta-mine factory in Philippi. Early that morning they raided it. It wasn't a big operation, four people arrested, a few hundred thousand rands' worth of tik seized. And this revolver, in the glove compartment of a minibus. The young gang member just said he didn't know where it came from or how it had landed in the cubby hole. The usual stubborn denial.

Milo was very worried, because he'd been the one to process the Smith & Wesson in May, doing everything by the book. So he didn't mention it to anybody, and back at work he looked it up on the system. 'And the gun wasn't on the system any more,' he said. 'Milo talked about eye-bus, that there was an eye-bus and now there isn't one . . . I didn't really understand.'

'IBIS,' said Cupido. 'It's short for Integral Ballistic Identification System. If the state confiscates firearms, for example when they've been used in a crime, we send them to Pretoria and they fire the weap-ons to get ballistic records, and they assign it an IBIS number. It's a sort of ID number for firearms.'

'Okay. Milo said, there was an IBIS number a few months ago, and then, that day after the raid at the tik factory, it had vanished from the system, and here was the gun again. He was not happy and he phoned the colonel. And the colonel said he didn't know anything about the gun, Milo should ask the state-capture people how the gun got into the hands of the gangsters.'

They interrupted her, asked her which colonel Milo had contacted.

She didn't know.

Griessel asked: 'Was it his station head detective?'

'No, I know that colonel, that wasn't the name he said.'

'He mentioned a name?' Cupido asked.

'Yes, he mentioned a name. It . . . It was a while back. If I remember correctly, I thought it sounded like that man who coaches the Western Province rugby, what's his name . . .'

'The Western Province?'

'Yes. The WP.'

'John Dobson,' said Cupido.

She hesitated. 'I'm not so sure now . . . Anyway, Milo was very angry, he talked fast, he only said the colonel's name once, I think, and

I can't think why it reminded me of the rugby coach. But it wasn't the way the colonel reacted that spooked Milo. It was the anonymous call. That afternoon someone phoned Milo, the number was hidden, and the *ou* said to him, drop the thing about the gun. Drop it now, go throw that gun in the sea, or we will ambush Chriselda, you understand? And Milo said it was a coloured man who made that anonymous call, because of the language and the accent. And how did that coloured man know about the gun and his talk with the colonel? He thought someone was bugging his phone. So he told me to be very careful, and he was going to lie low for a while. Milo was thinking, for two days, then he told me he had a plan. He had an idea about people he could trust . . .'

At that moment Griessel's phone began ringing in Kaleni's living room. They all jumped at the sudden noise. Benny took the phone out and saw that it was his son, Fritz. He badly wanted to know what the boy had to say. But he couldn't, not right now.

'Sorry,' he said, and cut off the call. 'Carry on, Chriselda, please.'

She swallowed the last of her tea. 'Then I asked him, Milo, what are you going to do? And he said he was going to contact the two Hawks who were suspended over the state-capture affair, because he was sure he could trust them. I sat next to him at the table while he was writing the two letters with the photo.'

'You don't know if he discussed it with anyone at work? Or with a friend?' Griessel asked.

'No. I don't think he told anyone. He was different, he was angry, very worried, I could see it. He just said he'd dropped the letters off with you, he'd asked you to come to the Waterfront. And on the Friday, the day before he was shot, he said he was getting paranoid, it felt like he was being shadowed. But when he checked, there was nothing. And then, that Saturday, they murdered him.' Her face crumpled, her voice cracking. She dabbed the tissue again. 'So sorry,' she said. 'So sorry.'

'Cry all you want,' said Kaleni again.

They asked her if he had discussed the case with any of his colleagues. Or his head detective, or the station commissioner?

She said she didn't know. She got the idea that he didn't want to confide in anyone at Mitchells Plain police station. Because he didn't know where and how the weapon had been taken off the system, it might have been done there. A favour for the commissioner? And there were strong rumours that the commissioner was one of the corrupt president's appointments. She knew for a fact, after he had decided to contact Griessel and Cupido, Milo had only spoken to her about it.

Were there any other threats?

No, just the one phone call, and the feeling that Milo had, that someone was watching him.

The detectives thought it over. Chriselda Plaatjies dried her tears, got more tea and ate her pancakes. Then she asked: 'Do you know who . . . Was it the state-capture people?'

'No, sister, we don't know. But we are doing our very best to find out.'

All three of them saw Chriselda Plaatjies off in her car. The rain had stopped. When she drove away, Griessel, Cupido and Kaleni stood for a moment in silence between the shining puddles that reflected the street lights, a moment of quiet, as if they were in the eye of a storm.

'Colonel . . .' said Cupido at last.

'It's not the provincial commissioner, Vaughn,' she said.

'We have to make sure,' he said.

'I am sure. There are things I need to tell you. Why don't you come back inside?'

'Milo April's phone records,' said Griessel. 'The colonel he phoned, and the call he received . . .'

'That is a line of enquiry we will have to pursue carefully,' said Mbali. 'But it must be done. Let me think about it . . . But first, there are things you need to know.'

As they reached the front door Griessel's phone rang again.

Must be Fritz.

He looked. It was the Stellenbosch detective branch office. He answered.

'Griessel, you and Cupido will have to come in urgently,' said Colonel Witkop Jansen.

'Back to the office?' He checked his watch. It was nearly nine p.m.

'As fast as possible.'

'We're on our way, Colonel.' Griessel rang off, told Cupido: 'Witkop Jansen. He wants us. Urgently.'

'Now?'

'Yes.' To Mbali: 'Sorry, Colonel, we have to go back to Stellenbosch.'

'What is it you wanted to tell us?' Cupido asked.

'It sounds as if it will have to wait.'

46

They drove down Voortrekker Road, then through Kuils River and the Polkadraai road. They discussed the names of the colonels they knew whose surnames might remind one of the name or surname of the WP rugby coach, John Dobson. They considered Robson and Johnson and Hobson, then they were stuck because it rang no bells.

Griessel phoned Fritz.

'Are you sober, Pa?' his son asked him.

'I was in a meeting, Fritz. I'm still at work.'

'Okay.'

'How are you?'

'Pa, are you going to be sober on Sunday?'

He suppressed a sigh. He would have to be patient, but at least it sounded as though his son wanted to go for a meal.

'Yes, I'll be sober on Sunday too.'

'Can we *braai*? At Aunt Alexa's house?'

'Of course.'

'Okay.' A short pause, before Fritz said: 'I want to bring a girl along.' In a tone of voice that would brook no further questions.

Benny knew he had to tread very carefully and say the right thing. 'Okay,' was the safe answer.

'She . . . she's fascinated by Aunt Alexa.'

'I'm fascinated by Aunt Alexa too,' said Griessel.

Briefly, amazingly, Fritz laughed, the first time in years that Benny had heard that sound.

'Cool,' said Fritz. 'See you about twelve o'clock . . . Oh, *ja*, Pa, Kayla is a vegetarian.'

'Your girlfriend?'

'Yes. Okay, bye.'

And then he was gone and Cupido was eager to know: 'What was that all about?'

'Fritz is going to bring a girl on Sunday for a *braai*, but she's a vegetarian. Kayla.'

'I wonder if she's skinny,' said Vaughn.

They took turns, making their dutiful phone calls. Cupido phoned Desiree to tell her he was still at work. And he hadn't been able to keep to his kilojoule allowance because the gods of diets hated him.

'It's a journey, lovey,' she said. 'Adonis wasn't built in a day. Have you found the boy yet?'

Griessel called Alexa to tell her about Fritz, and Kayla the vegetarian, and that he'd been called back to work. She too wanted to know if they had found Callie de Bruin yet.

He postponed the call to Annemarie de Bruin; it was becoming increasingly hard to give her bad news.

He did phone her eventually. To tell her they were still working full steam, they were making progress, that was all he could say. And they hoped that tomorrow would bring more insights.

She took the news stoically. She thanked him for not giving up.

After that they drove in silence.

Griessel struggled to focus; it had been a long day. His thoughts wandered. From Annemarie de Bruin's lonely vigil in a guest house waiting for news of the death that surely was coming. To Fritz and the fact that he wanted to introduce his girlfriend to his father, what a huge step that was, a breakthrough perhaps, even if his son had tried to downplay it saying *She's fascinated by Aunt Alexa*. To Milo April and the fat commissioner and the Smith & Wesson. To Callie de Bruin and what they would have to do tomorrow. Hopefully Capitec would let them know what the international payments were for. He wondered why the university security people hadn't let them know about the car registration numbers that they were trying to check. And through it all he knew his subconscious was trying to tell him something, like a searchlight trying to illuminate something in the dusty back rooms of his brain, but there just wasn't enough candlepower.

Just past the Asara wine estate, with the lights of Stellenbosch scattered against the mountain, Vaughn Cupido broke the silence: 'I know why Witkop Jansen called us. They must have found the boy. This isn't going to be good news.'

Witkop Jansen was sitting behind his desk when they entered. He looked old and weary. He waved his hand: 'Sit down, boys.'

Cupido was sure he was right, if *this* colonel was being so friendly then it spelled bad news about Callie de Bruin. They sat down.

'Jasper Boonstra has disappeared,' said Jansen, as if bringing tidings of death.

For a second they were taken aback at the unexpected turn of events. Then Cupido spoke up: 'Jasper Boonstra?'

'Yes . . .'

'That dude who made every chartered accountant and fund manager in the country look like an idiot? Schneider-König's Jasper Boonstra? The Superman of swindlers?'

'Yes,' said Witkop Jansen dryly. 'That one.' He looked at Griessel. 'I want you to take the investigation. Erin Riddles is waiting for you at the farm, she's there to back you up . . .'

Cupido drew a breath ready to protest, to say *he* was ready to 'back up' Benny, but Jansen held up his hand to stop him. 'No, wait, listen . . .' He looked from one detective to the other, as if searching for the right words: 'I'm going to be straight with you. This is a big mess. A huge mess. And it's going to become messier. We've got an hour or two, tops, before the media finds out . . .' He shuddered in disgust, rubbed his moustache. 'Boonstra's wife came to report it. Around seven o'clock. Captain Geneke phoned me, and I phoned the higher-up, because we know, this means . . . Chaps, this shit is about to hit the fan, do you receive me?'

They received him.

'The commissioner has decided to prepare a press release; they will present it to the media when this grenade explodes. And he is going to say that you have both been seconded from the Hawks to support Stellenbosch with the investigations into Callie de Bruin and Jasper Boonstra. Because we view each of these cases as top priority and because one cannot be seen as more important than the other . . .'

'*Jissis*,' said Cupido at the deception of it all.

'I don't want to hear a word from you. This is not about you; it's about something much bigger. You . . .' and he stared at Cupido, 'are going on with the boy's fifty-five. And if you need people or resources of any kind, come to me, but we have to produce some results. Benny, the same applies to the Boonstra disappearance. The commissioner said, everything possible must be done. Everything possible.'

'Which commissioner?' Griessel asked, just to be absolutely sure.

'General Khaba. He has the support of the station commissioner, the cluster head, the provincial detective chief, the whole lot. He has sent the PCSI, he has made all facilities available to you, but he expects results, and expects, if the media should ask, then you should just confirm it. The Hawks seconded you.'

They just stared at Jansen. Until Griessel stood up and asked: 'Where is the farm, Colonel?'

Cupido drove along. There was nothing he could do about the Callie de Bruin docket at the moment, he explained in the car.

And then he blew off steam. About the 'violation'.

'I feel violated, Benna, it's "hashtag me too" for policemen, that's what it is. You can't take my Hawkness away from me, and my rank and my dignity and then say, no, actually I'm still a Hawk when it suits them to say I am one. That's bullshit, that is a violation, that is cowardly, to be frank. That is, we'll kick you in the teeth, but we want you to smile for the camera when we say so. No, *fokkit, pappie*, I feel completely violated. You know what just happened, hey? When the Boonstra fifty-five came in, they knew, the spotlight was going to be shining like never before, and this spotlight is going to illuminate Cupido and Griessel like never before, the two famous detectives who solved . . .' and Cupido counted off the cases on his fingers: '. . . the Ernst Richter case, the Alicia Lewis case, the Johnson Johnson case, the list goes on and on, and what are these two brilliant crime-fighting minds doing in Stellenbosch, why is all this talent being squandered in Volvoville, while Rome is burning, Benna? That is why they are lying and cheating, fucking "seconded". Hashtag me too, we have been violated.'

Griessel was silent. He knew there was no way to sweeten this pill.

'Insult to injury,' said Cupido, 'they went and split us up. Us. The Mulder and Scully of the Hawks, the Holmes and . . . never mind who his partner was, you get my drift. It shows you the stupidity, Benna, it just shows you again, the very last criterion for advancement to the senior ranks of the SAPS is intelligence. I'm telling you now, if we don't get a new president in December, then I'm leaving, Benna, then I'm finished, completely finished. I am so fucking *gatvol* of all the shenanigans and politics and corruption and incompetence, and the great irony is, all that I got out of it, was to get fat. Because I'm telling you, if you're a working stiff in the SAPS, you can't *fokken* diet, it's impossible.'

It was the sight of the magnificent Baronsberg mansion that silenced him. In the dark of the night it shone like a citadel of light against the black mountain behind. The angles and textures of the architecture were all the more impressive in the mosaic of alternating reflections and shadows as they approached via the winding road.

They stopped among the police vehicles in front of the building. Outside was a black Range Rover. In the three garages behind glass doors were a Mercedes-Maybach G650 Landaulet, a yellow Ferrari and a BMW i3.

'*Jissis*,' said Griessel.

Cupido just whistled softly through his teeth.

Sandra held up through supper and bathing the twins and the long process of getting them ready and sleepy and into bed. She held up through sitting and talking to Josef over a glass of red wine. She thought she was coming across as she always did. Even if it took a superhuman effort.

She nodded in grateful relief when Josef said: 'Let's watch *Casablanca*,' because it was showing on one of the DSTV channels.

He sat on the couch, she lay down with her head on his lap, totally, totally exhausted, she couldn't keep her eyes open. But when she did close them, sleep would not come. She saw Jasper Boonstra on the stairs, with his staring eye and his genitals exposed, she saw him in the freezer. She saw the young man's face in the window of the Airbnb house. What *had* she seen? It didn't matter, she had to forget about it, she could not, must not, report it. Could not, must not.

Shoving Jasper Boonstra's naked body into the boot of the EcoSport, the feel of his cold flesh, the hairy body under her fingers.

She shuddered, opened her eyes.

'You okay?' Josef asked.

On the screen Rick Blaine was saying to Ilsa: *If that plane leaves the ground and you're not with him, you'll regret it. Maybe not today. Maybe not tomorrow, but soon and for the rest of your life.*

'I am,' she said.

How was she going to sleep tonight? She *had* to. Because tomorrow, when the storm hit, she would have to be ready.

47

There were too many police vehicles in front of the Baronsberg home-stead. A small squadron of uniforms stood around gaping at all the splendour, one eye on the front door in the hope of being allowed inside.

Griessel and Cupido had to navigate their way between them, and past the constable manning the entrance, to the reception lounge, where Sergeant Erin Riddles was seated with a man and a woman.

The man stood up. He was in his late fifties, a head taller than even Cupido, and impressive. His short hair was an elegant grey and care-fully styled. The dark suit and white shirt were fresh, even at this time of night. 'Meinhardt Sarazin,' he introduced himself. He had a voice of authority, matching the strong jawline. 'I'm supporting Mrs Boonstra . . .' and he waved a gallant open hand to the woman on the sofa '. . . as legal representative.'

They did not like 'legal representatives'. All it really meant was a lawyer disguising his presence with euphemisms. That was in itself an indication of what lay ahead. And lawyers by any name, euphemistic or not, interfered with a detective's progress.

They accepted Sarazin's firm handshake, noted his extraordinary-coloured eyes – a bright light green.

Then they looked at Jasper Boonstra's wife. She did not look like the wife of a billionaire. She looked like a home industry cake baker. Or a school secretary, or the organiser of the tombola table at the church bazaar. With her conservative hairstyle, the floral dress and sensible shoes, she was the kindly middle-aged aunt, and they doubted for a second that this was the real Mrs Jasper Boonstra.

She held out her hand for them to shake. 'Alet,' she said. 'Lettie.'

Griessel apologised for asking her to tell the story from the begin-ning again.

'Oh, no,' she said, 'it's not a problem.' A touch of a Namaqualand accent.

Meinhardt Sarazin said: 'For the record, gentlemen, there is a very strong possibility that Jasper is not missing at all. It is likely just a misunderstanding.'

Alet 'Lettie' Boonstra shook her head. 'I don't think so. Please won't you sit down?' She had a very deliberate down-to-earth quality, Griessel thought, as if she wished to distance herself from the formality of the lawyer. And all the ostentatious wealth surrounding her.

He, Cupido and Riddles took their seats on the large sofa, in a neat row.

Initially it wasn't a fluent narrative, thanks to the 'legal representative's' watchful eye and frequent interruptions. Sarazin sat with his head tilted towards Lettie Boonstra listening, like a judge at an art competition.

She said: 'Jasper and I have decided to divorce . . .'

'That is exceptionally confidential and sensitive information,' Sarazin said in his ringing voice. 'I would request that all three of you treat it as such. And for the record, it does not mean that Mr and Mrs Boonstra's marriage is on the rocks. There is still the possibility that the marriage might be saved.'

Lettie Boonstra ignored that interjection, and she said she and Jasper would have met this afternoon at two, to have an initial discussion about the divorce and especially the division of assets. They'd already met on Friday night at a restaurant in Clifton and tentatively and amicably agreed that the marriage was effectively over.

'Tentatively,' emphasised Sarazin.

When she arrived there was no one at home. At first she thought he must be somewhere out on the estate, and he would soon appear. She waited fifteen minutes, somewhat surprised by his poor manners. Jasper was usually on time. Not because he was a particularly responsible man, she said, purely because his schedule was always so full and being on time made his life easier. And then there was the question of Jasper's love of a good financial argument, he would not have wanted to miss their meeting. When fifteen minutes went by she tried to phone him. Just here, from the kitchen. And she heard his phone ringing upstairs in his home office. She went upstairs to see. The phone was lying there. He wouldn't have just left his phone lying around. She searched the whole house for him. It was most peculiar – the phone, his absence when they had agreed on a time, barely any sign that he was here. Jasper, with all his faults, wouldn't do that. She walked outside, went to look in the garden. She drove her little BMW i3 over to the wine cellar, only a kilometre away, and the people there said they hadn't laid eyes on Jasper today. Then she phoned the little guard house, where two people were always on duty, day and night, to keep the curious and the press and nuisance-makers away. Then they said, no, ma'am, Mr Boonstra must be home, he hadn't gone anywhere yet today. His cars must still be in the garage.

Indeed his cars were still in the garage.

She waited until three o'clock. Then she phoned Sarazin. He was Jasper's lawyer and advisor and friend, the only one who had stood by him through everything. Sarazin immediately agreed to help track Jasper down. He couldn't. 'I assume,' she said, quite cheerfully and calmly as she looked at the lawyer, 'that Meinhardt also contacted Jenna Abbott . . .'

She waited for a second to see if Griessel understood, then realised that he didn't know who Jenna Abbott was. 'Jenna was Jasper's midlife crisis. His mistress. A very pretty girl. Such a pert little bottom. Jasper told me it was over between them, but maybe he changed his mind on Friday when I told him it didn't matter any more, I thought we should get divorced . . .'

'His alleged mistress,' said Sarazin.

'Ay, Meinhardt,' said Lettie Boonstra. 'Can you stop working for Jasper, just for a second.'

'I want to state categorically,' said Sarazin, 'that Miss Abbott has had no direct contact with Mr Boonstra in the past ten days. She also told me this afternoon that she has no idea of Mr Boonstra's whereabouts.'

'And you believe her?' Lettie Boonstra asked.

'I have no reason not to believe her.'

'By five o'clock I decided to report Jasper's disappearance to the police,' said Lettie Boonstra. 'Meinhardt asked me to wait another two hours, to give him time to make some more calls, he was sure it was just a misunderstanding . . .'

'I am still certain of it. Mr Boonstra . . .'

'Ay, Meinhardt, for goodness sake just say "Jasper". He's not in some or other high position. He's a cheat, and you know it.'

Sarazin gave her a look of barely disguised dislike. Then he said to Griessel: 'Jasper had no reason to disappear. An official, public investigation will just create sensation and encourage wild speculation. Tomorrow, the day after, he'll be back, I'm sure . . .'

'Has he a history of being . . . out of reach?' asked Griessel.

'No,' said Lettie Boonstra.

'Frequently,' said Meinhardt Sarazin. 'Especially the past few months . . .'

Griessel sighed. 'Ma'am, do you . . .'

'Call me Lettie.'

'Do you have a suspicion as to where he could be?'

'Yes. I think he's skipped the country. I don't think he had the guts to take responsibility for all his fraud . . .'

'Alleged fraud,' said Sarazin.

'He once said maybe he should just disappear. Fly to Luanda and buy himself a new identity; in Luanda you can buy anything if you are prepared to pay the price. And I wouldn't be surprised if there was a new young thing in his life and that in a week or a month she also "disappears" after Jasper. I can tell you for sure it won't be little Jenna. Not after the public humiliation when Jasper threw her out of the Franschhoek house. Hell hath no fury, hey . . .'

'Lettie, please, I really don't think it's necessary to discuss this sort of thing in public . . .'

'Meinhardt, can I ask you a favour?' said Lettie sweetly.

'Of course.'

'Fuck off,' she said. 'Go and wait outside with the riff-raff.'

He stalked reluctantly out, the tall, dignified figure, but first he said over his shoulder: 'My advice to you is to wait. My advice to you is to say nothing. Lettie, please . . .'

When he exited the front door, she shivered, like someone shaking off a demon. She told Griessel: 'Now we can have a proper talk.' Sounding pleased as if she was looking forward to it.

He had to gather his thoughts, try to make sense of the dynamic between her and Sarazin. 'I . . . er . . . ma'am . . .'

'Lettie,' she said.

He checked his watch. 'Your appointment was for two o'clock, you and Mr Boonstra.'

'That is correct.'

'I . . . it's just over eight hours. That's, with a fifty-five . . . an investigation of a missing person, that is a very short period. And with the media, and your lawyer who is certain your husband is not missing . . .'

'Tell me your name again, please.'

'Warrant Officer Griessel.'

'No, your first name.'

'Benny.'

'Now, Benny, point number one, he is not my lawyer. He is Jasper's guard dog. And don't let that I'm-a-nice-guy appearance fool you. He's a pit bull in Labrador's clothing. I didn't ask him to be here, he invited himself. Point number two: I think he knows where Jasper is, he is just busy orchestrating this to suit them. And the last point: I really don't care what the media are going to do. Do you know the story of the crayfish in the pot?'

She was unmistakeably cheerful, as if she was enjoying this conversation very much. It made Griessel uncomfortable; he wasn't sure how to respond. 'I . . . er . . .'

'They say if you put the crayfish in the pot and heat the water up slowly, the crayfish just stays there, it doesn't matter if the water starts to boil. Because the crayfish gets used to it. Now, to be clear, over the past year I have become accustomed to the humiliation. First from Jasper's huge fraud, then from his little-bit-on-the-side. The endless gossip of this town, people staring at you, wherever you go. And the paparazzi behind every bush, the papers crowing about everything. Everything. That I must have known about Jasper's fraud, that I must have known about the mistress, that I don't care . . . This crayfish is accustomed to a lot, so let's turn the heat up high as we can.'

48

Griessel tried to get a word in, but Lettie Boonstra gave him no opportunity.

'As soon as you and I have finished talking,' she said in her chatty way, 'Meinhardt is going to take you by the arm, in his let's-sort-this-out-man-to-man way. And he is going to try to disarm you with that practised baritone, and with his great speciality, the I'm-looking-you-in-the-eyes-because-you-are-important-to-me technique. He's going to tell you Jasper is not missing. Yes, we can't find him now but he's just gone somewhere for a bit. Slipped away for a break, a little holiday, he does that now and then. Now, Benny, let me tell you why you must not fall for that. Jasper *is* missing, because Jasper is addicted to power. Why is Jasper addicted to power? Because Jasper has a chip on his shoulder as big as Table Mountain. And why does Jasper have a chip on his shoulder? Because his parents were so poor. Such simple people, so common. Not that *I* think they were, I'm just quoting Jasper. How he died a thousand deaths every time he brought his friends home. Ashamed by the poverty, their *commonness*. That chip on the shoulder had one boringly predictable outcome, just like Pavlov's dogs drooling when he rang the bell. Every time Jasper is humiliated, he has to try to prove something. His parents were the source of his greatest humiliation, and all his life he worked to prove he wasn't like them. That's what made him successful, that consuming ambition, but then he couldn't turn the engine off. He began to steal and cheat, because he craved more status, more respect, more admiration, more prestige, more acceptance. He wanted to keep proving that he wasn't like his oh-so-common Pa and Ma. Do you understand what I'm saying?'

'Ma'am . . .'

'Call me Lettie, please. What I'm saying, Benny, is that last Friday night at The Bungalow I told Jasper that I'm done. With the marriage.

With him. And all his tricks. I want the house at Rooi-Els, I want enough money to live comfortably, and I want it now. Because I know how much money and assets he has hidden, so he needn't tell me everything is frozen. Jasper didn't like that, Benny, because Jasper enjoys power. He loves control. If we're to get divorced, he wants to be the one to decide. And call the shots all the way, over the division of assets. He said we should try again, he wanted me, needed me. He'd even sent Jenna Abbott on her way – I don't know if you saw that, how the papers were full of it again, how she had to move out of the house in Franschhoek?'

'No . . .' said Griessel.

'I saw it,' said Sergeant Erin Riddles. 'It was even in *You* magazine!'

Lettie Boonstra looked at Riddles. 'Exactly. And when you saw it what did you think? Why was Jasper evicting Little Miss Sexybottom?'

'I just thought he had a change of heart . . .'

'Of course you did. Now, let me tell you why he broke up with her. Not because he turned over a new page, oh no, Erin. Jasper already had his eye on someone else. I am sure of it. Jenna Abbott wasn't the first one, and she won't be the last. Every two or three years he had a new one. When he could find another one of them who would sell her soul for gifts and a flash of cash. There were so many who said no . . . In any case, when Jasper told me that story that he had broken up with Sexybottom, I laughed at him. Because I knew that all he really wanted was to be the one to manage the end of our marriage. He wasn't willing to cede the power to me. No, he couldn't. Power is part of his DNA . . .'

'Ma'am . . .' said Griessel, his patience wearing thin.

'Lettie, please. I know, I know, I'm not getting to the point. Here's my point: the last chance for Jasper to try to wield his power over *me*, to make himself count, to show he wasn't his common father, was this afternoon at two. Because we would have discussed the settlement, here. Without Pit Bull Sarazin's presence. And Jasper would not have missed that for the world. He would have wanted to tell me I would get nothing. And that I would have to fight for everything, for anything. He would have waved his power around like a big penis, because that's what he does. And voilà, he wasn't here. So, Benny, something happened to keep him away. Something bigger than his obsession with power . . .'

'Like what, ma'am?'

'Oh, something that could take his power away from him. Like the threat of arrest. Or that his hidden assets had disappeared. Or were going to disappear, or were in danger of disappearing, if he didn't do something urgently. That made him choose. Stay or slip away. And it must have been a difficult choice, because he really wanted to wave his big powerful whatsit in front of me. He's not somewhere, as Meinhardt says. He's gone. And my money is in Angola.'

At last the monologue was over.

Griessel asked when she last had contact with Jasper Boonstra.

She took out her phone and showed him. There was a message in WhatsApp that she had sent at 07:56 that morning: *there at 2.*

Boonstra's reply was just the thumbs-up icon.

'And when you arrived here . . . Do you have a key?'

'Of course I have a key, Benny. But I didn't need it. The door was unlocked.'

'No sign that . . . Nothing is missing, nothing is disturbed?'

'Nothing that I can see.'

'Lettie,' he finally managed to call her by her name, 'there is just one thing that I don't understand.'

'Tell me, Benny.'

'You think he flew to Angola . . .'

'Well, not on SAA, I mean on a chartered flight. Just him, on the quiet. If you have the money, there's always someone who can make it happen . . . That's what he said, back then when it all came out about his fraud, in the first week or two when he went to bed thinking they would be banging on the door to come lock him up.'

'And then, from Angola . . .?'

'Who knows? New passport, he could choose anywhere in the world . . .'

'Okay. Now this is what I don't understand. If you think that is where he is, why do you want us to look for him?'

She looked at Griessel with new respect, then said: 'That is your first good question, Benny. And you might not like the answer, but here it is: when all Jasper's company fraud came out, I was consumed with fear that you would take him away. My clever, clever husband. My provider. My safety, my security. In those days I was blissfully unaware of all his mischief, financial and otherwise. But nothing happened to him. No police vans with sirens and flashing blue lights and men with guns coming to arrest him. Nothing. And Jasper said they were either too stupid, or too lazy, or too useless to prosecute him. And if he looked at how you allowed the president and his hench-men to strip the country, loot it into bankruptcy, then it is just laziness and uselessness. And I was only too glad of it, because what would I do if he had to go to jail? Then the press started to write about Sexybottom, and all the other stories about him carrying on with women came out. People I'd known for years, women who were my friends, began telling me all the things he'd been getting up to. Why only then? That was one of those questions I'll probably never have the answer to. But never mind, I digress . . . When it all came out, I began to pray that they would take him away, lock him up, that you would make him pay for all the pain he had caused. But no, you didn't turn up. Because you were too useless, or too lazy, or too stupid, or all three, who knows? So, Benny, you are going to get off your backsides for a change and live up to your responsibilities. Find the bastard. And bring him back. So I can get what I deserve. While he lies around on a Caribbean island somewhere with a new passport and a new sexybot-tom, I look bad and I have nothing, and I'll *get* nothing . . . Oh, and just so you get the complete answer: I want the media to report that Jasper Boonstra ran away like a coward. And I want everyone to know it. I want his photo everywhere on the internet, so that he can't hide anywhere. So, go do your work for a change, Benny. Or are you really all just too useless, too stupid, and too lazy?'

She stood up. 'The Pit Bull has my name and address. I will be in my house at Rooi-Els.'

Griessel also stood up. 'Lettie, no, I will have to go through the house with you first, to try to establish if anything is missing.'

'No, Benny. Call Sexybottom. She was here more often than I was. She might be able to help you.' And Alet 'Lettie' Boonstra walked to the front door, and left.

*   *   *

'*Jissis*,' said Vaughn Cupido.

'Amen, brother,' said Erin Riddles.

'Ay,' said Benny Griessel, as he saw the front door open again and Meinhardt Sarazin approach with the solemn gait of a giraffe. And behind him, Thick and Thin from Forensics – Arnold, the short fat one, and Jimmy, tall and skinny – making use of the open door.

'Warrant Officer . . .' said Sarazin. 'You're making a big mistake . . .'

Benny felt his temper rise, but he stayed calm, not without some difficulty. 'No. You wait outside,' he said.

'Who do you think you're talking to?' the lawyer said, suddenly much more attack dog than Labrador.

Later that night, as he drove back to Cape Town, he would try to work out why he'd so completely lost it at that particular instant. It wasn't just one thing, he thought, it was the confluence of many things bottled up over a long period. His frustration with this case, which looked like one big waste of time. Bloody rich buggers and their divorce disputes. It was his fear that he was letting down Annemarie de Bruin and her son. It was the legal man's pompous, insulting attitude, Lettie Boonstra's disdain for the police, how she talked down to him. It was a very long day, and the weeks and weeks of stress over his and Vaughn's suspension. And the spectre of Laingsburg and what his son Fritz would have to say about it, 'my alcoholic father who has been posted to the Karoo'. It was Milo April and state capture and his country, his world, his career, his existence that was going down the drain drop by fucking drop. It was how he had to cope with all of that and fight against the craving for alcohol too, all of that had conspired and combined to make him explode.

'Fuck you,' said Griessel, red in the face now. He walked up to Sarazin, threatening. He poked a finger in the man's chest, looked up at him and said: 'You wait outside, or I will arrest your arse and throw you in jail.' And then, with every consecutive word, he stabbed the finger like a dagger: 'Out, Now. *Cunt.*'

Deathly silence.

Jimmy and Arnold's eyes were like saucers; they had never seen Griessel like this before.

The lawyer's square jaw worked silently up and down.

Cupido and Riddles exchanged a satisfied glance.

Sarazin spun round and walked out – for the second time tonight – with as much dignity as he could muster.

When the front door closed gently behind him, Vaughn told Riddles: 'See that *oke*?' and he pointed with great pride at his colleague. 'That's my partner there.'

'Is it okay if we stay inside?' Jimmy asked cautiously.

49

Sandra waited until Josef was asleep.

Then very slowly and quietly she got out of bed and went to the bathroom. She took a Zolpidem out of the medicine lockbox that they kept under the basin. She had to get some sleep, and her heart would not stop racing, her mind wouldn't stop showing her images of Jasper Boonstra – on the stairs, in the freezer, in the boot of her EcoSport.

And what she had seen at the Airbnb house.

Had she really? She swallowed the pill.

What if it was the boy, the young student, and she had done nothing?

But what *could* she do?

She crept back into bed, lay down again, and waited for sleep to come.

Griessel asked Forensics to bring their ultraviolet lights, and then with Cupido, Riddles, Thick and Thin, they searched the house, thoroughly and methodically. He was out of sorts, angry at himself, and uneasy about something, something undefined. He tried to suppress the feeling so that he could focus on the task at hand, but it was a struggle.

By midnight he was certain there was no sign of a break-in, struggle or violence. The only evidence that anyone had been in the house at all, was the rumpled double bed in the master bedroom, where at least one person had been lying.

At 00:12 Witkop Jansen phoned to enquire about where things stood. Benny told him, as objectively as he could, and said there were still possibilities to be investigated.

'The media are at the gate,' Jansen said. 'Armies of them. The station men are keeping them out, Provincial has sent a spokesperson to keep them under control. The commissioner said, if you find anything, you must let me know, and I will let him know, and he will talk to the spokesperson. Are you reading me?'

The final refrain now without the usual edge. Griessel could tell that Witkop Jansen had also had enough of this by now. He said he understood, and rang off. He told Riddles and Cupido about the media.

'The end of the world as we know it,' said Vaughn.

Griessel tagged the cell phone on Boonstra's desk, and popped it in an evidence bag.

Then he asked the security personnel to come to the sitting room. Erin Riddles had sent for them earlier, the complete team of eight people who manned the guard house at the entrance, and at the same time patrolled the boundary fences, teams of two relieving each other every eight hours.

They told him that Jasper Boonstra had not left Baronsberg at all that day. This morning at eight he informed them he did not want to be disturbed, and once the estate agent arrived, they were to let no one else in.

'What estate agent?' Griessel asked.

'The pretty one with the little Ford,' the gate guard said, with a knowing look. When he saw that Griessel was not satisfied with that answer he added: 'He never had her sign in, so we don't know her name. But we can get her number plate off the camera.'

'Wait, wait, wait,' said Griessel, 'how many routes in and out are there?'

'That depends,' the security man said, 'if you're talking about the house or the farm . . .'

'What do you mean?' Griessel asked.

'Well, the house is on one side,' said the man, 'away from the cellar, the farm sheds and the wine tasting and all those things. If you want to get to the house, or leave the house, for example to go to town, the easy way is the way you came in, through the fancy gate, and past the intercom, and our monitoring point. The only other way is through the other gate. The one at the back that goes to the wine cellar, and from the cellar to the Jonkershoek road. But then you have to have the code for the gate between the house and the cellar, and you have to enter it on the panel. And we will see you on the CCTV.'

'And Boonstra didn't go out through either of them today?'

'Correct.'

'But he's not here, so how did he get out?' Griessel asked, increasingly impatient.

The security man looked at his colleagues as if asking for help with the answer. Then he said: 'The missus had two small pedestrian gates put in, so she could walk up the mountain, or to the cellar and the dam. Both have code panels. If you're on foot you can go out there. That's the only way Mr Boonstra could have left the farm, but then, he wouldn't have walked to town . . .'

'Are there cameras at the small gates?'

'No. The missus didn't want them.'

'How hard is it to climb over the fence?' Griessel asked.

'It's two-metre ClearVu Super Fencing, you can't get over it. And we patrol the fence every two hours, there are no holes cut in it or anything.' Now on the defensive, as if Griessel was suggesting it was their fault that Boonstra was gone.

'How can I see the CCTV footage?' Griessel asked.

'You can come and watch it in the guard house. But we have checked already. There's nothing for today. Only the agent who came in and out, and then the missus, and then the tall lawyer.'

'What about gardeners or domestics?' Griessel asked.

'Mr Boonstra said he wanted peace and quiet today. Nobody came near the house.'

'Did he do that often? Want peace and quiet?'

'Only when he brought in a little piece.'

'A little piece of what?'

The guard cast an apologetic glance at Erin Riddles, then back to Griessel. 'A little piece on the side,' he said.

Meinhardt Sarazin was leaning against his black Range Rover and straightened up when the detectives exited the house.

'Warrant Officer, please,' he said with exaggerated politeness. 'Just a minute of your time.'

Griessel stopped, Cupido and Riddles beside him.

'Surely you can see that Mrs Boonstra has an agenda,' the lawyer said.

'What is her agenda?' Griessel asked.

'She ... I suspect she wants to embarrass Mr Boonstra. In an attempt to ... I'm not sure of her reasoning, but it clearly has to do with the divorce and the settlement.'

'I thought that was all still tentative,' said Cupido.

Sarazin shrugged. 'Clearly the cat is out of the bag. That notwithstanding, she is speaking rubbish. There is no way that Mr Boonstra would have tried to leave the country without informing me. No way.'

'Then where is he?' Griessel asked.

'I don't know. But I bet you he calls me tomorrow, as soon as he finds out about the media hysteria.'

'With whose phone?' Griessel asked. 'His was here.'

Sarazin had no answer.

'Did he have any property on the market?' Griessel asked.

'But what is the relevance of such a question? I'm just telling you he wouldn't run off.'

'There was an estate agent here. This morning.'

'Oh.' A split second's hesitation. 'He did mention something ... That he wanted a valuation.'

'A valuation of what?'

'The house in Franschhoek, if I remember correctly . . .'

'Do you know who the estate agent was?'

The lawyer shook his head. 'I will try to find out . . .' He took out his wallet, produced a business card. 'Warrant Officer, forgive the er ... moment of tactlessness inside. Here are my details. I'll phone you as soon as I hear from Jasper. Meanwhile, if there is any way I can be of assistance . . .'

Griessel took the card. He watched the man turn and walk to the black Range Rover.

They walked to the guard house to watch the CCTV video recording.

They could see the spotlights of the TV crews at the gate, and the commotion of voices across nearly two hundred metres.

The security guard played them the video on a computer monitor, at high speed to emphasise only the sections with some activity. The white Ford EcoSport stopped at the big sliding gate at 08:55, paused a moment, and then drove through when the gate opened. The only occupant was a woman. The image was clear, her features reasonably visible. She looked attractive.

'That's the dolly. The agent,' the security man said.

Griessel wrote the registration number down in his notebook.

The same vehicle, the same number, drove out again at 11:54. She was alone in the car.

The 'dolly' gave the guards a friendly wave.

The next arrival was Lettie Boonstra's car, and after that the lawyer's. And then the police.

They watched the video material of the area outside the triple garage. It showed nothing new. Only the agent, Mrs Boonstra, Meinhardt Sarazin.

They watched the video footage of the big gate behind the house that led to the wine cellar and outbuildings. No movement the whole day.

Using powerful torches they walked to each of the two pedestrian gates that Lettie Boonstra had had installed in the high barrier of the ClearVu fences: one to the north-west that offered access to the mountain, the other on the east side that led to the big dam.

There were no signs of tracks at either gate.

'It rained all day,' said the gate guard. 'If there were tracks, it's no use now.'

Griessel took out his phone. He had to phone Witkop Jansen and tell him they had nothing.

Absolutely nothing.

50

They wanted to get back to the office. At the gate the uniforms had to forge a path for them through the media. Cameras flashed, TV lenses and big microphones were pressed against the windows, questions yelled at them.

'Never seen anything like it,' said Cupido, who was driving.

'Not even with the Hawks?' Erin Riddles asked from the back seat. 'Not even close,' said Cupido. 'But there you have it: the fraudster as celebrity. I wonder where the threshold lies. How much do you have to steal to be famous? Boonstra swiped about a billion rand, hey?'

'Something like that.'

'Those Indian businessmen who were in bed with the Prez, they must have looted four, five billion before they hit the limelight. Shows you, white privilege, even when you're a criminal . . .'

They drove past the last media van parked beside the Jonkershoek road. Vaughn looked at Benny. 'Interesting docket, Benna.'

'*Fok*,' said Benny with feeling.

'What do you think, partner? The butler did it?'

Griessel's grin was weak. 'The lawyer knows something,' he said. 'The question is: what?'

'And the aunty?' asked Erin Riddles.

'The aunty is pretty spooky,' said Cupido. 'All that anger . . .'

'That's what I'm thinking. Let's say he never comes back. How much will she get?'

'Who knows?' said Benny Griessel. 'The one thing I remember about all the stories when they caught him out then, was how clever he was. Clever at university, clever with his first businesses, and clever in his stealing. He wouldn't have put much of his stuff in his own name.'

'Is that why the aunty was so keen for us to look for him? And find him?' Cupido wanted to know.

'Ah, okay . . .' said Sergeant Erin Riddles, who viewed the cooperation with the two former Hawks as a good learning opportunity.

'Maybe,' said Griessel. 'And maybe that is why his lawyer doesn't want us to find him.'

'Aaah . . .' said Erin Riddles.

They brought the dockets up to date, finishing just before two in the morning.

'So, you asked to share an office?' Riddles asked from where she sat beside Griessel doing the computerised part of the Boonstra case administration on the ICDMS – the Integrated Case Docket Management System.

'No,' said Cupido, who was at his own desk adding to the Callie de Bruin file. 'Why?'

'But all the other detectives have their own offices. Even us sergeants.'

'Part of our punishment, I suppose,' said Griessel. 'It doesn't bother us.'

The calm of the night descended as they worked.

Cupido looked up from the docket. 'Benna, do you feel like . . . I don't know . . .'

'We're missing something?'

'*Yebo*. Like, something obvious, but I don't know what . . .'

'Ever since . . .' and he wanted to say Mbali Kaleni and Chriselda Plaatjies,' but then he realised it was better if Erin Riddles didn't know about everything, '. . . since this afternoon.'

'Exactly,' said Cupido. 'Exactly.'

They sent emails to Megan Daniels at Capitec and Veronica Adams at Campus Security, to notify them that Cupido would be handling the De Bruin disappearance case on his own from now on.

The last thing that Vaughn did before turning off the computer on his desk was to send the photo of Hoody – the one who went in and out of Callie de Bruin's hostel room – to the gang unit in the Cape. Without much hope, really to have one more item to write in the investigation journal, on the SAPS5 form of the dockets Section C, because he was worried that Witkop Jansen would find fault with their work again.

The last thing that Griessel did was to type the vehicle registration of the estate agent into the NaTIS.

He found her name.

Sandra Steenberg.

He found a home address and a telephone number. He wrote it down in his notebook, then looked at his watch. It was pointless to phone her at this time of night.

It could wait till tomorrow.

It was close to half past two in the morning when they walked out to their cars, knowing that they were going to get very little sleep. And tomorrow was going to be a very long day.

It was on the way home, the fifty-three kilometres between Stellenbosch and Tamboerskloof, on deserted roads, that Griessel pondered his outburst, the fit of rage that had taken everyone, even himself, by surprise.

It wasn't like him.

Perhaps it had been once, in the days before he began to drink and fuck up his whole life. Obstreperous and full of self-confidence, he would sometimes throw his weight around, especially early on in his detective days, when he was seen as one of the young Turks, an up-and-coming star.

But when he reached the far side of the addiction abyss, he didn't think he had the right to lose his temper.

Why now then?

He thought of all the things that might have led up to it, the combination of stress, all the bottling-up of things, for weeks. And this day, Boonstra and De Bruin, Milo April and his son Fritz, and how all of it made him crave the bottle, and how he simply dare not even take a drink.

Yes, he thought he understood, everything had just conspired together to make him explode.

And yet . . .

There was something more, something lurking in his subconscious, a slumbering monster.

He forced his thoughts elsewhere – what was it that kept evading him and Vaughn with the Callie de Bruin case? Like a word on the tip of the tongue, that would just not come out. Through his fatigue, in these early hours, he was struggling to think.

Only once he drove up Buitengracht, did he really confront the monster.

He and Vaughn were being exploited as 'co-opted Hawks'. After they had been humiliated and stripped of their rank. Milo April suspected the Smith & Wesson had been stolen inside the SAPS system, and ten-to-one, almost certainly, he was correct. Lettie Boonstra had said: *Because you were too useless, or too lazy, or too stupid, or all three, who knows?* And she was probably correct too, because Boonstra's crime was plain for all to see. Thousands of news articles, four books written about the Schneider-König scandal, a Dutch documentary film produced post-haste, the fraud exposed and explained, and still there were no repercussions. The mastermind was walking free. The country's president, unmasked as an arch-criminal. Along with a handful of ministers and at least two provincial premiers and a whole host of officials and accomplices. Billions looted. No consequences. Not a thing.

It was the monster that lurked in his subconscious. The monster of pointlessness. If crime was sanctioned by the state, why did you need anyone to fight it? If the odds were so overwhelming it meant that you could make absolutely no difference, you were useless. Then he was just as useless sober as he had been drunk. Every way you looked at it, useless. There was no point to it all.

A few weeks ago he had given Cupido his Mauritz Lotz monologue. He said being a detective was his home. That was where he was most himself. He might have added: that's where he was useful.

What are you if you have no use?

What was going to become of him?

He crawled into the bed, snuggled up to Alexa's back.

She gave him a clumsy, sleepy kiss, on his eye. 'I love you,' she whispered in the darkness.

'You too,' he said.

He laid his head down on the pillow.

Out of nowhere came the faint glimmer of an idea, like a curtain in his mind had been pulled back just a fraction. Perhaps born from his desperation not to be entirely useless.

He would look into it first thing in the morning.

51

The Cape is a fickle mistress. On Wednesday she was grey, cold and aloof; by Thursday she was poised to burst into the world as a bright and breezy coquette.

Sunrise was at 06:17. Sandra Steenberg stood in the kitchen, still in her pyjamas, cell phone in her hand. She had eventually fallen asleep, thanks to the pill. Her head was woolly, but her heart was racing because there was a message: *Police are going to contact you. Don't tell them about Donkerdrif. Call me urgently. I am JB's lawyer. Meinhardt Sarazin.*

Instinctively she glanced down the passage, towards the bedroom door. Like a thief, she thought. Always looking over your shoulder.

Josef was still asleep.

The WhatsApp had been sent that morning, at 02:41. That meant the police knew Jasper was gone.

What did they know? When would they come?

She walked through the kitchen and out the back door. She rang the lawyer's number.

It rang so long that she thought he wasn't going to answer. 'This is Meinhardt,' he said in a voice gravelly from sleep when he came on the line.

'My name is Sandra Steenberg. You left me a rather odd message.' She had to pretend she didn't know anything about it.

'Oh. Yes. Hello, thank you for calling me. Have the police contacted you?'

'Why would they contact me?'

'Mr Boonstra's wife has reported him as missing.'

Sandra noted the careful choice of words. 'How so?' she asked. 'I was there with him just yesterday.'

'Did he say where he was going?'

'No . . .' A hint of confusion added to her voice. 'He . . . He said we would speak again on Friday . . . tomorrow. About the Demeter transaction.'

'I must ask you a very big favour, Mrs Steenberg. It seems as though you were the last one to see Mr Boonstra yesterday. It's therefore unavoidable that the police will contact you. Please don't say anything about Donkerdrif. Please.'

She deliberately let the silence lengthen, as if she was considering the consequences. 'I understand. We don't want the sale . . . to be in jeopardy.'

'Precisely,' said Sarazin. 'Jasper was most relieved that the transaction was completed. And that you . . . handled it with such discretion, I have to add. I believe he has simply gone somewhere to unwind. Now, the police asked me last night if I knew why there was an estate agent visiting him. My reply was that it might be to do with the Franschhoek property. Stellenbosch is just around the corner, after all . . .'

'Or I could simply say that Jasper was talking to me about Baronsberg. That is what happened.'

'Baronsberg?'

'He told me if I play my cards right, one of these days we can put Baronsberg on the market.'

'You're not serious.'

She was on thin ice, Sandra knew. Sarazin was clearly Boonstra's confidant. He might grow suspicious about the forged mandate form on her desk. She would have to provide some context for it. 'Meinhardt,' using his first name to create a bond, co-conspiratorial, 'in all likelihood Jasper wasn't really serious about selling Baronsberg. It was just bait. He had ulterior motives. About me . . .'

'What do you mean?'

'If you are Jasper's lawyer, you ought to know exactly what I mean. Ask him when you speak to him again.'

Silence on the line.

'The police don't need to know every detail,' she said. 'I will just say we were talking about a couple of Jasper's properties.'

'That could work. Thank you. I will make sure that we remember your . . . discretion.'

*   *   *

Before Griessel left the house, Alexa made him the perfect omelette, with mature Cheddar. While listening closely to his tales of the previous day.

At sunrise he was on the N2, on the way back to work. He thought about the delicious omelette, amazed. A small miracle; that didn't happen every day. Maybe it was a sign. That this was going to be a good one.

But he doubted that. Today the circus was coming to Stellenbosch in all its glory. And his best hope was not to be the head clown. But he would have to keep his head if he wanted to avoid that. The lack of sleep was taking its toll. His thoughts were jumbled this morning, slippery. They slid back to last night, and his fear of being useless, redundant. Surplus to requirements. The whirling thoughts challenged him, asking what was he going to do about that? Then without rhyme or reason they leaped to his old Giant mountain bike, which he had noticed leaning against the garage wall when he drove out. Lonely. Redundant. He missed the cycling, early mornings on the slopes of Table Mountain. His body and mind and his mood missed it. One of his few pleasures. He wondered if it was worth it. To make all these sacrifices, while it seemed increasingly likely that his career was going to fade away, disappear, like a candle blowing out in the gloom of his utter uselessness. He told himself, *nee o fok*, that was enough of the heavy negative thoughts, he should focus on the glimmer of an idea that he'd had last night, the first thing he was going to look at when he got into the office. The fuckers could take his rank and his purpose away from him, but not his intuition.

Sergeant Erin Riddles lived in Tiobelle Crescent, in Jamestown outside Stellenbosch. Her husband, Neville, was an electrician and their three sons were in primary school.

She had made the children maize porridge with milk, butter and sugar for breakfast, and was preparing their lunch boxes for the day. Neville lent a hand. He put the ham on the sandwiches as he listened to her telling him about the strange disappearance of Jasper Boonstra, and the enormous castle he lived in.

'He's in Russia already,' said her oldest, thirteen years old.

'Russia? Why Russia?' asked Neville. 'There's only snow and vodka there.'

'That's where all the big criminal minds go,' said the child.

'I don't think he's gone anywhere,' said Erin Riddles. 'I think he's lying somewhere on that farm.'

'Who whacked him, do you think?' Neville asked.

'That wife of his. Means, motive, opportunity,' she said. 'And she's a bee eye tee see aitch.'

'We *can* spell, Mommy,' her oldest said reproachfully. 'We're not babies any more.'

Vaughn Cupido was busy getting dressed when Desiree came into the room, already fully groomed, bright and ready for the day. That was how she was. Always highly organised.

She had a Tupperware bowl in her hands. 'Lovey,' she said, 'I made this for you last night. If you're serious about this diet then we'll have to minimise the temptations.' She pulled up the lid from the bowl. There were four little cling-film packets inside, and a single banana. 'The baby carrots are for a snack. Have as many as you want. Low calories, nice and crunchy, they work well if you just want to take the edge off the worst hunger. The tuna, mayo and gherkins are for lunch. The blueberries are for dessert, loads of antioxidants and vitamins. The almonds are for energy, in the afternoon. I know there are only six, but they have a high calorie count. Lovey, the banana is for emergency only, if the day gets very long. Okay?'

He looked at the food. *Jirre* it wasn't his sort of thing. He was practically a vegetarian now. Like Benny's son's cherry.

He looked down at the trousers that he was trying to fasten.

'Okay,' he said. 'Thank you, lovey.'

Griessel was busy on the computer when Cupido arrived at the office.

'Come look here,' Benny said, and then realised Vaughn was hiding something half under the flaps of his jacket. 'What have you got there?'

'My skinny future self, let's not talk about it,' said Cupido and quickly put the object in his desk drawer. It looked like a Tupperware bowl. 'What you got, Benna?' he asked.

'Vusi's in-transit hijackers that we caught at the Slot van die Paarl, in July. When you shot the *ou* with RS200 . . .'

'No, I shot him with the Glock that day, *fokken* RS200 was a mistake . . .'

'That's right. Now, remember the AK47 with the ivory grip that the leader was carrying?'

'*Ja, ja,* the dude that scratched Ukufa on it. Death. Who nearly blew Zamisa in his *moer*.'

'That's him. This . . .' and Griessel pointed at his notebook that was lying open beside the keyboard, '. . . is the serial number of that rifle. And these are the IBIS and WR numbers that Silverton sent me after they tested and stored them.'

'Check.'

'I have put all those numbers into IBIS four times, and in the SVR, and there's nothing, Vaughn. Nothing . . .'

'Wait now, partner. You sent the AK yourself? To Silverton?'

'Yes. Vusi was snowed under by the admin of that case, with all those arrests. Frankie Fillander and I helped him.'

'The AK was forfeited, right? Because the whole crew took a plea deal?'

'Yes. I filled in the declaration of forfeiture myself and sent it off.'

'*Bliksem,*' said Cupido. 'Those are the numbers that they gave you?'

'Buddy Fick himself. There they are.' Griessel pointed at the notebook again.

'That's fucking weird,' said Cupido.

'Yes, but that's not all, Vaughn. It made me wonder about Milo. And something that Witkop Jansen said. It might be that . . .' said Griessel, but he didn't complete the sentence. Because Erin Riddles came rushing to the office door wide-eyed and out of breath and said: 'The general is here, he wants to see us urgently. And the TV is at the gate!'

52

'The general' was that bullfrog of a provincial commissioner, Mandla Khaba.

He wasn't alone. Accompanying him was the provincial head of detectives, the cluster commissioner, the station commissioner, a team of the SAPS media relations in the Cape and three colonels who were apparently purely part of Khaba's provincial entourage.

They were all sitting in the parade room when Cupido, Griessel and Erin Riddles walked in. Beside Khaba sat Witkop Jansen. He looked even smaller than usual, and ill at ease, as if he would rather be anywhere else but there.

The provincial head of detectives was the only one who greeted Benny and his colleagues out loud. Khaba's eyes remained lowered, fixed on the screen of his cell phone lying on the table. There was no place to sit down. Benny and his colleagues lined up against the wall, facing the firing squad.

The room fell silent.

'The commissioner is going to brief the media at the gate,' said Witkop Jansen to Griessel in his heavy Afrikaans accent. 'What do we have for him on the Boonstra fifty-five?'

He knew this game, the give-us-something-to-pacify-the-media-monster dance. Griessel addressed Witkop Jansen and the provincial head of detectives when he spoke, the only two people in the room that he trusted. He provided the same information that he had passed on to Witkop Jansen in the early hours – all airports and border posts were on the lookout for Jasper Boonstra, arising from information provided by the missing person's family members. That was, however, not the only part of the SAPS investigation, since all possibilities were being considered. A large team of the Boland cluster's police would search the Baronsberg farm today, with the help of, among others, the dog unit. Griessel would examine Boonstra's phone and phone records and individuals that he had been in contact with the previous forty-eight hours. There were still many lines of investigation to be followed.

'Is the wife a suspect?' asked Khaba still watching his phone. Condescending, as if talking to a child. 'My people tell me that is what the media really wants to know.'

Griessel heard the scorn in the general's voice and felt the same protest in his body as yesterday. He had also had very little sleep, he felt the fatigue creeping over him. He was a fuckup and an alcoholic, he'd made many mistakes in his life, but he was a good policeman, he fought the good, honest fight. Nobody had the right to talk to him that way. Last night he lost his temper and control, but not now. He remained calm, coldly formal: 'We prefer not to comment on or speculate about an ongoing investigation, General.'

He heard Cupido whispering enthusiastic approval beside him: 'Yes!'

Khaba was furious. He looked up from the cell phone and glared directly at Benny. 'I know that, Lieutenant, I do not need your answer for the media. I need to know for myself.'

He kept his voice level, without a hint of either exaggerated respect or disdain, gave just the facts: 'She is one of several persons of interest in the investigation. We have no reason to regard her as a suspect, and we have not discounted her. It's just too early to say. If and when this status changes, I will inform your office.'

Khaba stared suspiciously at Griessel and eventually decided being angry wasn't worth the effort. He turned on Witkop Jansen: 'And the boy? The student? Have you managed to make any progress?'

'Warrant Officer Cupido?' said Jansen.

'I believe we have, General,' said Vaughn. 'We will be approaching the court again today for a search warrant for the home of a Stellenbosch suspect, as well as subpoenas to access the phone and bank records of this suspect who has a criminal record. We are also waiting for information from the bank relating to international currency payments to the boy's account . . .'

'What payments? The boy received payments from overseas? Why was I not informed?' Khaba asked.

A colonel flew up and went to whisper in the general's ear. 'Oh,' he said. 'So we'll keep that quiet.'

'The boy's mother will be joining you at the news conference, General,' said the cluster commissioner. 'She is unaware of the foreign payments.'

'Yes, I understand. It is good that she is here. We want to show that we in the South African Police Service do not only serve the rich. I will tell her she has the full force of the police behind the investigation. Anything else?'

Jansen shook his head.

Khaba stood up. 'Okay. Let's go . . .'

The senior officers followed the commissioner out. The provincial head of detectives was the only one that came to shake their hands. 'Stay strong, boys,' he said and winked. 'Musad Manie sends greetings.'

Witkop Jansen nodded to them, barely perceptible, but clearly satisfied.

Sandra was with the twins on the way to the nursery school when her phone rang. She saw who it was, knew exactly what to expect.

'Charlie, you're on speaker,' she answered. Then to the twins: 'Say "hello" to Uncle Charlie.'

'Hello, Uncle Charlie,' they chanted in sing-song voices.

She suspected Charlie desperately wanted to talk about Boonstra. He must have watched the TV news, or heard about the disappearance on the radio. He wouldn't want to make baby talk now. But she had to pretend there was absolutely nothing to be worried about.

'Hello, hello, children,' said Charlie, as he could never remember their names. 'Have fun . . .' then suddenly serious, urgency in his voice: 'Sandy-san, did you see?'

'I didn't see, but his lawyer phoned me this morning.'

'What did he want? Sandy-san, it's a tragedy. The timing, it's . . . What are we going to do?'

'I think I have good news, Charlie. I'll call you back as soon as I've dropped Anke and Bianca off.'

'But . . . I . . . Sandy-san . . .' she could hear him wrestling with the consuming curiosity and anxiety. 'Okay, okay, as soon as you can . . .' Then he rang off.

'Uncle Charlie is funny,' said Bianca.

'Very funny,' said Anke. 'I like him.'

Twenty detectives from the Stellenbosch station stood outside the parade room waiting for the commissioner and his team to exit. They had seen the media crowd waiting at the detective branch gate in Adam Tas Avenue – a larger crowd than any they had ever experienced. The room buzzed.

Witkop Jansen called the meeting to order.

'We will not open with prayer this morning. Griessel and Cupido will tell you what is happening with the two fifty-fives,' he said. 'All other investigations are suspended, you will assist them in any way they need you. Only if they don't need you, may you go work on your own dockets. Do you receive me?'

When she called Charlie back from the car, he wasn't happy. 'You're making me sweat, Sandy-san, how long does it take to drop two children off?'

'When were you last on the R44 at this time of the morning, Charlie?'

'Oh, never mind now. What did the lawyer say?'

'He said the police are going to want to talk to us today . . .'

'Ooh, *Jitte Krismis*,' he said, panicking.

'Charlie, calm down.' The irony – that in these circumstances she was the one pacifying Charlie – did not escape her. 'The man asked that we say nothing about Donkerdrif . . .'

'How can we say nothing? It would look like we were hiding something.'

'Charlie, in the first place, the lawyer said Jasper has not disappeared, he's just lying low somewhere. In the second place, the sale of Donkerdrif is between two companies that Jasper has no official interest in. In the third place, I have the sole mandate on my desk that Jasper signed. For Baronsberg. I'm going to tell the police that is what he wanted to see me about. All completely true. Everything is going to be okay. Tomorrow we get our money.'

Just a moment of silence, then Charlie said: '*Jitte Krismis*, Sandy-san. I'm not built for this sort of thing. See you soon.'

He rang off.

It was suddenly quiet in the EcoSport. Her own voice echoed in her head, the self-assured, calm woman. In charge.

She looked in the rear-view mirror, saw her eyes.

She felt a deep loathing but also a sense of pride, and that was what bothered her most of all.

Griessel and Erin Riddles agreed that she would tackle the search of the Baronsberg grounds on their behalf. There were blood and cadaver dogs from the SAPS K9 unit at her disposal, and about fifty detectives and uniforms from the local station, Franschhoek and Paarl.

'We will have to post ten of them to man the farm's two gates just to keep the media out,' she said before she left.

Griessel went into the office, took out his notebook to find Meinhardt Sarazin's number, so that he could ask the lawyer and Lettie Boonstra to meet them on the farm. At eleven. Or suffer the consequences. And he wanted to ask the woman if she knew the password for Jasper's phone.

In his pocket, his phone rang. He took it out as he walked into the office. He didn't recognise the number.

'Griessel.'

'Hello,' said a woman's voice. 'My name is Sandra Steenberg. I hear you're looking for Jasper Boonstra. I saw him yesterday morning, if that helps . . .'

53

Cupido stood and explained to Witkop Jansen that he had a much better chance today of getting a search warrant for Roland Parker's house, because he could add the information about the Kruger Rand, the jewellery and the substantial overseas payments to Callie de Bruin's account.

'Do you want to go to court yourself?'

'Yes, Colonel, I know all the ins and outs, it will be faster. But I need people for the search itself.'

'How many?'

'As many as I can get. I want that *oke* to think Armageddon has come. I want him to tremble at the holy might of the SAPS, I want us to fill the whole street, so his mommy can get a proper fright. The more pressure she puts on his . . .'

'Twenty enough?'

Before Cupido could respond, his phone rang, and he answered: 'Hello, this is Vaughn.'

'Hello, it's Megan Daniels from Capitec. I think I have good news. We just received an email from Wells Fargo in the USA . . .'

'Who?'

'It's one of the banks that transferred a large payment to Callie's account. An American bank . . .'

'Okay, okay,' he said and felt a spark of hope.

'It has to do with the transaction of a hundred and ten thousand rand . . .'

'Right.' He took out his notebook and pen.

'Yesterday afternoon I sent an email to their international department where I explained the whole situation. About Callie, how he's disappeared and so on. Otherwise, if there is no context, if it's just numbers and codes, then it takes more time for the people to respond, if you know what I mean . . .'

'I understand,' said Cupido, willing her to get to the point.

'And when I arrived at work, there was an answer from them, from a woman at Wells Fargo who said, I'm also a mother, she could only imagine what it must be like for Callie's mother. And she immediately looked up the transaction and saw who made the payment. Then she contacted the client, and the man said you can contact him any time. His name is David Joy, he's from Dillsboro in North Carolina. I'm sending you his contact details. There is a telephone number as well. It's, let me see . . . about twenty past two in the morning there, if you want to call a bit later . . . I think it's a funny thing, this. This David Joy told the Wells Fargo people the payment of a hundred and ten thousand was for a rifle. A Webley-Fosbery, the email says. I didn't even know there *was* such a rifle . . .'

Sandra told the Stellenbosch police station over the phone that she had been with Jasper Boonstra yesterday and she would like to talk to the investigating officer. They gave her the number of a Warrant Officer Benny Griessel.

And now she was listening attentively to the man's voice. He said: 'Yes, thank you for the call, you were on my list of people. Can I come round to you in an hour or so?'

He sounded confused, as if his mind was elsewhere. 'Of course,' Sandra said. 'I am at Benson International Realtors in Dorp Street, opposite the Old College building.'

'Just hang on,' the detective said, 'I'm writing that down . . .'

She waited.

'Thank you,' said Griessel. 'Oh, in the meantime: Do you know where Boonstra is now?'

The question was so unexpected, making her heart skip a beat, and for the tiniest second she thought: What does he know? Then she said: 'He didn't say anything, no.'

'Okay, thanks, I'll come as soon as I can.' Then he was gone and she took a deep breath. Breathe, the first round had been fired, she'd done the right thing, contacting him. It was exactly what an innocent none-the-wiser Sandra would have done.

A Webley-Fosbery? He'd never heard of a gun called a Webley. Cupido phoned Bossie Bossert, the gunsmith at the Hawks in Bellville.

'Bossie, it's Vaughn. Listen, have you ever in your life heard of a Webley-Fosbery?'

'Yes, Captain.' Bossie still called him 'Captain' from force of habit. He let it go.

'What sort of rifle is it?' Cupido asked.

'It's not a rifle, Captain, it's a revolver. Lovely thing, they say it's the first automatic revolver. Very accurate, because there is less recoil.'

'Can *this* thing be worth a hundred and ten thousand rand?'

'Yes, Captain, especially if it's one of the first. They are rare, it came out around 1895, the English used them in the Boer War, but it wasn't very popular, too big and heavy.'

'So this is an antique firearm?'

'That's correct, Captain.'

'Collector's item?'

'Yes, Captain.'

'But definitely not a rifle.'

'No, Captain. You get your Webley & Scott air rifle, but you don't call that a Fosbery. Fosbery was the chap who designed the automatic revolver. He was a soldier in India.'

'*Fokken* women,' said Cupido. 'Anything that shoots is a rifle to them. Thanks, Bossie, thank you very much.'

Griessel phoned Meinhardt Sarazin and asked the lawyer to be at Baronsberg no later than ten. Then he asked for Lettie Boonstra's number. He had to check his notebook for the name of Jasper Boonstra's mistress.

'And Jenna Abbott, do you have her number?'

'I already spoke to her. She doesn't know where Mr Boonstra is.'

'Do you have her number?'

Sarazin was reluctant, but eventually surrendered it.

Benny sat quietly for a while before ringing Lettie Boonstra. He wanted to be calm; he wasn't going to allow her to get under his skin again.

'Yes?' she answered, as if the call was an annoyance.

He identified himself, and asked her to be at Baronsberg before ten o'clock.

'What for?' she asked.

'Ma'am, these are your choices,' said Griessel, 'you can be there and assist us in our investigation. You can come and fill in a SAPS ninety-two. Or you can be arrested for obstruction of justice.'

A pause before she asked: 'What is a SAPS ninety-two?'

'That is the form that has to be completed so that we stop searching for your husband.'

'You're wasting my time.'

'Let us hope, ma'am,' Griessel said, 'that you're not wasting *my* time. Another thing: do you know the pin code for your husband's cell phone?'

'Yes. It's zero, seven, one, nine, nine, seven. That's the month and year that he made his first million.'

A Webley-Fosbery? Callie de Bruin got a hundred and ten thousand rand from an American for a Webley-Fosbery? That he got where?

Cupido wanted to talk to Benny *now*, that's how they rolled, he got the info, then they tossed it around, considered it from all angles. But now Benny was on the Boonstra case. He wanted to phone North Carolina now, but he realised it was around three in the morning there, better to wait, he should get the court order to search Rolster Parker's place, to look at his banking, and procure his cell phone records.

He jogged outside to his car. His phone rang.

'Christ,' he said, this was one crazy morning. He answered on the move. 'Cupido.'

'Captain Innis of the Gang unit,' said a man's voice. 'We last saw each other at the seminar on sex discrimination . . .'

'*Jis, jis*, howzit?'

'No better here than with you, I hear on the radio. Listen, the photo you sent, the *outjie* with the hoody . . .'

'*Ja.*'

'We think we know the *laaitie*. He's a member of the Trojans in Elsies. Dogsbody and junior wing man for the gang leader, but up and coming. His name is Willie Gezwint, they call him "Hond", or "The Dog".'

'In Elsies?' said Cupido. 'Captain, with all due respect, are you absolutely sure?'

'Look, you didn't send us the best photo. It's a video screen grab, hey?'

'*Jis.*'

'Okay. The Dog has a tattoo here on his neck, on the left side. It says *Dance With The Devil*. On your screen capture it looks like you can see the "D" and the "a" of *Dance*. Maybe there is better footage, have a look. If that's the tattoo, then that's your man.'

54

'Hello,' said Jenna Abbott. Griessel could detect the hesitant caution in that single word.

He knew far too little about her. He remembered the photos in the newspapers, how some of his Hawks colleagues were all fired up about what a babe she was, especially the famous bum, the 'sexy bottom' that Lettie Boonstra had referred to last night. But information was scant about who and what she was. Or perhaps no one had gone to the trouble to go into that detail?

He told her his rank and name, and why he was calling.

'Yes,' she said. 'Meinhardt Sarazin WhatsApped me you were going to call. I don't know where Jasper is.'

'I understand it's a difficult situation for you, but I must ask you a few questions.'

'Ask away,' she said, resigned.

'When last did you hear from him?'

'I phoned Jasper last Wednesday, Mr Griebel. At about half past seven in the morning.'

He glossed over the 'Griebel', she must be anxious. 'That was the last contact of any kind that you had?'

'Yes.'

'Did he tell you he was going away? Mentioned the possibility at all?'

'No.'

'What did you talk about last Wednesday?'

'Is it really necessary to go into that?'

'Miss, your name was mentioned by those involved in the case. Some believe that you are party to Jasper Boonstra's plans to disappear. The more . . .'

'Probably Lettie. The bitch.'

'The more you tell me, the sooner I can remove your name from my list and leave you in peace.'

'Leave me in peace? The papers are camped out across the street. They keep calling me, they send me one SMS after the other, I don't know where those people even got my number. Do you think it will make any difference if *you* leave me in peace?'

Griessel tried to remain patient. 'What did you talk about last Wednesday?'

'I swore at Jasper. I told him he was effing rubbish, effing pathetic, he doesn't know what love is, he thinks he can buy everything. That's what we talked about, Mr Griebel. What else do you want to know? Don't you read *You* magazine? He chucked me out of my house. The house he promised would be mine. No matter what, I was getting the house, and then he got the hots for a new girl, she's probably going to move in there now. I told him he's just as greedy for sex as he is for money, he will never be satisfied with what he has, and it will eat him up. That was what we talked about, Mr Griebel.'

'Is there a new . . . another woman in his life?'

'Of course there is. Jasper always has to have a Plan B. It comes from growing up poor. He told me, he admits it, he always plans as if he's going to lose what he has. I mean, *I was* his Plan B, he said Lettie was going to leave him . . .'

'Do you know who it is? The new woman?'

Her voice rose an octave: 'Oh, I can describe her for you. She will have a pretty pair of tits, and you can be dead sure she's going to have a nice ass. That effing piece of shit Jasper Boonstra likes an ass like flies love a turd . . .'

He could hear her trying to control her breathing. When she spoke again she sounded despairing. 'Lord, Mr Griebel, listen to me, I sound just like the tart I am. How do you get yourself back again? What does your detective textbook say about finding yourself again after a mess like this.'

The news about Jasper Boonstra's disappearance was leaked two hours too late to make the morning issues of the daily papers, but at least a day too late for the local Stellenbosch rag, the *Eikestad News*. It appeared once a week, early on Thursdays. A whole stack were dropped off at Benson International Realtors, because they usually advertised numerous properties. The receptionist at the front door took delivery of the newspapers and then asked the tea lady to distribute them throughout the offices.

Sandra stayed out of Charlie's way. She wanted to save her energy for dealing with the detective, that was going to require her full focus and attention. She went to the kitchen to make herself some coffee, phone in hand, researching how to lie successfully to the police. These guys were old hands, they knew all the tricks. *Signs that someone is lying,* she typed into Google. She quickly scanned the first article, from a website on social psychology. It said that people who told untruths were guilty of:

Being vague; offering few details.

Repeating questions before answering them.

Speaking in sentence fragments.

Failing to provide specific details when a story is challenged.

Grooming behaviours such as playing with hair or pressing fingers to lips.

She picked up her coffee, read it while she walked back to her desk, trying to memorise the principles. At her desk she found the new issue of the *Eikestad News.* There was a photo of Callie de Bruin and his mother Annemarie on the front page. A big photo. Underneath the headline *STUDENT DISAPPEARS.*

And below that: *A mother's grief.*

She stood, mug in one hand and cell phone in the other, and stared. The photo was cropped so that only the head and shoulders of the mother and son were visible. They stood close together. Sandra could see they had the same skinny build, the same large round noses. Callie's eyes were different, large and innocent. And happy, she thought. Childishly happy, like someone who'd won a prize.

His mother's eyes were weary.

Sandra's conscience stabbed like a sudden dagger in her gut: Was this the face she'd seen yesterday in the house beyond the fence? This child? He . . . Looked like a farm boy, a carefree, naïve farm boy, whose life might now be hanging in the balance. What exactly was it that she'd seen? She was so upset, overwhelmed, shocked, traumatised . . . had she imagined it? This child looked too skinny, too . . .

She really couldn't be sure of what she'd seen.

Perhaps it was just her imagination. The phone on her desk shrilled, making her jump. She answered.

'Sandra, there's a Warrant Officer Griessel here to see you.'

So, here it was. The moment of truth, make or break. She felt the receiver in her hand begin to tremble and needed to sit down, suddenly weak.

'I'm coming,' she said. 'Take him to the conference room.'

She must just quickly read through the article on her phone again.

Cupido walked down the passage of the court building, cell phone at his ear. He told Veronica Williams at Campus Security: 'Just check for me if they can't get a better angle for a tattoo on Hoody's neck, any indication *Dance With The Devil* is there, please, my sister.'

'We'll look. I'm glad I'm talking to you. We're just about finished with the list of cars that drove down Merriman that evening. It's not perfect, but it's the best that we can do.'

'Okay, what have you got? Registration numbers?'

'We have a spreadsheet with the make, colour, model and registration numbers, but as I said, there are gaps in the data. For what it's worth. We just don't have the manpower to put it all through NaTIS.'

'Email me, sister, I'll put a couple of detectives on it so long. If you could just check out that tattoo for me?'

He was standing with his back to her, cell phone in his hand.

Sandra had no idea what to expect. She cleared her throat and he turned around, and she saw his ruffled hair, long overdue for a cut, curling over his ears and collar. She saw the fine network of red and blue veins on his nose, the mark of a heavy drinker. The way he held his head and shoulders, with a sort of embarrassment, as if he regretted the impression he knew he was making.

She felt relief. This was the best they could do, this . . . specimen – that was the word that occurred to her – to send this specimen to her.

But then she saw the eyes, the dark brown, peculiar eyes, almond-shaped, exotic, like something from the Steppes. They contained a certain wisdom, the reflection of a thousand things seen and experienced, and she knew instinctively she must tread very warily. It was the eyes that told the truth about him, not the slope of his shoulders or the tracks left by the booze.

Griessel stood with Jasper Boonstra's phone in his hand. He was look-ing at the WhatsApps of the past week or so, but saw nothing that gave any indication of where the man might be now. And why hadn't Boonstra taken his phone along? Because he was clever, because he knew he could be traced and followed through it?

Why leave the phone so neatly on his desk?

Was there a message contained in that act that he didn't understand?

He heard the woman enter the conference room. He turned and saw her standing there in her yellow sleeveless sun dress: she was lovely, alluring, a beautiful glow to her skin. He couldn't help it, he thought of Jenna Abbott's words: *She will have a pretty pair of tits, and you can be dead sure she's going to have a nice ass.* A description that matched this woman standing in front of him.

Sandra Steenberg put her hand out, her generous mouth smiling, and said: 'Warrant Officer Griessel, I am Sandra. Please, do sit down.'

She gestured at the round six-seater table. He said 'thank you', pulled out a chair and sat down.

'Coffee, tea? Water?' she asked, still smiling.

'No thank you,' he said.

She sat down opposite him.

'Thank you for calling this morning,' he said.

'Not at all,' she said and clasped her hands together.

He saw her right hand tightly grasp her left hand. He noticed the wedding ring. He noticed the fine sheen of perspiration on her upper lip, almost imperceptible. Then he smelt her. He smelt the subtle perfume and he smelt the faint perspiration and he thought, it's too early for sweat. It wasn't hot inside the building. Even outside it was moderate.

She's nervous, he thought.

Why was she so on edge?

He wished Vaughn Cupido was here to ask the questions, to draw her out, play cat and mouse with her, and leave him to watch her intently, and think.

55

Things are getting out of hand, thought Vaughn Cupido.

It was all very well for Witkop Jansen to say they could have twenty more people, but the Callie docket was on his mind and in Benny's, and now Benny wasn't here. He wanted to talk to him about a member of the Trojans from Elsies by the name of Willie Gezwint, how the fuck did that happen? Hoody was a gang banger? Couldn't be, Gang unit must have this one wrong.

And yet, and yet, somewhere a tumbler and a gear were trying to mesh. And Callie de Bruin had exported an antique revolver to America, and something there was also straining to connect, but first, right now, he had to get to the magistrate.

He found a different magistrate, a younger one, who'd read the *Eikestad News* that morning, who could tell these were desperate times. She signed with a flourish and told him: 'You go, Warrant Officer,' and he ran out, phoned Witkop, and said: 'Colonel, let's roll, send in the cavalry, I have the search warrant.'

'I'm sending them,' said Jansen.

'There's another thing now, Colonel, the varsity people sent a spreadsheet of all the cars that could have picked up Callie that evening, I need hands to process the data through NaTIS.'

'Can you get the spreadsheet to me?'

'*Yebo*, yes, Colonel, I'm sending it from my phone here.' And then he was at the car and he jumped in, he had to get moving, to Cloetesville. We're coming for you, Rolster, and we're gonna nail your arse, motherfucker.

But first he sent the spreadsheet of vehicle particulars to Witkop Jansen.

'How long have you known Boonstra?' Griessel asked.

'Let me check my calendar . . . He phoned me on the nineteenth of September. That's a little over two weeks ago.'

She had an attractive voice too, he thought, round and full like the second string, the open A on his bass guitar. 'How did you meet?'

'Oh, out of the blue, that morning. He found my number on our website and asked me to come and see him. So I drove out to him, on the estate.'

'About a property?'

'That's right. Not that he wanted to say immediately. He's a . . . I'll just say that he's quite a character.'

Griessel noted that she had started to relax a little. He had a sudden memory of 'Santa Maria', the tango song from Gotan Project, that Rust had to learn to play for a wedding. The bride and groom had seen the Richard Gere film and they wanted to do it. Benny enjoyed the bass part immensely; it was the engine of the song, different from Rust's usual songs. But at the wedding he had thought, this couple are not tango people, the music alone wasn't going to save them. And now, while he sat and watched Sandra Steenberg, listened to her speak he thought, *she* certainly was a tango woman, this sultry, smouldering beauty. Jasper Boonstra would have seen that too. And reacted to it?

'He wanted to sell the farm?'

She gave him an appraising look, as if judging how much of the truth he could handle, and then she said: 'Warrant Officer, to be frank, I'm not sure what Jasper's actual agenda is with me. But my husband and I are not rich, and Jasper's properties are worth a great deal. So, I ignored his advances and went back every time. He did eventually sign a sole mandate for Baronsberg.'

'Some of your company's forms were on his desk,' Benny Griessel said.

'Oh, yes, I left two extra ones there. He said if we exercised the necessary discretion with Baronsberg, there were other properties . . .'

'Did he say which?'

'Not directly, but I could deduce there was a house in Franschhoek.'

'So, he wanted to . . . offload quite a few of his properties?'

She released her clasped hands, Griessel noted, and leaned back slightly. 'Yes and no. When I came back to the office yesterday and researched Baronsberg's title deeds . . . It doesn't belong to Jasper. He didn't specifically say it was in his name . . .'

'Who does it belong to?'

'A company. Zircon Aere.'

Griessel asked her to spell it while he wrote down the name in his notebook.

'Ma'am, did he say anything yesterday that led you to believe he was intending to . . . go away?'

She thought for a second, then said: 'This morning when I heard you were looking for him, I wondered about that. The only thing I can think of is that he said his lawyer would talk to me in future. About Baronsberg. But at the time I just thought he'd grown tired of me.' Again she paused. 'Warrant Officer, to be frank, every time I was there, he . . . We were alone every time, and every time he was . . . inappropriate. Suggestive. There were certain innuendos. That I could get the mandate, but he said, it "was not for free". I don't have to spell it out for you. But not yesterday. Yesterday he was . . . I thought his mind was elsewhere. I thought he'd finally got the message, had lost interest, at least in that way. And so now he wanted to palm me off on his lawyer. To be frank, I'm not completely certain we really will have the opportunity to sell Baronsberg after all.'

Matters didn't work out precisely as Cupido had hoped at Roland 'The Rolster' Parker's house.

The cavalry rolled up in six police vehicles, lights flashing, wailing sirens. The dog behind the iron gate didn't bark, but ran with its tail between its legs to the back yard. Vaughn, search warrant in hand, and the twenty-one Stellenbosch detectives charged up to the front door. The aunty opened it. She said: 'Rolster has gone.' And then she began to cry.

Cupido steered her to the humble sitting room. He shut the door, to spare her the sight of the invading horde of detectives searching her home. He wanted to console her. He sat down on the sofa beside her, said: 'Sorry, aunty, I'm really sorry,' but she stood up and went to sit on a chair and said: 'You stay away from me.'

'Aunty, I'm genuinely sorry, but I'm just doing my job. Rolster can help us find young Callie de Bruin, all he has to do is tell us what he knows.'

The way she looked at him, leaning her body away from him as if she was afraid of a physical assault, made him suspect something was very wrong.

'Aunty, why are you so scared?'

She said nothing, just wept.

Cupido thought about The Dog Gezwint, the Trojans gang member from Elsies, and he had a feeling. 'Did Rolster tell you he's afraid of the gangs? Did he say the gangs threatened his mother?'

She just sat there.

'Aunty, I swear to you, those gangs won't do anything to you, and if Rolster comes to us, we will put him in witness protection. Whatever he and Callie had to do with the gangs, we will help you.'

'You?' she said in a voice both fearful and reproachful. '*You* will help us?'

'Yes, aunty.' And he thought, now he would have to defend the SAPS again, because here comes another accusation of 'you're all part of state capture'.

'It's you he's afraid of,' she said. 'You lot.'

'Us?'

She rose from the chair, still weeping, distraught. She waved her hands, voice shrill: 'My child stood there in the middle of the night, with his suitcase, and I said let's go talk to the Boere, they look like reasonable people, those two. He said no, Mommy, don't trust the cops, they killed Callie. And they're coming for me too, as soon as they know how much I know.'

'Us?'

'Yes, you lot. What have you done? My Rolster, living in fear, what have you done?'

'He said Callie was killed?'

She nodded her head, she was beyond words.

Cupido was dumbstruck. He wanted to tell her that her son was lying, big lies, and that to his poor mother. He saw how despairing and broken she looked as she sank back into the chair. His urge to console her battled with the rising tide of anger at Rolster Parker. But he had no words for any of it, as his mind struggled to comprehend the news that Callie was dead.

The sitting room door opened. A detective peered in. He nodded at Cupido: 'You better come and see.'

Warrant Officer Griessel stood up and said: 'Thank you, ma'am, thank you very much,' with that faint air of embarrassment, regret that he wasn't more impressive, it still seemed to her. His notebook and pen in hand. He snapped the notebook closed, as if there was nothing of any significance to record. Just another minute or two, and she could relax. It was going well, it was going well after all. She stood up.

He walked towards the door, opened it, and stood back so that she could pass through ahead of him. Then added: 'Boonstra made certain . . . suggestions . . .?'

'Yes,' she said.

'Did he . . . Try to touch you?'

Sandra saw how uncomfortable the detective was with the question, and she thought, all that booze, all that life and experience and things he had seen, but he struggled to ask her this. Strange world. 'No,' she said. 'Thankfully not.'

'Okay,' he said, and waved the notebook in the direction of the door.

They walked to the front door together. 'I may want to speak to you again, if something comes up,' he said. 'Thank you.'

'A pleasure,' she said. 'Goodbye, Warrant Officer.'

He looked at her half shyly and then he nodded and went out. She watched him as he walked out onto the pavement, and then jogged across the street. He was a peculiar figure. As policemen of his ilk probably were, she thought. Late forties. White. A lot of mileage on the clock, he looked like one of her father's drinking buddies. Incapable of finding a better job, trapped where he was.

She felt faintly relieved, one became so accustomed to the TV detectives, the sharp, young, dynamic and attractive people who would mercilessly home in on the minutest details.

She turned, went back to her office. She'd handled it well, she thought. Avoided all the traps. She hadn't been overly vague, she gave detail where necessary, she hadn't repeated a single question before answering. For the most part she had spoken in full sentences, and above all, she kept her hands still and in front of her, she hadn't fiddled with her hair or touched her mouth.

She drew a deep breath in an attempt to release some of the tension in her body.

Charlie hurried down the stairs, anxious. 'Sandy-san?' he asked. 'Has he gone?'

'Yes, Charlie.'

'Come,' he said theatrically, 'come and tell me everything.'

56

Griessel drove to Baronsberg.

Sandra Steenberg was lying, he thought. Strung as taut as a wire. The clasped, still hands, that sheen of perspiration. On edge because she was being questioned by a policeman? Because she had been drawn into the drama surrounding the disappearance of the notorious Jasper Boonstra?

Perhaps.

But she had been lying. Three times she'd said: 'Officer, to be frank . . .' Three times. It was a strong indication. Very strong.

Why had she lied? Why was she so tense?

She was married. *My husband and I are not rich.*

Was she tense because she'd slept with Boonstra? Afraid her husband would find out. Now, with all the fuss?

Boonstra had made advances, she admitted that. Boonstra had said she could sell the properties but *it's not for free.* If she and her husband were not well off, she could probably do with the money.

Had she slept with him because she was prepared to pay that price? . . . *and then he got the hots for a new girl, she's probably going to move in there now.* Jenna Abbott's words.

Was Sandra Steenberg lying because Boonstra was somewhere waiting for her, ready to start a new life with his new girl, now that his wife didn't want him back any more? Or something along those lines?

Why was she lying?

In Rolster Parker's mother's kitchen, on the counter top, were four large round, white tins with bright red lids. Each of the four tins had a word in red letters. *Salt. Sugar. Flour. Rice.* The lid was off the one containing sugar.

The detective who had called him, a sergeant, motioned Cupido to look inside.

Cupido looked. The sugar level was low. On top of the sugar were five rolls of bank notes wrapped with a rubber band. They seemed to be mostly two-hundred-rand notes, at least fifty notes to a roll, Vaughn made a quick estimate. A hundred thousand rand, more or less.

He whistled softly through his teeth.

And below that, visible between the notes, was a small, flat, transparent square box.

He made sure the sergeant was wearing gloves. 'Take that out,' said Cupido.

The sergeant removed the rolls of notes, arranged them on the kitchen counter. Then the perspex box.

They could see it contained a small gold coin. With the head of a man with a long beard minted on it.

'That looks like Paul Kruger,' the sergeant said.

He turned the box over. On the reverse side of the coin were the figures 18398, the three was considerably larger than the others.

'Is it a Kruger Rand?' the sergeant asked.

'No,' said Cupido. 'A Kruger Rand also has that head of Kruger on it, but on the other side it has a springbok.'

He became aware that Mrs Parker had come to stand in the doorway, her eyes damp with tears, worry etched deeply on her face.

The sergeant pointed at the cash and the coin: 'Tag it and bag it?' he asked Cupido.

'Wait,' said Vaughn. He walked over to the woman: 'Aunty, you know all that money, Rolster maybe didn't make it in an exactly legal way.'

'I know,' she said. 'I know.'

Sandra had to relate the entire interview to Charlie Benson before his knee stopped twitching. He asked her if she really thought the police wouldn't find out about the Donkerdrif deal.

'Who is going to tell them, Charlie? You?'

'Of course not.'

'Well, I'm not going to, you're not going to, and Jasper and his lawyer won't either. We all want it dealt with without anyone except us knowing who is involved.'

'So the detective . . . What's his name?'

'Griessel.'

'This Griessel knew nothing about Donkerdrif?'

'Nothing.'

'*Jitte Krismis.*'

'Charlie, relax. You'll see, tomorrow we'll receive the payment.'

He relaxed visibly, leaned back in his chair. 'Yes, Sandy-san ... It will be good if we talk about that again.'

'There's nothing to talk about. Demeter pays Stirling and Heyns, Stirling and Heyns pay us, and then they can all do what they like.'

'The percentages, Sandy-san. Because under the circumstances I think . . .'

She felt the anger reignite inside. 'Circumstances? What do you mean, circumstances?'

'You and I are equally deep in this thing. We have the same at stake . . .'

'What exactly are you saying, Charlie?'

'I say fifty-fifty.'

'It's too late to negotiate now, Charlie. We have an agreement.'

'You must think carefully about it. I know things now.'

'You know things? What things, Charlie?' she asked as the anger blossomed inside her.

'Now don't be angry, Sandy-san, I just want to say, you don't really want me to talk to Griessel.'

She sprang up from the chair. The words she wanted to snarl at Charlie Benson jostled in her mind, unleashed by the trauma of the past forty-eight hours, the tension, and her temper. On the tip of her tongue, the *Fuck you, Charlie, fuck you, you lousy little coward, you black-mailer*, but she wasn't the same Sandra that she had been yesterday morning, she was stronger, much stronger now. And Charlie knew nothing. Nothing.

She slowly sat down again, smiling at him. 'And what are you going to say to Griessel, Charlie? That we helped to sell Donkerdrif? And then he goes to talk to Stirling and Heyns, and Demeter cancels every-thing? And we both get nothing? Really? That's your master plan?'

She saw the flicker of hatred in Charlie's eyes, and she thought: How very greedy he is.

'I'd think carefully if I were you,' said Charlie venomously.

'I already have,' she said. She stood up and walked out. To her office, her heart thumping. What was she going to do if Charlie really did . . . get nasty.

Vaughn Cupido had only vaguely heard of chaos theory. And never really took in the common example used to illustrate it: the fluttering of a butterfly's wings in (let us say) Japan delicately disturbs the air current, and eventually, weeks later, a tornado is unleashed on another continent.

But if someone took the trouble to explain it in detail to him, he would immediately understand. He experienced it often: that tiny event that suddenly altered the direction, speed or feel of an investigation completely.

A word, perhaps, a footprint or a fingerprint, a video clip, some DNA.

Or a phone call. From Veronica Adams at the University of Stellenbosch Campus Security.

He was standing in front of Mrs Parker, uncertain how to handle the discovery in the sugar tin, and her distress. His phone rang. He checked the caller ID first; he really did not want to be disturbed right now. He recognised the number.

'*Jis*,' he answered.

'The hoody *ou* in the video has a tattoo,' Adams said. 'On the neck. We played it forward and backwards, you can almost make out the word "dance", at least the "d" and the "a" and the "n".'

Dance With The Devil.

'Shit,' said Cupido.

'Why are you saying "shit"?' Veronica Adams asked him.

'Gang banger,' said Cupido.

Mrs Parker was standing in front of him, still moist-eyed and despairing, and in that moment Vaughn was seized by the inspiration, strengthened by the fluttering of the butterfly wings. He looked straight at Mrs Parker and said to Adams: 'Veronica, I need your help please. I have Aunty Parker here in Cloetesville. Aunty Parker's son can help us to find Callie. But now her son told her not to trust the cops, that it's us who took Callie out. I want to give the phone to her, maybe you can convince her, *chlora* to *chlora*, that she can trust me, we're working with the university people, not against them.'

Adams had been a policewoman, she understood instantly. 'Okay,' she said.

Cupido handed the phone to Mrs Parker.

She took the phone reluctantly.

'Hello?' she said.

57

The media were still at the Baronsberg gate, their vehicles parked along Jonkershoek Road. Cameramen with long lenses photographing the policemen trudging in the distance across the farm, searching for signs of Jasper Boonstra, while the blood- and cadaver dogs sniffed back and forth between them.

The circus, in full swing, the whole shebang, Griessel thought as he drove in.

And he was not in the mood for it at all. Nor for this whole damn case. It was all just to pacify the press – his appointment and taking this fifty-five seriously, it sounded like a domestic dispute, at best, and a fugitive fraudster at worst. Or a choice blend of the two. While there was a young student he could be helping to find, a young student who was likely already dead.

He parked in front of the glass garage doors, got out. He phoned Sergeant Erin Riddles, to let her know he had arrived.

'So far nothing,' she said. 'It's as if . . . he's just vanished. Thin air.'

Griessel walked to the front door. A uniformed constable opened the door for him. Inside, Lettie Boonstra and Meinhardt Sarazin sat in silence, both occupied with their phones. A bit of an atmosphere, antagonistic, Benny felt.

Mrs Boonstra looked up. 'At last,' she said. This morning she was wearing a light blue blouse, jeans and a pair of brightly coloured running shoes. She looked like a kindly, middle-aged lady in trainers.

Griessel checked his watch. Just gone ten. The time he had asked her to be here.

'Good morning, ma'am. Would you please go through Mr Boonstra's bedroom and study again – or any other room where he might have stored something – and tell me if anything is missing . . .'

'I don't know what he kept in his study, Warrant Officer. It's a waste of time.'

Griessel sat down facing her. He said: 'Ma'am, I explained your choices this morning. Must I do it again?'

'I don't like your attitude.'

He'd had enough. He played his trump card: 'I don't like yours either. You have one minute, or I cancel the entire investigation, as Sarazin asked me to do yesterday.'

The lawyer looked up from his phone, approving.

Lettie Boonstra was not happy. She shot both men a dirty look, considered her options, and jumped up. 'I will look. But maybe you should ask Meinhardt to check the study. He knows more about what goes on there, don't you, Meinhardt? All the underhand shenanigans?'

'Where did Mr Boonstra keep his passport and ID book?' Griessel asked. 'His wallet? Is there a safe where he kept cash?'

She laughed at him. 'Jasper kept all his important documents in the top drawer of his desk. It's locked. And he keeps the key with him. You'll have to break it open, or call someone,' said Lettie Boonstra. 'He keeps his cash in Switzerland.'

Griessel's phone began to ring. He ignored it at first, because he remembered something he had seen during the search last night. 'Last night there was a key in a sweet bowl on his desk; go and see if it fits,' he told Lettie Boonstra.

She didn't react.

On his phone the screen read UNKNOWN. He answered: 'Griessel.'

'I can help you with the Boonstra affair,' said a male voice, muffled, as if he was making the call secretly.

'Who is this?' Benny asked, as he watched Lettie Boonstra walk reluctantly towards the stairs.

'I prefer to be anonymous.'

'How can you help me, sir?'

'Sandra Steenberg . . .'

'Yes?'

'I heard her say she could kill Boonstra.'

'Where and when did you hear that, sir?'

'Nearly two weeks ago . . .'

'Where?'

'I'd rather not say.'

'Who did she say that to?'

'I don't want . . . I just wanted to give you a tip. You must take a look at her. She said she wanted to kill him.'

'"Wanted"? Or "could"? Just now you said "could".'

'Want. Those were her exact words.'

Griessel sighed. 'Sir, I need more information if you want us to take you seriously.'

'I don't really want to get involved.'

'Then why did you call me?'

'Because I think it could have been San- . . . the Steenberg woman.'

'Who did what, sir?'

'He just disappeared, didn't he?'

'That's right.'

'It could have been her. Who did something to him.'

'What would have been her motive?'

Silence.

'Sir?'

'I just thought it was my duty, as a citizen, to let you know what I heard.'

'It is your duty, but I can't take you seriously if you won't give me more information.'

Another silence. Then the man said: 'Will you treat it with absolute confidentiality?'

'Sir, if your information results in her prosecution for anything, you may have to testify in court.'

'*Jitte Krismis.*'

'Do you want to provide more information?'

No reply.

'Sir,' said Griessel, 'I see that you have turned off caller ID on your phone. But I can still find out from which number you called me. Through the cell phone company.'

'I . . . You won't tell her where the information came from?'

'Not before the court case.'

The man hesitated before continuing. 'Very well. My name is Charlie Benson. Sandra works for me. About two weeks ago, she came back from seeing Jasper and she was very upset, it was plain to see. So I asked her: Are you okay, San-San? Then she said she was going to kill Jasper Boonstra.'

'Did she say why?'

'The entire town knows he's a sex pest, Warrant Officer. You don't have to be a genius to figure that out.'

Mrs Parker's knees trembled as she talked to Veronica Adams on the phone. For a long time. Standing with her in the passage, Cupido had to support her, and when the call was over, lead her back to the sitting room.

'Okay,' she said. 'Okay, okay.'

They sat down again on the sofa.

'Aunty, look here, look into my eyes.'

She looked, tearful, her entire body trembled.

'I want to promise, aunty, if Rolster helps us to find Callie, then I'll leave this tin with the cash and that coin . . .'

'It's a tickey,' she said. 'A Sammy Marks tickey. Rolster says it's worth a lot of money. He wanted me to keep it, he said for a rainy day, because he can't come back.'

'Well, if he helps us, then I'll leave that Sammy Marks tickey and the money in the sugar tin. No questions asked. And we'll see if he can maybe come back after all.'

'Really?'

'*Ja*, really. My job now is to find Callie, dead or alive. Because his own mommy is sitting here in a B and B and crying and worrying, just like aunty is. And my first responsibility is to take away her worry and her pain. So I'm willing to do the deal, but only if Rolster talks to me and tells me everything that he knows.'

'I'll ask him.'

'Where is he now, aunty?'

'He's gone north. I'm not going to say any more.'

'Okay. So here's what I'm going to do: all these detectives who are searching aunty's house, I'm going to tell them stop for now. Let me talk to Rolster. And if he says what I want to hear, then we walk away, and we leave the sugar tin here with aunty. Okay?'

'Okay.'

'And when I've found Callie, and there is nobody that lays a charge against Rolster, then I'll leave Rolster alone. Okay?'

'Okay.'

'Phone Rolster, on aunty's phone, 'cause he won't answer mine.'

'Oh, *ja*, of course . . .' She took out her cell phone.

Cupido stood up. 'Let me go and tell them to stop. And I'll bring the sugar tin, so aunty can hold on to it.'

58

Griessel sat in the reception lounge of the beautiful Baronsberg mansion. He was thinking he would have to get his arse in gear and start taking this fifty-five seriously, regardless of how crazy the case was.

The call from Charlie Benson, the malice in the man's voice, the envy. He was not a credible witness.

But if you didn't work through every vaguely credible tipoff, it could come back and bite you.

So he phoned Sandra Steenberg. When she answered, he asked her to please come to Baronsberg.

'Oh,' she said. 'May I ask why?'

'I just want to check a few things.'

After he rang off, he thought it might just be interesting to see how Mrs Lettie Boonstra reacted when she met Steenberg. The two women who had been here yesterday. Sandra Steenberg, the last person – as far as they knew – to see Jasper Boonstra. She said she left just before twelve. The CCTV confirmed that. Lettie Boonstra arrived at two o'clock. Again her testimony and the video at the gate agreed.

If they were both telling the truth, in the hours between twelve and two Jasper Boonstra simply disappeared.

There was no sign of a break-in, theft, or a struggle. Which suggested that Jasper Boonstra had slipped away of his own free will. To sidestep a potential court case?

It was possible. That's what Lettie Boonstra believed had happened. But why now? There wasn't even a whisper about possible arrest at this stage.

The alternative? Sandra Steenberg was lying about something. She was tense. Had she helped Boonstra escape, for a price? Ready to join him later?

You must take a look at her. She said she wanted to kill him.

Was Sandra Steenberg lying because she did something to Jasper Boonstra? Because Boonstra harassed her, if Charlie Benson was to be believed. Surely not impossible. Steenberg had been here for three hours yesterday, enough time to clean up after a struggle or a fatal shooting. But he battled to visualise *that* scenario – slender Steenberg against a relatively big man like Boonstra? Maybe if she had a firearm, but forensics hadn't found traces of blood. And surely she would have called the police if she'd done something in self-defence?

Unless romance was involved. A crime of passion? Jealousy?

Three hours was a long time. Enough time for sex *and* a fight?

That was hard to believe too. The circumstances just would not fit. She was the desirable one, she was married, she had a good job. Boonstra was the one with the reputation. The most likely scenario was that he was the one who wanted to do something to *her* out of jealousy or passion.

What then was Sandra Steenberg lying about?

He heard footsteps on the stairs. Sarazin and Lettie Boonstra. The woman was holding an electronic car key.

'We have to show you something,' the lawyer said and pointed towards the first floor. The man looked worried. Beside him, Mrs Boonstra looked merely irritated.

'Not yet. Wait,' she said. 'Just wait here, I want to check something in the Merc . . .' She walked to the kitchen. Then they heard the door to the garages open.

'The problem is there in his study,' said Sarazin, in his sonorous baritone.

'What problem?'

'Jasper had . . . That grand desk of his is hand-crafted. To order. With African Blackwood. The hardest wood there is. He had a specially reinforced top drawer built in, with a unique key, only one of its kind. It's practically impossible to get it open without the key, you would have to use some sort of saw and a crowbar. And he always carried the key on his person . . .'

'That's not completely true,' said Lettie Boonstra, coming back from the kitchen. She had an item in her hand, which she now held aloft. 'He usually kept the key in this . . .'

A brown leather wallet.

'And this wallet,' she said, 'was in the Merc's safe.'

'The Benz has a safe?' Griessel asked.

'The Mercedes G650 Landaulet. The SUV in the garage. If you have more money than sense, and a helluva chip on your shoulder, then you don't just buy your usual Merc G-class, you buy a Landaulet. It costs ten times more than the usual one. And then you hear that your super-rich friends have bought a Bentley Bentayga with a safe in it, a little one, between the two front seats. That you can open with your fingerprint or a key. Then you spend hundreds of thousands more to have one built into your Landaulet too. Because you can never bear to be second best. So that's where Jasper usually kept his wallet, when he was at home. Like yesterday . . .'

She opened the wallet. A few hundred rands cash and a bunch of bank cards. 'Everything is here, except the key . . .'

'But Lettie, we know that,' said Sarazin. 'The key is there upstairs, in the ostrich egg.'

'Ah, the legendary mantra shell. *Half an egg is never as good as the whole egg.* Jasper's I-am-a-greedy-fraudster mantra . . .'

'Lettie, please,' said Sarazin, tight-lipped and sanctimonious.

'The key,' Griessel steered them back to the subject of the conversation.

'Jasper would never have left it there on his desk,' said Sarazin. 'Not out in the open. It would have been in the wallet, or he would have taken it along.'

'It wasn't necessary to hide the key any more, because the crook book is gone,' said Lettie.

'There is *no* such thing,' said Sarazin.

'Of course there is,' she said.

'Is not,' he said.

Griessel just sighed.

'Come and see,' Sarazin told Benny, and walked up the stairs.

He and Lettie followed. 'By the way,' she said, 'there is a small suitcase missing from his wardrobe.'

'Just the suitcase?' asked Griessel as they climbed past the knight's metal suit.

'I really can't say. Jasper has more clothes than the Queen of England. Or Imelda Marcos. He could have taken half of them and I wouldn't have a clue. But the suitcase is not there. That's the one that he used when he went away for a night or two. Or, like now, when he wanted to travel light.'

Sarazin was waiting at the study door. 'Jasper kept all his most important documents in that drawer . . .' He pointed inside while he waited for Griessel to walk in.

The top drawer was wide open. Griessel had a look. The drawer was spacious and sturdy, reinforced inside with metal. The lock was nearly industrial size.

'Jasper really only kept his crook book in there,' Lettie said.

'Lettie, please,' said Sarazin.

'What is a crook book?' Griessel asked.

'There is no such thing,' said Sarazin.

Lettie laughed dryly.

'The crook book,' she said, 'is how my dear husband kept a record of all his fraud. You see, he's a very clever man . . .'

'Lettie . . .' said Sarazin.

'Be quiet, Meinhardt,' she said. Then to Griessel again: 'If you commit extremely complex fraud, Benny, you have to keep a record of it somewhere. If you hide all your assets, your money, your properties, your shares, you have to keep a book of all the companies, the bank account numbers and pin codes, and the safe deposit boxes, from Bermuda and the Cayman Islands to Luxembourg and Switzerland. So that you don't get your own crafty wires crossed later on. And that's why he needed the book – what I called his crook book . . .'

'That's nonsense,' said Sarazin. 'Jasper kept his passport and his ID and a few other documents in the drawer.'

'And those are also gone,' said Lettie. 'Along with the crook book.'

'Not true,' said Sarazin.

'And that, friends,' said Lettie Boonstra, 'is how we know that Jasper has done a runner. Because only he and Meinhardt knew about the crook book and how it worked. Passport and ID gone too. He left the wallet behind, because he knows if he uses a bank card, you will find him . . .'

'It seems to me you knew more about the contents of the drawer than I did, Lettie,' said Sarazin. 'It makes one wonder . . .'

'Really, Meinhardt?' she said. 'Really? Me? You are also a clever man. Spell it out to me and Benny here, the most likely explanation. I got my hands on the key, unlocked the drawer, took the crook book, ID and passport, put the key back nicely in the egg shell, and made Jasper disappear. Come on, tell us, how do you think I managed that?'

'I didn't say you did it.'

'Then who, Meinhardt? Who?'

Downstairs, the front doorbell chimed.

Griessel knew Sandra Steenberg had arrived.

59

'I don't want to talk to you,' Rolster Parker said over the phone to Cupido. 'I don't trust you.'

'Rolster,' said Cupido. 'I get that. But here are your prospects. I reckon you're in Joburg or somewhere round there, and if I really want to, I will find you. Phone tracing, traffic cameras, call in the full force of the SAPS, it might be a week, it might be two, but find you I will. But here's the thing, Rolster: my priority is Callie. That is my case, and I'm going to focus just on that. Your choice: your ma told you about the deal. And she's sitting here with the sugar tin in her hands. If you help me, the tin stays here. Including the contents.'

'I don't trust you.'

'You don't have a choice, *bra*.'

Cupido heard hip-hop music in the background. He wondered if Parker was in a bar somewhere in Johannesburg. They listened to a whole stanza.

Then Rolster replied: 'Have you got a ma?'

'Of course I have a ma. She lives there in the Belhar Six.'

'Then swear to me on your ma's name you're a man of honour.'

'I swear, Rolster, for what it's worth,' but Cupido suspected that Parker was just trying to soothe his own conscience, he knew he had no choice. 'Tell you what; I'll sweeten the deal a little. If you give me information that helps us find Callie, then I'll drop the general broadcast on you ...'

'What's a general broadcast?'

'That is what the Americans on TV call an APB, an All Points Bulletin. We tell every policeman in the country to arrest you, wherever they find you. If I drop the general broadcast, it means you can come back after a week or so, and see for yourself that your mommy is okay. Without fear of arrest.'

'How can I believe you?'

'Rolster, for fuck's sake, how many times do I have to say it: this isn't about you, *bra*. It's about Callie. Once we find him, no one's going to worry about a two-bit housebreaker in Cloetesville.'

Rolster thought.

'And the sugar tin, Rolster. Think about the sugar tin.'

Rolster thought.

'So,' said Cupido, 'I'll ask you again: why did you go and say that the SAPS nailed Callie?'

He heard Rolster inhale deeply, then slowly breathe out. 'Callie got into the Boere databases.'

'That we know, Rolster, that's how he wiped out your record. Give me something new.'

'I'm talking about the other databases. The ones for the firearms.'

'Why would he want to go in there?'

'First it was to sell. The data. Then later for the collectables.'

A light went on for Vaughn: 'Collectable firearms? Like a Webley-Fosbery?'

'That's right.'

'Okay, okay, explain to me *mooi*, Rolster. So he hacked into the SAPS databases for firearms, then he looked for collectables. And when he found them? What then?'

'Then he looked up what the stuff was worth in the USA. Then he or I went and made an offer to the local owner, whose details we got on the database. Lots of times, it was a little old lady, she didn't have a clue what the firearm was worth. We would buy it, and then Callie would sell it in the USA. Other times, when the owner knew what he had, he would just say, no thanks.'

'Rolster, but that sounds almost legal. That's not what made the trouble, is it?'

'No.'

'You'll have to tell me all of it.'

More music, more silence, more breathing. Cupido let him stew, Rolster had to decide himself to spell it all out.

'You were right. Callie did find me in the database for criminal records. He was looking for my skill set . . .'

'The big cat burglar. But why?'

'Well, he saw he could hack into all the short-term insurance data-bases. That's this treasure trove of stuff, rich whiteys who . . .'

'Wait, wait, short-term insurance? Like what?'

'All of them. Santam. Outsurance. Discovery. First for Women, the whole lot. Where all the rich whiteys conveniently list their valuables. So Callie had all this info, goods and alarm systems and addresses, but he couldn't get his hands on the stuff. Then he contacted me and said as a signing bonus he would wipe out my criminal record. And then we'd be partners, fifty-fifty.'

'Okay. That's where the jewellery and the Kruger Rands and the Sammy Marks tickey came from. He gets the info, you go break in. And he gets buyers for the stolen goods.'

'Basically, yes. But we got too successful. There just weren't enough gold and coin dealers and pawn shops to sell to without them getting suspicious. Then Callie said that is just the tip of the iceberg, we must diversify, 'cause data is free, and there's lots of it, and it's all accessible if you know how to get it. He went looking in other places too. Like the SAPS. 'Cause he saw, when he cleared my record, to get into govern-ment systems, that's easy, their stuff isn't very secure. So, in the begin-ning, when Callie found the firearms data, about which whiteys had guns in their houses. Hunting rifles, pistols for self-defence, that sort of thing. Then I told him I don't steal guns. That's another sort of trouble. But what I can do, I can sell the info to the syndicates, addresses, gun details, particulars of the gun safe. Then they go break in to steal the guns. No risk for us . . .'

'The syndicates? The township syndicates, or do you mean the gangs in the Flats?'

'No, no, the township syndicates. Those that specialise in armed robberies, cash-in-transit heists, carjacking, all the crimes that need guns.'

'Fuck,' said Cupido. 'But wait now, if you didn't do business with the Flats gangs, how did you piss off the Trojans from Elsies?'

'The Trojans? I don't know.'

'You're lying.'

'I'm telling you, I don't know.'

'You're lying, Rolster. The *outjie* who went into Callie's room on Sunday night, is a member of the Trojans from Elsies.'

'*Jirre, bra,* I swear, I don't know about that. Makes no sense . . .'

'Who has got Callie, Rolster? Why are you lying to your mommy, saying the Boere have him?'

'Because you . . . they do have him.' Desperation in Roland Parker's voice, almost begging Cupido to believe him.

'Where did you get that from?'

'Callie told me.'

'What did he say to you?'

Parker gave a deep sigh over the hip-hop that was still playing in the background. 'Last week, I think Tuesday, Callie phoned me, and he said, let's go eat a sirloin and egg at De Akker. So we went. And he told me we have a big payday coming, and then we can stop all these other small-fry things. And I said, how does it work? And he said, with the hacking into the SAPS databases for guns, he saw, something's not right. There was monkey business. Someone is fucking around with the gun data. There's guns: today they are there, tomorrow they're gone. He kept an eye on that, for months. And he saw that it looked like they were taking guns off the system. And there are a lot of things pointing in the direction of the SAPS selling those very same guns. Illegally. I don't know the technical details of how they did it, but the way I understand it, he put software in there to set a trap for the *okes* who were doing the monkey business. And then he caught them, there are three of them. Police, all three. And he sent an email, and he said, okay, we know what you're doing, and we are going to let *Carte Blanche* . . .'

'*Carte Blanche?* The TV show?'

'Yes, that one that exposes all the corruption. Then the guys wrote back to Callie and said, hang on, let's first have a chat about this. That's what Callie was hoping for, *nè.* That they would come with an offer. Then it was backwards and forwards, and finally, Callie said, okay, we want two million, and we'll let it go. Callie told me there in De Akker, that's one million for him, one million for me, then we're finished, then we have enough, time to shut down the whole operation. He told the Boere he wanted cash, before the end of the month. September. And they said okay. Then I said, Callie, you gotta be wide awake, the Boere don't just give you two million and say, cool, *lekka*, thanks. Then Callie said no, I mustn't worry, he had all these safety measures. Data bombs, he called them that. And the Boere knew it, they wouldn't mess with us. We left there and on the Thursday Callie phoned and he said, Rolster, they are coming Friday with the money, and with a proposition, they say they can use his skill set, two million is small potatoes, it's time to make big bucks. They want to come talk. And I said again, Callie, you gotta look out, and then he said, don't worry, Rolster, I have safeguards, those little data bombs that can explode, they can't do anything to us. Come Friday, Callie phoned me just past five, and he said the colonel is coming to fetch him, he'll phone me later. Last I heard from him.'

'The colonel?'

'That's right. The colonel.'

'Did he say the colonel's name?'

'*Nay*. He just said the colonel is the one in charge of the firearms, the main man, the big fish.'

'And then?'

'Then nothing. I never heard from him again. Next thing I know, you came knocking on my ma's door, and I thought that colonel sent you, that you nailed Callie and now you wanted to nail me too.'

'Okay,' said Cupido.

'Okay what? Are you going to leave my ma and the sugar tin now?'

'*Ja*, Rolster. I'm a man of my word. I'm going to leave her and the tin, and I'm going to get Callie. And then we'll see how the cookie crumbles.'

60

Griessel asked Lettie Boonstra and Meinhardt Sarazin to please wait in the study while he talked to Sandra Steenberg in the sitting room.

'Who is Sandra Steenberg?' Lettie wanted to know.

'The estate agent,' said Sarazin.

'What was Jasper selling?' Lettie asked.

The lawyer shrugged. 'Maybe Franschhoek. Maybe this ...' He indicated the house and the farm around them.

'He wanted to sell property? And you don't believe he was planning to run, Meinhardt? Do you still say that he only wanted to lie low somewhere for a few days?'

'That's right.'

Griessel walked out and down the stairs, heading for the front door. He heard Lettie laughing derisively at Sarazin.

What did he want, what did he want? Sandra kept thinking, all the way from town to Baronsberg.

Then she saw the *Eikestad News* posters on the lamp posts displaying huge photos of Callie de Bruin, with the headline below:

WHERE

IS

CALLIE?

And it made her think: I know where Callie is. Most likely. Probably. But she daren't say, she dare not risk a huge invasion of police vehicles in the street, detectives knocking on doors, detectives wondering what was going on in the house next door, the one where Jasper Boonstra's ice-cold, naked body was stashed in the freezer.

Just tell that Griessel guy. Just tell him, the day before yesterday or even the Monday she had seen the people in the Airbnb. Just tell him and lift this curse from her. The gods, the universe will help her if she just told Griessel about Callie de Bruin.

No, no, no. He would think it was a deal, a way of shifting attention away from her. He wouldn't believe her.

She drove past the long line of media vans and turned in at the Baronsberg gate. She could see police taking dogs through the vineyards. She went ice cold inside.

Did they know Jasper was dead?

Oh, lord. Had they found something in the house?

I just want to check a few things, Griessel had said over the telephone.

What things?

The guards in their little guard house waved her through with their customary smiles. That helped her relax a tiny bit. Maybe the detective just wanted to clear up a few routine matters. Was this where they'd left the sole mandate forms? Was that where she had last seen Boonstra?

She sat still for a moment in the EcoSport in front of the garage; there where she had loaded Jasper into the car boot.

Breathe, Sandra. Calm down. Hear what he has to say first.

Breathe. Calm down.

Benny opened the door. She was standing there in her pretty yellow dress. She seemed relaxed and she smiled and said: 'I came as quickly as I could.'

'Thank you,' he said. 'Come in, please.'

He stood to one side, allowed her to walk ahead. 'We can just talk in the lounge,' he said. 'Mrs Boonstra and the lawyer are up there . . .' He watched her closely to see how she reacted to that news, but her expression gave nothing away.

Only the faint perspiration-and-perfume scent, a little sharper now.

In the reception lounge he said: 'Sit down, please,' and waved at a chair with its back to the staircase, so that he could keep an eye on the stairs.

She sat down primly, knees together, hands folded on her lap, looked at him expectantly.

The picture of innocence.

'Ma'am, I had a call this morning. From someone who said you threatened to kill Jasper Boonstra.'

He kept watching her intently: her eyes, her hands, her body.

First he saw confusion, then outright astonishment. 'Me?' she said.

Could it be relief, a barely perceptible lowering of her shoulders?

'That's right,' he said.

She shook her head. Griessel could see she was trying to think who it could be. Then realisation dawned. 'Charlie,' she said. A short, relieved laugh. 'Charlie.'

'*Did* you say it?' he asked.

She wanted to laugh louder. She wanted to laugh hysterically. Charlie, the yellowbelly, the coward. Charlie, who was doing his damnedest to get his sweaty little hands on the entire fee. Was he trying to find an excuse to fire her? *Sorry, Sandy-san, if the police are investigating you, I have to let you go, and you won't get a cent.*

Fuck you, Charlie. Respond to Charlie's allegations – was that all she had to do now?

Relief.

'No,' she told the detective, and she knew instinctively – and because of her father's impressive example as a habitual liar – that it was best to tell him the truth. 'What I said, if I remember correctly, was that I *could* kill him. And I meant it, Officer, at that moment I meant it. Because I'd been here with Jasper. In the kitchen. And he was telling me about my stupid pa, because he'd had me and my husband investigated. Even our parents. By private investigators. To make sure he was doing business with the "right people". And I found it arrogant, judgemental, when he told me my pa was a weakling. Not that my pa isn't one. My pa is white trash. But for a rich man to tell me that to my face, made me very angry. And I suppose you're going to ask me now, why I didn't tell him to go to hell? Well, Officer, because my husband and I are poor. Not white trash though, my husband lectures in literature at the university. He, at least, is reasonably sophisticated. But we are battling financially, because he's on sabbatical and we have twins, so you can understand, if it's a choice between a couple of million in commission and your pride, then it isn't a difficult choice.'

Maybe she's just the sweating type, Griessel thought. Because he *did* believe her, everything indicated that she was actually telling the truth.

And then he remembered, this morning he'd been so certain she was lying. It was as if suddenly a whole lot of tumblers dropped into place, as if he could picture a possible scenario where it all fitted. He decided to keep at it, stir the pot some more.

'Ma'am,' he said, 'did you have more than a business relationship with Boonstra?'

'You're not serious,' she said with what looked like genuine disgust. 'Have you seen him?'

He shook his head. 'Why were you here for three hours yesterday?'

She sighed. 'He spent two and a half hours flirting and showing off how rich and sexy he is, and only then getting down to the business. If he knows you *have* to wait for him to sign the forms, he abuses his power. That's why I was here for three hours.'

'Did he offer you money to help him disappear?'

Again that blend of confusion and surprise. 'No,' she said.

'Did he hide in your car when you drove away?'

Again surprise but this time just a little bit forced. And the shoulders rising again. A slight stiffening, or was he imagining it?

'Of course not,' she said. With a hint of reproach in her voice; how could he ask such a thing?

What did he know? Sandra wondered and her gut contracted. She had to focus and concentrate, stay calm, stay calm.

She saw him nod, patiently. 'You know, the more weight you load in a car, the lower it rides on the suspension,' the detective said.

Oh, Christ, she thought. 'Yes?' Her voice sounded calm to her; keep it that way, keep it that way.

'I have video footage of you driving in, and video footage of you driving out. If I asked our forensic people to analyse it, do you think there will be a difference in the height of the car?'

She stifled an almost irresistible impulse to touch her face, her hair, to repeat the question.

Being vague; offering few details.

Repeating questions before answering them.

Speaking in sentence fragments.

Failing to provide specific details when a story is challenged.

Grooming behaviours such as playing with hair or pressing fingers to lips.

She settled on a small frown and a 'I don't think so?'

She waited for his response. He kept on looking at her with those peculiar eyes of his, like those of a Slavic barbarian racing a horse across the Steppes.

'And if I asked our forensic people to test your car for Boonstra's hair or clothing fibres . . .?'

Her heart felt as though it was about to explode.

She couldn't sit still any longer. She drew her handbag onto her lap and did the only thing she thought appropriate. She took her Ford's keys out and offered them to the detective. 'Please,' she said, 'if it would help you . . .'

She saw him look past her, up at the stairs. She followed his gaze. She saw a woman walking down towards them. She recognised her from the photographs. It was Mrs Boonstra. Not nearly as elegant as she imagined the woman would be. She looked like a housewife. In jeans and trainers.

The woman looked at Sandra with a great deal of interest.

'Hello,' said Sandra.

61

Outside the Parker house in Cloetesville Cupido asked the uniforms to take him to Baronsberg. 'I need speed, *pappie*,' he said. 'Sirens and lights, whatever it takes. We're in a hurry.'

They drove, very loud and conspicuous, in the single-cab van, and he turned it all over in his mind and hoped like hell he was wrong. He had looked at all the pieces of the jigsaw puzzle, this way and that, and the picture that formed sent cold shivers down his spine.

Perhaps he'd got things upside down, the picture skewed. That's why he needed to talk to Benny Griessel. He was the intuitive one, the gut-feeling detective, Benna the sounding board, the critic. 'You're the sober partner, Benna,' he'd said, and then chuckled at the irony.

The pieces of the jigsaw – Witkop Jansen who'd said a few days ago: *It's the people at the courts who don't do their jobs properly. I'm not surprised. The CFR is even worse, full of errors lately. Everyone puts in data any old way. No standards any more.* And Sergeant Milo April's letter, and the whole question of the boomeranging Smith & Wesson, and Benny Griessel's AK47, and something that Mbali Kaleni said that his brain hadn't fully registered. And everything that Rolster Parker had just told him. And Chriselda Plaatjies, Milo's fiancée, he thought she'd made a mistake, he thought she'd made a rugby mistake, but perhaps his picture was wonky. And then there was something right at the start, before they came to Stellenbosch, that was bugging him now, like an itch that he couldn't quite scratch.

'Faster,' he urged the constable. He felt he was so close to a breakthrough, he just needed Benna to help him straighten out the crooked angles.

Griessel left all three of them behind – the lawyer, Lettie Boonstra and Sandra Steenberg – sitting in awkward silence in the sitting room, while he went outside to fetch his murder case from his car.

It was a big briefcase that he'd carried with him since his days at the old Murder and Robbery unit. There was an array of basic forensic equipment in it, including rubber gloves and evidence bags, fingerprint material, tweezers, a torch, a camera, a few SAPS forms, and the main thing that he was looking for now: the tape measure.

He opened the boot and thought of Sunday nights, when he and Alexa came home from the Green Door Alcoholics Anonymous group that met at the Dutch Reformed Church in Upper Union Street, Tamboerskloof at five o'clock. The AA meeting psychologically exhausted both of them and then Alexa always wanted to sit back and watch a movie. Something light and relaxing. Her favourite winddown films, ever since she and Benny had been living together, were old detective dramas: *Murder on the Orient Express* and *Death on the Nile* and *The Big Sleep* and *Presumed Innocent*. He watched along with her, even though it annoyed him when Alexa, without exception, would comment: 'Oh no, my master detective would have spotted you were guilty long ago.'

Also the films bore no resemblance to reality, but he held his tongue; she enjoyed them so much, and he could just switch off. He was thinking about that now, and how there was always a scene where the detective brought all the suspects together in one room, so that he could reveal to them all of his brilliant deductions. The three inside could have stepped out of a scene just like that. The only trouble was, at the moment he had no brilliant deductions. Only a suspicion and a very vague plan.

Let them stew. And sweat. Let them wonder.

He got his case and walked towards the Ford EcoSport. He took the measuring tape out.

He heard a siren approaching. It was getting louder.

Had Sergeant Erin Riddles and her team found something? He would be very surprised.

He crouched down beside the Ford's rear wheel. He measured the distance between the lower wheel arch of the body and the rear wheel. At the moment it was seventeen centimetres.

He walked a distance away, about as far as the video camera was from the car when it went in and out the gate yesterday morning. He looked at the Ford, gauging the seventeen centimetres by eye at this distance.

The siren was very close now.

What he needed was something that weighed about eighty or ninety kilograms. To put in the car. That was what he estimated Jasper Boonstra's weight to be, judging by the photographs that he had seen on the study walls.

The siren was right here. He heard the van's engine and then the SAPS patrol vehicle came around the corner of the driveway and he saw Vaughn Cupido was in it, and he thought, perfect, Vaughn can measure and he, Griessel, would get into the Ford himself, he was eighty-six kilograms, that ought to be a good indication.

Cupido jumped out. 'You can go now,' he told the uniforms, and he came jogging up to him and said: 'Partner, I need your counsel. I scheme there's a shit storm brewing here.'

An awkward silence reigned in the lounge: Meinhardt Sarazin and Sandra couldn't afford to let slip to Lettie Boonstra that they had already spoken to each other, though each so badly wanted to check what the detective, Griessel, had asked or said to the other.

'What's he doing there outside?' Lettie asked, breaking the silence.

'He thinks I smuggled Jasper out of here yesterday,' Sandra said.

'Did you?' Lettie asked, amused.

'Yes,' said Sandra. 'He's in my cellar, chained up. I'm going to use him as a sex slave until I'm bored with him.'

Meinhardt Sarazin pulled up his nose at her flippancy, but Lettie Boonstra looked at Sandra and then threw her head back and laughed. 'Come on then, tell me everything.'

They stood leaning against the front of the EcoSport. Cupido was talking urgently, excited and fast, repeating the key points of his conversation with Rolster Parker. '*Bliksem*,' was all Griessel could say when Vaughn was done, his brain racing to keep up. He had to collect his thoughts on this, set the details of the Boonstra case to one side for now.

'Okay, Benna,' said Vaughn, 'so, when I put everything together, I thought, Silverton, right? I mean, with your AK, and the Smith & Wesson, that is the logical conclusion, right?'

'Right.'

'Okay. So I schemed: there was one thing in Milo April's letter that bothered me, that whole time, I couldn't quite get my head around it. Now, the whole way here, I was thinking, what was it? And you must tell me what you think of my logic. 'Cause why, I'm thinking some dangerous thoughts, Benna. I'm making connections and I'm wondering, am I out of my mind? Because if it's true, then we have a shit storm . . .'

'Okay,' said Griessel.

'Let me go back to his fiancée. Chriselda Plaatjies. Remember when we talked about the colonel, when she said it reminded her of the WP rugby coach . . .?'

'Yes.'

'And I said "John Dobson". 'Cause why, he's the WP rugby coach. The Currie Cup team, *the Western Province*. But now, on the way over, I made other connections, Benna. What if Chriselda isn't really rugby literate? I mean, she's a chick. What if she doesn't properly understand that the WP and the Stormers aren't the same team? They're in the same union, Western Province Rugby Union, but it's two separate teams. The Stormers are the Super team. And their coach is Robbie Fleck . . .'

Griessel nodded, but he wasn't sure where his colleague was going with this.

'Right. Which brings me to Milo's letter to me. Why did he write: *There's an adder in our bosom, gahzie*? I mean, he doesn't know me. But he throws a '*gahzie*'. Why not 'bru' or 'brother', that's how we coloureds talk to each other when we're not big friends. Not once has a lower rank called me '*gahzie*', never happened, not in twenty years in the force. There's a certain respect, despite the skin tone kinship. So, I now believe, it could be a message, Benna.'

'What message?'

'A *gahzie* is a pal, Benna. A *buddy*.' The last word with emphasis.

Comprehension slowly dawned on Griessel, and when he understood he said: 'Fuck.'

'Fuck indeed. Buddy *Fick*. Fleck can remind you of Fick. And who's the colonel in charge of Silverton?'

'*Jissis*,' said Griessel.

'An adder in our bosom, Benna. That is what Milo meant. Buddy "The Flash" Fick. The *ou* who Callie de Bruin wanted to blackmail for two million. Buddy *fokken* Fick.'

Griessel grasped the consequences, the damage to the reputation of the SAPS. Again. 'We will have to talk to Witkop Jansen . . .' And then something else penetrated his consciousness, something that had been lurking in his mind all week. 'And Mbali. I think . . . No, I don't believe in coincidences . . .'

'What, Benna?'

'No, Vaughn, let's go and talk first, it's just too . . .'

'Benna, this is a weird country here. Coincidences happen. What is it?'

'I . . . It's just . . . You know what I said, about why we didn't go to Laingsburg. I said it's a problem that someone wants solved, sending us to Stellenbosch. Someone made that call for a reason . . .'

'Yes . . .?'

'Witkop Jansen talked about how the firearm register is so messed up. And then . . . *Bliksem*, I think Callie is the coincidence. A helluva coincidence, can't be. Maybe . . .'

'Partner, I'm not following you?'

'I don't understand myself entirely . . . When we were with Mbali last night . . . She said . . . She said the commissioner, Khaba, he didn't have anything to do with the Smith & Wesson, she was dead certain. But there was something she had to tell us. I think she wanted to . . . No, *fok*, Vaughn, let's go and discuss this first, I don't want to make a complete fool of myself.'

'I do that every day . . . I think we are in the same ball park, Benna, we just aren't seeing the same ball.'

'I'm nearly finished here, then I'll go with you, we'll have to call Mbali. Buddy "The Flash" Fick. What a balls up.'

'I'm telling you. Shit storm. But how's it look here?'

'I think I know what's going on. If you'll just help me a minute, I want you to measure something for me . . .'

62

Sandra was sweating. Anxiety threatened to overcome her.

And if I asked our forensic people to test your car for Boonstra's hair or clothing fibres . . .?

How did he know? How?

Lettie Boonstra wanted to talk to her, so warm and friendly, and Sandra had to concentrate, she had to try to gain control of her thumping heart. She wondered if they could see how stressed she was? Lettie and the lawyer. Sarazin just sat there, pecking at the screen of his phone.

Lettie bombarded her with questions, and responded with exclamations. Married? Children? Twins? Oh, how precious! How old are they? Cute! And what does your husband do? An author! Marvellous! When Sandra was exhausted by the effort of trying to be calm and friendly, she asked if there was a bathroom she could use.

'Of course. Just there around the corner, the guest room bathroom.' Sandra fled, shut the door, and scrutinised her face in the mirror. Perspiration on her forehead, her upper lip: the strain was so obvious. What was she going to do?

She picked up a wash cloth, wet it with cold water and wiped her face. Put it down. Stood with her palms on either side of the basin, head bowed. He would find traces of Jasper's DNA and hair in her car; she should at least have vacuumed it. She was an idiot, but there just hadn't been time. What would she have told Josef if he found her in the garage, hoovering? The truth was, she hadn't thought that far. Oh lord. She wanted to cry, she wanted to get away from here. Run away. Flee.

For a split second she saw herself in court: in an orange jumpsuit like the guilty on TV. Being led away, handcuffed . . .

She would never see her children again, she thought, and that was the straw she grasped at: her children. Think of Anke and Bianca. Be strong for them. Be positive. The detective had no evidence. Nothing. Just suspicions. It took time to take DNA samples and analyse them. And if they found something, she could say, yes, Jasper gave her something. Wine. A case of his wine. He put it in the boot, that's why his hair was there . . .

Griessel didn't have a thing.

Except Charlie's phone call. Charlie, the pig, another reason to be strong, she would not give that pathetic excuse for a man the satisfaction . . .

Sandra slowly calmed herself. Sat down and peed. Washed her hands. Put her handbag down beside the basin. Dabbed away the sweat, refreshed her make-up. Carefully, methodically.

Then she walked back to the lounge.

She saw Lettie Boonstra and Meinhardt Sarazin standing at the front door, with the detective and coloured man, much better looking and with far fewer miles on the clock than Griessel. Taller, though a little paunchy.

'I'll let you know if I need you,' said Griessel to Sarazin and Lettie Boonstra. 'Thank you very much.'

Lettie said goodbye to Sandra: 'So good to meet you. I am sure we will talk again.' Then she waved and they walked out, the lawyer and the housewife in her jeans and trainers.

'Are we done?' Sandra asked Griessel. She saw the coloured man watching her intently.

'Just a moment, please,' said Griessel.

Her stomach clenched again. 'Of course,' she said.

He took his cell phone out as she sat down.

He dialled.

She heard him say: 'Erin . . . I was thinking . . . can you do me a favour? I have to go to the office with Vaughn. Can you just go to the guard house for me . . .' Sandra saw both detectives look at her, '. . . and look at the videos from yesterday. Nine o'clock, and twelve, when a Ford EcoSport drove in and out. See if the suspension shows that the vehicle was heavier going out than coming in. Get the videos for us for Forensics.'

Sandra felt her knees go weak.

★　　★　　★

Griessel and Cupido watched Sandra Steenberg drive away in the EcoSport.

'Benna, she's so hot, she gives me heat rash. Why didn't you tell me?'

'Well, I thought you have Desiree already, and so . . .'

'Partner, I'm a one-woman man. I'm just saying. I feel like phoning the fire brigade about that hotness. Look, if I was a billionaire, I would also get her to flog my wine farm.'

They walked to the car. 'Did you notice?' Griessel asked. 'She was sweating.'

'From hotness! Ha, sorry, Benna, bad joke. She looked pretty calm and collected to me, but then, I was distracted. And you scheme she took Boonstra out in the car?'

'It's just about the only possibility I have. I think he paid her to do it. There's only a small case missing from his room, his passport, his ID and a book where he listed all his investment codes . . .'

'That's not a crime, Benna. The man hasn't even been charged with anything yet.'

'That's the point. We're wasting our time, when we should be looking for Callie de Bruin.'

'Yes. About Callie . . . I have a bad feeling, Benna.'

'I know . . . Let's go and tell Witkop Jansen about Buddy Fick. And phone Mbali.'

'*Yebo*, yes,' said Cupido and took his phone out of his pocket. 'Hot,' he said as he tapped the number in. 'So hot she'll set off the smoke alarms.'

Yes, of course her car would show that there was a load at the back. There was an easy explanation: Jasper Boonstra gave her a case of wine. Two cases. Three?

Sandra drove. She hardly knew where. Towards town. Her thoughts were a jumble.

And where was the wine now? Show it to me.

I gave it away.

No.

She could buy wine. Stash it at the office. Here it is, Warrant Officer Griessel, Jasper's gift to me.

She prayed, now, for the first time in years. Oh, God, help me.

She saw Callie de Bruin's face on the lamp post.

Her conscience was telling her she couldn't pray for help and then do nothing for the missing boy.

But what? If she phoned Griessel now and said she knew where Callie was . . . Too many questions. Why are you only telling us now? Oh, so it was just after you were with Boonstra? What were you doing at the house in Brandwacht?

She had to do something.

An anonymous phone call.

The police would keep a record of calls. They could trace any cell phone number these days.

She would have to use another number. And phone the university. This morning in the *Eikestad News* there was a university number for people to call if they had any information about Callie.

She saw the Lanzerac on her left.

What if she called from there . . . She could tell them her phone had been stolen, she would pay, just a quick call.

That's what she would do.

Over the phone Cupido told Mbali everything he knew.

'*Hayi*,' she said.

'*Yebo*, Colonel,' he said.

'Where are you going now?' she asked.

'We have to inform Colonel Jansen.'

'I will meet you there.' She put the phone down.

It was a while before Cupido realised the phone was dead. 'Smack me with a *snot snoek*,' he said to Griessel. 'I'll meet you there, The Flower says, and then she hangs up on me.'

'She knows something, Vaughn,' said Griessel. 'I don't believe in coincidences.'

'Coincidences happen, Benna. They're like black swans, don't diss them because you haven't seen them.' Then his cell phone rang and he didn't recognise the number. He answered.

'Vaughn, this is Rowen Geneke,' said the senior on-call detective at Stellenbosch station. 'That list of registration numbers that Campus Security supplied – Colonel Witkop asked us to feed them through NaTIS.'

'Yes, Cappie, those are the cars that went past Callie de Bruin's hostel on Friday evening.'

'That's it. I have the list in front of me. Can I bring it to you?'

'No, that's okay, we're on our way back to the office . . .' And then Cupido took a shot in the dark: 'Cappie, just for interest's sake, is there maybe a Fick on that list?'

'Funny you should ask,' said Geneke. 'The only one that is a rental vehicle. A Chevrolet Spark. Friday, from Thrifty Car Rental at Cape Town International Airport. A mister Christoffel Lodewyk Fick. From Pretoria.'

'Bingo,' said Cupido. 'Bing-fucking-go. Cappie, big favour, please. Can we put out a general broadcast on that car? Like in right now?'

63

Colonel Witkop indicated they should take a seat across from him, then said: 'I asked Captain Geneke to hold back on the bulletin on Fick's rental car for now.'

Cupido was stunned. 'But why, Colonel?'

'Just sit, and we'll wait for Kaleni. In the meantime, how is the Boonstra investigation looking?'

'Colonel, with all due respect, we have to find Buddy Fick, he will know where Callie de Bruin is. Our problem now is, if we call Silverton, they are going to get suspicious. 'Cause why, I don't think The Flash is in this alone. There's no way he could manipulate the databases himself, not IBIS and the Firearms Registry. You need an IT guy, I scheme there's a whole den of them up there . . .'

'Colonel Kaleni already phoned Silverton to talk to Fick. They say he applied for leave. They don't know where he is.'

'There we go. All the more reason to chase his *gat* down now.'

'No. We will wait for Colonel Kaleni. The Boonstra case . . .' And he turned to Griessel.

'Colonel,' said Griessel, 'there was an estate agent by the name of Sandra Steenberg with Boonstra yesterday, for three hours. I have reason to believe she smuggled him out of there. The only way for us to prove that is through the video footage of her car arriving and leaving. We will look at the height of the Ford's suspension. Sergeant Riddles is doing that now, but we will ask the PCSI to review it. I know it's not much, but it's all we have.'

'Where do you think he is?'

'His lawyer confirmed that he has put some of his properties on the market, and his wife says he wants to skip the country. Seems she may be right. His passport has gone, along with a book where he kept all his bank account codes.'

'*Bliksem,*' said Witkop Jansen. 'They will crucify us. He hasn't been charged yet.'

'They will crucify us when this whole Buddy Fick story breaks, Colonel.'

Jansen gave a deep sigh and rubbed his moustache. 'I know.'

'Colonel, can you tell us why we're waiting for The Flower . . . for Colonel Kaleni?'

Griessel's phone rang.

'We will let you know when she arrives,' said Jansen.

Benny's phone screen indicated that Erin Riddles was calling. He got up as he answered and walked out the door.

'On the video it does look like the car is riding a bit lower when it leaves,' she said.

'How obvious is it?'

'The video at the gate doesn't show it so well. But when I checked the other video, the one from the camera at the garages . . . There the car is closer to the camera, you can see it clearly, when she reverses, the suspension is definitely lower.'

'Thank you, Erin, that's good work.'

'Do we keep searching the farm with the dogs?'

'Let's make absolutely sure. At least it will hold the media's attention for now.'

Griessel saw Mbali coming up the stairs. She was hurrying and out of breath. 'I have to go now, Erin, talk later.'

'I wanted to tell you last night,' Kaleni said once all four were seated around Jansen's desk. 'But then the Boonstra affair broke. You did not come to Stellenbosch by accident. Perhaps you should start at the beginning, Witkop,' she said.

'Can I speak in Afrikaans? You know my English is for self-defence only.'

'Of course.'

Witkop leaned forward, rubbed the moustache and, in Afrikaans, said: 'The first burglary was eighteen months ago, here in Mostertsdrift. And the only things they took were the weapons. The husband is a hunter and quite an enthusiast, they got three pistols and seven hunting rifles. Knew exactly where the safe was, and how to open it. Professional job, quick in and out, all the security cameras could show us was that it was five men, armed, all wearing balaclavas. Then

four weeks later, another one. Same story, balaclavas, in the morning
when there was nobody home, just went for the weapons. In and out.
Never the same vehicle, always stolen, always false number plates.
Another one went a bit wrong, an anaesthetist who just happened to
be home, and they ran away. Nevertheless, all five break-ins in
Stellenbosch suburbs, and as far as we could determine, they had
knowledge of the CCTV in and around the town. After the fifth one,
I was pretty certain that someone was feeding the syndicate with
information from the Firearms Registry, because they didn't put a
foot wrong, every break-in was at a house with a minimum of four
firearms, the MO identical every time. My suspicion grew that it had
to be a member of the Service, either here with me, or at the station.
I began looking at everyone who had access, but then the break-ins
suddenly stopped. And then other things demand your attention and
you let it go. Then, in January, we were at a seminar in Cape Town
and the head of detective branch in Durbanville began talking about
the same thing happening with them. A few wine farms, just over the
boundary of our jurisdiction, and a few houses. Every time only
places with a lot of firearms. It was like someone knew to leave
Stellenbosch alone for now, not to attract too much attention. It was
then that we went to see Colonel Kaleni . . .' He nodded to her to
continue the story.

    'I took it very seriously, as you can imagine,' Mbali said. 'One of our
own, feeding the syndicates that type of information. So, I kept an eye
on the stats. In May, the same thing happened in the Paarl district.
Also just across the border from the Stellenbosch jurisdiction, as if
someone knew to be careful about it. I called in Sergeant Reginald
Davids, because I wanted to know, can we trace online access to the
Firearms Registry from the Stellenbosch SAPS terminals? He said it
would be much easier with the cooperation of the Registry's systems
administrators, but I did not want anybody else to know yet. So,
Sergeant Davids did it the hard and slow way. I don't understand the
technical details, but the problem was that he could only tell me the
access was indeed happening from Stellenbosch. He could not
pinpoint it without involving the Registry people. Witkop and I still
thought it was a member of the Service, but we did not know who to
trust. It could have been any of the Stellenbosch staff. So, when I

heard that the commissioner wanted to send you two to Laingsburg, I saw the opportunity. Everybody knew you were being disciplined, so it would not make the perpetrators suspicious that two former Hawks were sent to this station. And I knew we could trust you, and we wanted you to look into the whole matter. Witkop and I wanted you to settle in first, and then put you on the case. But then, the student went missing . . .'

'Colonel, how did you manage to convince the commissioner to send us here?' asked Cupido. 'He seemed to be extremely piss— . . . I mean, upset with us.'

'It wasn't easy. But I told him, if we found the culprit stealing the Registry information, it could be managed internally and quietly. The alternative was that it would become a very public matter, which would look very bad for his province, and his command. And that is the only thing our commissioner does not like. Something making him look bad in the eyes of the president.'

Griessel frowned: 'Colonel, so it was just a coincidence that Callie de Bruin was abducted the day before we started?'

'Indeed.'

Griessel shook his head. 'I don't believe it.'

'Black swan, partner, it's a weird world,' said Vaughn.

'First time in twenty years,' said Griessel.

Cupido's phone rang. Veronica Adams from Campus Security.

He declined the call. 'Sorry,' he said.

'Look at it this way, Benny,' Kaleni said. 'We finally got a little bit lucky. Witkop had been looking at this matter for eighteen months, Sergeant Davids and I for almost six months, and the robberies just kept happening. We were getting no closer to a solution.'

'Okay, Colonel, but why are we not putting out a general broadcast on Buddy Fick? The boy may still be alive.'

'Well, Warrant Officer, let's stop and think for a moment. You told Witkop you believe that Colonel Fick is not the only Silverton staff member involved. That means, if we issue a general broadcast, there is a good chance he will be alerted. If the boy is still alive, it would put him in grave danger. Secondly, we know how quickly the media gets wind of something like that. We already have one circus in town . . . And thirdly, to prevent you from being sent to Laingsburg, I had to promise Commissioner Khaba that I would be discreet. I intend to honour that promise as far as possible.'

'I get that, Colonel, I really do. But there's something else that's scaring me big time.'

'What is that, Warrant Officer?'

'The guy who got into Callie de Bruin's residence and into his room, is a member of the Trojans, the gang from Elsies River. The Smith & Wesson that Milo April confiscated and sent to Silverton, came from the Restless Ravens – another Cape Flats gang. Benny does not believe in coincidence, and mostly he is right about that. It looks to me like Buddy Fick was selling confiscated weapons to the Flats gangs. And he got them involved to help with the abduction of Callie de Bruin. I mean, according to Roland Parker, Callie had a few safety measures lined up. What Parker called "data bombs". Maybe information that would expose the whole thing if something happened to him. That's why Fick sent a Trojans member to Callie's room. To get his hard disk, because they believed, no hard disk, no data bomb, or something like that.'

'I see,' said Kaleni thoughtfully.

Cupido heard a WhatsApp notification on his phone, but he didn't look at it . He said: 'That is why we need to find Fick very, very quickly, Colonel. Because the gangs will kill Callie without batting an eyelid.'

Kaleni nodded slowly. 'Let's get a two-oh-five on Fick's cell phone,' she said. 'To try and locate him. Witkop, the town's CCTV? Could that help?'

'Maybe,' Jansen replied with a shrug.

'Callie's last known location was Paradyskloof,' Griessel said. 'If they have cameras there . . .'

'The neighbourhood watch has some cameras,' said Witkop Jansen. 'They work with the private security firms. It's worth taking a look.'

Sandra drove to the Tops bottle store in Die Boord to find some of Jasper Boonstra's wines. As an excuse if that detective Griessel found proof that there had been something in her car.

She had made the phone call to Campus Security from the Lanzerac Hotel. Breathless and frightened, no need to pretend, she simply channelled all her very real fear into her voice. She had made up a story.

She had to, to divert attention from the Schoemans' Brandwacht house she was selling. She said she'd been driving past in this particular street, when she saw two men pull Callie de Bruin out of a car. Yes, yes, she was sure it was the boy; she saw his face clearly when he was pulled out of the vehicle, the car that the men had driven up to that house in. She was right beside them. She saw the posters this morning with the photo on, that's why she was only phoning now, because you know, you didn't want to get involved. But when she saw the picture . . . Yes, she was absolutely sure.

Sandra gave the exact street name and number, three times. And then she rang off, before they could ask her who she was, and drove away from there in a hurry.

She got out of her car and walked to the bottle store.

Her phone rang. Not a known number.

'Hello, this is Sandra.'

'Hello, Sandra, it's Lettie Boonstra. I want you to come and have lunch with me at Decameron.'

'When?'

'Now.'

'Oh, thank you very much, but it won't be possible.'

'I think it *is* possible, Sandra. You see, I know about you and Jasper. And what happened on the stairs yesterday morning.'

64

Cupido was outside Witkop Jansen's office when he read the WhatsApp: *Just got a tip-off about Callie. Woman is dead sure he is at a house in Brandwacht. Call me!*

It was from Veronica Adams at Campus Security.

He stopped and called her number. 'Is it credible?' he asked when she answered.

'The staff member who took the call, said the woman sounded distressed. She thinks it's genuine.'

'Do you have the number?'

'Of the woman who phoned? No, she didn't say. Probably doesn't want to be involved. That's the way this town works.'

'Damn. Okay, what did she say?'

'Two men dragged Callie out of a car in front of the house. The woman was driving past, she said she was right beside them.'

'A Chevy Spark?'

'She didn't say.'

Cupido thought for a moment. 'Right, give me the address, but I'm not convinced.'

'It's something,' said Adams. 'It's the only credible tip we've had all week.'

Cupido turned around and went back into Witkop Jansen's office.

Lettie Boonstra was sitting right at the back of the restaurant at a four-seater table, with a bottle of wine in an ice bucket beside her and a full glass in front of her. A thick folder lay beside her cell phone on the table. She smiled when she saw Sandra walking towards her.

'Sit down, please. And don't look so worried. We're going to be good friends, you and me.'

She sat down. Lettie beckoned to a waiter. 'Another glass, please.'

'I won't have any wine now, thank you,' said Sandra. She could barely breathe, she felt suffocated by fear.

'Bring the glass,' Lettie said to the waiter, 'and menus.'

Sandra put her handbag down on the chair beside her. She was aware her hands were trembling and gripped them together tightly on her lap. She stared at the woman in front of her.

'I am burning with curiosity about what you did with my husband, but we'll get to that. First, look at this . . .' Lettie said, with a faint, amused smile.

Lettie Boonstra picked up the cell phone, pressed the screen, looked around to see if anyone was nearby, and passed it across to Sandra. 'Play the video. I will warn you if anyone comes close.'

Sandra took the phone from her.

'Shame, you poor thing,' said Lettie. 'Look how you're shaking. Just relax, I'm sure we can come to some kind of agreement. Go on. Watch the video.'

Sandra started the video.

It showed the stairs in Jasper Boonstra's house, no people visible. Taken from the top. The camera must have been hidden somewhere. But where, there was no . . .

Then she understood. 'The knight,' she said to Lettie.

'That's right. In the breastplate of the knight. Symbolic, don't you think?'

On the video Sandra came around the corner, Jasper Boonstra behind her. There was no sound, only two people walking upstairs and talking, the woman's face tense, the man's eyes fixed on her bum, a cynical look to his mouth.

Jasper's lips moving. *Never is a long time, Sandra,* she could both remember and decipher.

Her answer too: *I'm sorry?*

You said I would never have the privilege of fucking you. I say: Never is a long time.

On the video, Sandra's eyes narrowed, stung.

There are two questions that you have to ask yourself. The first is, how badly do you need the three million? Really, when the chips are down, as they say.

Fuck you. Rage on her face.

She saw Jasper grinning on the screen: *We all have a price, Sandra. What is yours? Three million not enough? For a few days' work and a bit of fun?*

Fuck you.

And then she was right in front of the camera, as if she had flinched away from Boonstra and whirled around, the sword touching her buttocks. Jasper behind her, and only her arms were visible at the moment when she pushed him.

She saw the surprise on his face, captured in that single second. And as he lost his balance and toppled backwards, an instant of fury, of *how could you?* Until his head was no longer visible and he tumbled down, bumped down a further step, and lay still.

The video ended.

'That's how I know,' said Lettie.

Sandra's mouth was dry. Her entire body shook.

'I swear, I didn't . . . It was an . . . The things he said to me. If you look, you can see he's talking. He was saying . . .'

Lettie Boonstra took the phone out of Sandra's hands. 'I know. The video does have sound, I muted it because it's very public here. You don't understand. I'm here to thank you.'

'He wanted to . . . I thought it was him grabbing me . . .' The incredible pressure, the unbearable stress and strain and anxiety finally broke Sandra. Not gradually, but a dam breaching, so that she shuddered and wept, her body spasmed.

'Can you hear what I'm saying? I want to thank you. Your secret is safe.' Lettie Boonstra waved the waiter away as he approached the table with the wine glass and menus.

She stretched her arm across the table, took Sandra's hand.

Griessel didn't want to go back to Baronsberg just yet. He couldn't stomach the circus of a search for a millionaire who'd fled the country. He wanted to be part of the hunt for Buddy Fick.

He knew what his shrink would say about that.

His urge wasn't to save Callie de Bruin; it was about his son, Fritz.

If he could save Callie, he could save his relationship with Fritz.

Or something along those lines. The psychologist explained it to him as 'omnipotent responsibility guilt'. The omnipotence because he felt he had the power to do everything, protect everyone. It was common among policemen, because they grew accustomed to the power of being protectors, of ensuring that justice was done. And that had a big impact when it came to their own loved ones. You saw death and murder all around you, and you knew it was your responsibility to protect your wife and children. And then you realised you couldn't. That drove you to depression. It drove you to drink.

Thoughts that circled in his mind as he drove to Baronsberg to collect the video footage, so that Provincial's forensic video analysts could examine it.

Cupido told Witkop Jansen about the tip-off about the Brandwacht house. Colonel Mbali Kaleni was still there. Everyone was sceptical, but they agreed they should at least check it out.

So Vaughn asked Captain Rowen Geneke if he would apply to the court for an article 205 subpoena, to investigate and trace Buddy Fick's cell phone. To free Cupido to take a look at the Brandwacht house immediately.

He headed to the street and drove past the house, at forty kilometres per hour, as was proper in a residential area. He saw four cars parked outside.

One of them was the Chevrolet Spark.

Sandra wept for ten minutes, powerless against the emotion, while Lettie sipped her wine patiently and made the occasional sympathetic murmur.

At last Sandra said, in a small voice like a child looking for comfort: 'You want to thank me? My secret is safe?'

Lettie took a bundle of tissues out of her handbag, then said: 'That's right,' and beckoned to the waiter again to bring the wine glass and menus.

After casting Sandra a nervous glance, the waiter put the menus down, filled the new glass with wine and hurried away. Lettie said, 'I can only imagine what hell you've been through. I'm sorry I didn't say anything earlier. I just didn't expect the detective to be so on the ball. When he kept you back this morning, I knew he had something . . .'

Sandra dabbed her tears and wiped the smudged mascara away, just nodding.

'There you go, have some wine. It will make you feel better. Then we'll order something delicious, and I'll tell you the whole story.'

'Thank you,' said Sandra. And started to cry again.

Griessel had to thread his way through the barking dogs of the K9 unit from Paarl to reach the guard house at Baronsberg. Erin Riddles was sitting at the video monitor.

'K9 want to know if they still have to stay.'

'No,' said Benny. 'They can go. The search team too.'

Erin Riddles stood up. 'Take a look at the footage so long. I will go and tell them.'

Griessel sat down. The security guard played the two clips back for him. The first, where Sandra arrived at the garage, and then parked out of sight under the roof. He rewound the video to the point where the best angle of the rear of the EcoSport was visible. He pressed a plastic ruler against the screen, and took the measurement from the spare wheel cover that clung like a hunchback on the rear door of the Ford. 'Look at the distance of the spare wheel from the ground . . .' said the security guard.

He forwarded to the next clip, where Sandra reversed out of the garage. He stopped at the same spot. Measured again. 'Do you see? It's clear.'

Griessel did see. But it was the lid of the baggage area, just inside the rear window, that drew his attention.

'Show me the first one again,' he asked.

The security guard went back to the first clip, where Sandra was driving in.

The lid was level and tidy.

'Now the second.'

Griessel looked carefully when it appeared. The lid was crooked. As if something – or someone – was just a little bit too big to fit in.

But there was something else about the images that intrigued him.

65

Sandra Steenberg's body language was different in the two videos.

In the first, when she arrived, she sat leaning back comfortably against the seat. One hand on the steering wheel.

When she drove out of the garage again, made her U-turn and left, both hands were clamped to the steering wheel and she sat forward like someone who was in a hurry. And very anxious.

The resolution was good, but not brilliant, so he didn't want to jump to conclusions about her facial expression. Perhaps he was imagining her nervous frown as she drove away.

But there was no doubt: there was something making the back of the Ford sit lower. Something that might be just a fraction too bulky to fit in the baggage space, nudging the lid up. Something like a man between eighty and ninety kilograms.

The thing that was bugging him, that didn't gel with the rest, was the woman's nervousness. Here it was again, on video, her stance behind the steering wheel. And when they spoke this morning, the perspiration. If he accepted that she had indeed helped Boonstra to get away unseen – it was not a crime. It was the sort of thing one confessed to a police-man when pressed, with a 'Yes, I did. He paid me. What about it?'

Why this level of anxiety?

Afraid her husband would find out?

Perhaps. But why?

He asked the security guard if they had a good internet connection here. When the man said yes, Griessel asked them to send the video clips to PCSI.

But he was already reasonably certain that Sandra Steenberg had smuggled Jasper Boonstra out of the estate in her EcoSport. Let Forensics confirm it scientifically, and then he would confront her. At the very least she was guilty of obstruction of justice.

★   ★   ★

'You see,' said Lettie Boonstra, 'I was in an impossible situation. Jasper and I got married in December 1984. Out of community of property. One month after the accrual system became law here. That meant, if we were to divorce today, I would get half of the growth of our joint estate. And you'll be thinking how marvellous, she's a rich woman. Because according to the media, Jasper is worth around three-hundred-and-fifty million dollars. The trouble is, nothing is actually in Jasper's name. Okay, not nothing, there is about three million in a bank account for daily expenses, general living costs, but apart from that he hid everything. Properties, cash, shares, *everything*. In every tax haven on earth, in companies and accounts and safe deposit boxes. That snake Meinhardt Sarazin knows all about it, but only Jasper had the details, the places and names and codes . . .'

She took a sip of wine. 'And just to be clear, it's not just a divorce that would leave me with nothing. If something were to happen to Jasper, or if he skipped the country, I would *also* sit with peanuts. After a lifetime of sacrifice and humiliation. In any case, I don't believe a wife should just accept her lot. If you want something, you have to do something. I found myself a private investigator to advise me, and put two cameras in the house. One in the suit of armour, and one in his study, in the book case. I wanted to find out two things: just how much he was actually cheating on me, and where he was hiding the book with the numbers and codes. His crook book. He hated me calling it that, but that is what it is. If I could get hold of it, and if I had a couple of videos of a mistress or two, I thought it would make a big difference in the divorce court. I would be able to prove he *did have* assets *and* he was unfaithful. Oh, and I got myself a lawyer too, a little anxious grey man in Durbanville, and he said I mustn't get too excited. Jasper is clever. If the crook book only had codes in, it proved nothing. And Jasper had enough money to stretch out a divorce case interminably, and to move the assets to other places. I think the little grey man was scared to take Jasper on, but there you go. What was I to do? The book was my only hope. And then there was another fly in the ointment: on the camera in the study, I could see where he kept the book, but he guarded the key to that drawer with his life. Whenever he went some-where, he kept it in his wallet. When he was at home, he kept it in his trouser or jacket pocket. And when he was asleep he kept it in the drawer beside his bed. No matter how I tried, I couldn't get my hands on it . . .'

At that moment Lettie Boonstra's phone rang. She looked at the screen and told Sandra: 'You must focus now. In the next ten minutes both our lives will change forever. I am going to answer this call, and then I'm going to phone that Benny detective. And then, my dear Sandra, we'll be free.'

She picked up the phone and answered: 'Hello.' Then just: 'Thank you . . . Thank you . . . Thank you. Okay, thank you very much . . .' And she rang off.

13:34

Griessel noticed the activity in the detective branch parade room, he saw Vaughn Cupido and Witkop Jansen around a table, Rowen Geneke scowling with a cell phone to his ear, and he walked in.

He felt the electricity and he knew something had happened.

Cupido looked up from a computer screen where Google Earth was open.

'We've got him, partner,' said Vaughn, and showed him the screen. 'Buddy Fick is here, in a house in Brandwacht. It looks like an Airbnb, we're just waiting for confirmation. And if he's there, Benna, then Callie is also there. I bet you.'

Rowen Geneke ended the telephone call, then said: 'Gentlemen, it's not going to be so easy. Those other cars in front of the house – the Gang unit checked the registrations for us. They say those are Trojan's cars. Definitely.'

'Shit,' said Cupido. 'Soldiers.'

'*Ja*,' said Geneke with heavy irony. 'With firearms supplied by the SAPS.'

The worried silence that ensued was broken by Witkop Jansen. 'Call Colonel Zamisa,' he said, referring to Lieutenant Colonel Phila Zamisa, leader of the Boland cluster's special task force. The man whose life Griessel had saved three months ago. 'Tell them to come. But quietly.'

Griessel wanted to say he was going too; when the task force struck, he was entitled to. But before he could do that, his phone rang. The number looked vaguely familiar.

*   *   *

Deon Meyer

Lettie Boonstra looked at Sandra. 'Now for step two. Listen closely, and enjoy . . .'

Sandra watched Lettie search through her call register until she found a number. She rang, looked at Sandra again, and smiled.

'Hello, Benny? It's Lettie Boonstra. What did you call it, the form when a missing person isn't being looked for any more? That's it. Now, you can you fill in a SAPS ninety-two. Jasper has just phoned me. He didn't say where he was, but the number begins with a two-six-four code. I think that's Namibia . . . So, Jasper is no longer missing, and I want to drop the whole matter. No, all he said was that we won't find him. Because you are too hopeless and I am too poor . . . Yes, of course, just hold on . . .' She swiped her finger across the screen to check the call register again. She read the Namibian number back to him slowly and listened to something the detective was telling her. Then: 'Of course. Where must I come to sign it? Is three o'clock okay? I see . . . Yes, if that's necessary, I will talk to the press. Good. Good, thank you, Benny. 'Bye.'

Lettie gave a satisfied sigh and her smile broadened. 'Come, we'd better order,' she said to Sandra, 'I have to be at the police station at three.'

In the parade room Griessel told them that, according to his wife, Jasper Boonstra was in Namibia. 'Now she wants a ninety-two.'

'*Fok*,' said Cupido, and all the air seemed to be sucked out of the room.

Witkop Jansen rubbed his moustache. '*Bliksem*.'

Griessel waited for the colonel to respond.

'Fucking rich whiteys,' Cupido said. 'All the hours of effort, all the manpower . . .'

'That's the way Stellenbosch is,' sighed Jansen. 'I'll phone the commissioner. We will have to hold a press conference.'

'She said she will address the media. Three o'clock.'

'Call the liaison officer. It will have to be at the station, just not here.'

'Right, Colonel,' Griessel said.

But he didn't phone the liaison officer immediately. Instead he tapped in the Namibian number that Lettie Boonstra had read out to him.

The subscriber you have dialled is not available right now. Please try again later.

There was something about this whole affair that didn't sit right with him.

'I really should start at the very beginning again,' Lettie Boonstra said. 'Tell you that I am one of three, the children of a plumber from Vredendal. I met Jasper here at university. I was studying to be a teacher. He was . . . there's only one word for it: charming. Clever too, of course, but charming is what made the difference. He's not hand-some, not ugly, just okay. He had these chubby cheeks, back then. But the charm made him attractive, to everyone. He could talk people into things, not overbearing, just quietly. Subtly. A wonderful sense of humour. He had the ability to fake self-confidence, even in those days. And not the in-your-face sort of self-confidence, just *there*, fundamen-tal. You knew this guy was going to succeed. You felt it, the ambition, you saw it, never in your wildest dreams would you imagine he could have a chip on the shoulder. He charmed me. Very quickly. In my second year. The day he asked me to marry him, he said: "Let, we're going to be rich." I never once doubted it. And you know, the first five, six years were good. We had nothing. I was teaching, he did his articles and began working, we began to set up house, make a home, and it was good. That feeling of hard work brings rewards. Then it was . . . The thing about Jasper I could never understand was why we always had to *show* that we had money. The cars, the house, the hi-fi, the watch, the friends . . . But then you didn't begrudge him his success, because he was the one who made the money, not me on my teacher's salary. But to hear the way he talked, *this* car cost so much, and *that* plot in Plett cost so much, and you watched how he dumped old friends and replaced them with new, richer ones, and slowly you began to realise that something was not quite right, there was something lacking in him. In the end I recognised the chip on his shoulder, from his parents being so dirt poor. And then . . . Look, I know I'm no oil painting, no pin-up. I think I was sexy in my way at university, but . . . I mean, look at me: long legs and big boobs and flowing locks – that was never *me*. And the time came when that was also something that Jasper craved. To trumpet his success. To hide the chip. And . . . I always use the story of the crayfish in the pot, you know, the book that André P. Brink wrote, *Die kreef raak gewoond daaraan*? At first you're oblivious, you just sit there in your pot. Okay, it's a very grand pot, you have everything your heart desires, except a man that desires you. And you hear stories about your husband's philandering, and you see and smell and feel things, but you don't want to believe it. And in the end when the water boils, it's too late, by then you are this middle-aged woman with nothing to your name, and you don't have the power or the money to climb out of the pot. And then the pot breaks, when you discover your husband is the biggest white-collar crook in the history of the country. Then you start to wonder, when you've recovered from the shock and disillusionment, how the fuck are you going to find a new pot now?'

66

Every twenty minutes they drove past the house in Brandwacht Street, every time a different, unmarked car.

They took cell phone videos of the house, carefully, discreetly.

Over the course of the afternoon they used a pharmacy delivery motorbike, a detective disguised as a hobo, and a female detective with a briefcase to ring the gate and front doorbells at the neighbours across the street, next door, and at the back. At the house to the left of the Airbnb, the house of André and Joan Schoeman who were in America, the house with a freezer in the garage, there was no response. Nobody – including Cupido – put two and two together connecting the *For Sale* sign with its Benson International logo and phone number with Sandra Steenberg. Their focus was on the Airbnb, the double-storey where Buddy Fick and the Trojans gang members were possibly – hopefully – detaining Callie de Bruin. They phoned Benson International Realtors for information, but the receptionist said the agent responsible for the house wasn't currently in the office.

At the house across the street from the Airbnb they spoke to a domestic worker. She said the owners would only be home after five. They asked for phone numbers and contacted the couple who lived there.

At the home behind the Airbnb two pupils of the Afrikaans girls' high school, Bloemhof, answered the intercom. They had the girls phone their parents, and explained the situation. The parents gave reluctant permission for the SAPS to use their house as a lookout post, but made arrangements for the girls to be collected and stay with friends.

Everyone was asked, very firmly, not to say a word about the situation. 'It's a case of life and death,' Cupido and his colleagues said.

They traced the owner of the Airbnb. He lived in Pretoria. He said there was an alarm system in the house, but no cameras.

They acquired the plans of the house from the municipality. In the parade room they spread them open on the big table, and began building a model of the yard and house, using whatever they could lay their hands on – empty KFC containers and rulers and pens and unused docket files that they bent and folded. All so that Lieutenant Colonel Phila Zamisa and the Boland cluster's special task force could plan their entry and raid as soon as they arrived in Stellenbosch.

At the Decameron restaurant, the food was delivered to the women's table, but neither of them ate much, although the dishes were tasty.

Sandra still had no appetite, and Lettie Boonstra was too busy telling her story.

She said Jasper's fraud with Schneider-König was the beginning of the end. That was when the papers and magazines and social media also found out about the mistress in the fancy Franschhoek house, and that was the last straw. For the first time Jasper's former colleagues, friends and strangers found the courage to tell her about all his skirt-chasing escapades. Only then did she realise the full extent of it, only then did she understand quite how big that chip on his shoulder was. How little she really knew about her husband, the extent of his weaknesses.

No, she didn't hate Jasper. Hate is a useless, destructive emotion. Just nothing. That's what she began to feel for him. A cold, empty nothing. And in that chill void, a space for sober reflection, time to plan and act without rage or fear.

But still the dilemma remained: how to avoid walking out the other side stripped completely naked? Her plan was divorce. Getting rid of him, stepping away from the spotlight, the humiliation, the whole shebang.

She did her homework about private investigators, and eventually contacted one with a good reputation. An Englishman in Kenilworth. The cameras were his idea, to gather information on the mistresses and find the crook book. And once they had that, the search for the damned key, which had her tearing her hair out in frustration. Jasper guarded that key like his life depended on it.

So she decided she would present the video material about the mistresses and the crook book in his study to the divorce court. Throw herself on the mercy of the judge. Or at least heavily influence the settlement negotiations.

Which brought her to yesterday. They were due to have a first meeting about a settlement at Baronsberg, she and Jasper. And she planned to hint that she had some serious ammunition.

She arrived at Baronsberg, but Jasper was nowhere to be seen. She called him, looked through the house, waited, tried to phone him, then heard his cell phone ringing upstairs. She walked up to the study and found the phone. And the key. Right there, in the ostrich shell bowl, on top of the jelly beans. She couldn't believe her eyes. Swiftly, she unlocked the drawer and grabbed the crook book and a few other files, hoping that they too might be worth something. She locked the drawer again, took the documents down to her car, replaced the key in the ostrich egg, and returned to the sitting room.

Where slowly she came to the conclusion that something was not right. Jasper was never late, and he would never, ever have left the key there.

She downloaded the camera video onto her phone and watched it. And only then did she realise what had happened.

Yes, she was shocked. It took her over an hour to regain her equilibrium, to think the matter through and decide on the best course of action.

Why hadn't she told the police what had happened and shown them the video?

Meinhardt Sarazin, that's why.

The lawyer would have known she had the crook book. Because the video showed Sandra taking the key out of Jasper's dressing gown pocket and disappearing upstairs with it. The study camera would show how the key fitted in the drawer. Sarazin knew that was where the crook book was kept. And Sarazin for sure had some way or other to access some of the hidden assets. Or perhaps he would at least be notified if they were tampered with: if she began transferring or withdrawing, he would know it could not be the deceased Jasper. And he was just as sly as Jasper, he would get court orders or summonses or interdicts against her to get his hands on the book.

The very best outcome was for nobody to suspect that Jasper was dead. Jasper had skipped the country. And so it would be Jasper that was withdrawing money, or opening safe deposit boxes, or whatever.

Then Lettie phoned the private investigator. All she asked him was to arrange for someone – anyone – to phone her from Karasburg in Namibia, today between one and two. With a burner phone. So she had proof.

'I thought your secret would be safe, Sandra, because you did such an excellent job of getting rid of him. But then that Benny detective began sniffing around this morning, and I could see how frightened you were, and I wondered if you would hold out or whether you were going to fold. I thought, you really don't deserve this. You don't deserve to worry for the rest of your life that they are going to catch you. Now I want to say you don't have to thank me. But please explain to me why you didn't just call the police when he fell down the stairs. With his reputation they would surely have believed you.'

14:40

Griessel stepped outside for a smoke. Trying to get the frustration of the Boonstra case out of his system.

That was where Witkop Jansen found him. 'The commissioner wants you to be at the press conference,' the colonel said. His compact body radiated discomfort, his voice was low and apologetic. 'You must tell the media the SAPS search for Boonstra, along with the National Prosecuting Authority, is progressing well. As soon as the docket is prepared, we will have him extradited via Interpol.'

'Where will we find him then, Colonel? With all his money . . .'

A helpless shrug: 'I know, Warrant Officer. The commissioner said you both did good work; he will keep that in mind. He said you must remember to mention that you were seconded from the Hawks. He will appreciate that too.'

Griessel drew on his cigarette.

'I'm sorry, Warrant Officer. It doesn't feel right to me at all. I wish there was something I could do.'

'Colonel,' said Griessel, and flicked the cigarette butt into the long grass, 'it's okay. This morning, when the commissioner and his men were sitting in front of me, I was thinking about what you said, that we work for the people of Stellenbosch. I don't agree. I'm not a police-man because I want the respect from the rabbits. Because we won't get that any more. And I'm not a policeman because I can get a higher rank and praise from the top brass. That is not going to happen. I'm a policeman because I want to be one. That's all.'

They stood there for a while, each thinking his thoughts.

'What's happening to us, Benny?' Jansen asked. 'What's happening to us?' It was the first time that the commander had used his first name.

It was a huge relief to Sandra, to be able to be honest. To tell the truth to someone, to share all the lies and the trauma and stress. To unburden herself. She was on the edge of tears as she spoke, but she remained strong.

She told Lettie Boonstra exactly what had happened. From the first call from Jasper, through the marketing of Donkerdrif and the repeated harassment, to the reason why Jasper's body had to disappear: to save the transaction.

'Thank you for telling me,' said Lettie, and pushed the thick file across the table towards Sandra. 'You are entitled to have this. It's a report from Jasper's spies, about you and your family.'

'Did you read it?'

'I couldn't help myself.'

'My husband . . . Is he being unfaithful?'

'Good heavens, you surely didn't believe Jasper, did you? That's one of his classic tricks. Disinformation. They say in here that he's dreadfully dull, your husband. And now, I have to run, because I'm late for the big news conference.'

15:00

Griessel stood in front of the cameras and microphones on the scrappy lawn of the Stellenbosch police station, beside Lettie Boonstra. He blinked at the blinding lights and flashes. He read the statement that the media liaison officer had helped him prepare.

'I was seconded from the Hawks to lead the investigation into a missing persons report late on Wednesday evening, the fourth of October. Mister Jasper Boonstra was reported missing by his wife, Alet Boonstra. The team from the South African Police Service worked tirelessly, night and day. A general broadcast to law enforcement and all border posts was issued in the process. This morning, it was ascertained that mister Boonstra was probably transported from his home, voluntarily and secretly. The investigation was terminated at about fourteen hundred hours today, after Mrs Boonstra informed us that she wished to withdraw the form fifty-five report. She has had contact with her husband, who has allegedly fled the country . . .'

The media crowd stirred, there were gasps, exclamations, hands shooting up, questions shouted out. The liaison officer stepped up to the microphone, held up her hand and called for order. 'Warrant Officer Griessel and Mrs Boonstra will conclude their statements before we take any questions, thank you.'

It took a while before the hubbub settled down.

Griessel carried on: 'The South African Police Service, in conjunction with the National Prosecuting Authority, will continue its investigation into the alleged fraudulent activities of mister Boonstra, and will work closely with international law enforcement agencies to ensure that we find him and have him extradited. Thank you.'

He read the statement with a conviction that he did not feel. And as Lettie Boonstra read her statement and tried to field the barrage of questions from yelling journalists, he simply could not shake off the nagging sense of disbelief.

67

Outside the offices of Benson International Realtors Sandra sat in her Ford listening to the news conference on CapeTalk. When it was over, she wept from pure relief. Also over Josef, dull, dull, darling Josef. Her faithful husband.

It was over. The pressure, the suspense, the strain was over.

Finally she walked in at 15:21 and the receptionist told her the police had phoned, she was to call a Sergeant Julies back, it was urgent. It was about the house in Brandwacht, the house of André and Joan Schoeman.

She felt as if her heart would stop. 'Why?' she asked, the worry so clear in her voice.

'He didn't say. Here's the number,' the woman said and passed her a note.

Sandra went outside onto the pavement in Dorp Street. She rang the number.

Sergeant Julies answered promptly. 'Ma'am,' he said, 'thank you for calling. We have a situation in the house next door. We urgently need to get into that house to set up an observation post, and deploy the task force.'

'I . . .' She started shaking again and began to search desperately for a way out, for excuses. 'It's not my house, I don't have permission,' she said. 'The owners are in America.'

'Ma'am, we just want to put two people in the house to watch the neighbours' place, that's all.'

'I can't . . . The owners will have to give permission, and it's the middle of the night in America . . .'

'Ma'am, this falls under chapter two, article twenty-six of the Criminal Procedure Act that says we do not need permission. Can you please take us there and unlock the house? As in *now*.'

15:32

Lieutenant Colonel Phila Zamisa and the members of the Boland cluster's special task force arrived in a range of vehicles at the Stellenbosch detective branch, to attract as little attention as possible.

Now they were filling up the parade room. When Benny Griessel walked in, released from the Boonstra fifty-five, there was barely room to stand.

His colleague Vaughn Cupido was in charge of proceedings. He displayed the house plans, the street map of the neighbourhood, the model that they had constructed. He said they had an observation post in the house behind the Airbnb, they had just heard that the house which was for sale next door would be unlocked for them too. That observation team was on their way. Based on the fact that Buddy Fick was still in Stellenbosch, and the three other cars had most likely brought other members of the Trojans gang, they believed that Callie de Bruin was alive and also in the house. That made matters more complicated, as they didn't want to walk into a hostage situation. They wanted Callie alive. And the longer they waited, the greater were the chances that their activity would be noticed, or that details would be leaked. Because the town was still heaving with the media, due to the Boonstra case. And they suspected that Buddy Fick was not acting alone in this matter. Should a SAPS member here deliberately or accidentally let the news slip – the police bush telegraph could spread like wildfire – and should information on the developments reach Fick's colleagues in Silverton, they were in big trouble. So, the quicker, the better. He believed they had two choices: strike just after five, when homeward-bound traffic in the suburb would be at its height, or wait for dark.

Colonel Zamisa said: 'No, let's wait for dark. Get the municipality to cut the power to that part of town, so that we have the advantage of night-vision gear. Sunset tonight is at 18:51 exactly, I'd like us to go in at 19:15.'

'Cool bananas,' said Cupido. 'Everybody happy?'

Everybody was happy.

The Julies detective explained carefully to Sandra over the phone what she should do. She must wait for the two police officers to come to her office, then they would drive with her in her car to the Brandwacht Street house with all their equipment. It would be quite normal for her vehicle to be seen there. It wouldn't attract attention, and that meant no additional traffic.

She must then open the gate, drive in and park in front of the garage. Then she must get out, unlock the front door, open the garage doors, come out, drive the vehicle into the garage, and close the doors.

The policemen would get out and find the best room from which to observe the Airbnb.

She could leave again once they were satisfied. The police would let her know once it was all over. Sometime tonight perhaps, or perhaps only tomorrow.

Sandra almost forgot to ask, because she already knew; only at the last minute, when Julies was about to ring off, did she add quickly: 'What's going on there?'

'I'm not permitted to say, ma'am. And you must keep it quiet. It's a case of life and death.'

It was the bit about the garage that stressed her most, almost to breaking point. The two policemen would be less than a metre away from Jasper Boonstra's corpse in the freezer.

They would hear the freezer running, and they would say: 'If there are no people here, if the owners are in America, why is the freezer on?'

And then she would have to lie and hedge and try to disguise her agitation, in this exhausted, anxious state. She couldn't carry on. She simply didn't have the strength.

Things didn't quite work out that way.

They arrived at 16:02 at Benson International Realtors offices, a man and a woman, with four cases of equipment. They were friendly. She walked with them to her car. Just as Charlie arrived.

'And now?' he asked.

'It's police business, sir,' the female detective said.

Charlie saw Sandra's discomfort, her stress. To the police he said curtly: 'She works for me.' Then to her: 'Are they arresting you?' Blatantly hopeful.

Sandra wanted to say: 'Fuck you,' but she checked herself.

'Sir, Mrs Steenberg is assisting us with an investigation.'

'Oh.' Disappointment.

Sandra looked back once she was seated in the EcoSport. Charlie was still standing there, hands on his narrow hips. Like a jackal waiting to get at the carcass once the bigger predators were done with it.

It was in the garage that Sandra knew she wouldn't be able to handle this pressure much longer.

The policeman got out of the EcoSport, picked up one of the cases, and put it on the freezer.

Her knees buckled, she felt faint, panic rising, and she had to cling on to the car door. She was going to fall over, she was going to pass out. Oh Lord, not now. She smelt her own perspiration, her heart raced. How much could her body, her very being, still handle? She was going to give in, give over, give up.

The second case, also plonked onto the freezer.

'Ma'am, are you okay?' asked the policewoman.

Sandra stood as if turned to stone.

Until the man shut the back of the Ford, picked the first case off the freezer and walked to the inner door. She drew inspiration purely from muscle memory, reaching back to when her body had felt this way before. 'I think I'm pregnant.'

'Oh! Awesome! Congratulations!'

'Thank you. But I haven't taken a test yet.'

'I'm holding thumbs . . .'

And so she survived the garage and the wave of panic, while they moved upstairs, two cases at a time. And the police chose the room where she had hidden the freezer keys, deep at the back of the cupboard.

'How long do you think it will take?'

'We aren't permitted to say.'

'Can I go now?'

They said yes and thanked her. The woman said: 'Have a test,' when she said goodbye.

Sandra drove to the nursery school to pick up the children.

Would this day never end?

17:49

Planning for the Great Brandwacht Invasion was complete. The team had discussed it over and over again, until each one knew exactly what their role would be.

Phila Zamisa and his special task force were going to attack in four groups – from behind, from left and right, and from the front.

The first teams to move would be the rear, and the flanks. The one from the front would move last. Vaughn Cupido and Benny Griessel would be part of the front line. They also received the night-vision headsets. They had to practise how to operate them, because the equipment was new and unfamiliar to them.

At the armoury Cupido once again chose the RS200 shotgun with the pistol grip.

'Are you sure?' Griessel asked, remembering the previous occasion, the in-transit robbery.

'This is my good luck gun, *pappie*. And besides, it's indoors this time.'

Colonel Zamisa came to stand with them. 'So, are you going to save my life again, Benny?'

'You never know, Colonel. It looks like this is my week for coincidences.'

Sandra and the children drove home.

She pushed ahead of the twins to give Josef a hug. She held him tight. Her husband, her dull, darling, faithful man.

He asked: 'And now?'

'Now, I am tired and dirty and very hungry. And I love you very much. I have a story to tell also . . .'

'Goldilocks,' said Anke, 'please, Mamma.'

'Snow White!' said Bianca.

'Later,' Sandra laughed. 'I'm going to shower first, and then I want to tell Papa about the day when the police came to talk to Mamma twice.'

With the hot water streaming over her, her mind turned to many things. To the two policemen in the Brandwacht house – so close to Boonstra's body in the freezer. To the big, strong padlock she had put on it. To the keys stashed in the cupboard, so close to them. And to what she should tell Josef now: a version of the truth.

About the Donkerdrif deal. (Tomorrow would bring them financial freedom!) About Boonstra's constant harassment and the stress of trying to push the deal through. (That's why I was so irritable, please forgive me!) About the police coming to talk to her because she'd been the last person in the country to see Jasper (Can you believe that?) And about the detectives in the house in Brandwacht. (What do you think they're doing there?)

Then she set to scrubbing her body, with fierce determination.

68

Colonel Mbali Kaleni found Cupido and Griessel in their office, busy checking their weapons and fitting their bulletproof vests.

'It is my fault that you have had to share an office,' she said.

'Why, Colonel?' asked Cupido.

'I asked Colonel Jansen to keep you together, and away from the other detectives. You know how it is; once you start making friends and working with other people, it is hard to stay objective. It could have been any one of them leaking the firearms information. But I'm happy it wasn't.'

'There are still enough good cops, Colonel.'

'Yes, Warrant, that is very true. Which brings me to why I came to talk to you. I called the commissioner. I told him Benny did everything that he asked in the Boonstra case, including the media conference. And, if all goes well tonight, you will close both the Callie de Bruin and firearms dockets. So, I would like to see that your rank is reinstated. Right away.'

'What did he say?' asked Cupido.

'He will think about it.'

'Thank you, Colonel,' said Griessel.

'And getting back to the Hawks, Colonel?' asked Cupido.

'How do you eat an elephant, Warrant Officer?'

'I feel you, Colonel. I feel you.'

'Just don't get yourselves shot tonight,' were her parting words.

18:53

The operation to save Calvyn Wilhelm de Bruin and arrest Colonel Buddy Fick was, as Cupido commonly described this sort of chaotic, everything-going-wrong operation, 'a clusterfuck of majestic proportions'.

But at least not from the start.

The twelve members of the special task force were divided into four groups of three men each – teams Alpha, Bravo, Charlie and Delta. Alpha consisted of Colonel Phila Zamisa and another two, who took up their position in the house behind the Airbnb. Bravo came from the house on the left – the one that was for sale – and had a folding ladder with them so they could climb up to the balcony on the first floor of the Airbnb. Team Charlie attacked from the right flank. These three teams got into position without hindrance with the concrete wall as cover for the rear and sides of the Airbnb. Just as the sun disappeared behind Table Mountain in the distance.

Team Delta were the three task force members in the RG-12, the tactical vehicle of the SAPS also known as a Nyala. It resembled a prehistoric creature, with its big sturdy bull bar on the nose, and the angular, armoured lines. Benny Griessel and Vaughn Cupido were also inside. It was waiting around the corner from the Airbnb. Behind the RG-12 two ambulances were parked, just in case. If everything went according to plan, the Nyala would break open the gate at exactly 19:15, and Team Delta would then force and enter the front door. Griessel and Vaughn were instructed to form the rear guard. Allowing the task force members to execute their well-oiled, orchestrated expert plan of assault on the front door of the target house.

At 19:04 all the teams confirmed over the radio that they were safely in position.

The Stellenbosch municipality control centre notified Captain Rowen Geneke that the electricians who had to cut the power to this section of Brandwacht, were at the substation. Ready to go.

Geneke phoned Cupido. Cupido communicated the news via radio to Phila Zamisa.

19:05

In the back of the Nyala Griessel and Cupido tested their night-vision headsets again in the dark of the interior. They were feeling uncomfortably hot in the bulletproof vests. There was a sense of expectancy in the cab. And tension. They believed Colonel Buddy Fick was there, and they believed the armed gang members were there. But despite all the scopes, binoculars and eyes on the Airbnb house since that afternoon, they didn't know the exact number. They suspected there might be twelve – four men to each of the suspected gang vehicles outside. They didn't know for sure.

Nor did they know in which room Callie de Bruin was being held. If he was there at all. The one thing that Witkop Jansen and Phila Zamisa had told them over and over again, was that the chief aim of the operation was to extract Callie de Bruin safe and sound.

Easier said than done. So much could go wrong. As usual. That was why Benny wanted a cigarette.

Or a drink, if only he could.

19:10

With their police vans, members of Stellenbosch SAPS station blocked all access routes to the block of houses where the Airbnb was situated.

19:11

The first trouble arose when the municipal electricians switched off the electrical supply to the wrong section of Brandwacht. Accidentally. The switches were side-by-side.

Phila Zamisa waited two minutes before he asked Cupido over the radio why the lights at the Airbnb were still burning bright.

Cupido phoned Captain Rowen Geneke, the operation's link with the municipality.

In the meantime the municipal control centre received the first complaint call from a furious resident.

Geneke phoned the municipal control centre to tell them the power supply was still on where it should be off. The control centre phoned the electricians and gave them hell.

The anxious electricians switched off power to the correct section of Brandwacht.

The operation was running nine minutes late.

19:24

Phila Zamisa gave the order to all the teams: 'Go, go, go.'

Alpha, Bravo and Charlie moved as smooth as silk in the dark. They slid easily over the concrete wall, their night-vision headsets bathed the house in front of them in a grainy green.

The Nyala with Cupido and Griessel accelerated, raced around the corner at the highest possible speed and headed for the Airbnb.

Zamisa and Team Alpha reached the back door of the Airbnb unseen.

Bravo and Charlie moved into position beside the house. They used their radios to report to each other that they were ready.

Team Bravo unfolded the ladder, leaned it quietly against the side of the balcony.

The Nyala driver told them they were two hundred metres away.

'Go,' said Zamisa again. The two task force members with him swung the heavy ram against the back door. The door burst open with a dull thud. They threw down the ram and followed Zamisa inside.

Bravo climbed the ladder up to the balcony. Team Charlie broke a window down below, on the right side of the house, and entered a room that was apparently used as a study.

The prehistoric Nyala beast used the bull bar to smash the front gate completely off its hinges, and stopped. The three task force men leaped out.

Griessel and Cupido waited.

The municipal control centre received the sixth phone call from an irate resident complaining about the power cut.

19:27

Colonel Zamisa and his two team members surprised five armed members of the Trojans gang sitting around the kitchen table eating baked beans in tomato sauce out of tins, using the light of a cell phone. Their weapons were on the table beside them. The shocked men cursed, screamed and reached for their weapons. Zamisa ordered them to freeze. The gangsters ignored him. They picked up their weapons; three pistols, two assault rifles. Zamisa shot two of them, lightning fast and with deadly accuracy. His two adjutants shot at the other three. One Trojan managed to get two shots off, both hit a task force member in the chest, which was protected by a bulletproof vest. The task force member toppled over backwards from the force of the bullets, but he was unharmed. The reek of firearm propellant filled the room.

All five Trojans were down.

Zamisa stepped forward and smashed the cell phone, so that the light of its screen wouldn't hamper their vision through the night-vision headsets.

He heard the front door crash open and knew his Delta team members who'd come in the vehicle were in.

At the same moment the municipal control centre called the electricians at the substation and asked them to please turn the lights back on to the part of Brandwacht that they had cut off in error, as the people were phoning like crazy.

Zamisa heard shots from the first floor, to the left of the house. Automatic gunfire.

19:30

The night-vision headset was irritating Griessel. His wouldn't fit properly; it kept slipping down, he kept having to push it up. He felt detached from reality, the greyish green of the scope created a disorienting sense of distance that made him uncomfortable.

He saw Team Delta break through the front door. He had his Z88 in his hand, Cupido beside him with the stubby shotgun. They ran, waited for Delta to go inside, counted to ten, followed the task force through the front door into the hall.

The electricians at the municipal substation threw the switch for the wrong section of the neighbourhood.

Suddenly the lights burned brightly in the Airbnb, blinding all the members of the task force. Six of them, Colonel Zamisa included, had the presence of mind to rip off the night scopes instantly, cursing. But that meant the advantage of darkness was gone, the Trojans could see them clearly now. The vital seconds were decisive. Zamisa and his two mates were on the stairs, and one of the Alpha team members was shot in the shoulder. Zamisa was hit on the bulletproof vest, three shots, practically simultaneously. The brute force lifted him momentarily, he lost his footing on the step and fell.

Upstairs, in the main bedroom, Bravo had broken through the sliding door from the balcony. Two Trojans opened fire on them. They hit one member of Bravo on the back of his trigger hand. The other Bravo troops mowed them down.

Downstairs in the entrance hall, Griessel and Cupido had been too slow to take off the night-vision headsets; they were new to this sort of operation. So they didn't see the Trojans in the dining room, the two who'd crept under the table when they heard shots booming from the kitchen.

One of the gang members fired a Sig MPX K, a short-barrelled semi-automatic 9 mm machine pistol. There were thirty rounds in the curved magazine, which he fired off in one clattering barrage. It was a small miracle that only a buckle of Griessel's jacket was shot off. Otherwise he was unharmed.

Two of the bullets struck Cupido in the upper thigh.

Griessel saw Cupido fall. He shot at the Trojans, hit one. He heard his colleague say: '*Jirre*,' and saw Cupido grimly raise the shotgun and shoot the other gang member full in the chest. The blood made a fine red spatter pattern on the white wall behind.

The sound of shots boomed from all parts of the house. Griessel made sure both Trojans were down, then he bent down at Cupido. The leg looked bad, blood pumping.

'Partner, I'm gonna die here tonight.'

'Not a *fok*,' said Griessel and called for an ambulance over the radio.

The electricians at the municipality realised their error, turned off the power to this part of Brandwacht again. And to their doubtful credit they at least restored supply to the correct part of the neighbourhood.

A clusterfuck of majestic proportions.

69

Griessel focused entirely on Cupido.

He just said '*Fok, fok, fok,*' when the lights went off again. In the dark he stripped off his belt and wrapped it around Cupido's leg, as fast as he could.

They both knew how quickly you could bleed to death if your femoral artery was shot to pieces. They'd seen victims like that, and they'd stood at the graveside of their colleagues. They knew you had to apply pressure at all costs, as much pressure as possible. Without letting up.

Griessel pressed his knee on the wound, his full weight on it. Cupido bellowed in pain. Griessel pulled the belt tight and said: 'Don't worry, the ambulance is on the way.'

'There's no time, Benna.'

'They're coming. Lie still.'

'Benna, yesterday morning . . . I was proud of you, partner. I just wanted to tell you.'

'*Ja,* and tomorrow morning you'll be just as proud, because I saved your life. You owe me. Muffins.'

Cupido's smile was weak. 'Just tell Desiree she's the love of my life.'

'*Jissis,* Vaughn, leave the fucking last words and help me hold on to this.'

'Hell, Benna, I'm drifting. I can feel it . . .'

Griessel heard the ambulance outside and he screamed: 'Here, here, medic, here!'

Then, on the first floor, shots boomed, and he thought, tonight I'll have to tell Annemarie de Bruin her son is dead.

Phila Zamisa stood up, at the foot of the stairs, adrenaline surging. Along with a wave of rage. At the municipality, at the Trojans, at this almighty balls-up. He charged up the stairs.

The lights went off.

He swore. He pulled his headset over his eyes. He reached the top step, peered around the corner. One of Alpha team was just behind him.

The passage was clear. Movement, right at the end.

His own men. Bravo. One was holding his hand, the blood a strange dark spatter through the green vision of the scope.

They indicated with hand signals that the main bedroom was secure.

Zamisa motioned, you take *that* bedroom, we'll take this one.

They shuffled up to the closed doors. Bravo waited for his signal.

Then they went in.

Zamisa saw Callie de Bruin sitting, in the faint reflection of the laptop screen in front of him. He could tell the student had been beaten, bloody around the mouth and nose, swollen eyes. But he could still see the terror in them. Behind Callie, he saw Colonel Buddy Fick, with the Heckler & Koch VP9 Tactical pistol barrel pressed to Callie's temple. Fick's eyes were crazed. 'I'll shoot him, I'll shoot him!' he screamed. 'Get out, or I'll shoot him!'

'Put down the gun, Buddy.'

'I'll shoot him, get the fuck out of here! I swear to God I'll shoot him!' The VP9 shook in Fick's hand.

Callie de Bruin had been kept in this room for six days. Buddy Fick and various members of the Trojans had tortured him, daily. With electric shocks, fist blows to the head. Held burning cigarettes to his chest and belly. This morning, an electric drill through each foot. While one of the gang members held his mouth shut, so the neighbours wouldn't hear his screams.

They left only his hands unscathed. He needed them for the laptop they had put in front of him. So he could delete the data bombs. The data bombs he had already warned Fick about last Friday night.

'If you kill me, the data bomb goes off.'

'What data bomb?'

'I recorded everything you did on your database, all the guns you didn't destroy, that you sold. And how you did it. The data bombs are emails that go to the newspapers, with everything. If you let me go, I will stop them.'

'Who's going to send the emails?'

'Not who. What. I wrote software. It's all automatic.'

'You're lying, you little shit.'

'We'll see on Friday.'

'Friday. You're sending the emails on Friday?'

'Friday morning six o'clock'

'You're lying.'

'We'll see.'

So they began to torture him, to stop them. With the laptop in front of him. 'All you have to do, Callie, is log on and stop the data bombs. Then we'll stop. Then we'll let you go.'

Callie was a very clever young man. He knew if he did that, he would die. And the excruciating pain of torture was preferable to death.

Even six days of torture.

He hated Buddy Fick. With a terrible, white-hot hatred. He put all that hate into his legs when he braced them against the bottom of the table leg, and launched himself backwards, against Buddy Fick. He knew instinctively he had to disturb the man's balance to the maximum. It was the only chance that he and the policemen at the door had.

He kicked.

Zamisa couldn't shoot. Callie and Fick were entangled on the floor behind the small desk. He did the only thing he could. He pulled off his headset, dropped his firearm, and dived onto Fick in a desperate attempt to reach the big pistol.

He hoped his Alpha colleague would cover him from the door.

Callie kicked wildly. He kicked Zamisa, he kicked Fick, he writhed and screamed.

And then the VP9 boomed.

Griessel gripped the belt tight around Cupido's leg while the two paramedics loaded his partner on the stretcher.

He kept his grip on it as they pushed the trolley at a jogtrot towards the ambulance.

Cupido was silent now. His eyes were closed.

Upstairs in the Airbnb a single shot boomed.

'Vaughn!' Benny shouted. 'Vaughn!'

He got no response.

'He has to get blood,' Griessel said.

They loaded the stretcher into the ambulance.

'Go!' yelled the paramedic.

The ambulance pulled away before the doors were fully closed.

Griessel watched it go.

Vaughn you better not go and die on me now.

He realised he was gasping for air, and his hands were covered in blood. He wiped them on his jacket.

Where was his Z88? Inside. He'd better go and pick it up.

God, Vaughn better not go and die. He would shoot Buddy Fick dead.

He walked into the hall. He couldn't see much inside. He found his headset, put it on. Picked up his pistol from the floor.

Where was Buddy Fick? He walked to the stairs. Then up them.

In the passage he saw the figures emerging from a doorway. Two members of Alpha, with Callie de Bruin between them. The boy was limping badly. He looked a mess. Blood everywhere. He'd been beaten. Beaten badly. What sort of man beats a defenceless kid like that?

It could have been Fritz.

Rage overwhelmed Benny. Rage over the abused boy, rage from his omnipotent responsibility guilt, his bottled-up rage over the disparaging remarks he'd had to listen to at Baronsberg, rage at the commissioner's malice in the parade room, rage about Vaughn, and about Milo April, the young sergeant murdered on orders of Buddy Fick, rage at his own uselessness. Silent fury, deadly calm fury.

'You okay, Callie?' he asked.

'Yes,' the boy answered hoarsely.

'Where is Buddy?' Griessel asked.

There inside, the Alpha member indicated.

Griessel tightened his grip on his Z88 and went in.

Fick was sitting on the floor. Zamisa, wearing his night-vision headset again, had his pistol barrel to the Silverton officer's neck.

Griessel stopped, holding the Z88. 'I'm going to shoot you,' he said. 'This one is for Milo April.'

'Benny, no,' said Zamisa, his voice pleading.

Fick couldn't see anything in the dark, but he heard the intensity in Griessel's voice. 'Please,' he said, and raised his hands in defence. 'It was them, it was the Trojans, they shot April.'

Griessel raised the Z88 and aimed it at Fick.

Phila Zamisa did the only thing he could do. He shot Benny Griessel in the middle of the chest.

And when Benny fell down, he said: 'Now we're even, Benny. I've just saved your life.'

70

The police phoned Sandra Steenberg at 21:37 to tell her she could come and lock up the Brandwacht house, the operation was over.

She got in the car and drove. She was less worried now, because the female detective only sounded tired, not threatening.

They were waiting for her in the driveway, because the gate was shut.

She used the remote control to open it and drove in.

They thanked her.

'What happened?' she asked.

'It's the Callie de Bruin disappearance,' the woman said. 'We rescued him.'

'He was here? Next door?'

'Yes. They kept him there the whole week.'

'I'm very glad he's safe.'

'We are too. One of our people is wounded. Critically.'

'I'm so sorry,' she said.

Then they picked up their equipment cases and walked out the gate, towards the Airbnb.

Sandra waited until they were out of earshot before she let out a long, slow sigh of relief. Then she locked the house up securely again.

Tonight at least she would sleep.

At 21:58 they sat in the waiting room at the Mediclinic in Die Boord, Stellenbosch – Griessel, Desiree, her son Donovan, Colonel Witkop Jansen and Captain Rowen Geneke. They didn't talk much. They drank coffee. Donovan was eating a muffin. 'Uh-huh,' he said, 'my and Uncle Vaughn's muffins are much, much better.'

His mother stroked his head. She was on edge, as they all were.

Benny sat with his now clean-scrubbed hand resting on his bruised ribs. They were bloody sore. One might even be broken.

Fucking Zamisa. But the colonel was right, he had saved his life with that shot. Because Griessel would have gone to prison.

What he appreciated most about the colonel, was what Zamisa had said afterwards: 'We won't talk about this, Benny. Not ever.'

If he was going to lose it like that again, he might as well go back to the bottle.

The only thing that had made him feel better was phoning Annemarie de Bruin to tell her that her son was safe. Injured, traumatised, admitted to hospital, but safe.

She laughed and cried.

The surgeon was approaching. With a grim expression. His heart contracted.

Desiree sprang to her feet. The others followed suit.

'Are you here for Warrant Officer Cupido?' the woman asked.

'That's right,' said Desiree.

The surgeon shook her head. 'It was touch and go,' she said.

'He's okay?'

'He's okay.'

Desiree hugged the doctor.

Griessel didn't want to show the depth of his emotion. 'I'm going to phone Mbali,' he said and hurried away.

71

6 October

The data bombs went off at six o'clock on Friday morning.

Which meant that by 08:30 the circus was back in town. Television, radio, newspapers, all gathered at the Mediclinic where Callie de Bruin was. Their vehicles even packed the parking lot at the Spar shopping centre, to the general dismay of the Eikestad's residents, already frustrated by the lack of parking.

The hospital group's media spokesperson and the liaison officer for the SAPS were posted at the front doorway to fend off the ravening pack. They provided what information they had: Yes, he was severely traumatised and his injuries were serious, but Calvyn Wilhelm de Bruin was conscious, stable, and should be in hospital for no longer than a week. His mother, Annemarie, was currently with him, along with three members of the police. The provincial commissioner, Lieutenant General Mandla Khaba, was on his way and would address the media later, along with Mrs De Bruin. No, they could not say at what time precisely that would be.

The detectives who were sitting with Callie and Annemarie de Bruin in the ward – with permission of the medical staff – were Benny Griessel, Witkop Jansen and Rowen Geneke.

Nobody in the room had had much sleep.

To begin with, Griessel explained to mother and son what Callie's rights were in terms of Chapter Three, Section Twenty-Five of the South African Constitution. Callie could remain silent, he needn't say anything that might incriminate himself. Callie could ask for a lawyer. But before he made up his mind: they had just come from the local office of the National Prosecuting Authority. The NPA said that if Callie turned state witness and testified against Colonel Buddy Fick, and if he pleaded guilty to charges of cyber theft and complicity to housebreaking, he would not serve prison time. He would receive a suspended sentence.

He could take time to think it over.

'No,' his mother said. 'There is nothing to think about. That is what you are going to do.'

Callie looked at her, and started to cry. And then he talked. It was a partial confession, halting and raw. It was a slow process, what with his bruised and swollen mouth, his black eyes and the impact of the pain-killers. 'I'm sorry, Ma,' the boy kept saying. 'I'm sorry. I wanted to buy you a house, Ma.'

Callie told them Buddy Fick had come to the hostel alone on Friday afternoon to pick him up. Fick pointed to the back seat and said: 'There's your money, but let's have a chat first. We're going to work very well together, you and me.'

Callie got into the car, because the data bombs were his insurance policy. They drove to Paradyskloof chatting all the way. Up at the Eden plantation they parked beside two other cars, where the gang members were waiting. Five of them grabbed him, and took his cell phone off him. Fick was extremely worried about the cell phone and the possibility that Callie could record their conversation, the possibility that Callie could be traced via the phone.

Then they took him to the Brandwacht house, handcuffed him to the desk chair in front of the laptop, and ordered him to disarm the data bombs, or they would hurt him, badly.

He flat-out refused. And so they tortured him. On Sunday evening Fick sent one of the Trojans to collect the hard drive from Callie's computer, because they believed that would automatically stop the emails. The Trojan also stole Callie's PlayStation. And a wad of notes from his cupboard.

They kept on torturing him, yelling at him, threatening to kill him. But he knew his only chance for survival was to say nothing.

By 09:17 Charlie Benson still wasn't at the office. Unusual.

Sandra knew why. He was avoiding her. He couldn't look her in the eyes. The old snake.

At 09:20 her phone rang. It was Mareli Vorster from Stirling and Heyns. She said: 'Shoo, Sandra, lots of excitement over there.'

You have no idea, Sandra thought. But she kept her cool, because she'd had a wonderful night's sleep. 'And just the other day we were talking about Jasper Boonstra,' she said. 'Can you believe it?'

'Yes, it's a small world, hey? I suspected he would try to disappear some time or other. That's what I would have done . . . Listen, I'm just phoning to say we have just transferred your money by EFT. We're with the same bank, it should show today already.'

Waves of relief washed through Sandra. She felt like jumping up from her desk and dancing around pumping her fists in the air, cheering and shouting.

She said: 'Oh, thank you. It was a pleasure doing business with you.'

Then she phoned Charlie Benson to tell him what a cunt he was.

Colonel Buddy Fick sat across from Griessel, Geneke and Jansen in the detective branch interrogation room.

He wasn't flashy now. He was tired and dirty, his eyes bloodshot. There was a bruise on his cheek where Zamisa had hit him. And in the coat-tail of the expensive brown jacket was the big hole left by the VP9 bullet. Only the wall and the jacket had been damaged. And Fick's giant ego. But his attitude was still patronising, scornful, arrogant.

Griessel shoved a printout of Callie de Bruin's data bomb across the table. 'Buddy, the boy basically wrote out the charge sheet for us.'

'I want a lawyer.'

'What for?' Geneke asked. 'You're finished anyway.'

'I want a lawyer.'

'Your two colleagues were arrested in Pretoria last night, Buddy,' Griessel said. 'They're singing like canaries.'

'Fuck you. You should have shot me when you could.'

'I should have, Buddy. Because you had a Member murdered. And fucked up the reputation of the entire Service.'

'*I* did? *I* did? The reputation of the Service was fucked up a long time ago, you moron. You all are just too dumb to realise it. You whites who still arse-lick the brass.'

Griessel knew the only way to get Fick to lose control was through his ego. He wished Cupido were here. His colleague could have accomplished that very quickly. He wondered what would Vaughn have done next? 'Not as dumb as you, Buddy,' he said. 'Caught out by some puny student. Just a green student kid . . .'

'Fuck you.'

Griessel could tell he was on the right track. 'And he'll be there in court to testify to the fact that you are a dumb sonofabitch. The whole world will be laughing at you, Buddy "The Flash" Fick. Oh-So-Important Buddy Fick, who orders everyone around like a general. Where are you now? In your *moer* in, because of a rookie student.'

Fick started to rise from the chair, face flushed bright red, spit spraying as he screamed: 'I should be a general! Me! Ten years ago already! I earned it, not you lot . . .' he pointed at Captain Rowen Geneke, '. . . who get everything because of your fucking colour!'

Geneke smiled. 'And that's supposed to hurt me, Buddy? Coming from a crooked cop who sold guns on the Cape Flats? Now I get why a *laaitie* caused your downfall. You're just useless.'

'Fuck off!'

'Is that why you did it?' asked Colonel Witkop Jansen. 'Because you weren't promoted? That's how you justify it?'

Fick folded his arms defensively, as if he knew they could see right through him now.

Annemarie de Bruin addressed the media first.

In her simple, humble way she said her thoughts were with Warrant Officer Vaughn Cupido who was also here in the hospital. He had almost given his life to save her son's. She wanted to thank him and Warrant Officer Griessel very much for bringing Callie back to her. She would be eternally grateful to them and the other policemen who had helped. Thanks also to the media who had helped to broadcast his disappearance to the world.

'My son did some wrong things, and it breaks my heart that with all his talents he chose that path. That is not the way I tried to bring him up. Perhaps I failed as a mother. We will both bear the consequences of that now. This morning I told him it is a hard lesson to learn. A horrible lesson. But I stand by him. I love him still. Thank you.'

The provincial commissioner said he had never doubted that the South African Police Service would return Callie to his mother. That was why they seconded two Hawks detectives to handle this case and the Jasper Boonstra case. Because he believed everyone – rich and poor – deserved the same level of investigation.

And he wanted to make it abundantly clear that he would not answer questions about Colonel Buddy Fick. He pronounced the surname as 'Feek'. He said: 'Fick is not from this province. Fick works in Silverton, in Tshwane. You will have to ask them how this happened. Our house in the Western Cape is squeaky clean.'

Charlie Benson couldn't look her in the eye.

He sat behind his desk and stared at the poster on the wall.

Sandra said: 'You thought if you could get me arrested, you could keep all the money, you greedy old runt of a man.'

'How dare you speak to me like that . . .' His leg twitched wildly.

'I will talk to you how I wish, Charlie. You're a snake.' She smacked the letter of resignation down on the table in front of him. 'And you have an hour to pay my money over.'

'Or what?'

'Or I tell the *Eikestad News* everything. How you harass me, every day. "Pretty thing" and "honeybun" and "sexylegs". You've honed your own special brand of harassment, turned it into an artform. All the "sweet" little names, the whole patronising attitude, the mindset that all the women who work here have to be reminded, constantly, that they are inferior. So cowardly and subtle, Charlie, just on the very edge of the safe side so you can always justify yourself. But let's see, Charlie, how many people will still want to do business with you after I speak to the papers.'

72

Josef and Sandra and the twins were in the Spur at 12:49. It was the children's favourite spot.

She heard her cell phone beep. She picked it up and saw that it was an SMS from the bank. Her account had been credited with precisely three million rand.

She took her husband's hand. 'I've been thinking about starting my own agency. When your book is finished.'

'What's an agency, Mamma?' Bianca asked.

'I also want to start one,' said Anke.

'This calls for champagne,' Josef said. 'Do you think the Spur will have any?'

Benny and Alexa were only allowed to visit Cupido that afternoon at 16:00.

Only briefly, because he was still in intensive care. On drips with pipes and sensors in and on him. His eyes were still dull, his colour pale.

Alexa shed a few tears, and said she was so glad he was going to be okay, she had been so shocked. And the flowers outside were for him.

Griessel put a flat parcel, gift-wrapped, down on the bed beside Vaughn.

'What is this, partner?'

'Must I open it for you?'

'*Yebo*, yes.'

'I thought,' said Griessel, 'while we still have to share an office for a while, I'll have to make a plan to be sure there's room for me.'

'What do you mean?'

Griessel tore the gift wrapping off and showed Cupido the book. *The Complete Low Calorie Cookbook.* 'There's even a recipe for muffins.'

'That is so thoughtful of you, Benna. Fuck you.'

'I knew you'd love it.'

73

Alexa had made a butternut tagine for Kayla the Vegetarian. From her Moroccan recipe book.

She wasn't good at Moroccan cuisine. Griessel tasted it, just before the children arrived at 12:00. He suspected this would be the last time they would be entertaining Fritz's girlfriend.

He was out the back at the *braai* corner salting the steaks, when the pair approached with Alexa.

He noted that Kayla the Vegetarian had tattoos all over her arms. Lots of them. But her smile was broad and her eyes were lively. He noted Fritz's faint frown. The constant anxiety of being the child of an alcoholic: will my father be sober today?

Guilt burned through him.

They said hello. Fritz relaxed. Kayla the Vegetarian talked. A lot. She didn't call him '*Oom*', she said: 'Wow, Benny, I saw you on TV, it must have been awesome to investigate that thing. What's she like, Jasper's wife? Is she nice? Please say she's nice, spill the beans, all the beans, don't leave anything out . . .'

From there on it was plain sailing. Fritz loved that his girlfriend liked his somewhat famous *and* sober father so much. Benny started out a little reluctantly, but Kayla responded so spontaneously and with such genuine interest that he even began to enjoy himself after a while. He told the story of the investigation, and what he believed had happened. With the attractive estate agent, and the EcoSport, and the fact that Forensics had let him know that there was indeed a load of somewhere in the region of ninety kilograms in that car.

And while the meat was on the *braai*, Alexa prodded him to tell them about Callie de Bruin as well.

Which he did.

When Kayla began to eat the tagine, Alexa immediately asked: 'Is it okay?'

'It's delicious, thank you, Alexa.'

Benny could tell when someone was lying. He knew all the signs. He could spot at least two of them now.

By the time they moved on to the vegan ice cream and chocolate sauce he'd told the whole story.

'It's so weird,' Kayla said. 'There are so many things in our country that divide us. But we are united in our greed.'

They stayed till half past four, and when they left, Fritz gave him a hug, a man hug, just shoulder to shoulder.

He watched them drive away and thought how this was the best thing that had happened to him this entire year.

Sandra Steenberg was in the lounge reading a magazine, just before four in the afternoon, when her phone rang.

She had to get up to fetch it from the kitchen counter.

She didn't recognise the number, but answered.

'Hello, Sandra, it's Joan Schoeman, how are you?' The owners of the Brandwacht house.

'Very well, thank you, and you?'

'*Jong*, not so great. André's stepfather is sick, we're on our way back, things don't look good.'

Sandra felt a chill come over. 'I'm so sorry to hear that. When are you coming?'

'That's the reason I'm phoning. We're in Johannesburg now, we're landing in Cape Town at seven. I just want to arrange to get the keys from you.'

ACKNOWLEDGEMENTS

One of the great challenges in writing a crime novel is to keep the blend of reality and fiction on the right side of credibility, without sacrificing pace, suspense or entertainment. Because reality and story are often at odds with each other. The life of a real, flesh-and-blood Hawk or station detective consists of long days of waiting to testify in a court case, investigations that lead nowhere, a few days of sick leave, and a host of other activities that wouldn't contribute to the success of a book.

As author, one is continuously confronted with choices: when does one allow the hard facts to determine the progress and direction of a novel, and when does one exercise one's right to poetic licence?

If I have made the wrong choices in *The Dark Flood*, I have only myself to blame. Because the long list of people that shared their knowledge, insight, experience and time so generously, did their best to keep me on the straight and narrow.

Very many thanks to:

Major General Jeremy Veary, Western Cape Commissioner of Detectives, for the story that began it all, and for vouching for me with the Stellenbosch detectives.

Colonel Damon (Deon) Beneke, former station commissioner and now Chief of Detectives at Stellenbosch, also for the privilege of attending morning parade. And Captain Hilgard Holster who allowed me to experience the 'Crime Office' and answered a multitude of questions.

Advocate Grant Smith, former Murder and Robbery detective and the dream of any crime writer, for the inputs into Case number G 641/2015 – The State versus Christiaan Lodewyk Prinsloo.

And, as usual, Lieutenant Colonel Elmarie Myburgh of the SAPS Investigative Psychology Section for Forensic Services.

Viljoen van der Walt, head of the Stellenbosch University Campus Security.

Brian Coode, weapons expert and collector.

Albert Marais of Marais Müller Hendricks who answered my legal questions so patiently. And Anneli, for the soup and bread.

Mari and Deon Carstens of Anna Basson Properties in Stellenbosch, and especially Janitha Livingstone-Louw who shared her experiences as a young, female estate agent.

Neighbour Johann Steytler, the anaesthetist who foiled the firearms thieves and who is now known as the street's Benny Griessel.

Primarius Liam Cloete and the house committee of Eendrag residence.

Angus McGregor, thank you for your part in Benny's care. You know what I mean.

My agent Isobel Dixon, UK editor Nick Sayers and the team at Hodder, and USA editor George Gibson and his colleagues at Grove Atlantic. It remains an honour and a privilege to work with you.

Laura Seegers and all my other translators, overseas editors and publishers, who each in their own way contributes to my books, as well as all the proofreaders, for their eagle eyes.

My wife, Marianne, for her endless patience, love, care and support. And the children, who are still prepared to laugh at my dad jokes.

Thank you also to all the people whose names were lost between written notes, digital notes and curtailed phone calls.

The Dark Flood is fiction. The characters in the book only exist in the imagination of the author.

GLOSSARY OF AFRIKAANS WORDS

Ai – Afrikaans, meaning Ah, oh, ow, ouch, mostly used a little despairingly.

Aitsa – An exclamation that depends on the context: ouch, hey, yipee are all possibilities.

Bakkie – the word all South Africans use to refer to a pick-up truck.

Bergie – Cape Flats Afrikaans for a homeless person, often a vagrant, living on the side of Table Mountain (berg = mountain). Cape Afrikaans or Cape Flats Afrikaans refers to the Afrikaans spoken on the Cape Flats, a vast area east of Cape Town, where the majority of 'Cape Coloured' people reside. 'Coloured people' refer to the descendants of Malaysian and Madagascan slaves in South Africa (forced migration by the Dutch East India Company), who inter-married with white farmers and local Khoi people – as opposed to Blacks (descendants of the Bantu people) and Whites (descendants of European settlers).

Bliksem – Mild profanity, used as an exclamation or adjective ('Damn!' or 'damned'), or a verb (I will 'bliksem' you = I will hit you hard).

Blougatte – Police slang for freshly trained constables, the lowest rank in the SAPS.

Bra – Abbreviated form of 'brother'.

Braai – South South Africa's national pastime, to barbecue meat over the coals, mostly outdoors.

Chlora – Cape Flats Afrikaans for a coloured woman.

Drol – Mildly profane term for excrement. A turd.

Fok – Fuck.

Fokken – Fucking.

Fokkit – Fuck it.

Fokkol – Fuck all.

Fokkop – Fuck-up.

Frans – Cape Flats slang for someone who is not a gang member.

Gahzie – Cape Flats slang for a friend.

Gat – Arse.

Gatvol – When you've had enough of something. Fed up.

Haas – Police slang for a member of the public. A 'haas' is the Afrikaans word for a rabbit.

Hayi – IsiZulu for 'No!'. (South Africa has 11 official languages: Afrikaans, English, IsiNdebele, IsiXhosa, IsiZulu, Sepedi, Sesotho, Setswana, SiSwati, Tshivenda, Xitsonga. Township slang transcends all 11.)

Ja – Yes.

Jirre – Cape Flats slang for God, approximates 'Gawd'. (Afrikaans.)

Jis – Yes.

Jissis – A harsh version of the exclamation *Jesus*! (Afrikaans.)

Jitte Krismis – A very mild version of the exclamation *Jesus Christ!*, similar to 'Jeepers Creepers'. (Afrikaans.)

Jong – Literally means 'young', but is often used as an address, such as 'Yea, man'. (Afrikaans.)

Klaar – Finished. (Afrikaans.)

Kwaai – Mostly used in slang form to indicate coolness, it is an Afrikaans word with a very wide application. Literally meaning someone who is hot-tempered, bad-tempered, ill-natured, harsh or severe, it is also often used as an exclamation: 'Kwaai!' = 'Cool!' (or 'Heavy!').

Laaitie – From the original South African English expression 'lighty', referring to a young man, still a lightweight.

Lekker – Afrikaans word widely used for anything that is 'good', 'delicious', 'tasty'. ('Lekka' is Cape Flats vernacular, 'lekker' is formal Afrikaans.)

Loslit – Literally means 'loose at the joints', and mostly means easy-going, laid back.

Maaifoedie – Cape Afrikaans slang for a ne'er-do-well, a rascal, an unstrustowrthy or criminal person. In its original form, it literally means 'motherfucker', but the word has lost its harsh vulgarity.

Manne – Men, or guys.

Moer – 'Moer' is a wonderful, mildly vulgar Afrikaans expletive, and could be used in any conceivable way. Its origins lie in the Dutch word 'Moeder', meaning 'Mother'. Being the 'moer in' means 'to be very angry', but you can also 'moer someone' (to hit somebody), use it as an angry exclamation ('Moer!', which approximates 'Damn!'), call something or someone 'moerse' (approximates 'great' or 'cool'), or use it as an adjective: I have a 'moerse' head ache – I have a huge head ache. 'Moer toe' means 'fucked up', or even 'dead'. 'In its moer in' is used to indicate that something is gone or destroyed.

Mooi – Pretty, or beautiful.

Mos – Surely/evidently.

Nay – No.

Ndiyoyika – An IsiXhosa exclamation of fear or apprehension. It literally means 'I am afraid'.

Nè – Hey.

Nee o fok – Fuck, no!

Nogal – An almost untranslatable Afrikaans word, used in many different forms: sufficiently, enough, plenty, quite.

Oke – A guy, a man.

Oom –Respectful Afrikaans form of address to a male ten or more years older than yourself. Means 'uncle'.

Ou – Literally means 'old' in Afrikaans, but often used as a substitute for 'guy'.

Outjies – Guys, sometimes 'little guys'.

Pappie – Daddy.

Photie – Slang for a photograph.

Scaly – South African slang for someone or something looking suspicious or dodgy.

Sights (as in: we're not in the mood for your sights) –Tantrums.

Skedonk – Afrikaans word referring to a battered, run-down vehicle.

Snot snoek – Snoek is one of South Africa's piscine delicacies, a fish found in the cold Atlantic waters off the west coast. When a snoek is no longer fresh, it is referred to as a 'snot snoek'.

Stompie – Police slang for the custom Beretta RS200 shotgun.

Takkies – Running shoes, trainers.

Tjommie – A friend.

Wragtig –Very strong form of 'really'.

Yebo –Township slang for 'Yes'.